# Maids of Misfortune
A Victorian San Francisco Mystery


## A Novel

## By M. Louisa Locke

*Dedicated to all the family and friends who supported me during the long years it took to finish this book. Special thanks to Ann Elwood, Abigail Padgett, and Janice Steinberg, Jim and Victoria Brown, the Hawkins family, Terry Valverde, Kathy Austin, and my loving husband and daughter.*
*But most of all, Cynthia, this one's for you.*

## Chapter One:
## Monday morning, August 6, 1879

*The bastard!*

Annie Fuller gasped, shocked at even allowing such an unlady-like expression to enter her mind. She had been enjoying her tea and toast while sorting through her mail in splendid solitude. This was one of the privileges of being the owner of a boarding house, and absolute heaven after the dreadful years she had spent living off the charity of her in-laws, not a room or a moment to call her own.

However, this morning, the mail contained a slim envelope that had blasted her peace to shreds. With trembling hands she reread the letter, which followed the standard business formula, direct, very much to the point, and devastating in its implications.

*Mr. Hiram P. Driscoll*
*New York City, New York*
*July 25, 1879*

*Mrs. John Fuller*
*407 O'Farrell Street*
*San Francisco, California*

*Dear Madam:*

*I hope that this letter finds you in good health. It pains me to have to introduce such a difficult subject, but it is my duty to remind you of your obligation to repay the loan I made to your late husband, John Fuller, by September 30, 1879.*

*To reacquaint you with the particulars: the original loan was for $300, to be paid back within six years. Under the terms of the loan, interest was to be paid monthly at a rate of 5% until the loan was repaid. In respect for your departed husband, for whom I had great affection, and in recognition of your financial difficulties at the time of his death five years ago, I did not insist that this part of the agreement be met. However, since none of the interest has been paid, you are now responsible for the original loan, plus accrued interest, a total sum of $1,380.00.*

*I confess that I have been quite concerned about your ability to meet your obligations, and I was greatly relieved when I heard from your esteemed father-in-law about your good fortune in inheriting property in such an up-and-coming city as San Francisco. I must be in your fair city the last week of August on business. I would like to take the opportunity to stop by and visit with you at that time. I am quite sure that we will be able to come to some agreement of mutual benefit.*

*Your obedient servant,*
*Hiram P. Driscoll*

Annie's skin crawled as she thought of Mr. Driscoll, one of New York City's most successful entrepreneurs. "Your obedient servant." The hypocrite! She realized some women found his unctuous manner attractive, but after each encounter with him she always felt soiled. At parties he had leaned close, his husky voice whispering inanities as if they were endearments, his hot breath blanketing her cheek and his hands roving unceasingly over her person, patting a shoulder, stroking a hand, squeezing an elbow.

Annie shivered. Standing up abruptly, she crossed the room to close the window, shutting out the chill early morning fog. She had suspected that Driscoll had played some role in her late husband's dramatic slide into financial ruin, but she hadn't realized the man played the part of loan shark. Not that she was surprised at the debt. Creditors swarmed from the wainscoting in the months following

John's death, picking over what was left of his estate. Few of them got a tenth of what was owed, since her father-in-law, as John's executor, hired an expensive but skilled bankruptcy lawyer to ensure that at least his own assets would not be touched. But Annie had been left destitute and dependent on John's family.

Dependent, that was, until she inherited this house from her Aunt Agatha last year. She had returned to San Francisco where she had lived as a small child and turned the old mansion, located just four blocks from Market Street, into a respectable boarding house. Annie's features softened as she walked to the fireplace and turned to look at the room that had grown golden with the sunrise. The furnishings were sparse. There was an old mahogany bedstead and mismatched wardrobe and chest of drawers, a simple round table on which the morning tea tray sat, and a comfortable armchair, next to the fireplace. A worn Persian carpet covered a dark oak floor, and the only decoration was the two simple blue jugs holding dried flowers sitting on either side of the mantel clock. These jugs and the clock were all that was left of her inheritance from her mother, who had died over thirteen years ago. She didn't care if her surroundings were unfashionable because she loved everything about the room and the house and the freedom they represented.

Oh, how unfair to have Driscoll and his loan surface at this time, when she finally felt safe. He was clever to have waited, accumulating the interest. If he had tried to collect on the original loan five years ago, he would have gotten very little, perhaps nothing, back. Everything she had brought into her marriage, including the house her father gave her, had gone to settle her husband's debts. But now she had Aunt Agatha's house, and Driscoll wanted to take it from her. The last part of the letter implied as much.

Annie began to pace. The house was small, built in the early 1850s, and she had only six rooms to let out. After all the expenses of running a boarding house, she barely broke even. There was simply no way that she could, on her own, pay off Driscoll's loan, without selling the house itself. Fighting Driscoll in a New York court would be equally expensive, as he would be well aware. He probably counted on being able to frighten her into turning over the house. The lawyer who was executor of her Aunt Agatha's estate had suggested that she might get nine hundred, or even a thousand dollars for the property, located as it was near the expanding commercial sector of the city. Clearly Driscoll had figured this out.

"The God-damned bastard!" This time Annie said the words out loud.

She may have been only twenty-six, a widow without any immediate family to protect her, but she refused to let Driscoll, or any other man for that matter, rip her home and independence away from her a second time.

When Annie finally left her bedroom, it was a quarter to seven. Descending the narrow uncarpeted backstairs, she caught the tantalizing odor of the morning bread baking and heard the faint clatter of breakfast dishes interspersed with bursts of conversation emanating from the kitchen below. She yearned to go down one more flight and join in whatever joke had caused the sudden laughter, but she couldn't, she had work to do. She turned off the stairs on to the first floor and entered a small room at the back of the house.

At one time this room had been a gloomy back parlor where her Uncle Timothy had retired with his port after Sunday dinner to smoke his cigar and subsequently snore away the long afternoons. Annie had remodeled it by having a small entrance cut from this room into the larger parlor in front, installing a washstand and mirror in one corner and replacing the horsehair sofa with a small desk and book shelves.

Annie stood in front of that washstand and began a curious morning ritual. First, she liberally dusted her face with a flat white powder that rested in a box on the top of the washstand, effectively erasing all signs of the freckles sprinkled across her nose. Then she dipped the little finger of her right hand into a small tin containing a sticky black substance, which she applied liberally to her eyelashes, normally the same reddish-gold as her hair. Using her middle finger, she transferred a minute quantity of rouge from another tin to her lips, turning their usual soft pink into a strident scarlet. After washing the black and red stains from her hands with the rough soap she kept beside the washstand, she bent and opened the cabinet door under the stand and removed a disembodied head.

She placed this apparition, a be-wigged hairdresser's wooden form, on the stand. After tethering her own braided hair securely with a net, she carefully lifted the mass of intricately entwined jet black curls off the form and pulled it snugly onto her own head. The transformation was startling. Her eyes seemed to grow instantly larger, turning from the color of heavily-creamed chocolate to the deep rich hues of coffee, taken black. Her features, normally pleasing but unremarkably Anglo-Saxon, emerged as flamboyant and Mediterranean. Annie smiled mockingly at her image in the mirror. Then, after putting the mute, scalped hairdresser's form away, she draped a silken shawl of scarlet and gold over her severe black dress and opened the door to the front parlor, where she would spend the rest of her day at work, not as Annie Fuller, the respectable, widowed boardinghouse keeper, but as Sibyl, one of San Francisco's most exclusive clairvoyants.

## Chapter Two

"Mr. Harper, please, do not be so impatient. The reading I took last week was quite explicit. For a Taurus like you, there will be a definite improvement in financial status in the months to come. But this will take time. The signs were not for a sudden windfall, but a gradual improvement."

Annie kept her voice pitched carefully in the lower registers, with extra emphasis on her sibilants. She had always had a good ear for accents, and she found it easy when she was speaking as Sibyl to call up the cadences of the Italian porter who had worked in her father's investment firm in New York City.

She stared at the man who stood at the fireplace with his back to her, noting the tension in his curved shoulders and the nervous way he scrubbed his hands, trying to capture some of the fire's warmth. While it was chilly this morning, as was usual for August, it was not cold enough to explain why Mr. Harper had hovered next to the fireplace throughout this whole session.

"Mr. Harper," she spoke more sharply. "You did sell that stock in Furngell's Cable Company, as we discussed last week? The notice of bankruptcy was posted Friday. You should have been able to unload the shares before then."

The dispirited droop of his shoulders eloquently foreshadowed his answer. "Oh, Madam Sibyl, I didn't sell. I got to talking with Mr. Heller later that day, and he swore he'd heard the company was about to be bought out by Hallidie's company. I thought I'd just wait another week."

In her guise as Sibyl, Annie frowned and scolded him for failing to heed the advice of the stars, but inwardly she smiled. Mr. Harper was an indecisive little man who tended to follow every tip he heard. His constant buying and selling of stock as San Francisco lurched its way slowly out of the terrible depression of the mid-seventies nearly ruined him. Since he only owned a few shares of Furngell's now-worthless company, this last mistake would not seriously hurt him. But it might make him more willing to follow her advice in the future. So she decided to let the poor man off the hook.

"Mr. Harper. Come and sit down. It is not the end of the world. It takes great strength of will to avoid what fate has prepared for you. Last week when I cast your horoscope, I saw a small obstacle in your way. Perhaps you might have avoided it if you followed my advice. But, I understand. Fate this time was too strong for either of us. Do not worry. The stars also forecast success for you in the long run, and you will not be easily able to avoid that future either."

She smiled briefly at him as he came and sat across the table from her. A man in his mid-fifties, he dressed conservatively in brown worsted as befitted a hardworking retailer of lady's sewing notions. But the yellow silk vest that peeped from under his frock coat testified to the more daring side of his personality. From the first she had found him easy to read. She saw her task as trying to harness the two aspects of his nature in tandem.

Taking up his right hand and softly tracing the lines in his palm as she had done each session, she began to speak. "Mr. Harper, see how this line is strong and reinforced in several places? Remember how I told you this represents the conjunction of the both the moon and Venus ascending?"

She noted, as her patter continued, that the worried lines in the man's forehead began to smooth out, and he began to nod with each point that she made. "Now, Mr. Harper, I believe that by the middle of next week you shall have good news that will greatly relieve your concerns about financing your September trip."

Annie mentally crossed her fingers, although she was feeling fairly confident in her predictions. The close reading she had made that weekend of the *San Francisco Commercial Herald and Market Review* revealed that a particularly good wheat harvest was going to increase the value of the investments Mr. Harper had made in local flourmills. She was certain that some of the increase would be reflected on the California Stock Exchange before the end of next week, since she would not be the only one who would have drawn that conclusion. Within the month, he should be able to sell at a tidy profit, enough to bankroll his annual buying trip to New York.

He had resisted buying the stock originally. Agricultural-based investments were always risky; however, she had based her advice on sound information gleaned from the small central valley newspapers. Yet, to Mr. Harper it would seem that Madam Sibyl was truly clairvoyant.

*"Clairvoyant, specializing in business and domestic advice, consultations by appointment only, fee $2"* stated her simple advertisement that ran weekly in the *San Francisco Chronicle*.

Unlike the other men and women who listed themselves as mediums or fortunetellers in the city, Sibyl did not have open consultations nor did she hold séances. She neither promised to contact the dead through slates, move tables, speak in a trance, produce materializations, nor tell amazing information about the past. Through the casting of horoscopes and reading of palms, she offered only to see clearly into the future and give advice. After less than a year at the business, Sibyl had twenty-six regular clients, a few who had biweekly consultations. Her fee was twice the going rate, because she had found that the higher fee and the "appointment only" rule kept away those individuals who were shopping for news from the spirit world and helped her develop a steady clientele that really could benefit from her expertise. She brought in a substantial sum each month, enough to pay for the additional expenses connected to transforming a family home into a boarding house.

She had even accumulated a few hundred dollars so she could make some investments of her own. But all of this would have to be liquidated if the importunate Mr. Driscoll had his way. This thought distracted Annie, and she found Mr. Harper looking puzzled at her momentary silence. She mustn't permit her own concerns to interfere with her work.

The clock over the fireplace chimed the half-hour as she leaned forward and stared at Mr. Harper's hand as it lay face up on the table. She looked up and gave him a strong, encouraging smile.

"Mr. Harper. You will have a very good day today. You will be kind but firm with your head clerk, Mrs. Parker, inquiring after her daughter's health, but insisting that she be pleasant with the customers. You will eat lightly at lunch, and when Mr. Rosenthal needles you about the Furngell bankruptcy, you will not become angry. You will realize that, as a Gemini, Mr. Rosenthal is simply a talker who speaks from his envy of those who are willing to take a chance in this life. And you will know that you have done no wrong, simply followed what the stars had planned for you.

"Then, after a very productive afternoon, you will return home early, surprising your wife with the brooch you bought for her birthday. You will find your evening congenial, your wife amiable, your children full of high spirits, and your appetite good. I will see you at eight next Monday morning, and I am sure you will have good news for me then."

Mr. Harper sighed lightly and smiled as if in anticipation of this pleasant future. He stood up and briskly crossed to the coat rack by the door, where he retrieved his hat and cane. Bowing with surprising grace, he said, "Thank you, Madam Sibyl. As usual your advice makes a good deal of sense." Then he left the room.

Annie slumped for a minute, listening to the murmuring in the hall as her maid, Kathleen, escorted Mr. Harper out the front entrance. She now had nearly an hour to prepare for her next client, a young, newly married woman who was having a good deal of difficulty with her mother-in-law. Pushing herself up from the table, she moved to the front windows and pulled open the thick dark green curtains that so effectively shut out sounds from the city street below. She opened one window a crack, since Mr. Harper, like most of her male clients, had smoked when he had first come in. Kathleen would soon bring in several vases of flowers to help sweeten the air.

Moving around the room, Annie made other changes in preparation for her next client. She pulled a comfortable armchair close to the table she always sat behind as Sibyl. Women who had been on their feet since early morning were quite content to remain stationary throughout their consultations. A large tea set would be placed at the armchair's side, with some of her housekeeper's delicious pastries temptingly arranged on a plate. She found that in this cozy atmosphere women were more likely to unburden themselves willingly, with little hesitation.

Men, on the other hand, seemed to require a different atmosphere. For them she lay out Uncle Timothy's crystal decanters, filled with a variety of expensive alcoholic beverages, and she placed, invitingly near at hand, all the little accoutrements of cigar or pipe smoking for those who indulged. In addition, since she had found men seldom stayed sitting, Annie provided a few carefully placed objects d'art for them to look at while roaming around the room.

Aunt Agatha's father had been a sea captain who plied the Orient. Annie had culled a number of interesting pieces from his collection. It amused her to observe that most men felt much more comfortable turning their backs on her and confessing their fears and hopes to the small jade horse they held in their hand or to the ancient painted leather globe of the world they idly spun in rapid orbits.

She banished this loot from the Orient, along with the whiskey decanters, to the dark paneled cabinets along the walls, replacing them with the numerous knickknacks that had been her Aunt's pride and joy. When she finished she surveyed the parlor with satisfaction. Fortunately she only had to make the changeover twice a day, once in the morning and again in the afternoon, when women needed to be back at their homes supervising the preparations for dinner and men scheduled appointments for the other end of their work days. Today she'd only two male clients scheduled in the morning; the rest were in the late afternoon, including her favorite, Mr. Matthew Voss.

The thought of Mr. Voss lifted her spirits. Maybe he would be able to help her solve the problem of Mr. Driscoll and his loan. Matthew Voss was a well-respected manufacturer who had come west in '49 to make his fortune in the gold fields of California. Along with Malcolm Samuels, a man he had met on the trail, he had failed at mining but succeeded in business. In time, their firm, Voss and Samuels, had become one of the leading manufacturers of fine furniture on the west coast. The company, like many other local firms, had faced a difficult time during the recent national panic and depression, and it had been Voss's desire to put his personal finances on a sounder footing that first brought him to visit Sibyl.

"Sounds crazy to me," Voss bluntly told Annie the first day he had come to Sibyl for advice. "Can't see why the lines in my hands, lines that come from plain old-fashioned toil, should help me decide what stocks to buy. But I'll try anything once. And if you do half as well for me as you done for Porter, well, maybe you'll just make a believer out of me!" Voss had laughed at this point, a wheezing sort of cackle that had become comfortingly familiar.

Most of her male clients had developed this way. One satisfied customer had inevitably led to several more. She was really doing the job any good investment broker would do, but of course as a respectable woman she could never hold that position. However, as a clairvoyant, Annie found that most men willingly listened to her advice and freely talked about their own ideas for investments. They didn't worry about whether she could understand the masculine world of finance capital, real estate speculation, and commercial markets because they thought she got her advice from the stars.

Mr. Voss was different. He took her seriously and she felt a glow of satisfaction when she thought about how, with her guidance, he had begun to recoup his fortune. Recently, their discussions were more about how he should spend his money than how he should make it. He'd been particularly interested in pleasing his wife; he worried that he hadn't been able to devote the time and attention to her that she deserved. "She's a good little thing," Voss once said, "and I haven't liked to worry her about problems with the business. I think we both deserve to start having a bit of fun. Never put much faith in the idea that 'Virtue is its own reward.'"

So Annie and Mr. Voss had held some lively sessions on the relative merits, astrologically speaking, of the kinds of earthly rewards his wife might like. She suspected a surprise for his wife lay behind the "grand plans" he had referred to in the note she received from him last Wednesday, rescheduling his regular Friday appointment for today. She had been amused by the note, which was, for Voss, uncharacteristically dramatic. Thinking of Voss made her feel more optimistic. She had no doubt he would be able to advise her, perhaps help her get a loan to pay off the debt, if necessary.

Hoping to find some nugget of financial advice that would further brighten Voss's own financial outlook and perhaps give her some ideas about how to get out of her own predicament, she picked up the morning edition of the *San Francisco Chronicle*. She would look specifically for the steamship lists that so often revealed interesting information about the region's commercial health.

A headline on the second page arrested her attention. MYSTERIOUS DEATH OF RESPECTED CITIZEN. What new scandal was the Chronicle manufacturing? Then she noticed in the first paragraph the words "Geary Street." Since Voss lived on this street, she read on, thinking that Mr. Voss would certainly be full of the news if a neighbor had died.

As the meaning of the words began to sink in, she found it difficult to breathe. "Respectable Furniture Manufacturer Voss ...found dead by his wife early Sunday morning...cause of death unknown...no sign of unlawful entry...question of recent business reversals...survived by sister, Miss Nancy Voss, wife, Mrs. Amelia Voss, and son, Jeremy."

Annie stared at the words that seemed to bleed into each other. The unexpectedness of death always left her feeling betrayed. People she cared for seemed to die someplace else, without warning, without her, without giving her time to say good-bye. Voss had been so alive. She had felt no hint of his impending death; she never did. Why was she so blind to death when she was able to see life so clearly?

## Chapter Three:
## Monday evening, August 6, 1879

Annie slowly rocked back and forth in a chair set next to a window crammed with pots of pungent geraniums. The window was open, letting in wisps of fog and the soft sounds of a summer evening. The damp coolness of the breeze was welcome since the old wood cook stove across from her gave out the steady heat necessary for baking bread. An enormous cat lay in a comforting, rumbling mass on her lap. Across the room her housekeeper, Beatrice O'Rourke, leaned over the dishpan, scrubbing the dinner dishes.

Beatrice was a short woman of ample proportions, but somehow her contours suggested lightness rather than weight. Nearly sixty, she had the energy of a much younger woman. Her husband had been a well-respected captain in the local police force, gunned down ten years earlier in a battle with one of the Barbary Coast gangs. The pittance that the St. Mary's Benevolent Association provided a police captain's widow forced Beatrice back into domestic service, where she had served Annie's aunt and uncle as housekeeper and cook. Annie, a widow herself, could well imagine the bitterness this might have produced. But Beatrice was always unfailingly cheerful, and it had been a godsend when she had agreed to help run the boarding house. Annie hadn't had the heart to tell her about Driscoll's letter yet. For Beatrice's sake, as well as her own, she had to find a way to save the house.

Slowly, as she watched Beatrice's broad back expand and contract and the dimples above her plump elbows wink in and out of sight, the huge knot of misery she had been carrying around all day began to loosen. As she rocked and stroked the cat's soft black fur, she found herself taking long, deep breaths. She realized that all day she had been carrying herself tightly, as if trying to compress herself into the smallest space possible, becoming invulnerable to assault. Where was the immediate threat? Certainly not here in her own kitchen with Beatrice a comforting few feet away. Yet the shocks of Driscoll's letter and the death of Mr. Voss had rekindled emotions from her past when unexpected events had irreparably torn the fragile fabric of her world.

The cat under her hand stiffened and the rumbling purr ceased. At first she feared that in the thrall of her dark thoughts she had carelessly hurt the animal, but then a small scratching could be heard at the back door, followed by an excited volley of yips. Beatrice turned around and their eyes met. The last knot of the day's despair unraveled as Annie turned to the contemplation of life's real problems and said, "Oh, Bea, Jamie's dog! I'd forgotten. What are we going to do?"

Beatrice chuckled. "Right now I think we had better let him in, for if he barks much longer we'll have Jamie down here to see to him, and then the fat will be in the fire."

Jamie Hewitt, a lively eight-year old, and his widowed mother were boarders who occupied the third-floor back room. Jamie had arrived home that afternoon with a stray dog he rescued from a local bully. He'd pleaded with Annie and Beatrice to let him keep it, claiming that it would make an excellent watchdog. At the time Annie had been fairly brusque with him, thinking angrily, why get a watchdog when in a month she might no longer have a house to watch? But this evening she rejected that attitude as unnecessarily defeatist.

Watching the older woman wipe her hands on the dishtowel, Annie asked, "Did you get a chance to talk to any of the boarders to see if there would be any objections to keeping a dog?"

Beatrice replied as she crossed over to the back door, "Well, Miss Lucy isn't home from work yet, but if I remember correctly she mentioned having dogs when she was young, so she probably won't put up a fuss. Neither Mr. Harvey nor Mr. Chapman raised any objection. In fact, Mr. Chapman offered to help Jamie care for it. You know, I think that young gentleman would help take care of an elephant if he thought it might make Jamie's ma take notice of him."

She laughed. "Oh Bea, you're quite right. But I am afraid it will do him no good."

Miss Lucy Pinehurst, a no-nonsense woman in her late forties who lived alone in a small room on the third floor, was the cashier in one of the more prestigious restaurants in town and usually worked late. Mr. Harvey and Mr. Chapman shared the small room behind Annie's on the second floor, since they couldn't afford anything larger on their minuscule salaries as clerks in the city. Mr. Chapman had been showing distinct signs of being smitten with Jamie's mother, Barbara Hewitt, who taught English literature at Girl's High. But the departed Mr. Hewitt had evidently ruined her trust in all men.

Bea paused before opening the door and turned. "The Misses Moffet expressed great delight at the idea of having a watchdog. Well, at least Miss Minnie was delighted. As usual Miss Millie didn't say a word. It seems that they had been worrying a good deal about burglars. What I think is that Jamie had been campaigning for their support before dinner. That boy has a way with him for certain. Do you suppose he'll grow up to be a senator?"

"Heavens, I hope not! At least not one of those dreadful ones under the railroad's thumb!"

"Of course not. Not our Jamie! He'd be a champion for the working classes," replied Beatrice, as she opened the door. "Anyway,

Mrs. Stein was of your mind. She felt a dog might be good for the boy."

By this time the object of concern had come prancing in. He was a small bull-terrier mix, with the pugnacious, squashed-in muzzle of a dockside tough and the soulful brown eyes of an Italian poet. After sticking his non-existent nose into everything he could reach, the dog came and sat at Beatrice's feet, thrust his skinny chest forward, cocked his head to one side, and looked up expectantly.

Annie chuckled. "Well, it looks as if he is a smart young thing, for he clearly knows who will cast the deciding vote. You have enough to do around here, without adding the care and feeding of a dog."

Beatrice responded by looking significantly at the extremely alert cat in Annie's lap. "It seems to me that the deciding vote must come from that old puss, for if she won't put up with him, there will be no peace in this household. I know she is getting old and crotchety, but I won't have her bothered, even to please the young lad."

As if she knew she was being spoken about, the cat sat up in Annie's lap, drew herself tall and then sprang lightly down onto the kitchen floor. After arching slowly, she walked sedately across the floor until she stood facing the young bull terrier. He sat very still, without blinking. Annie could see that the effort he made not to bark was tremendous. Then, with a swiftness she found remarkable, the cat stretched out her right paw and lightly batted the dog on his forehead, right between his ears. Beyond emitting the smallest of yips and producing the fleeting impression that he had gone cross-eyed, the dog did not stir. The cat then stalked majestically across to her basket in the corner, circled twice, and curled up into instant sleep.

A collective sigh of relief from both Beatrice and the dog followed this performance, and then the sound of laughter came from the doorway leading to the front part of the house.

"I could have told you they'd get along, Ma'am," said her servant Kathleen. "That old cat already showed him who is queen of the castle this afternoon in the backyard. No, Ma'am, as long as he stays in his place and acts the gentleman, they'll get along just fine."

As always, Annie was cheered by the sight of Kathleen Hennessey, who, while only seventeen, was already very wise in the ways of the world. Some family misfortune had orphaned her and sent her into service at the age of twelve. Beatrice had taken her under her wing and brought Kathleen to work for them as soon as they had opened the boarding house. She had proved to be a prodigious worker. Annie was amazed that such a slip of a girl could do so much in any given day. Annie, moderately proportioned and not more than 5'4" tall herself, felt like an Amazon next to her. Kathleen's coloring was unremarkable, dark-brown hair, pertly tilted nose, and clear blue eyes. But even the curls that fringed her face seemed to wiggle with excess energy, and her laughter was a tonic to weariness all by itself.

Stepping into the kitchen, Kathleen bustled around assembling the materials needed to soak the table linens so they would be ready to wash in the morning. As she did so, she asked, "So, is it agreed Jamie gets to keep the dog? I do think I would feel safer sleeping back of the kitchen with that dog here to sound the alarm if any one tried any funny business. Patrick is always going on and on about how unsafe this neighborhood is."

Patrick was a nephew of Beatrice's, a current member of San Francisco's police department. He dropped by quite frequently to "check on his Aunt Bea," but Annie had long suspected that the real object of his visits was Kathleen, who had several admirers vying for her attention.

Kathleen continued, "Even in the posh neighborhoods in the Western Addition past Van Ness you can't always sleep safe at night. Patrick really thought there had been another burglar at work when that old lady pulled him off his beat yesterday morning. She was sobbing and screeching something terrible about robbers and murder."

At this point Kathleen turned and looked at Annie, her usual dimples banished and a serious expression in her eyes. "It was your gentlemen that usually comes Fridays. I recognized the name when Patrick said it was a Mr. Matthew Voss. You did know, didn't you, Ma'am, that he's dead?"

Annie nodded mutely, fighting to hold back the tears this reminder called forth.

Kathleen went on. "Patrick said the dead gentleman's wife found him early yesterday morning, just lying across his desk, cold as can be. Patrick says it couldn't be a robber, no matter what the old lady said, because the wife said all the doors were locked, and there wasn't anything taken. She, the old gentleman's wife, told Patrick that it must have been his heart. He had been working too hard. Patrick said she's a real sweet lady, the wife is, and terrible upset by it all. But Patrick said the police doctor said it looked more like he drank something that didn't sit right. Maybe he drank poison, by accident or something."

At this point Beatrice sharply interrupted. "That's enough of your gossip, girl. 'Patrick said this and Patrick said that.' Since when did Patrick McGee become the fountain of all wisdom? A good-for-nothing boy who wouldn't know how to button his own coat if his mother didn't show him how every morning. He'd better watch his tongue. When my sainted husband was on the force, no man would have dared talk about a case off-duty. He would have had young Patrick on report, nephew or no nephew. Now you just tend to your own duties and stop chattering."

Quite startled by the ferocity of Beatrice's scold, Annie realized that her distress over the death of Mr. Voss must be pretty obvious if Bea had felt the need to snap at Kathleen in that way. But what had

Kathleen meant, something Voss drank? The newspaper story hadn't mentioned any poison. She was just about to question Kathleen further when the bell connected to the front door rang. Kathleen wiped her hands, curtsied, and swiftly made her escape, running up the stairs.

Once Kathleen was out of the room, Annie turned to Beatrice and said, trying to make her voice sound calm, "Bea, you really shouldn't have been so hard on her. She didn't mean to upset me. And I do want to know more. I'd like to understand how this terrible thing could have happened. Do you know anything more about it?"

Beatrice shrugged. "Well, Patrick did stop by here when he got off duty this morning. He was practically reeling from lack of sleep. That poor Mr. Voss was discovered very early yesterday morning, toward the end of Patrick's watch. Since Patrick was the first to see him, his chief expected him to stay on duty for most of the day to answer questions. By this morning he'd been awake for nearly two days. It's his first death, so he was terribly excited and...."

Annie interjected at this point, "But what did he say? Was Mr. Voss poisoned or not?"

Bea looked searchingly at her, and continued, "Daft boy, he said a good deal, most of it nonsense. I sent him home to calm down and get some sleep. He'll probably stop by here tomorrow morning and be talking his fool head off again. But what I think, dearie, is that it would be better for you not to dwell on this. I know you were rare fond of the old gentleman, but what is done is done, and fretting isn't going to bring him back."

Annie frowned slightly. Beatrice was just trying to protect her, but she was no longer a child and didn't want to be shielded from the truth. She was trying to frame these thoughts into words when Kathleen reappeared, short of breath.

"Mrs. Fuller, it's a gentleman, come asking after Sibyl. I did as you told me always to do, said she wasn't available and that he should leave his name and address so she could get in touch with him. But he wouldn't do it. He insisted that it was very important he get in touch with her tonight. Said if she wasn't in, he would like to see who was in charge. I didn't know what to do, so I put him in the drawing room and said I would see. He looks to be a fine gentleman and ever so handsome, but he seems awfully angry about something. Do you think Mrs. O'Rourke should see him and find out what he wants? Oh, here is the card he gave me."

Annie's heart fluttered as she took the embossed card from her. It read, "Nathaniel Dawson, Attorney-at-law. Hobbes, Haranahan, and Dawson. 246 Sansome Street."

*A lawyer! How odd.* Maybe he was representing Driscoll. But no, that didn't make sense; he had asked for Sibyl. Was he a potential customer? But why would he appear angry? Was one of her clients trying to take some legal action against her? Oh, she didn't want to leave the warmth and safety of the kitchen. But it wouldn't be fair to send Beatrice in her place, and she certainly wasn't going to the trouble to get back into her Sibyl disguise.

Stifling a sigh, she rose and said, "That's all right Kathleen, you did just fine. I'll see what he wants." As she followed her up the back steps she prayed that Mr. Nathaniel Dawson brought good news, because she wasn't sure she could stand any more bad news today.

## Chapter Four

When Annie followed Kathleen into the drawing room she saw a tall, lean young man, perhaps in his late twenties or early thirties, standing in front of the fireplace. For a second after Kathleen had done her duty by announcing "Mrs. Fuller" and then withdrawn, Annie and the stranger stared at each other in silence. He wore the requisite tailored black evening clothes of a gentleman, although the coat was cut a bit looser than was the fashion of the day. His thick dark hair, unusually long, covered his ears and the whiteness of his starched collar contrasted starkly with the rich brown tones of his skin.

When she was six, her father dissolved his brokerage firm and moved his family from San Francisco to the outskirts of Los Angeles in the hope the southern climate would help his ailing wife. Looking at the stranger, she was forcibly reminded of the tall, tanned, taciturn men that had helped her father run their ranch. The clean-shaven state of his face was highly unusual. It became him, she thought. It would have been a shame to hide the defined jaw or the high cheekbones that complemented his dark brown eyes. Eyes that were glaring directly into her own.

Abruptly conscious of her rudeness in staring, Annie glanced downward, feeling her face grow hot. Then, eager to cover her embarrassment, she moved forward, her hand extended in greeting.

She recoiled in surprise when the man exclaimed, "My God, you are so young! What the hell are you doing running an establishment like this!"

She stiffened and withdrew her proffered hand. How dare he challenge her authority, in her own home? Who was he anyway? His clothes and bearing might have been that of a gentleman, but his manners certainly weren't.

Annie lifted her chin and replied with some asperity, "Excuse me, Sir. I am not too young to run any sort of establishment I please. I suppose that you are the kind of man who believes that women are incapable of conducting business. I have no patience with that attitude. Would you please state your purpose here, if you indeed have any?"

The man gave a short bark of laughter that contained no mirth and said in an exaggerated drawl, "Well now, clearly looks can be deceiving, Ma'am. I'll be glad to leave as soon as you tell me how to reach the woman called Sibyl. I have a number of questions to ask her about a Mr. Matthew Voss."

This statement completely mystified her. Why would a lawyer connected with Mr. Voss want to interview Sibyl, and why would he question whether she was old enough to run a boarding house? Maybe this man was a close friend or relative of Mr. Voss, and perhaps extreme grief prompted his odd behavior.

With that thought, Annie moderated her tone somewhat. "Mr. Dawson, I am sure Madam Sibyl would be very glad to speak to you about Mr. Voss. She valued him highly as a client and is very upset at his sudden passing. But you must understand that, as a professional, she never takes walk-in business. It's late, and it would be much better for you to make an appointment for one of her regular consultations. I believe she could see you at nine o'clock tomorrow morning."

She looked at him hopefully. "Or, if this is not convenient, perhaps you should write her a note about the nature of your business."

Her attempt to placate Mr. Dawson apparently had the opposite effect. By the soft lamplight, Annie could see his jaw clench, and he grew very still.

"A professional? She gives consultations, you say? That's a new euphemism for what she does, isn't it? I guess it is a useful blind for businessmen who are trying to cheat on their wives, though most professionals of her sort work late at night don't they? Well, you just tell your Madam Sibyl that I don't want a consultation, even though I am quite sure she gives good value for the money. I am the lawyer representing Mr. Voss's estate, and, unlike her other clients, I just want to speak with her. But it must be tonight."

As the meaning of the lawyer's words sank in, Annie experienced the distinct impression that the floor had tilted under her. A real earthquake couldn't have surprised her more. This man thought that Sibyl was some sort of a prostitute. A prostitute!

The idea was so unexpected and absurd that she felt a laugh begin to well up, but before it could surface a second thought replaced her amusement with cold fury. If this idiotic man thought Sibyl was a prostitute, what did he think she was, the owner of a brothel? *Of course, that was exactly what he thought! That would explain his earlier comment about me being too young to run this sort of establishment.*

Literally speechless with rage, she stood for a minute trying to figure out how to respond. How could he have possibly made this mistake? How could she possibly explain to him the mistake without subjecting herself to further embarrassment? She should just leave the room. But she couldn't just let the misunderstanding continue. And she still wanted to know what business he had with Sibyl.

The sounds of voices in the front hall broke the silence and indicated that two of her boarders had just entered the house. This gave her an idea, and she acted swiftly. Trying to keep her voice as neutral as possible, she said as she crossed over to the door that led into the hallway, "If you insist, I will get Madam Sibyl for you. Please wait in here until the maidservant comes to direct you to her."

The couple standing in the front hallway, being assisted by Kathleen in the removal of their wraps, were Annie's prize boarders, the Steins. Mr. Herman Stein was a prosperous city merchant and banker, and his wife, Esther, was on the board of virtually dozens of local charity organizations. They had been very good friends of her Uncle Timothy and Aunt Agatha, and they had welcomed her when she moved back to San Francisco, over a year and a half ago. Because Mr. Stein was away so much on business, and Mrs. Stein no longer wanted the time-consuming care of running an entire household herself, they had been delighted to become the occupants of Annie's most elegant upstairs suite of rooms. Mr. Stein had also been very supportive of her decision to set up as Madam Sibyl.

The Steins, both in their mid-sixties, radiated a sense of well-being. Mr. Stein, almost entirely bald, more than made up for this loss of hair by the luxuriousness of the sideburns, mustache, and beard that bloomed below. Esther Stein's hair was now pure white and tightly braided into an intricate circlet that defied dislodging by stray Bay winds or the exploring fingers of grandchildren. Both were dressed in quiet elegance, but the cut of the clothes of both testified to their greater love of rich food and comfort than of fashion. Annie suspected that Beatrice's excellent reputation as a cook had been almost as important in their decision to move into her boarding house as had been their desire to help out the niece of old friends.

Breaking into their usual good-natured greetings, Annie whispered urgently, "Please, could you do me very great favor? In the drawing room there is a young lawyer, Mr. Nathaniel Dawson. He has come to see Sibyl, something about the death of Matthew Voss. Mr. Dawson seems to have gotten an entirely wrong impression of everything. Could you please go in and introduce yourselves and perhaps impress upon him the respectability of both this establishment and Madam Sibyl? He has met me as Mrs. Fuller, but I am going to change into Sibyl. For now I don't want him to realize the connection. I'll explain later."

Esther Stein laughed and said, "Oh Annie, what mischief are you up to now? Of course, we will go in and vouch for you. But if you mistrust this young man's intentions, maybe Herman should go into your interview with you?"

Herman Stein broke in at this point. "Young Nate Dawson? His father's a rancher outside of San Jose, but he's in his uncle's law firm. Good, respectable firm. I've not met the young fellow. Harvard law degree. I've heard he's a go-getter, but with a good head on his shoulders. Whatever would he want with Madam Sibyl?"

Mr. Stein frowned for a moment. "Well, in any case, I don't think we need worry about leaving our Annie alone with him, Esther. He may be part of this new modern generation, but he will be a gentleman all the same."

Annie wasn't so sure about that, but, then again, she wasn't sure she would be acting like a lady in their upcoming meeting, so she didn't quibble. Instead, she profusely thanked both of the Steins and ran up the stairs to change out of her dress and begin her transformation into Madam Sibyl, one extremely angry clairvoyant.

## Chapter Five

By the time the maidservant announced that Madam Sibyl was waiting for him across the hall, Nate Dawson was a shaken man. For twenty minutes he had listened to one of the most respected businessmen in the city portray Mrs. Annie Fuller as a paragon of virtue. He learned how she had bravely survived the ordeal of her mother's death when she was a child, and how she left California to go to New York with her father to become both companion and housekeeper to him, until she married. He heard the tragic story of how she had lost both her beloved father and her husband within a year, and how her fortune had been lost as well in the terrible economic collapse that had started six years ago. Finally he listened to her praised for her valiant efforts to support herself by running an elegant boarding house.

As Nate followed the maid into a smaller but stylish parlor his only thought was the hope that no one would learn of his mistake. He hadn't wanted to come on this errand in the first place; he had thought they should contact the woman Sibyl by post. Now he had potentially alienated a respectable woman with important friends. Worst of all, he hated feeling the fool.

As the maid shut the door behind him, he looked around. While a fire was crackling in the grate, the oil lamps scattered around the room were turned down low and provided little illumination. Across from him stood a small round table, draped to the floor by dark green velvet. The woman behind the table motioned peremptorily, clearly indicating that he should sit. Nate tried hard not to stare at the woman as he took his seat. Her skin appeared almost ethereally white in the lamplight, and her eyes glittered in their black depths. He'd never seen eyes so large. She was wearing some sort of scarlet shawl that matched the color of her lips. Then there was the woman's hair! Nate was reminded of an old engraving in his Latin grammar of Medusa.

Clearing his throat, he got right to the point. "I expect Mrs. Fuller told you I represent the estate of Matthew Voss, and that I have come tonight to ask you a few questions."

When the woman across from him nodded, he continued. "First, is it true that you are the woman known as Sibyl? And if so, just what was the nature of your relationship to Mr. Voss?"

The woman stared at him for a moment and then in a soft, lightly accented voice replied, "Yes, I am Madam Sibyl. I consulted with Mr. Voss twice a week to give him personal and financial advice. I have done so for over seven months."

Nate went on, "Just what sort of financial and personal advice were you giving him?"

"Excuse me sir, but I don't see that it is any of your business," the woman replied. "Please explain yourself."

Nate could tell that for some reason his questions annoyed her. Despite the vetting the Steins had given this Sibyl, he wondered if perhaps his Uncle Frank had been right all along. There was something suspicious about such a well-regarded businessman going to see a damned fortuneteller.

"It seems to me that it's you who need to explain yourself." Nate leaned forward. "Here we have a man, Mr. Voss, who apparently had everything to live for: a beautiful wife, a fine upstanding son, an assured position in society. Yet, for some indiscernible reason, he begins to see a fortuneteller. I find it difficult to believe it was simply coincidence that not long afterward he died in mysterious circumstances."

He clearly caught the woman off-guard. She started to rise and then sat back abruptly, two vivid red patches staining what he could now see were highly powdered cheeks.

"I don't believe it!" she hissed at him. "You are trying to blame me for the death of Mr. Voss! What am I supposed to have done? Broken into his house and slit his throat? Or am I more diabolical than that, did I put some sort of curse on him?"

"Don't be ridiculous," Nate interrupted. "Voss wouldn't be the first man to become so addled by the ranting of some so-called spirit medium that he was no longer responsible for his own actions."

At this the woman did rise and swept over to the cabinet to her right, putting her back to him. She reached out and picked up a carved ivory elephant on the cabinet in front of her, and Nate could see her take several deep breaths. Putting the carving down with a click, she turned and spoke quickly. "I am so sorry, sir, but it's you who are ridiculous. First, for no apparent reason you mistake a respectable woman for a keeper of a house of prostitution."

Nate scrabbled his chair backward and stood, leaning over the table, trying to staunch her flow of words. "Oh no! Listen, that was an unfortunate mistake; I had hoped she didn't realize. If I could only explain to Mrs. Fuller."

She continued, ignoring him, "... and now you accuse me of being some kind of a fraud who is responsible for a good man's death. What a fool you are! Tell me, do you really think a sober, responsible man like Mr. Herman Stein would have encouraged people to come to me for advice if I were a charlatan?"

Nate was appalled that Sibyl, or more importantly, Mrs. Fuller, had discovered the mistake he had made in thinking the house a brothel, but he was damned if he was going to let some painted pretend Gypsy lecture him.

"Well," Nate snapped back, "obviously the advice you gave to

Matthew Voss wasn't very good if it left him so desperate he decided to kill himself!"

Abruptly there was silence.

"Killed himself," whispered the woman. Then she began shaking her head. "No, no, you must be wrong. Why would he have done that? He was doing so well, he had such great plans! He would never kill himself; he wasn't that sort of man. Suicide! Wherever did you get that idea? You must be mistaken!"

Nate was startled by the sudden change in the woman's speaking voice and demeanor. Reacting to her clear note of anguish, he replied more quietly. "I am not mistaken, Ma'am. The police surgeon confirmed it at the inquest today. Voss drank enough poison to cause almost instantaneous death. It couldn't have been an accident, there was...."

Annie no longer heard the voice of Mr. Dawson saying those terrible things. She was no longer listening. She found herself pulled back across time and a continent to a suffocating overheated room in a fashionable New York City town house. She could hear hushed whispers behind her and from a nearby room a steady sobbing. She felt so cold inside, yet the roaring fire seemed to scorch her very skin. Ice, she was made of ice. The ice maiden. That was what her husband John had called her towards the end. And now he was dead. Killed by his own hand. Her poor husband had been too weak to face the disaster he had made of his life, and he had taken the coward's way out. Mr. Voss had been no coward.

Annie felt herself swaying. She vaguely registered that the lawyer had moved over to her and was gently supporting her to the chair by the table where she sat down abruptly. Feeling as if she was enclosed in a glass wall that muffled sounds, she rested her head briefly on her arms. The astringent smell of brandy unexpectedly assaulted her. She reared back; only to have him thrust a tumbler full of the amber liquid into her hands. She took a small sip, and the glass enclosure dissolved.

"Feeling better?" Mr. Dawson's voice seemed unusually loud.

Looking up at him she saw he was staring at her intently. Annie glanced quickly away, putting the glass on the table before her. Her momentary weakness embarrassed her and his close scrutiny made her uncomfortably aware of being in her Sibyl disguise. His next words confirmed her fears.

"Mrs. Fuller, what in heaven's name prompted you to play this abominable charade? Why are you pretending to be this woman Sibyl!"

She stiffened, declaring, "I am not pretending. I am Madam Sibyl."

He began to sputter. "But why, Mrs. Fuller? A woman of your obvious class and refinement."

"Whom you mistook earlier for a brothel owner!" Annie cut in.

"But that was only because we, my Uncle Frank and I, thought that Sibyl was a...well that Voss and she were engaged in some sort of illicit relationship. I mean there was every reason to believe so, and that was the root of the misunderstanding. Oh hell! How can I...."

She noted the flush on his face and thought how it made him seem younger. He sat down heavily in the chair across from her and took a deep breath.

"It happened this way. Early this morning my uncle, Frank Hobbes, called me into the office to tell me about Matthew Voss's death. I'd been out of town visiting my family, so I hadn't heard about it. Probate is my responsibility, and usually it's a pretty simple business. But Uncle Frank told me there had been a good deal of confusion about the cause of death, and that there was strong evidence of suicide. He said that, although Voss's business partner had assured him that the business was on a secure financial footing, Matthew's personal finances seemed to be in disarray. According to his bank, there is currently very little money in Voss's account. In fact, at this point, except for the house and the business, Voss appears to have been practically insolvent."

Annie responded quickly. "But that isn't true. He has been steadily investing for at least the past six months in a variety of money-generating schemes, almost all of them successful. He bought a good deal of property, stocks, and bonds. Granted, his liquid assets would be rather low at this point, but I would estimate that overall his net worth has increased significantly in the past few months."

She stopped for a moment, trying to order her thoughts. She wanted to appear composed in order to convince him she knew what she was talking about.

"You should have found records of these transactions. Deeds of property, stock certificates. Haven't you looked in his safety deposit box in the bank? I know he has one. That would clear up this so-called mystery."

He shook his head. "Of course we looked there. Uncle Frank opened that and his safe at the factory. There were the usual documents you would expect to find, but none representing the assets you describe or any cash."

"Mr. Dawson, you've still not explained why any of this led you or your uncle to decide that Mr. Voss was regularly patronizing a prostitute, or that the prostitute was Sibyl. Are you one of those men who simply assumes that any working woman must be a woman of easy virtue?"

He said, "Look, Mrs. Fuller. It was my Uncle Frank's idea. We were trying to find an explanation for his apparent insolvency. Uncle Frank simply speculated that if Matthew Voss was entangled with some woman, perhaps his wealth had gone for her support or to keep her quiet."

He added, "You must, in all fairness, admit that this would not be the first time that a respectable merchant of this city found himself in that position."

"I would strongly question whether any man who found himself in that sort of position could be called respectable," Annie replied tartly. "But this still doesn't explain why you decided Sibyl was the woman in question. Did Voss's wife make this accusation?"

He seemed shocked. "Good heavens, we have not even hinted at our suspicions to Mrs. Voss. She is already suffering enough. She keeps insisting his death must have been some sort of accident and the money must have just been misplaced. No, it was the appointment book and Mr. Voss's will that put us on to Sibyl. When my uncle talked to Mrs. Voss this afternoon, she suggested that Voss's pocket diary might reveal something about his finances. My uncle and I went over the diary thoroughly, and for the most part we simply found what you would expect for a man of Voss's standing and occupation. There were references to, and appointments with, the usual group of bankers and businessmen. Also the occasional social engagements, birthdays noted. Nothing unusual. However, there was one odd sort of entry we couldn't explain. Regularly, once or twice a week, the word Sibyl was jotted down. This had been going on for months."

Annie wrinkled her forehead, still trying to understand how either Mr. Dawson or his uncle could have jumped to the conclusions they did from this piece of information. She said, "But how did you find me? I mean, if you had seen my card, or advertisement, or talked to anyone about me, they would have told you that Sibyl was a clairvoyant. But you obviously didn't know this when you came this evening."

"Ah, but this is where the will came in. Mr. Voss had recently added a rather odd codicil to his will. Well, guess who was mentioned in the codicil!"

"Not Sibyl!" was her startled response.

"Yes, Sibyl, giving her address as well. That is how we found her, or, rather, you. And it seemed to confirm our suspicions. Why else would he have put a woman he wasn't related to in his will?"

*Of all the wrong-headed, idiotic, tortured twisting of logic, this seemed the worst,* she thought. In low, fierce tones she began to tell him so in no uncertain terms. "Did you ever think that maybe, just maybe, he might have done so because they were business associates, or even friends? Of course not. Well, you were wrong, about everything. Matthew Voss was not an adulterer, nor was he a coward. Even if he had some recent financial reversals, which I don't believe, he would never have taken his life." She stopped, fighting back tears.

Turning her face away and looking in vain for a handkerchief, she suddenly felt indescribably weary. She also felt self-conscious remaining in front of Mr. Dawson dressed as Sibyl. Her head ached under the tight wig, and she was sure that her tears were making a mess of her face. She just wanted this man, and his infuriating suspicions, to be gone.

Blotting her face with the edge of her shawl, Annie said quietly, "Please, I have answered your questions, and you have answered mine. Will you now leave?"

"Listen," he said, leaning forward and briefly reaching out as if to touch her shoulder, "I know I have behaved abominably tonight. You have every right to be angry, and I am sorry. Clearly my uncle and I were very mistaken in some of our conclusions, certainly in those regarding you. My younger sister Laura would rip me to shreds if she heard what a foolish mistake I made. She says that I am hopelessly out-dated in my attitudes towards women. I suspect the two of you would get along famously."

She looked up and caught a glimpse of a wry smile. His expression then turned serious.

"Mrs. Fuller, please say that you will forgive me. You must understand, from our perspective our speculations made some sense. We were wrong about you, obviously, but that still leaves us with the problem of Voss's suicide."

Annie started to speak, but he continued. "The evidence is really very convincing. The coroner clearly stated that Voss died of a poison called cyanide, which is evidently not something one would take by accident. There is no indication anyone else was with him, and then there is the note."

Here she successfully interrupted. "What note? Are you saying that he left a suicide note?"

"Yes, on his desk was a half sheet of torn paper. It said, 'I am sorry.' At the bottom was his signature."

Her indignation rose. "That is absurd, and not at all like Mr. Voss. If he had decided to take his life, he would have explained, made sure that everything was straight, orderly. That note could have meant anything, been torn off of a letter about something entirely different."

"I know...I know. You believe he was in good financial shape, but perhaps there was some problem in his life that required him to sell all his assets, or some sorrow that you didn't know about."

"But there wasn't. He would have told me. In fact, he was very excited about how he was going to spend all the money he had been making. Even if he had already liquidated his stocks and property to make a large purchase, another business, a piece of property, well, there still would have been something to show for it!"

"Maybe you're right. I can't argue with you because I didn't know Voss personally. Perhaps you are also right about his assets. I certainly hope so, because otherwise his family will be in some difficulty. Over all he owned sixty percent of the furniture company, his partner the other forty percent. Voss left ten percent of his shares of the company to his sister and divided the rest equally between his son and his wife. His wife also got the Geary Street house and property. There are a few small legacies, to his manservant, for example, and to a local orphan society. The rest of his estate, which at this point seems to be non-existent, is to be divided equally between his wife and his son."

Annie frowned, wondering where the assets might have gone, when she noticed a quizzical expression on Mr. Dawson's face.

He said, "You know, you still haven't asked what Voss left you in his will. Perhaps as a clairvoyant you already knew."

Annie wasn't in any mood to be teased. "I am not that sort of clairvoyant!" She then continued with more composure. "Frankly, I doubt that he left me more than a token. I thought of him as a friend, but it was clear to me his family came first. I take it the will has been read already."

He answered, "The will itself will be read formally tomorrow after the funeral. That is one of the reasons why I had to see Sibyl tonight. Apart from our suspicions, we needed to contact her, or you, before that time."

"Oh, must I attend? I couldn't go as Sibyl, and I really would prefer to keep the connection between Sibyl and my real identity as separate as possible."

"Well, you could come to the law office later and fill out the necessary papers. Perhaps it would be better that way. Actually, you were right; the amount of money willed to you is very small. The codicil was rather odd. He left you ten dollars and two hundred and fifty shares of some mining stock. However, you may not see any of either, since we haven't found any sign of the stock certificates. If some other assets don't show up, after the primary legacies are distributed, there simply may not be even ten dollars left."

Annie interrupted. "Did you say ten dollars? And was the mining stock for the Last Hope Arizona Silver Mine?"

Startled, he nodded yes, and she went on. "Oh, isn't that just like Mr. Voss. Some months ago, after looking long and hard at the prospectus, I advised him to buy stock in that mine. I wanted him to buy the miner's survey reports. They cost ten dollars and he grumbled on forever about the expense. Said that as a clairvoyant I shouldn't need surveys. I finally bought the surveys myself. Don't you see, he was paying me back?"

"I'll say he paid you back, since he left you the mine shares as well. Do you know what they are worth now?"

"The mining ventures in Arizona have been very risky, some very good strikes and as many worthless," Annie replied. "The biggest problem seems to be early strikes petering out, so that the value of the stock rises sharply at first, then declines. But this one seemed like it could be the exception. We argued over whether he should sell after three months, when the price rose enough to let him recoup his investment, or whether he should hold on to it. I said he should hold on. He thought he shouldn't. So far I have been right. The price for that stock is now selling for around five dollars a share."

He whistled. "That is a hefty legacy! He must have valued your advice."

Annie noted the tone of amazement. "Well, I think he was also teasing me a bit. Think about it. Assume that he was not planning on dying and when he made out the will he expected to live a good many more years. And I am convinced he had every intention of doing so. If I were right about holding on to the stock, by the time he died, I would certainly have benefited. But so would he, by receiving substantial dividends all those years. However, if I were wrong about the stock, by the time he died my inheritance would probably be worthless, just like my advice!"

She thought for a minute about Matthew Voss. She could see him in this very room, the firelight glinting off the glasses he was forever polishing while he talked. He would laugh dryly at her spirited defense of some investment scheme or another. He was one of the few clients who had seemed willing to treat her palmistry and star charts as the amusing contrivances they were. As they had plotted and planned for his financial recovery, she had been reminded of the games of speculation she had played with her father when she was growing up. She could just imagine Matthew chuckling to himself during one of their consultations, thinking of the codicil and how surprised she would be by it someday. He had liked secrets; in that way he could be almost childlike. Just the way he had been in that last cryptic note, canceling his Friday appointment because he had some secret plans to work out.

"Don't you see? He would never have left me that stock in his will if he needed the money. He would have left it to his wife so she could sell it. And if he committed suicide for some other reason, then where are the stock certificates? They must be somewhere. When you find them, I am sure you will find the other assets he had. No, Matthew Voss did not commit suicide, I am sure of it."

Annie froze. *Two hundred and fifty shares of stock, worth five dollars a share*. Matthew Voss had bequeathed her over twelve hundred dollars, nearly enough to cover her debt to Driscoll! The importance of that information hadn't sunk in at first; she had been so intent on proving to Mr. Dawson that Voss couldn't have committed suicide. But what if the certificates were never found, or what if he had redeemed them and planned to rewrite the will? What then?

Mr. Dawson interrupted these thoughts by rising and saying, "I will not argue with you any more. It's late, and I really must go. If it is convenient, perhaps you could stop by the office tomorrow afternoon around four o'clock to sign the papers? You still have my card?"

Annie rose and looked blankly for a second at the hand he extended toward her. Then she took the hand and shook it, but as she did so she said, "That's not the end of it, is it Mr. Dawson? You will try to find out where Mr. Voss's money has gone, won't you? People must be made to see that he had no reason to kill himself. You do believe me when I say he can't have committed suicide?"

He sighed. "I don't know what to believe. I do promise we will try to discover more about his financial status. But, Mrs. Fuller, you must realize that the police are convinced it is suicide. There was nothing to indicate otherwise; no sign of illegal entrance, no sign of a struggle."

Gently withdrawing his hand from hers, he continued, "Now I really must go. And, again, I apologize for any distress I might have caused you tonight."

As he turned and made his way out of the room to the front door, Annie followed him, feeling rather bereft. It was terribly important to her to prove that Matthew Voss hadn't been the kind of man who would make a financial mess of his life and then leave others to deal with the consequences. But she knew it was unreasonable to insist that he remain just so she could go on trying to convince him.

She unbolted and opened the door, saying, "Of course I accept your apology. And I am grateful you have been so frank with me in discussing Mr. Voss's death. Many gentlemen would have insisted that the entire subject was unsuitable for a woman. But do keep in mind what I have told you. I promise you that I will not let it rest until I have discovered the truth."

After collecting his hat, gloves, and cane from the hall table, Nate Dawson turned at the door's threshold and looked straight into Annie's eyes. "Mrs. Fuller, I don't think you have really considered the implications of what you are saying. If Matthew Voss did not die by accident, or by suicide, then...."

"Quite so, Mr. Dawson," Annie said, not blinking under his gaze. "Then someone killed him. And I think when you find out what happened to Matthew Voss's assets, you will have discovered who killed him. Goodnight, sir. Until tomorrow."

## Chapter Six:
## Tuesday morning, August 8, 1879

The next morning Annie was again dressed in her plain black gown. This time a delicate collar of black lace, instead of a scarlet shawl, graced her shoulders, and on her head, instead of the wig, perched an imposing black hat. She hadn't worn the hat since arriving in San Francisco. Then it had been a painful reminder of the deaths of her father and husband; today it was a useful badge of respectable mourning, behind whose veils she could hide while attending the funeral of Matthew Voss.

After Nate Dawson had left last night, she found that the more she thought about what she had learned, the more convinced she became Mr. Voss must have been murdered. But why? By whom? When she had discovered the Steins were going to attend Matthew's funeral, she asked if she could come along. At the time she'd some bright idea that if she could at least meet Matthew's family, she would find answers to her questions. This morning, as she sat primly in the Stein's carriage on the way to Laurel Hill cemetery, this idea didn't seem so very bright, and she rather regretted the loss of her morning's income, since she had had to cancel one of her clients to attend.

Part of her low spirits stemmed from exhaustion. Half-formed plans to deal with Mr. Driscoll's threatening letter had jostled with questions over Matthew's mysterious death to keep her awake until early that morning. When she'd finally fallen asleep, vague menacing shapes had filled her dreams. At breakfast, Beatrice had probed

unmercifully about Mr. Dawson's visit and had been visibly hurt
when Annie put her off. But she feared that if she got into the question of Mr. Voss's will the problem with Driscoll might come out,
and she wasn't ready to tell Beatrice about the debt until she had a
plan for handling the problem.

Driscoll wasn't due in the city for at least another two weeks. She
should be able to figure something out, get a loan; maybe she could
use the house as collateral. But she found it hard to concentrate on
this problem with the questions of Matthew Voss's death still unan-
swered. She had planned to discuss some of her concerns with the
Steins as they rode to the cemetery; until she learned they were picking up Hetty, their youngest daughter, on their way.

Unfortunately, of all the Stein children, Hetty was the one Annie
had met most often and liked the least. Hetty seemed to find it a personal affront that her parents had chosen to give up their home and
move into Annie's boarding house. As a result, she was not surprised
when Hetty began to complain the minute she set foot in the carriage.

"Mother, I am so sorry to have inconvenienced you this way.
This carriage can barely hold three comfortably, let alone four. I
would have gone with Adela, but she had to stop at her dressmakers'
on Larkin first, and I couldn't leave until I had given instructions to
Mrs. Phelps. She has been simply impossible all week, ever since
the little dinner party I had last week. She's all in a huff about the
scolding I gave her about the sauce for the salmon. It was inedible.
Of course she blamed it on the stove, and she does have a point. I'm
sure that half the reason your Mrs. Kelly did so well, Mama, was the
wonderful kitchen she had to work in. I just can't fathom why you
gave the house up. Not that Mrs. Fuller's cook isn't adequate, but
really one can't expect boardinghouse cooking to compare."

Here Hetty had nodded vaguely at Annie and paused for a breath,
giving her mother a chance to get a word in edgewise.

"Dear, I am sure neither you nor your Mrs. Phelps would ever want to trade your nice new modern kitchen for that old inconvenient basement room we had. But enough of these domestic concerns. I hoped you would be able to tell Mrs. Fuller a little about the Voss family while we were on our way to the cemetery. As you know, she goes out little into society."

Hetty seemed pleased at this request. Sniffing delicately and throwing her nose sharply up in the air so she could more effectively look down it at Annie, Hetty responded, "Well, Mother, if Mrs. Fuller wants to know about the Voss household, I will be more than happy to oblige. I suppose that she must find the doings of fashionable society fascinating, even on such a sad occasion as this."

Esther Stein looked apologetically at Annie and sternly said, "Hetty, Mrs. Fuller was a good friend to Mr. Voss, which is why she is attending the funeral. But she never had an opportunity to meet the rest of the family."

Hetty replied, "Oh, of course," but it was clear she was thinking how odd it was that Annie would have known the old gentleman but not be acquainted with any of the Voss ladies.

"I've known Jeremy Voss simply forever," Hetty began. "Why, I can remember him when he was in short pants and long curls, leaning up against his mamma's knee when they came to call on visiting day. One time, when we were about ten, he pulled my hair and I kicked him in the shins during some sort of musicale. There was a large lady singing very shrilly, and Jeremy and I were both bored."

Mrs. Stein inserted here, "Yes, I remember. He howled and you stuck your tongue at him! I was mortified that I was raising up such a young rapscallion!"

Annie found the image of Hetty in a scrape with young Jeremy Voss rather amusing, and for the first time she could imagine liking the young woman.

Hetty continued, "He disappeared into some boarding school for a number of years, and I only saw him every so often during the summers. Then he simply vanished from San Francisco society."

Mrs. Stein again interrupted. "He attended college back east, and I believe that he spent every summer abroad."

"Well, all I know is that two years ago he reappeared and took all the girls by storm. He had turned into a terribly interesting young man, very sophisticated, not at all rough like most of our California boys. An artist, you know. Very sensitive. He writes poetry and he is forever threatening to kill himself or someone else in a duel for love."

"Now, Hetty," said Mrs. Stein.

"No, Mother, it's true. I remember not long before my George proposed to me; he heard some silly rumor that Jeremy had written me a sonnet. George was simply furious. But I told George that any girl would be a fool to prefer a man like Jeremy, always talking so extravagantly but never doing anything, to a man like him. George might not have much to say, but at least he's a real doer."

Annie noticed that Mr. Stein, who had been silently listening to the conversation, smiled briefly at this remark, and she suspected Hetty was probably quoting her father here. Annie wondered what he thought about Matthew's death. Perhaps he could help her convince Mr. Dawson and his uncle that Matthew's death couldn't possibly be the result of suicide.

The carriage arrived at the cemetery just then, halting all conversation while everyone disembarked and made their way up a short hill. Normally a funeral for a man of Matthew Voss's status would have been a larger, more elaborate affair, with notices in the paper, a viewing, and some sort of ceremony in the church. However, Mrs. Voss had evidently requested that there only be the short ritual at the gravesite, and no public notices had been made of the time or place. As a result, only a small number of the family's friends and Matthew Voss's business acquaintances were in attendance.

The gravesite was nestled in a little hollow that had captured tiny wisps of the early morning mist and swirled them around the feet of the small group representing Matthew Voss's family, who stood to one side of the casket. The other mourners stood just a short distance away on the sunnier slopes across from the family. Annie, standing with the Steins, had a very good view of all that was going on. The sound of sea gulls and the sharp tang of the sea air wafted in on the cool morning air; she took deep breaths, feeling her tiredness ease. Looking around her she decided coming to the funeral was not such a bad idea. After all, experience as Sibyl had taught her to read faces and divine information from how people held themselves or related to each other. The important people in Matthew's life now stood before her, open for her scrutiny.

Annie easily recognized Matthew's son, Jeremy, from Hetty's description. With his height, black curly hair that tumbled over his forehead, dashing mustache, and furrowed brow, he reminded her of some brooding hero from a Gothic novel. She had not been surprised by Hetty's portrayal of Jeremy, which fit the image she had already developed from her talks with Matthew. Annie knew, for example, that the summers abroad, when Jeremy evidently spent his time traveling, writing poetry, and painting, had been a source of contention between the father and son. She also knew, when his company had encountered financial difficulties a few years ago, Voss cut off all funding to his son and demanded he return to San Francisco to take up a position in the furniture company. Matthew had hoped this would settle the young man, but he had indicated that it had not had that effect.

Matthew recently hinted he had some new scheme in mind to get Jeremy to change his ways. "I'll teach the young jack-a-napes the value of honest work, even if it kills him," had been Matthew's exact words. She wondered what the scheme had been and whether Jeremy had known about it before his father's death.

On either side of Jeremy stood two women dressed in deepest mourning. The striking young blonde on his left, dressed in an extremely smart black silk, leaned close to Jeremy, staring intently up at him. She was biting down on her full rosy lip and wrinkling her delicately arched brows above clear blue eyes in quite a fetching manner. Jeremy seemed oblivious to her. Annie was wondering who she was, since she knew Matthew had no daughters, when Hetty turned and whispered to her.

"Do you see to Jeremy's left? That's his fiancé, Judith Langdon. We were all really surprised when they announced last month. No one ever expected him to get caught so soon. Her mother was ecstatic. Judith is one of my most intimate friends, and I know for a fact that she is frightfully poor and needed to marry money. She's welcome to him. Just look at him. I'm sure he'll be a trying husband. My George never bothers me with a fit of bad-temper."

Only vaguely listening to further revelations about what Hetty's George never did, Annie continued to study the scene in front of her. The motive of the young blonde's mother might have been mercenary, but judging from Miss Langdon's expression, the daughter's was not. She wondered why Matthew had never mentioned the engagement.

A small movement turned her attention to the woman standing to Jeremy's right. With shock she realized the small, ethereal creature with an astonishingly tiny waist must be his mother, Amelia Voss. Even her long gauze veils couldn't hide the fact that Matthew's wife was much younger than her husband had been. Matthew had mentioned his wife's youth, but Annie realized that she had been picturing a woman who, after over twenty years of marriage and the birth of a child, had faded into a comfortable middle age. While it was impossible to distinguish much about her features or coloring from behind her veils, the bare hand that reached up and clutched her son's sleeve appeared exquisitely slender and pale. His fiancé may have been focusing all her attention on Jeremy, but all of his attention was turned to his mother. He took Amelia Voss's hand in one of his and drew his other arm around her waist, gently supporting her.

As he did so, Mrs. Voss tuned her head to look over at a man who had moved to her other side. Just as Annie was wondering who he was, Mr. Stein enlightened her by muttering to himself, "Ah, there's Samuels. Good fellow. They'll need his support now more than ever."

So, that was Malcolm Samuels--Matthew's business partner and oldest friend. Matthew had talked at great length about this man: stories of how they had met at a muddy river crossing on the way west, of the difficulties they had surviving the terrible year they spent panning for gold, and the risks they had taken in opening up San Francisco's first wholesale furniture enterprise. Quite soon a division of labor between the two partners had developed. Matthew ran the day-to-day affairs of the company, including managing the factory. Samuels took care of the supply and sales sides of the business. He traveled up and down the coast, even taking trips back east and abroad to contract for lumber and to maintain their markets. Matthew had felt badly that the peripatetic nature of the business had kept Samuels a bachelor all these years.

Annie remembered him saying, "I had the best of the deal. Poor old Malcolm never got to settle down. He says the traveling suits him, but I know he feels the lack of a family. My wife and I have done our best to make him feel our home is his, but it just isn't the same."

As she watched Mr. Samuels shake hands with the minister, who had finally arrived to begin the service, she mused that traveling and bachelorhood certainly agreed with him. He looked at least fifteen years younger than Matthew had, although she had assumed they were nearly the same age. Although of moderate height, Samuels had a commanding presence, carrying his considerable weight well.

Only the tiniest frosting of grey at the temples marked his thick, neatly brushed head of hair. His sideburns, beard, and mustache curled crisply around his mouth. *What a striking contrast the two men must have made*, she thought. She pictured Matthew, tall, stooped, with thinning grey hair and small paunch, wearing one of his rusty old black suits, standing next to this vigorous, handsome, elegantly-dressed man. She found it difficult to believe that Samuels hadn't remained single by choice.

The minister then began to speak, and Annie realized she had been carefully avoiding the primary reason for being in this place at this time. Matthew Voss lay in the highly polished wooden casket standing slightly below her on the edge of the grave. And it was time for her to say her farewells and face the truth of her friend's death. On the surface their relationship had been a business one. But she knew it was more than business. She had revealed a little of her history to him, something she had done with no other client. In turn, he had needed her, needed the chance to talk about his worries, to try out his ideas, to speculate about the future. And he had paid Annie the supreme compliment of accepting from her what help she could give. They had been true friends. Now he was gone and she would miss him.

Remembering the first days of her own bereavement, Annie looked over at Matthew's wife, Amelia, and wondered what she was feeling at this moment. Would she truly mourn his passing? Or would there be anger, a sense of betrayal, or even relief? Would she have resented the fact that he turned to another woman, Sibyl, to share his thoughts and ask for advice? Perhaps not. From what Matthew had said about his wife, it was possible that Amelia Voss had been relieved that he had turned elsewhere with his concerns.

"Such a sweet Angel," Matthew once said, "but completely at sea when it comes to worldly things. It was her Southern upbringing, you know. Yankee girls are taught to be more practical. Her mother made me promise when I asked for Amelia's hand in marriage that she would never ever have to worry her beautiful little head about money. And I have been able to keep that promise up till now, and will continue to keep it, God willing."

Annie smiled at this memory, thinking of how fervent the old gentleman had looked as he made this vow. Then the sight of Matthew's wife placing her wreath on the coffin as it was lowered wiped away her smile. Matthew was dead now, and if his assets remained missing, Amelia Voss would have to begin to worry about money. His promise would have been broken. Oh, how he would have hated that!

Moving slowly down the slope with others to place her flowers and give her condolences, Annie tried to say her silent goodbyes. But she was too angry to feel at peace. As she looked up, she saw she wasn't the only mourner with anger in her heart. Standing across from her, slightly apart from the rest of the family, an older woman glared fiercely into the grave being rapidly covered with flowers. She bore a remarkable resemblance to Matthew, but a Matthew filled with fury and despair. Almost as tall as Matthew had been, the woman had the same thinning grey hair, tied in a severe knot and covered by an ancient black hat with a veil thrust back to reveal her features. The thin shoulders that had drooped on Matthew were rigidly straight on her, and her long thin arms and the black-gloved hands were held equally rigid and straight at her sides. Annie found herself speculating whether or not this woman had a small paunch similar to Matthew's hidden under her tightly-laced corset. But it was her eyes, grey and piercing, that most reminded Annie of Matthew, and it was her bruised-looking, unblinking eyes that revealed a woman in anguish.

*Who could she be?* For a moment Annie simply stared. Then several fragments of conversations over the past two days came together, and she knew the answer. First, the newspaper article had mentioned that Matthew was survived by a sister. Then Kathleen talked about an "old lady" who had fetched Patrick off his beat, an "old lady" who had clamored that murder had been done. At the time Annie had assumed that this referred to Matthew's wife. Finally Nate Dawson had said that a small percentage of the company shares would go to Matthew's sister, who must be the woman standing there at graveside.

Yet how odd. Another person, like Judith Langdon, that Matthew had never mentioned. She could understand him not mentioning his son's fiancé, but a sister! Maybe she didn't normally live with them. Had she been visiting by chance? Annie turned and made her way to Mrs. Stein, who had moved up the hill after shaking hands with Amelia Voss.

"Oh, I do feel for the poor woman." Esther Stein sniffed into her handkerchief. "We have never really been that close. Amelia was always more part of the younger set, but I can't help but think how frightening it would be if Herman was gone."

Annie gave the kind-hearted woman a quick hug and said, "Now Mrs. Stein, your husband is not going anywhere--you are much too good to him. Besides, you have six children who would line up to take care of you. Your only problem would be that they might start fighting with each other over the privilege."

Mrs. Stein chuckled at this and replied, "Oh my lord, what a thought. I just know they would plague me to death, giving me advice and help I didn't need. I'd better tell Herman he must promise to out-live me. I couldn't stand the aggravation!"

Annie then turned Mrs. Stein gently to the side and nodded at the woman who was still staring into the now flower covered grave. "Is that Mr. Voss's sister?"

"Of course it is, poor soul. That's Miss Nancy Voss. She will be bereft. She followed Matthew out west after their parents died and has kept house for Matthew ever since. Over twenty-five years, and

in all that time she's never been apart from him. I wonder what she'll
do now?"

Annie was even more mystified. How could Matthew have lived
most of his life with his sister, and yet had never once mentioned
her? And why did she look so angry?

Almost as if to answer her question, Miss Voss tore her eyes
from the grave and turned her baleful look on a little tableau that had
formed to her right. There was Mrs. Voss, leaning her head against
her son's chest as if she was faint, with Jeremy tenderly murmuring
in her ear. At the same time, Malcolm Samuels hovered over her,
ineffectually trying to drape a shawl around her bowed shoulders,
while Miss Langdon kneeled at her feet, offering to Mrs. Voss the
black lace handkerchief she had dropped. Looking back at Matthew's sister, Annie saw her raise her upper lip in a sneer, then turn
swiftly and walk off, alone.

## Chapter Seven:
## Tuesday afternoon, August 7, 1879

Annie wove her way through the crowded sidewalk along Sansome, in the thick of the San Francisco business district, trying in vain to keep up with Nate Dawson, who was striding in front of her. He had insisted in accompanying her home from the law offices of Hobbes, Haranahan, and Dawson, where she had dutifully signed the necessary probate forms to ensure that Madam Sibyl would get her inheritance--if they ever found the missing mining stocks. But he had immediately set a pace that seemed intended to leave her behind. From the moment she had arrived at the scheduled meeting, she had been confused by Nate Dawson's behavior. Certainly their first meeting had been odd: a jumble of mistaken identities, sharp suspicions, and small kindnesses, resulting in a disconcerting sense of intimacy. At the end she had thought they had parted on good terms. This afternoon, however, he had been treating her as if she were a complete, and very unwelcome, stranger.

By contrast, his uncle, Frank Hobbes, who she had dreaded meeting, turned out to be a charming man. The family resemblance to his nephew was strong, but age had greatly tamed Frank Hobbes. At one time he must have been as tall and dark as his nephew, but middle age and too many years spent hunched over an office desk had reduced his stature, curved his back, paled his skin, and streaked his dark hair with white. He had the same high cheekbones and beak-like nose as his nephew, but the small pair of round, tortoise-shell glasses that perched on this nose turned these hawk-like features into the face of a rather amiable owl.

Hobbes had completely disarmed Annie by first apologizing for the misunderstanding about Madam Sibyl and then telling her that he was interested in her assertion that Mr. Voss had recently been successful in his business investments. He said he had even directed his nephew to look into the list of assets that she had brought with her to substantiate that claim.

"Mrs. Fuller's father, Edward Stewart, was one of the best brokers on the New York Stock Exchange in the fifties," he said to Nate. "Made his fortune and then moved out to California and dabbled in mining stocks. He was a good friend to me when I started out as a lawyer, gave me excellent financial advice. If Mrs. Fuller is half as smart as her father was, you would do well to listen to her."

Nate had not seemed at all pleased by his uncle's remarks and had turned to the desk to shuffle various papers, completely ignoring her. In fact, the whole time she had been at the crowded and untidy law offices, he had barely said two words to her. *Irritating man.* This thought was interrupted when she was forced to slow down by the crowd of people waiting to cross Market Street. She saw that Nate was looking toward her over his shoulder.

Noticing the difficulty she was in, he turned back and adroitly shepherded her through the crowd and around the corner, saying, "Are you all right, Mrs. Fuller? Are you sure you don't want me to hail you a hansom cab?"

"Mr. Dawson, I am quite all right," Annie replied. "As I said before, there really is no need for you to accompany me. However, it would be nice if you could try not to turn it into a foot race and let me pause for a second to catch my breath."

She turned away to look back at the Bay, which could be seen over the dockside buildings at the end of Market Street. Market was even busier than Sansome had been; in addition to the pedestrian traffic, several heavily laden wagons lumbered up from the docks, and numerous carriages swept by smartly. Yet there was a stillness and sense of peace to the afternoon. Dark-blue water flashed diamonds through the light fog that was accumulating, and a light breeze fluttered the feathers in her hat and lifted small scraps of paper into a miniature whirlwind.

"Oh. I apologize, Mrs. Fuller," Nate said. "I get irritated when my uncle feels the need to treat me like some inexperienced clerk. The disadvantage of working for someone who once dandled you on his knee. I fear that I was taking my ill humor out on you, and I am sorry. We can certainly walk as slowly as you wish." Then taking the list Annie had given him out of his jacket pocket, Nate continued, "I wonder if you would mind if I showed this list to Mr. Voss's son, Jeremy, and perhaps to Malcolm Samuels, his business partner? They might be able to help me track down the investments." This statement was followed by the first smile Annie had seen on his face all afternoon.

Heartened by both the apology and the smile, she replied quickly. "Of course not, although from what Mr. Voss said about his son's lack of interest in business, I would be amazed if he had confided in Jeremy. Did anyone in the family have any idea where his assets had gone?"

"No." Nate shook his head. "In fact, they were all rather stunned when my uncle explained the financial situation to them earlier today. Of course, there is the furniture business and the house. But with the economy still so sluggish they can't depend on the company generating significant amounts of income for some time. Certainly there won't be enough to permit Jeremy to set up a separate household upon marriage; and, since the house they are living in now is relatively new, there is still a substantial mortgage to account for there."

Annie remembered the panic she had felt when she'd confronted similar financial difficulties in the months before her husband's suicide. The suffocating shame when she had had to dismiss Susan, her young servant, because she could no longer afford to pay her. No matter how she contrived, she hadn't been able to make the small monthly sum that John gave her cover the necessary household expenses. She wasn't sure who had been more upset that morning, the financially straightened wife trying to maintain her dignity, or the young maid facing unemployment.

A bleak thought intruded. The debt she owed Driscoll threatened to return Annie to that time of financial insecurity. Pushing back the small whispers of panic this idea produced, she consoled herself with the reflection that at least she had learned to deal with adversity. For the Voss family, it would be new and all the more distressing.

Annie turned to Nate and said, "Oh, they must be upset. To have lost Mr. Voss and then to discover the precariousness of their economic situation. With no forewarning that anything was wrong."

"Yes, they really seemed taken aback. Mrs. Voss stated quite positively that her husband would never have left them with any financial worries, and his son, Jeremy, insisted the money must be somewhere. He got very agitated and practically shouted at Uncle Frank, calling him a liar. Said he knew for a fact that his father was doing well financially."

"Oh, don't you see? I am sure he is right. That is exactly what I have been telling you!" cried Annie.

"Yes, but where is the proof? Maybe Mr. Voss lost more than he gained from his investments and didn't tell you. Maybe he was a secret gambler. There are lots of ways that a man can go through money quickly."

*Oh, yes, a million ways*, Annie thought to herself, *and poor John had found every single one.* Out loud she replied, "His family would have known, had some hint...."

Nate broke in, "Not necessarily. In my experience, the family is the last to know. He would have kept any knowledge from his wife and son, out of pride. But just think; if he knew that he had lost everything, wouldn't that explain his decision to kill himself, so he wouldn't have to face the humiliation? I mean, what man would...."

Nate stopped speaking and Annie glanced curiously at him. He seemed flustered. It dawned on her that his uncle had probably told him of the rumor that her husband had killed himself after losing her fortune through reverses on the New York Stock Exchange. She knew that look, usually seen on the faces of men. They seemed to feel ashamed that one of their own had failed so miserably in upholding his duty to protect and to provide. Annie decided to ignore his apparent discomfort and simply responded to his last statement.

"Your argument isn't logical. Apart from the fact that I just don't believe it was in Mr. Voss's character to commit suicide, there wasn't any need. It wasn't as if he was completely insolvent. He had a company that was doing well. His partner confirmed that, didn't he? And he had an extremely valuable piece of residential property. They could have always sold the house, moved to smaller quarters, retrenched. I am sure that he could have gotten loans to tide him over. Suicide based on financial grounds just doesn't make sense. Not for someone like Matthew Voss."

Annie stopped, noting Nate's frown. She sighed. She knew she was being too argumentative and that men found this unbecoming. Mr. Dawson had seemed less concerned than most about issues of female conversational propriety, but perhaps she had gone too far.

Surprisingly, he also sighed and then said, "All right, I will admit that what you are saying makes sense. But if we are to convince the police that Matthew Voss didn't kill himself because of financial difficulties, we need proof. Malcolm Samuels did say that the business was on sound footing, but he also said that keeping the company afloat the last few years had depleted both of their savings. And he didn't know of any new investments on Matthew's part."

Elated at his concession, she said with more confidence, "So that simply means that Mr. Voss didn't confide in his partner. What about his son? Didn't you say he had proof?"

"Well, that's interesting," said Nate. "Now that I think of it, he never did go on to tell us why he was so sure that his father was well-off. Let's see. He was shouting at Uncle Frank, and his mother rose to try and calm him down. Then she felt ill and asked him to fetch her some water. That's it. By the time he came back, Mrs. Voss had decided that she wanted to leave, and off they went. So he never did finish what he wanted to say."

"Well, you really must talk to him," she replied. "Perhaps when you show him the list of assets I gave you, he will be able to shed some light. And what of Mr. Voss's sister? What did she think about it all?"

Nate put the list away, and they turned and resumed walking. "She didn't say a word the whole time. Just sat and glowered at us all."

Annie frowned, thinking back to Miss Nancy's expression at the funeral and what Beatrice's nephew had said. Musing out loud she said, "I think she knows something. Patrick said she insisted that her brother had been murdered."

"Where did you hear that? Who is this Patrick?" said Nate.

She tossed her head and laughed. "Don't sound so suspicious. Patrick is my housekeeper's nephew, and he just happened to be the patrolman on duty the morning Mr. Voss's body was discovered. I assure you that I have no first-hand knowledge on the subject. Or, Mr. Dawson, do you still think Sibyl was directly involved in Mr. Voss's death?"

Nate turned toward her and said, "Mrs. Fuller, I am harboring no suspicions about you whatsoever. However, since you persist in making a mystery of Mr. Voss's death, let me repeat what I said last night. According to the police surgeon, after writing the suicide note, Voss drank a glass of whiskey laced with the poisonous substance called cyanide. He then evidently convulsed, falling forward, cutting his temple against the edge of a sharp object on his desk. This cut bled freely for a short while. Perhaps this was what caused Miss Voss to conclude that her brother had been killed by someone."

"Oh," said Annie, feeling rather deflated. Then another idea occurred to her, and she suggested, "Couldn't it have happened the other way around? Couldn't someone have knocked Mr. Voss unconscious, poured the poison down his throat, and then taken any money or assets he had in the house?"

"You are just grasping at straws." Nate shook his head vigorously. "Supposing it was even possible to pour poison down an unconscious person's throat. Who would have done it? A burglar who just happened to have the cyanide with him? Anyway, the police are convinced it was impossible for an intruder to enter the house. Uncle Frank insisted that they look into this thoroughly. When Mr. Voss was discovered Sunday morning, all the windows and both the front and back doors were locked. There are only four keys to the house. One was on Mr. Voss's person, one was in his son's possession, one hangs beside the back door and the fourth hangs by the front door. It was that key that Mrs. Voss used to open the front door to let her sister-in-law out to call for help."

"But why are you assuming that it had to be an intruder?" she asked. "There were people in the house at the time of his death weren't there?"

"Just stop it!" Nate said. "That is an unconscionable suggestion. There were four people in the house that night, besides Voss. His wife, his sister, his son, and a perfectly respectable maid. Good heavens, you don't think any of them were capable of murdering Matthew Voss? What earthly reason would any of them have for doing so?"

Annie stood still, shocked by his vehemence. As she began to speak, she struggled to control her voice, saying, "There are all kinds of reasons to wish someone dead. Love. Hatred. Fear. Revenge. Even incredible weariness. How can you presume to know what any of those people were incapable or capable of doing? You barely know them."

"But neither do you," said Nate, quietly.

Annie paused. Then, thinking out loud, she replied. "No, you are right. But from everything you have just said, it seems clear that the answer to Matthew Voss's death lies somewhere within that household. So, we must get to know the members of that household better if we are to solve the mystery of his death. We owe it to him to do so."

With that statement, she briskly resumed walking. Across the street from them rose the mammoth Palace Hotel, and its rows of bay windows glowed golden in the afternoon sun. "Ralston's Folly," Beatrice always called it. It was, in its way, magnificent, but people said it had bankrupted Ralston and driven him to suicide four years earlier. Because of this too painful reminder of her own husband's death, she had so far avoided even entering the carved archway that led to its central court. Looking up at the building's symmetrical facade, Annie found herself fervently hoping that she could prove that Matthew Voss had not died in a similar fashion, crushed by fortune's fickleness. Nate caught up with her, and they continued walking side by side in silence.

"Mrs. Fuller, why did you decide to become a clairvoyant? Do you really believe in spiritualism?"

Annie, who had been lost in her own thoughts, was startled. She took the opportunity to pause, grateful for the chance to rest again and let the air cool her heated brow. Although Market was not one of the city's steeper hills, her dress made walking difficult. She had chosen to wear one of the outfits that had been remade recently by the Misses Moffet, her seamstress boarders. The tightly fitted skirt may have looked very fashionable, but it was extremely confining. She realized now that she had wanted a chance to show Mr. Dawson that she didn't always dress like some actress from a variety show. *As if he would even notice what I am wearing? And why should I care?* Nate's question had interrupted this thought, and the unexpected nature of the question about clairvoyance so surprised her that she answered him honestly, without thinking.

"I don't disbelieve in it. I suspect that ninety-nine percent of it-- the table rapping, ghostly manifestations, voices from the great beyond--is completely fraudulent. But that doesn't mean I discount the possibility of there being spirits or ghosts, or that there might be some people who are able to communicate with them. It has always seemed to me pretty arrogant to assume there are no mysteries in the universe that cannot be explained away. However, what I actually do is cast people's horoscopes or read their palms."

"You really use that astrology rigmarole to advise people on their business ventures?" Nate said. "And men like Matthew Voss and Herman Stein take it seriously?"

She laughed, "Well, to be honest, Mr. Stein doesn't take the astrology or palmistry seriously, and I suspect Mr. Voss didn't either. I don't, of course, but most of my clients do. I use the palmistry and star charts as a way of getting to know the people who are asking my advice. You can tell a lot about a person through touching their hands; for example, their state of health, how nervous they are, how much physical activity they engage in. The discussion that precedes the casting of a person's horoscope, plus the person's reaction to the predictions, tells me a great deal. From that knowledge, I can do a better job of giving them advice, whether it is over a personal matter or a financial one."

"But if you don't believe in these things, why do you do it at all?" said Nate. "Dressing up that way. It seems so demeaning. Why not just ask people what you want to know, and then give the advice? If you are half as good as your father supposedly was, wouldn't people be knocking down your doors, without all the fakery?"

"Because, Mr. Dawson, people, men in particular, would rather trust their lives to the stars than to the advice of a woman.

She knew she sounded harsh, but he had probed an unhealed wound. "Don't you think I tried a different way? When I came to San Francisco, I wrote to several brokers on Montgomery Street, men who knew my father, asking for any sort of position. I would have been glad to start out as a clerk, work for free, anything to prove myself. Do you really think that one of them would take me seriously? Would you have?"

Annie saw Nate wince at the anger in her voice. But if he were honest he would admit she was right. She went on, as Nate stood staring at his feet. "I thought not. Well, finally I met Mr. Stein. He was one of my uncle's oldest friends and he also knew my father. First he and his wife moved into my boarding house, which of course was of great help. Then, when it became obvious that I needed some additional source of income, he supported my decision to set up as a clairvoyant. There are already several mediums in town who specialize in business predictions, so he knew a market existed."

Nate shook his head slowly from side to side, wide-eyed, looking for an instant quite like his uncle. "I still can't understand why you would agree to take up such a strange occupation!"

They again moved forward, crossing over to O'Farrell to walk up towards Annie's home. As they reached the sidewalk Annie replied, "You see, I had done something similar before in New York. After my husband died, I was dependent on his family for support, passed round from branch to branch until I finally found a more permanent place with one of my husband's aunts. She is a kind person, but much addicted to spiritualism. So, to please her I began to conduct séances for her and her friends at home. It seemed preferable to letting her get into the clutches of some of the unscrupulous mediums in the city. She developed a great faith in my nonexistent powers and appeared to have a wonderful time. I, in turn, found I had a talent at giving all sorts of advice, and that people would take that advice more readily if I pretended it came from some supernatural source."

"But why the odd get-up? I mean, do all clairvoyants look that way?"

"No," she replied, "but I found that if I looked slightly exotic it seemed to reassure people, kept them from thinking about who I really was. Anyway, I think that from the time I was a child I have always enjoyed dressing up and playing a part."

Annie slowed her steps. Playing a part, she mused. Perhaps that was the answer to the problem of getting to know the people in Matthew's family better. Annie turned to Nate and said, "Mr. Dawson, you said that there was only one servant in the Voss household the night he died. How could that be? They must have more servants than that?"

His confusion at the shift in topic showing plainly in his voice, Nate said, "Yes, of course they do. I believe the servant who was in the house the night that Mr. Voss died was Mrs. Voss's personal lady's maid. There is also an old Chinese male servant, Wong, who doesn't live in, and a young parlor maid, Nellie, who was also away, since it was her night out. Evidently this Nellie has already given notice and left the house, as if Mrs. Voss didn't have enough to deal with. But what does that have to do with anything?"

Annie didn't answer at once, having just noticed that they had reached her doorstep. She looked up at the house with affection. Although it didn't sport the intricate woodwork of the new houses past Van Ness, its tall, plain, but stately facade pleased her; and she was proud of the way the glossy black paint smartened up the trim fram-

ing the front windows and the front door. Red splashes from the geraniums in the boxes in the first floor windows nicely relieved the
overall somberness of the house. A fierce determination swept
though her. She would find out who killed Matthew Voss, she would
track down his missing assets, including her own inheritance, and
she would use that inheritance to stymie Mr. Driscoll's designs on
her home. And she knew just how she would accomplish her goals.

Turning swiftly to Nate, she extended her hand, saying, "Thank
you so much for accompanying me. Our conversation has been quite
enlightening. I do hope that you will let me know if you discover
anything of importance in your inquiries. As for your question about
what the Voss household servants have to do with anything. Well, I
was just thinking, maybe I can do something to help out Mrs. Voss.
You know, don't you, that good servants are so hard to find."

## Chapter Eight:
## Wednesday, early afternoon, August 8, 1879

Damn that Annie Fuller! Yesterday afternoon she left him standing like a fool in the middle of the sidewalk, without the foggiest idea what she was talking about. Today he felt an even bigger fool, this time standing in the middle of Mrs. Voss's parlor, wondering what in the world he would say to her when she came in to the room. And it was all Mrs. Fuller's fault. She had argued so forcefully that a mystery surrounded the death of Matthew Voss that he'd decided to visit Jeremy today to ask some questions. What he hadn't planned on was Jeremy's absence and an invitation to tea from Amelia Voss.

Nate strode over to a chair across from the fireplace and sat down, then immediately stood up again; his frustration made sitting impossible. He knocked his ankle painfully against a footstool he'd overlooked in the dim light. Thick curtains eliminated any hint of the sunshine that sparkled outside, and the two oil lamps failed to dispel the general gloom. Dusty surfaces, musty vases of flowers that were past their prime, and a plethora of black crape that covered every available piece of furniture. God, how he hated formal mourning rituals.

He and his uncle had been in this room earlier in the week, and nothing seemed to have changed, except the accumulation of dust and the decay of the flowers. This time Nate had sent a note making an appointment to see Jeremy Voss. He wanted to show him Mrs.

Fuller's list of investments and ask him why he was so certain his father faced no financial difficulties. However, when he arrived at the house the manservant informed him that Jeremy had just left and then had extended the tea invitation from his mistress. Nate never expected to see Mrs. Voss on this visit; he assumed she would be in seclusion the day after the funeral. It seemed ungracious to decline her invitation, but he wasn't happy about it. Being in charge of probate meant that he often had to meet with the newly bereaved, and he hated this part of the job.

Nate thought of his own mother, weeping inconsolably when the letter came telling them about Charlie's death at Chickamauga. When his brother Frank had fallen at Shiloh the year before she had just gone quiet. But somehow the death of Charlie, her firstborn, had been different. Nate had been only fourteen and felt helpless in the face of his mother's grief. The only thing he could think to do was sneak off to join up--get the bastard johnny rebs who had killed his brothers. His father had found him the first night, twenty miles from home and sleeping in a hay barn. He had never seen his mother that angry. Her fury had raged unceasingly until his father sold the farm and successfully resettled the family across the continent, on a ranch outside of San Francisco. His younger brother, Billy, only ten at the time, had thought that life on the trail was one grand adventure. His sister Laura was just a baby. But Nate knew that somehow a woman's grief had changed their destiny.

"Mr. Dawson. How kind of you to visit. I am afraid that I was not at my best when you came last." This soft speech provided the first indication that Mrs. Voss had entered the room.

Startled, Nate whipped around, almost tripping over the treacherous footstool, and stammered, "Oh, Mrs. Voss. Of course. My pleasure. I apologize for disturbing you. Hadn't meant...expected your son, Jeremy. There seems to have been some mix-up."

Mrs. Voss glided across the room, shaking her head slightly in protest, and she gracefully gave him her hand, saying, "Please, Mr. Dawson. So kind. It is I who must apologize for my son. That is one of the reasons I asked to see you. But where ever are my manners. May I pour you some tea?"

Nate then noticed that while they were speaking, the servant, Wong, had been setting up the tea tray. At a nod from his mistress, he bowed and left them alone. Mrs. Voss sat down next to the tea tray, indicating that Nate should sit down across from her, and she began to pour out the tea. He took the opportunity to examine his hostess more closely.

She wore deep mourning, from the black ruffled cap atop her head to the black lace-edged handkerchief she clutched in her left hand. The black accentuated her paleness. Like the fine bone china of the teacup she held, her skin appeared translucent, and her elegant hands fragile enough to break at a touch. Those hands trembled slightly as she handed him a cup, and Nate felt an unexpected impulse to take them into his own to steady them.

Uncomfortable, he searched for something to say. But what do you say to someone whose husband just died and left you destitute? He couldn't ask her about her husband's finances; she had already indicated she didn't know anything. It didn't feel right to push for personal details about her family or servants, even to please Mrs. Fuller.

To his relief, Mrs. Voss didn't seem to have noticed his hesitation, since she had risen to pinch off an offending blossom on one of the bouquets scattered around the room. Shrugging perceptibly at the bedraggled state of the flowers under her fingers, she turned back to Nate and smiled.

"Mr. Dawson, I must apologize for the state of the house. Wong can only do so much, and I am afraid we are sadly missing Nellie, our former parlor maid. But these domestic trials were not why I asked you to tea."

Mrs. Voss hesitated and then moved restlessly to another vase and recommenced her pruning, while Nate mentally tried to calculate Mrs. Voss's age. She couldn't be more than her mid-forties, and, if he hadn't known she had a grown son, he would have sworn she was much younger. *Too young to be a widow.* Of course, Mrs. Fuller was even younger. An image of Annie Fuller flashed before him. She was offering him her hand, her warm brown eyes looking directly at his, her mouth flirting with a smile, her light brown curls capturing the sunlight with a hint of fire. Younger, yes, but she had a depth and experience that Mrs. Voss lacked. Looking over at Mrs. Voss, Nate doubted she had much experience beyond managing her house and arranging flowers. What should he say to her? His uncle always had a string of platitudes in situations like this.

Having naturally risen when Mrs. Voss had stood up, Nate placed his teacup on the table and tried again to make conversation. "Mrs. Voss, I wanted to say again how deeply sorry I, we, I mean my uncle and I are for your loss. And if there is anything in particular we could do, please let us know. I mean, anything...." Disconcerted by the warmth of the smile Mrs. Voss directed at him and the tears that filled her huge blue eyes, Nate's sentence petered out.

Limpid pools. He remembered eyes being described in that fashion once in a book, but he hadn't know what it meant until now.

Mrs. Voss dabbed at those overflowing pools with the black lace handkerchief and whispered, "Thank you so much, Mr. Dawson. You and your uncle have been most kind, but there is really little you can do, I am afraid." She then swept up the wilted flowers she had picked and stood looking helplessly around for someplace to dispose of them.

Relieved that Mrs. Voss had turned those eyes away from him, Nate searched for something helpful to say. "Mrs. Voss, I think that there is some hope your financial position may be better than we first supposed. I have been making inquiries this morning, and there are some indications of investments we didn't know anything about. I will be meeting again with your husband's banker later this afternoon. I hoped to speak with your son first, to see if he could shed any light on the issue. He seemed so sure that Mr. Voss was doing well financially; we thought he might know something that would help."

Mrs. Voss simply dumped the flowers back on the table and came back to sit across from Nate, saying, "Oh, Mr. Dawson, I am sorry Jeremy isn't here. He just isn't himself since Matthew's... I mean, Jeremy has always been highly strung, but now... it really isn't that he wants to be uncooperative. But he feels everything so deeply. He has refused to talk to the police. I'm afraid they will think he is hiding something. I don't know what to do. Normally we are so close. But he won't confide in me. I am so worried."

Noting that Mrs. Voss had dropped her handkerchief, Nate bent over and retrieved it for her before resuming his seat. "Now, there is no need to get so upset. Look, I'll tell you what. I'll leave this copy of a list of possible investments for Jeremy to glance over; ask him to get back to me. Then maybe I, or my uncle Frank, could have a talk with him. Find out what's bothering him. Give him a little advice."

Nate pulled the list out of his inside jacket pocket and handed it to Mrs. Voss, who frowned at the pieces of paper as if they were written in Sanskrit.

"Oh, that is very good of you. I'm afraid none of this makes any sense to me. I have been wondering and wondering how Matthew planned to pay Malcolm for his shares in the company if we have no money."

Nate exclaimed sharply, "Mrs. Voss! What ever gave you the idea that Matthew planned on buying his partner out? We have heard nothing of this from Samuels."

Mrs. Voss shook her head slightly and said, "No, I don't think

Malcolm knows, and since Matthew's death I really haven't known whether or not to even mention it. I think Matthew planned it all for a surprise. He only told the family Saturday night at dinner. The last time we were all together."

At this point she began to weep in earnest, and if Nate hadn't been so impatient to find out what Mrs. Voss was speaking about, he would have pulled the cord for her servant and fled. Instead he leaned closer and said softly, "Please, Mrs. Voss, try to tell me about that dinner. I think it might be very important."

Mrs. Voss nodded and said, "Please forgive me, Mr. Dawson. Silly of me to cry so much. I will try to help." She then took a deep breath and began to speak in a quiet voice, staring in front of her as if she could see the scene she began to describe.

"Everyone was at dinner but Malcolm. Matthew, Jeremy, myself, my sister-in-law. Malcolm was supposed to dine with us, but didn't. I remember having Nellie remove his place. Actually it was unusual for us to have a guest on Saturdays, as it was the maid's night out. Usually we do our entertaining on Friday nights. On Saturdays, I try to have our large meal at mid-day, so that Nellie can leave early. But Matthew had asked us all to be there. He seemed put out at first, when he arrived home around five and found the telegram from Malcolm saying he couldn't come. But then his mood changed. All the way through dinner he was in such a playful mood, teasing us all as he had when Jeremy was just a boy, making us laugh, putting me to the blush."

Mrs. Voss stopped at this point, smiling softly. Before he could say anything, she continued with a sigh, "Then, when we'd concluded the main course, and Nellie had served the dessert and left the room, Matthew took his spoon and tapped it on his wine glass for attention. Just like he would do if he were making a toast at a grand banquet. 'What was the special occasion?' I asked him. He said he had an announcement, but that having all his family sitting down together under one roof was special occasion enough."

Mrs. Voss again paused and glanced at Nate. "You see, Jeremy hasn't been dining at home much. A young man, he has his friends, his club. It's only natural. But I don't think Matthew understood."

"But the announcement? What was it about?"

"Well. There were several parts to it, each really more unexpected than the last. I think he had been planning this surprise for some time. He did so like surprises. Every Christmas he'd be just as he was that night at dinner. Gleeful, hugging his grand secrets to himself. He could be so generous, even extravagant. But he didn't always consider if the recipient would want what he gave them."

Mrs. Voss again faltered. Her memories now seemed darker. Giving her head a little shake, she sat straighter. "He had three announcements, really. First, that he had decided to buy Malcolm out. Said it was time for Malcolm to stop his traveling. Said the money he'd give Malcolm for his share of the company would let him start some local enterprise, settle down, and start a family. Then, he said he planned to give Malcolm's share of the business to Jeremy. The company would be now Voss and Son. After running the business in partnership for six months, he intended on turning full control over to Jeremy as a wedding present. Finally, and perhaps the biggest surprise to me, Matthew announced that he would then close up the house so the two of us could go on an extended three-year tour of Europe. Something I have always wanted to do, ever since we married."

Mrs. Voss stopped and looked questioningly at Nate. "So you see. I can't understand how Matthew could have hoped to buy out Malcolm, or turn the business over to Jeremy, or take us on a tour of Europe if there was no money. It just doesn't make any sense, does it, Mr. Dawson? No sense at all."

## Chapter Nine:
## Friday evening, August 10, 1879

Annie thought she had never been quite so tired in all her life. She had started her job as a maid in the Voss household only that morning, but she felt as if she had been on her feet for days. As if on cue, her feet began to ache in an agonizing fashion. The desire to sit down on one of the heavily carved dining room chairs and rest her weary head on the soft linen tablecloth almost overpowered her. But she dared not. *Servants did not take such liberties.* No doubt Cartier, Mrs. Voss's lady's maid, would find out somehow and tell Miss Nancy.

*Cartier, what a silly, affected name,* Annie thought. *I bet she wasn't born with it. She's probably a plain old Jones or something. I wonder what her first name is? Of course, lowly parlor maids don't warrant the privilege of addressing upstairs maids like Miss Cartier by their first names.*

This was just one of the many rules for proper servant behavior that Cartier had been pontificating about for the past twelve hours. "I sure would like to lay down a few rules for Miss Cartier," Annie grumbled aloud, as she angrily shoved the chair up against the table and tugged the cloth straight. Rule number one would be to treat a new fellow servant with a little kindness and concern, instead of trying to make life miserable for her.

Cartier was a very handsome woman in her mid-thirties. Apparently she had been able to parley a brief job as an assistant nursemaid in London into a career as a highly paid "lady's maid" back in the States. Annie knew that American women were often willing to pay high wages for a maid with European "polish." Cartier was quite tall, and she used her height effectively. She displayed much of her ample salary on her back, dressing so elegantly that Annie wouldn't have been surprised if a visitor mistook Cartier for the mistress of the house.

A searing pain snaked across her shoulders and down each arm to her fingers, banishing all thoughts of Cartier. Annie, in the process of lifting a pair of heavy silver candelabra from the table to the sideboard, came close to dropping these unquestionably expensive pieces before getting them safely to their allotted places.

"Would have fractured my toes," she muttered. *The blasted things feel like they are lined with lead. And they're ugly as well. Oh, for pity's sake, what am I doing? I'll never make it through tonight.*

Throwing caution to the winds, she pulled out one of the chairs and sat down. This alleviated the ache in her feet somewhat, but did little to ease the persistent pain in her shoulder. She hadn't known that ironing could be so difficult. It wasn't as if she'd never ironed before. But there seemed to have been mountains of wet sheets, pillowcases, towels, tablecloths, shirts, petticoats, and handkerchiefs. Thank goodness she hadn't had to wash everything first. She could swear that the irons had become heavier and heavier as she used them, until they'd felt like massive blocks that she could barely lift from the stove. As she grew more tired, she had become increasingly clumsy, wrinkling sections that she had already ironed, having to do them all over again. She must have burned herself in a dozen places trying to determine whether the irons had heated or cooled sufficiently to be used.

Massaging the back of her neck, Annie thought, *What a wretched job! How in heaven's name does Kathleen do it every week for a house full of boarders? I really must get Beatrice to hire a laundress to help her. No wonder she was worried about how well I could play the part of a maidservant! But did I listen? No!*

Tuesday afternoon, when she left an obviously bewildered Mr. Dawson at her doorstep, Annie had been supremely confident of the brilliance of her plan for solving the mystery of Mr. Voss's death and her own financial problems. She would apply as a temporary housemaid at the Voss's, to replace the departed Nellie. This would give her the chance to get to know everyone in the house, plus any frequent visitors. She could look for the missing assets, find out exactly what happened the night Matthew died, and determine who killed him.

Annie had not counted on the strong opposition she would encounter the next day from the three women--Kathleen, Beatrice, and Mrs. Stein—that she had assumed would help her carry out her plans.

First Beatrice had told her she was "daft to think of such a thing!" And then Mrs. Stein, who was sitting in the rocking chair by the window, put down her knitting and had added, "Annie, dear, I am afraid I must agree with Mrs. O'Rourke. I understand you are convinced there is some mystery to Matthew Voss's death, and you think you would be able to uncover the truth if you could find a way into the household. What I don't understand is the urgency you seem to feel."

Beatrice had turned around, wiping her hands on a towel. "My point exactly, dearie. I know that for those that aren't familiar with their methods, the police can seem a might slow. But from what I hear, Detective Jackson, what's in charge of this case, is a through and through professional. Not some do-nothing boss appointee. I warrant he'll get to the bottom of it, if you just give him time."

Annie had responded impatiently, "Well, even if the police can be convinced that Mr. Voss's death wasn't suicide, no matter how professional Detective Jackson is, you can't really expect him or his men to have the financial expertise or the time to track down stray investments, or even recognize the significance of records referring to those investments if they did run across them. And that is why it is crucial that I be involved. I was the one who made the recommendations to Mr. Voss, so I would be the best one to try and track down those missing assets of his."

Kathleen had chimed in, and Annie couldn't help smiling at the memory of how earnest she had looked as she made her argument. "But Ma'am. Didn't you say Mr. Dawson was going to look into the missing stuff for you? A smart lawyer feller like him would know all about such things. And being the family's lawyer and all, he could ask questions without getting into trouble. And pardon me, Ma'am, but I can't help but think some parlor maid snooping around, looking into the master's desk drawers, would raise quite a ruckus. That is if you could pass yourself off as a parlor maid in the first place. Which would be a miracle, as I've said before. A fine lady like yourself!"

Then Kathleen had grinned at her, no doubt trying to take the sting out of her words. But, nevertheless, she had been sending a clear message; she thought Annie simply would not be able to carry off her plan to work as a servant.

Annie had finally prevailed, but only later Wednesday evening after she had been forced to confess to the three women why getting into the Voss household was so urgent. It had been the perceptive Mrs. Stein who had winkled it out of her. Once again the four of them had been in the kitchen, arguing about Annie's plan, as Beatrice and Kathleen cleaned up after dinner. Annie had come down as usual for a cup of tea after transforming out of her Sibyl persona for the day.

"Annie," Mrs. Stein's voice had been stern. "I think there is something you are not telling us. Is it the inheritance, dear? Is that why you are so anxious? I know it must be frustrating not knowing if you are going to ever get your legacy from Matthew Voss. But to rush into things won't help. Even if the stocks are found, from what Herbert explained to me, it might take months before probate is completed and you would be able to call them your own."

"Yes, but Mrs. Stein, don't you see, once they are found, I could borrow on the expectation of receiving them...." She had stopped, aware she had revealed too much, but it was too late.

Dear Beatrice had reacted first. She had trotted across the kitchen and sat down next to Annie, grasping both her hands in her own. "Now, Annie, love. What is this all about? Why would you need to borrow money? What's gone wrong? I just knew that something more than that poor man's death was eating at you." Here Beatrice had looked over at Mrs. Stein with a significant nod. "Didn't I say that our Annie was worrying herself about something?"

Annie had gazed at the concerned faces surrounding her, basking in their affection, and then she had taken a deep breath and told them everything. She told them about her husband's debt, and Mr. Driscoll's threatening letter, and her hopes that the mining stock that Voss left her might help save the house.

And all three women had begun to talk at once.

"Well, I never, Ma'am! Can a man really do that, take the house right out from under a poor widow...."

"Saints preserve us! Just when were you planning on letting me know about this, young lady, or did you think...."

"Annie, you should have told us, I am sure Herbert would have been able to...."

Annie had been torn between laughter and tears at her friends' indignation. She explained to Kathleen that creditors were often successful in attaching wives' estates to settle their husbands' debts, and she apologized to Beatrice for not telling her earlier, and she had pointed out that since Mr. Stein had left on a business trip that Wednesday morning and wouldn't be back for a week that she really couldn't wait for his advice. There had followed a good deal more discussion, but when all was said and done, she finally had the women on her side.

From that point on, events had moved swiftly. Early the next morning Mrs. Stein sent a note to Mrs. Voss asking if she could use the services of a reliable housemaid. By midday she had received a gracious note in return asking if the servant in question could start early that Friday morning. Annie then had sent Jamie with a notice to the *Chronicle* announcing that, as of Friday, Madam Sibyl would be out of town for a week. Annie certainly hoped this wouldn't lose her too many clients, but the consequences were so much worse if she had to sell the house that she felt the temporary loss of income was necessary.

After dinner Kathleen had gone through Annie's clothes, picking out what would be suitable for a maid, and added one of her own starched aprons and caps to the suitcase that Annie was assembling. Kathleen also promised that she would try to track down the servant, Nellie, who had left her job right after Matthew's death. She seemed to feel Nellie could tell them more than Annie would ever find out in a few days snooping. At this point Annie couldn't help but think she was right. The rest of the evening had been spent with Beatrice and Kathleen trying to tell her everything they thought she should know to pull off her masquerade. Rubbing her sore right shoulder, Annie again thought how foolish she had been to dismiss their concerns. It turned out there was an enormous difference between managing a servant and being one.

A muffled noise outside in the hallway brought Annie sharply back to the present and she swiftly got to her feet. By the time the dining room door opened, she had stood up and was busily engaged in sweeping imaginary crumbs from the tablecloth. Her heart beating furiously, she turned and bobbed a short curtsey to the woman who had entered. She then covertly examined the older woman who was surveying the room. Up close, Miss Nancy Voss looked even more like a washed-out version of her brother Matthew. Somewhere in her late fifties, with a tall, spare frame and ramrod-straight back, Miss Voss had encased herself in an uncompromising mourning that eliminated any life or color that might ever had existed in the shades of grey that dominated her hair, skin, and eyes.

Miss Voss broke the silence with a voice that reminded Annie of flint. "That will do, girl. You can return to your duties in the kitchen now. You did all right tonight serving at dinner, a sight better than you did at ironing Master Jeremy's shirts this afternoon. Remember in the future that you mustn't let them get too dry, or the creases will never come out."

"Yes, Miss," responded Annie, who curtsied again and then left Nancy Voss staring into the dying embers in the room's large ornate fireplace. She longed to stay and talk to the older woman, but she had already discovered that in this household, except when acknowledging an order, servants were to be seen and not heard. So Annie did as she had been directed and made her way down the stairs to the kitchen.

"No gossiping with the other servants!" That was one of Cartier's rules, although Annie had noticed she had plenty to say, but it was all about Annie's duties as a servant. In contrast, the other servant in the household, the Chinese manservant Wong, had spoken not a word to her the whole time she'd been here, even when they had worked together getting dinner ready. She wasn't even sure he spoke English.

As for the Voss family itself, well! She hadn't gotten a glimpse of Matthew's son, Jeremy, who appeared to have taken up permanent residence at his club. And Matthew's grieving widow, Amelia Voss, hadn't yet left her room; Cartier took all her meals to her. Except for a short visit from the dressmaker, who came to the house to do the final fitting for the new black morning dresses that she had ordered,

Mrs. Voss wasn't seeing anyone. This meant the only member of the family Annie had had any contact with had been Matthew's sister, Miss Nancy. And she wasn't exactly chatty. This evening was particularly odd, as Annie served the older lady in the dining room in solitary splendor. Although she was glad to have that practice before being asked to serve the whole family at once, it meant she had so far learned precious little, except how tiring it was to run up and down the stairs from the basement kitchen to the dining room.

She had arrived at the house this morning at six o'clock and had been busy doing the ironing and helping Wong prepare and serve meals since then. As a result Annie had found few opportunities for exploring. So far she had access only to the kitchen, the dining room, and the front parlor, and none of these rooms had revealed anything of interest, except that Matthew's family had dutifully draped every possible surface of the public rooms with black crape. Even more frustratingly, Miss Nancy had explicitly instructed her not to go into Matthew's first-floor study, the room she most wanted to search for clues about the missing assets.

She had learned one piece of information. Cartier seemed jealous of Miss Nancy's position in the household. Miss Nancy made it clear she was responsible for the day-to-day management of the house, but Cartier kept insisting on checking with Matthew's wife before she carried out any command. This, however, seemed to be a long-standing struggle; the icily polite conversations between Miss Nancy and Cartier contained a well-rehearsed quality to them. And Annie couldn't see how it had any bearing on Matthew's death.

Entering the warmly lit kitchen, Annie paused in surprise. Wong had completed the dish-washing. Miss Nancy had informed her that since Wong was responsible for cooking the dinner, it would be her duty to clean up afterwards. Because of her aching feet and shoulders, she had been dreading this task. Wong turned from the sink and waved her towards the large kitchen table, where he had set out a late snack for her.

No, Annie thought, not a snack, a piece of artwork! A thick blue kitchen plate sat squarely in the middle of a woven mat of burnt orange. Echoing the colors of plate and mat, a sky-blue vase held a single golden chrysanthemum. Continuing the autumnal color scheme, on the plate rested a thick slice of apple pie, its buttery crust baked so delicately that it was difficult to determine where the pie-crust ended and the slab of mellow cheddar cheese beside it began. And as Annie sank gratefully into the seat in front of this culinary masterpiece, Wong added the finishing touches to the picture by placing at her side a delicately crafted cup of robin's-egg blue, in which strong, fall-colored tea swirled.

"Oh, Wong," Annie sighed. "You are wonderful! I don't know that I have ever seen anything so beautiful in my life." Her stomach then growled out its opinion, and she continued, laughing, "I am certainly sure that I have never seen anything as beautiful and utilitarian at the same time. It seems almost a sacrilege to disturb it by eating, but I am afraid that while the mind is strong, the flesh is weak."

With this, Annie picked up the fork and began to eat. She didn't know if he understood her, but hoped that at least her tone of voice conveyed her sentiments. As she finished up the pie and sipped at the tea, her spirits unaccountably rose. Wong sat down across from her and beamed. She smiled back, nodding in pantomime her appreciation. He was older than most of the Chinese she had known, with white hairs that looked like thin white wires threaded through the black braid that hung down his back. She thought Matthew had once mentioned that his manservant had started working for him in the mining camps. Wong must have some insight into who might have wanted his master dead. She wished she could remember some of the Cantonese she had learned from Choy, who worked for her family on their Los Angeles ranch while she was growing up. But she couldn't.

She knew that many Californians despised and mistreated the Chinese, called them dirty heathens, and worse. She felt quite differently. Since her mother had been frequently confined to bed by illness and her father was usually out managing the ranch when she was young, Annie had often been left to the care of Choy, their cook. She had found him a wise and gentle friend.

These bittersweet memories were swept away when Wong began to speak to her in clear, excellent English. "It is a pleasure to cook for one who finds joy in the harmony of what the eye sees and the tongue tastes, Miss. You seemed to be in need of renewal of both body and spirit."

Annie found herself staring, open-mouthed. Then she laughed. "Wong, for heaven's sake, why have you been pretending not to understand English?"

Wong smiled slightly and then shook his head gently. "Excuse me, Miss, I have not been pretending anything. I simply chose not to speak. I have found that there is often less misunderstanding that way. It seems to me that it is you who have been pretending, pretending to be a servant when you are not."

Annie felt a rising sense of panic. Had her secret already been discovered? She should never have let her interpretation of a dim-witted servant lapse in front of Wong. Or was he just referring to her ineptness? Was he going to give her away? She had to say something, quickly.

Trying to sound unconcerned she said, "Oh dear, have I been doing such a bad job of it? I am afraid I haven't had as much practice as I ought. And I've been out of service for a while. I guess I've gotten rusty. Please, will you help me? You see I really need this job. I intend no harm, and I believe that I can do some good."

Annie had leaned forward as she spoke, trying to impress upon Wong her sincerity. She found it difficult to read the old man's response because of the softer, flatter planes of his features. She was used to seeing harder angles and the telltale lines around eyes, nose, and mouth that pain, worry, fear, and laughter etched on even the youngest person. She wondered, as they both stared solemnly at each other, if Wong was having an equally difficult time reading her expressions. But no, she thought, as a servant he would have had to learn years ago how to discern the hidden meanings found in the faces of his alien employers.

Annie was anxiously awaiting his response, when the sound of a bell from behind drew her attention. With some relief Annie smiled tentatively at Wong and said as she rose, "Can we talk later? I have to see what Mrs. Voss wants."

## Chapter Ten

Annie stood in front of Amelia Voss's sitting room door and took a deep breath. She had to lay aside her concerns about Wong's statement so that she could make the most of this opportunity. This would be the first time she saw Mrs. Voss up close, and she realized that she had been curious to meet Matthew's beloved wife in person. She knocked on the door to the sitting room, and, at a quiet "come in," she entered. The different quality of this room from the rest of the house struck her immediately. First of all, the room seemed bathed in a warm rosy glow, as the light from the fireplace and the oil lamps filtered through thin embossed screens of red and pink. In addition, there didn't appear to be a hard or dark surface in the room. She saw none of the ornately carved tables and chairs and dark paneling that characterized the rest of the house. Mrs. Voss's room, without the slightest hint of black, was papered and draped and upholstered and cushioned in a dazzling variety of bright-colored silks that seemed to give out light rather than to absorb it. Annie found the effect charming.

She felt no doubt about who was responsible for the room's decor. Wearing a richly embroidered-dressing gown of deep burgundy that was elegant enough for street-wear, the woman sitting on one of the well-padded armchairs clearly belonged in this setting. Annie was again surprised by the youthfulness of Matthew's wife, for Mrs. Voss appeared even younger when no longer obscured by heavy mourning veils. There were some of the marks of maturity that testified that she was indeed a woman in her early forties and the mother of a full-grown son. But the sprinkling of grey hairs, the small lines around eyes and mouth, the slight softening of the flesh at the base of the throat only served to make the overall beauty of the woman even more remarkable. Her thick black hair swept down from a center part, massing in an intricate coil at the nape of her neck. Dark eyebrows, delicately arched, and equally dark eyelashes of unusual length emphasized the extreme whiteness of her complexion. But it was her eyes that dominated all of her other features. As Mrs. Voss looked up from her embroidery frame, Annie mentally reviewed all the terms for the color blue, trying to hit upon just the right word to describe these eyes. Azure, indigo, cobalt, turquoise. No, Annie thought, no word quite fit the unique color of the eyes of Amelia Voss.

Eyes whose depth completely contradicted the shallow torrent of words that began to issue from her mouth.

"Oh, my, it's the new girl, how simply lovely!" said Mrs. Voss, with just the hint of her Southern birthplace. "Do come closer and let's get acquainted. You must think me terribly remiss to have engaged you without taking the time to even meet you. You will forgive me, won't you? I'm sure we will get along just splendidly now that we have met. Oh dear, I've dropped my thread. Oh, well, never mind."

Annie could well understand why Matthew had wished to spare his wife any knowledge of his financial difficulties.

Mrs. Voss gushed on, "I'm afraid that you will find me a terribly muddled sort of mistress, particularly now. But my sister-in-law, Miss Nancy, is so practical, and she takes care of everything. She always has."

At this, Mrs. Voss turned her head and threw a brief smile to her left, and Annie, following her glance was startled to realize that Miss Nancy had been sitting silently in the corner the whole time.

There was no answering smile on Miss Nancy's dour face. In fact, Annie could have sworn that Matthew's sister shuddered abruptly, as if Amelia Voss's words had been the flick of a whip.

As Annie drew closer, Mrs. Voss continued. "Well, now, Lizzie, that is your name isn't it? I remembered it especially because when I went to Miss Henderson's Finishing School there was a lively young girl who served at table there. She was a great favorite with all the young ladies because she would buy chocolates and other goodies for us on her day off and sneak them to our rooms. Sweets were strictly forbidden. I did so love cream puffs, but that was certainly way before your time."

Annie had given her name as Lizzie when she had come about the job, wishing to prevent anyone from making a connection between Annie Fuller and the new servant. She had chosen Lizzie in part because it sounded so maid-like, and in part because for a brief time in sixth grade friends had teased her by using that diminutive of her middle name, Elizabeth. She hoped that this tie to the past would be enough to ensure that when anyone called for Lizzie, she would remember they were referring to her. So far it really hadn't been a problem, because everyone simply referred to her as "girl," an appellation she found increasingly irritating.

Mrs. Voss continued to chatter on. "So Lizzie, I hope that you will be comfortable here. We certainly do appreciate you helping us out in our time of trouble. With my husband's death, such a sad accident, so unexpected, we are simply at sixes and sevens, and...."

"Amelia, don't be a fool," Nancy Voss's harsh voice cut across her sister-in-law's gentler tones and effectively silenced them. "The girl doesn't want to hear about Matthew's death. What she does want to hear is why she was called up here. Girl, fetch us a pot of tea. Wong will show you what is needed and will help you bring it up if you can't manage it yourself. That woman Cartier has gone to bed with what she calls a sick headache. More likely an excess of spite.

So you will have to tend to Mrs. Voss for the rest of the evening. Well, don't just stand there, get along."

Annie curtsied in response and turned to execute her orders. But in doing so she collided sharply with Jeremy Voss, who at that instant entered his mother's sitting room.

"Oh, I'm sorry, terribly clumsy of me," Jeremy apologized with a smile that quite transformed him from the brooding Byronic hero to a rather engaging schoolboy. "You must be the new girl. Won't Cartier have her nose out of joint! She's used to being the only handsome servant in the house. The last girl, Nellie, wasn't nearly as elegant as you. But don't you let Cartier get you down with that sharp tongue of hers. Its just jealousy!"

Mrs. Voss interrupted her son at this point, chiding, "Jeremy, do stop. You know I don't like you teasing Miss Cartier, and you are making poor Lizzie blush. Stop making mischief and let her get on with her duties."

Annie was indeed blushing, much to her irritation. Her husband had displayed just that sort of flirtatious charm, and she had grown to detest it. What was even more annoying, she had deliberately tried to look the part of a mousy domestic by wearing one of her most out-of-date and worn dresses and by pulling her hair severely back into an unadorned bun. The last thing she wanted was any unusual attention. Of course, judging by the smell of whiskey that emanated from Jeremy, he would have flirted with any female he ran into, and his mother was probably used to it. However, his jab at Cartier did bear further thought. Might the stylish lady's maid have set her sights on the young master of the house? If so, how would she have reacted to his recently announced engagement?

As she left the room, she heard Jeremy say, "Mother, darling, you're out of bed. Are you feeling better? I'm sorry I've been out so much, I just couldn't stick it here with all the old vultures stopping by to make their insincere condolences."

Annie paused after the door was shut, hoping to be able to catch more of his words, but the door was too solid. Jeremy's voice was immediately reduced to an unintelligible murmur. She admonished herself for having shut the door completely. She must stop acting so well-mannered and get a bit more devious, otherwise she'd never learn anything at all.

A short while later, when she returned to the sitting room, it was clear that something had happened to disturb the room's three occupants. Jeremy leaned against the fireplace, with his back turned to both his mother and his aunt, kicking moodily at a small cinder that had popped out onto the hearth. His mother was stitching furiously at her embroidery, eyes down and her breathing uneven. His aunt still sat silently in the shadows, her face a rigid, unreadable mask. But the glint of firelight reflecting off her eyes revealed that she was shifting her glance rapidly between her nephew and her sister-in-law, as if trying to read their minds. The air in the room palpably vibrated with the after-effects of a heated exchange abruptly broken off by Annie's entrance.

As she slipped quietly back and forth from the hallway table, setting up the tea service, silence in the room grew ever more awkward. Finally, the social habits of Mrs. Voss reasserted themselves, and she rose and went to the tea table to start pouring.

Nodding graciously to Annie, Mrs. Voss said, "Thank you, Lizzie. I do hope that Wong was able to help you with the tea things. When you have finished here, could you please prepare my bedroom? I shall probably retire soon. I haven't been well, you know, since the terrible ordeal of the funeral, and I really am completely done in."

Then, clearing her throat nervously, Mrs. Voss turned to her son and sister-in-law and attempted to change the mood by introducing a neutral topic of conversation. Annie watched in fascination as this gambit met with disastrously little success.

"Well, Jeremy, I received the sweetest little note of condolence from Judith this morning," Mrs. Voss remarked. "I meant to show it to you, but you had gone out already. You can't imagine how pleased I am that you have the love and support of such a wonderful girl to help you through these times. I remember how much...."

Jeremy turned around and snapped, "Mother, don't be such a romantic. Do you honestly think that Judith will stand by me? I'm surprised she hasn't broken off the engagement already!"

"Oh, Jeremy," said Mrs. Voss, "why would you say such a thing? Judith adores you."

"Well, that's hard to believe since I haven't been permitted to see her since the funeral. Somehow, she is never *at home* when I call. And, I am quite certain that her mother will find someone else for her to *adore* quite easily, someone untainted by scandal who won't disgrace her proud Southern heritage," Jeremy replied.

His mother reached her hand out to him, and in a plaintive voice she said, "I am sure you have misjudged the situation. I can't understand why you are insisting that there will be scandal, anyway. Your father died of an unfortunate accident. Where is the dishonor in...."

Stepping back from her as if her touch might burn, Jeremy barked out, "Unfortunate accident! No, mother, you cannot continue this charade. Father committed suicide. Mr. Dawson told you what was said at the inquest. To go on pretending that it was all some sort of accident just makes all of us look ridiculous."

Annie, who had silently crossed over to Mrs. Voss's bedroom during this conversation, turned and paused just inside the doorway, hoping that no one would notice her. From this vantage point she watched Mrs. Voss begin to weep. When Jeremy noticed this he immediately turned contrite.

Going over and pulling up a chair next to hers, he said softly, "Oh, mother, don't cry. I'm sorry. I haven't gotten much sleep lately and I feel like my whole life has crashed down around my shoulders.

I should never have taken it out on you. But don't you see, pretending only makes it worse. We've got to face up to the facts. It's no use otherwise."

"But Jeremy, I still don't understand how it could have happened. Your father was so happy at Saturday dinner with his grand plans. Buying Malcolm out, making you a partner in the firm as a wedding present, and taking me to Europe! Why would he promise to do all that and then kill himself? It just doesn't make any sense, it must have been an accident."

Mrs. Voss gently shook her head, blotting her wet cheeks with the handkerchief Jeremy had retrieved from its newest resting place on the floor. She continued, in a rallying voice, "In any event, you mustn't despair. You have your whole life ahead of you and you must not let your father's death or any of this interfere. If there has been a misunderstanding with Judith, talk to her and straighten it out. Your father would want that. I am sure she is just waiting to hear from you."

Jeremy sighed, "Mother, you haven't been listening. I can't go on as if nothing is changed. Somehow we must try to straighten out our financial affairs. Even if Judith still wanted me, I couldn't afford to get married now. There's not enough money. I know we have been all over this, but as much as you and Aunt Nan don't like the idea, I can't see any way around selling our shares in the company. It's all my fault. If only I hadn't been so stubborn and selfish."

Mrs. Voss sat up straight at this and exclaimed, "No, my darling boy, don't ever let me hear you say that. None of this is your fault. Besides there must be money, how else could he have planned to pay Malcolm? I know the lawyers say there isn't any, but your father..."

Jeremy's aunt stepped forward from the shadows. Annie almost gave herself away at this point by gasping; she had been so engrossed in the mother and son that she had forgotten Nancy Voss was even there.

The older woman rapped out in her rough way. "Jeremy, for once your mother is right. This tragedy is not your fault. And you should not have to bear the brunt of its consequences."

She then turned towards her sister-in-law and began to speak in a low, fervent voice. "Others are to blame, others who sucked your father dry, who took and took and never gave in return. It was by their hand that your father died. They are to blame, and they will suffer for it. I will see to that. As the good Lord said in Job, 'Look on everyone that is proud, and bring him low; and tread the wicked in their place.'"

## Chapter Eleven:
## Very early Saturday morning, August 11, 1879

Annie found herself awake, her heart pounding. For some reason she was curled-up in a tight ball under a thin unfamiliar blanket. When she tried to straighten out, her body seemed to be frozen into a kind of *rigor mortis*. It was dark, and the material beneath her cheek was rough and smelled of carbolic soap. Where was she? Then she remembered. She was lying in a narrow bed up in the attic in Matthew Voss's house. She vaguely recalled climbing the long back stairs to her room around ten o'clock, after having tidied up the tea things. She must have just stripped down to her chemise and drawers, too tired to properly undress. This was a mistake, since clearly the attic got very cold at night, even in the summertime, and the blanket was certainly inadequate.

It was still dark, so maybe it wasn't time to get up yet. Stifling a groan, Annie tried to wake her protesting limbs from their premature death, as she pulled her unresponsive body to the side of the bed. Barely enough moonlight came in from the narrow window under the eaves for her to make out the face of the traveling clock she had brought with her. She groaned more loudly when she saw it was only twelve-thirty. She had been asleep just long enough for every ache and pain of her over-worked muscles to flower into their full glory. Death didn't seem like such a terrible alternative.

Annie slowly turned onto her back, pulled the blanket up, and tentatively stretched herself straight. Barring one excruciating moment when her right calf cramped, the new position was a definite improvement. Wishing to distract herself from her bodily complaints, she began to review what she had learned on her first day as a maidservant. She hadn't been able to continue her conversation with Wong because, by the time she had finished getting Mrs. Voss ready for bed, he had already left the house. She could only hope he wasn't planning on voicing his suspicions to Miss Nancy when he came back in the morning; it would be humiliating to be dismissed without having learned anything definitive. It had been his discreet knock at the sitting room door that had broken the appalled silence that had followed Nancy Voss's extraordinary lapse into biblical prophecy. Wong had come to ask Jeremy to let him out of the house so he could return to his lodging in Chinatown.

Earlier in the day Miss Nancy had explained that Mr. Voss had insisted the house remain locked at all times. This meant that if any servant wanted in or out, someone would have to be present to unlock and re-lock the bolt. Evidently, decades before, Matthew had been robbed during the daytime and consequently had been quite fanatical about taking this precaution. This must be why the police dismissed the possibility of an intruder.

Annie had used Wong's interruption to cover her stealthy movement from the sitting room into Mrs. Voss's bedroom. She hoped that everyone, if they bothered to think about her at all, would assume she had been there the whole time. Jeremy and Miss Nancy must have left the sitting room with Wong, for almost immediately Mrs. Voss followed Annie into the bedroom and wordlessly began preparing to retire. Unfortunately this had meant she hadn't had time to search the bedroom for the missing assets.

Annie lay in the dark pondering the enigma of Mrs. Voss. She could swear she had seen a spark of intelligence in her beautiful eyes, and yet her conversation struck her as childish and naïve. Actually, much about the conversation she had over heard confused

Annie. Why was Jeremy so adamant that his father's death was suicide? Could it be that he wanted to divert attention from the possibility that Matthew was murdered? But why would he then blame
himself for his father's death? And hadn't Mr. Dawson said it was
Jeremy who had insisted that Matthew was financially solvent? If
so, what would the motive for suicide be? Then there was Miss
Nancy's extraordinary accusation. She couldn't possibly mean that
Mrs. Voss had killed her husband. Yet Mrs. Voss was afraid of
something; her protests to Jeremy that everything would be just fine
held a clear note of panic.

The one thing that had made sense to her was the idea that Matthew planned to buy out Samuels. This might explain what he had
done with the assets he had been accumulating. In fact, she wished
she could get word to Mr. Dawson about this, because it might be
that Matthew had cashed in his assets in preparation for making an
offer to his partner. But then where was the money?

Having thought of Nate Dawson, she experienced a twinge of un-
easiness. It was possible that he might stop by the boarding house if
he had any additional information about Matthew's financial affairs,
but she had left strict instructions with Kathleen and Beatrice not to
divulge her whereabouts to anyone. The more disturbing thought
was that he might discover her whereabouts himself if he called on
the Voss household. He was such mystery; so gruff and humorless at
the law office then quite personable on the walk home. She could
just imagine what he would say about her decision to come to work
as a maid. Unbidden she had a vision of him standing at the Voss's
front door, frowning down at her from his superior height, those
fierce brown eyes boring into her own.

Feeling inexplicably warmer, Annie sat up, and hugged her
knees. Thank goodness Miss Nancy had agreed to let her take Saturday night and all of Sunday off, despite the fact that she had just
started work. Beatrice had made her promise that she would ask for

this, saying that she would need the additional day to recuperate. At the time she had scoffed at Beatrice's concern, but now the idea that she would be spending the next two nights in her own bed was heaven. Evidently the previous servant, Nellie, had gotten only Wednesday afternoons and Saturday nights off, but clearly Miss Nancy was so desperate to engage a new maid she hadn't quibbled about this request.

Thinking about her night off led Annie to consider why the former servant, Nellie, had left her position so precipitously. Except for Jeremy's brief mention of her looks, and a few disparaging comments by Cartier about her leaving without notice, there had been no mention of her or why she left. *I wonder what she was like? Did she like working here? Was she lonely?* Annie was afraid to ask Wong about her, because it might further his suspicions. Could it be Nellie was involved in Matthew's death? Perhaps she had been bribed to let someone into the house before she left that evening-and was afraid she would be blamed for Matthew's death? But then, how could this person have gotten out of the house without leaving one of the doors unlocked?

Cold again, she pulled the blanket around her shoulders, thinking how odd it was to be sitting on a narrow cot, under Matthew's roof, seriously considering who might have killed him. *Oh, if only I could talk to Matthew about what happened!*

She swung her legs to the edge of the bed. *This is useless,* she thought angrily. *Sitting here wishing I could talk to a dead man isn't going to solve anything. I'm wide awake now so I should be spending the time searching for the missing assets rather than in idle speculation. At least if I get up and move around I will feel warmer!*

Annie decided that she would change into her flannel nightgown and robe and slip quietly downstairs to Matthew's study on the chance it was unlocked, since this seemed the logical place to start looking for the missing stocks and bonds. Miss Nancy had told her that she should use the water closet behind the stairs on the first floor for her personal use, so at least she would have some sort of an excuse for being on that floor if she ran into anyone. Kathleen's comment about the "ruckus" that would result if Annie were found snooping rose unbidden in her mind. She paused for a second, her nightgown hanging from her cold fingers, then gave her head a shake. *What is the worst that would happen? Miss Nancy might give me a terrible scold. Or, maybe I would be dismissed, which would be a shame. But that's all! What else could possibly happen?*

## Chapter Twelve

Annie closed the heavy wooden door, very slowly, waiting for the soft snick of the latch. She then took a deep breath and turned around to get her first look at the room that was at the heart of Matthew's domain. So far, her night-time foray had gone remarkably well, including finding Matthew's study door unlocked. Once she had gotten past the creaky attic stairs undetected, her progress the rest of the way down three flights of stairs to the first floor had been eerily silent. The pale glow from the hallway gas jets had helped. Miss Nancy had told her these lights were to be kept on low all night. Annie hadn't been surprised to discover that Matthew's house had been built to accommodate gas, but so far none of the gas fixtures in all of the rooms she had entered had been turned on. Instead the rooms continued to be lit by the old-fashioned oil lamps or candles. These were expensive alternatives to kerosene or gas, but Annie approved of the soft clear light they produced, and she was frankly glad that her own house didn't have gas fittings. Her mother-in-law had installed gas throughout her New York City town house and Annie had never liked the harsh glare they created. But in this case, the gaslight that burned in the hallways had made it possible for her to make it to the first floor study without bumping into anything.

With the door closed behind her, the only light came from the candle she carried, and the room seemed small and cave-like. Annie thought she detected the faint smell of wood she always associated with Matthew, but there was an underlying whiff of something metallic she didn't think she wanted to identify. She listened intently for a second, but the thick silence reminded her of how little noise passed through these wooden doors, and she began to feel a little safer.

Lifting the candle up in front of her, she turned slowly to let the light slide over each wall. First she saw floor-to-ceiling book cases that marched along the wall directly to her right, wrapped around the corner and continued along the street side of the room for about three feet. Next came the large bay windows that looked out to the street in front of the house. These were matched by another set of windows that overlooked the narrow passageway between the Voss household and the neighbors. Both sets of windows were curtained in some heavy dark material that kept out the slightest hint of moonlight. Moving a few steps into the room she saw that in the corner between the two sets of windows stood a drinks cabinet, an armchair, and a small table, with a lamp and a pile of papers on it. Continuing to turn to her left the candle light revealed more bookshelves and a desk that jutted out perpendicular to the long interior wall. Moving closer to the chair near the windows, the candlelight throwing her shadow up the curtains to her left, she began to notice some additional details. There was a silver platter on the drinks cabinet, but it was missing the decanter and glasses she would have expected to see. When she leaned closer, she saw that the newspaper on the table next to the armchair was dated Saturday, August 4, which made sense, since this was the day Matthew died; she also noticed that there were several rings where the printing was blurred as if a glass had been repeatedly placed on top of the papers. She could imagine Matthew sitting in his study sometime on Saturday evening, having a whiskey, perhaps thinking about the reactions to his announcements at dinner.

Was the poison found just in the glass of whiskey or also the decanter? This would make a difference. If it was also in the decanter, then any one of the servants, well, probably not Cartier, but certainly Nellie or Wong, would be a suspect, since they both would have been able to put the poison into the decanter at any time during the day. But then there would be no guarantee that Matthew wouldn't offer the poisoned whisky to someone else, like Malcolm Samuels, if he had showed up for dinner. *I will just have to ask Patrick, he will know.*

Patrick had come by to see his aunt Bea on the previous evening, while everyone was sitting around giving Annie advice on how to be a good servant. He had been very willing to tell her everything he knew, despite his aunt's patent disapproval. For example, she now remembered that he had said that a white packet had been found on the floor at Matthew's feet, in the bottom of which they had found a residue of the poison.

"That's what cinched it for Detective Jackson, Ma'am," Patrick had said. "Proved it was suicide, finding the packet like that, where the poor man most likely dropped it before finishing off the fatal drink."

As Patrick described what the police had found, Annie had thought to herself that the murderer had certainly done a good job of setting up the scene to look like suicide, note and all. Now she also realized that this meant that the person who poisoned Matthew had probably been in the room with him as he died, or at least had access to the room after he was dead, in order to place the fake suicide note and the packet. This would make it less likely that either Wong or Nellie were involved, since Patrick said both of them left the house while Matthew was still alive and had arrived back in the morning after the body was discovered.

According to Patrick, Wong told the police that he had let Nellie out the back door at eight o'clock, as was usual for her night out, and Mr. Voss had let him out the front door at ten. This would seem to rule out involvement by these two servants. But what if Wong lied about letting Nellie out, couldn't she have simply hidden up in her attic room and then come down in the middle of the night and let someone, like Wong, back in? But then, how would that someone have gotten Matthew to drink the poison? It was even possible that if Nellie stayed hidden in the house she could creep downstairs in the early morning hours to see if Matthew had indeed had his poisoned nightcap and was now dead. Then all the she would have to do is plant the evidence to make it look like suicide, steal whatever money or documents were at hand, and sneak out of the house. *Oh dear, that was a problem, how could Nellie, or her unknown accomplice, have gotten out of the house without leaving some door or window open?* Annie was sure Patrick had said he had made a complete circuit of the house as soon as he was called in, and he didn't find any openings, except of course for the front door, which Mrs. Voss swore was locked until she opened it to let Miss Nancy go get the police.

Patrick had clearly been very impressed by Mrs. Voss. He spoke about how brave and composed she had been to answer Detective Jackson's questions, with her "poor husband's lifeless body still lying right across the hall." He said she told the police that she had been at the top of the stairs, after having just been downstairs to say good night to her husband, when she saw Wong leave and saw her husband lock the front door behind him. She thought that this was just about ten; she said she had then retired for the night. It wasn't until she woke early in the morning that she discovered that Matthew had not come to bed. She said it was her husband's habit to stay up until at least one in the morning, that he didn't need much sleep, but that he had never before been absent when she awoke.

Annie thought it spoke well of Wong that his mistress would be so quick to verify that he wasn't in the house. Patrick said she was less specific about the rest of the household. She wasn't sure when

either Cartier, who had seen her right before she retired, or her sister-in-law, had gone to bed. She believed her son had gone out after
dinner and wasn't sure when he returned, although he was there the
next morning when Matthew was found. Jeremy evidently told the
police he had come in at eleven and gone right upstairs without
speaking to his father. Not surprisingly, none of the four who were
still in the house the next morning had any idea what the other three
were up to during the rest of the night. Annie tried to imagine any
one of them coming into Matthew's study, pouring him a drink, and
standing by to watch him die.

She shuddered and her shadow danced crazily along the walls.
*Better concentrate on finding Matthew's missing assets. Its stupid to*
*stand here wondering if anyone in this house hated him enough to*
*kill him.* With that thought, Annie began to look around the room in
earnest, looking first at the desk. Besides the lamp and an inkwell
and pen there was nothing on top of the desk. She refused to think
about why the desk blotter was missing. She was very surprised
when she opened the file drawer and found nothing in it. In fact, accept for a few odds and ends--a ruler, magnifying glass, some pencil
stubs, a box of matches--that she found in the shallow drawer underneath the desk top, the desk was empty.

*This can't be right*! Annie thought. *The police would have found*
*the lack of any files suspicious!* Then she mentally kicked herself.
Probably the police, or most likely Nate or his uncle, had taken the
files to go over them. She would have to talk to him to find out if
this had been his and his uncle's handiwork. If it had been the police, maybe Nate could get access to the missing files and look
through them. Then again, it might be that Matthew kept only
household information in his study, and that the place needing a
more thorough search would be his office at the furniture factory.
She couldn't remember whether Nate had mentioned if he or Matthew's partner, Samuels, had looked there.

Annie scanned the room again and thought with a sigh that the only place left to look was the bookshelves, and that could take all night. She leaned over to look at the clock she had noticed on the desk and almost let out a gasp when she saw the hands at 4:30. *No, that can't be right,* she thought, *not that much time has passed.* Then she realized that the clock was silent, probably hadn't been wound since Saturday. *So what time was it?* No more than fifteen minutes could have passed since she entered the room. She stood and listened carefully, but could hear only the sound of her own breathing. *Well,* she thought, *I should at least look closely enough to see if it looks like any papers have been stuffed between any of the books.*

Annie crossed over to the end of the shelves to the right of the door and had just raised the candle up high to get a better look at the top shelves when a soft sound at the door gave her barely enough warning to snatch the candle down and snuff out its flame. The door was shoved open to its full extent, effectively boxing her into a tight triangle, with her back against the wall, the bookshelves to her left and the door a few inches from her nose. Annie held her breath and hoped that the candle, which she held clutched to her breast, didn't have enough heat left in the wick to set her robe on fire. Clearly whoever had entered the room had their own candle, since flashes of light cut through the edges of the door against the bookshelves and then jerkily stabbed through the long opening between the door and the doorframe. She slowly turned her head to the right so she could look over her shoulder through this opening. She was so relieved not to see an eye peering through the door hinge at her that she almost let out a sigh. Instead all she could see was a narrow strip of the end of the book shelves on the other side of the door, but the concentrated brightness of the candle light indicated that the person who had entered that room was standing right next to those shelves.

There was a light click, and then a sound of wood sliding against wood. A small rustling noise was followed by the sliding wood sound again. Before Annie had time to blink, a figure moved rapidly past the strip of light, closing the door behind them, and Annie stood alone, in the dark, trying to make sense of the image that had flashed before her eyes.

She had seen a person, in a dressing gown, holding some sort of oversized folders or books. But that was all she could recall. No face, since the head had been turned away. A dressing gown, but that didn't help; she couldn't tell if it belonged to a man or a woman. She did think that the person had been taller than she was, but that would only rule out Mrs. Voss, not Cartier, Miss Nancy, or Jeremy, and there was no one else in the house. Standing there in the dark, Annie finally took a breath. Minutes ticked by where the thump, thump of her heart was the only thing she heard. Then, as her heart and breathing slowed, she noticed the small sting on her thumb and forefinger where she had pinched the candle flame. A small bubble of relief tickled its way into a giggle, which she quickly stifled.

Annie finally got up enough courage to pull out her matches from her robe pocket and relight the candle, her hands shaking. Ruthlessly repressing the small voice in her mind that was saying, *that could have been the murderer*, she went over to the bookshelves and stood, moving the candle back and forth and looking for what might have made the sounds she heard. Running her left hand across the books in the middle shelf, she noticed a section that felt different. Instead of leather, what she felt was carved wood; as she looked more closely, she could see the wood was painted to look like books. She pressed and heard a click, and this whole section slid to the right to reveal a hidden shelf. *Oh Matthew! How this hidey-hole must have delighted you*, she thought. She wondered if anyone had told the police about it. Certainly, his family, and Nellie, who would have discovered it during dusting, must know about it.

The candlelight revealed a metal box sitting on the hidden shelf, with its lid open, empty. Otherwise there was nothing else in the hiding place. She didn't think that the box was big enough to hold the items she saw being removed from the room, but it was certainly big enough and deep enough to hold a stack of property deeds, stock certificates, or even money. She didn't think whoever had just been in the room had had time enough to open the box and take things out, so she had to assume it was already empty. So what had just now been removed from the hiding place? *And why had anyone come down in the dead of night to get it?*

# Chapter Thirteen:
## Saturday evening, August 11, 1879

"His name is Jack O'Sullivan, Ma'am," Kathleen said, "And as I told you, my friend Moira says he's been courting Nellie Flannigan for nearly six months. Moira says she can't imagine them missing this dance for the world."

"Are you sure this is the Nellie that worked for Mr. Voss?" said Annie. "Seems an awfully common name. Do we have any description of her, or this Jack?"

"Oh yes, Ma'am, I'm sure it's her. Moira worked with Nellie in another position two years ago, and they kept in touch. She knew all about her working for Mr. Voss. Told me Nellie is short, got a good figure, has striking red hair, and frizzes her bangs something awful. Said Jack's a typical Irishman--all blarney and a big mustache."

It was nine o'clock in the evening, and Annie and Kathleen were standing just inside the entrance to the Parker House, where the St. Joseph's Annual Parish Masked Ball was in full swing. The foyer of the hotel rang with excited chatter, and small groups of laughing people coalesced into a tight mass at the entrance to the ballroom. The entrance fee was twenty-five cents, which, at half the usual ticket price for most city amusements, made it a real bargain. The purpose of the event was to raise money for parish charities, and a good number of the individuals dispensing punch were dressed in the elaborate black robes and white wimples of the Sisters of Charity. These good women's august presence did not seem to be dampening the enthusiasm of the young people dancing. The three famous gas-lit chandeliers in the Parker House ballroom illuminated a swirling kaleidoscope of dancers twirling around the floor, some dressed in full costume, others merely masked.

Annie hadn't been in a gathering with this many people in years. Indeed, most of the Irish population of San Francisco appeared to be in attendance this evening. This was, of course, why they were there. Where better to find Voss's former maid, Nellie Flannigan, and her beau, Jack O'Sullivan?

When Annie had arrived at her home a few hours earlier for the start of her night out, she was feeling discouraged. After she had finally gotten up the courage to return to her attic room from the study earlier that morning, only four hours remained before her morning chores began, and the day had turned out to be a frustrating repetition of the day before. Jeremy went out, Mrs. Voss stayed in her rooms, Cartier continued to irritate, and Miss Nancy kept ordering her around as she did her chores. When she returned to work on Monday, she would finally get a chance to check out the upstairs rooms and she hoped to finish looking through the rest of the house in a day or two. At this point she wasn't sure she had learned enough to justify the two days of lost income as Sibyl.

The only odd thing that had happened was that as she was leaving the Voss house to come home, an extremely tall and slender gentleman stopped her in the back alley. Fashionably dressed, he had pulled the brim of his top had down to shadow his face, and he acted very nervous. He politely asked if she could tell him if Jeremy Voss was at home; when she said no, he had tipped his hat and slipped quickly down the alley and vanished. She supposed that if she hadn't been so tired she might have gone after him to find out what he wanted with Jeremy; instead, she had just plodded down to the corner to catch the horse car home. She was so tired she even fell asleep on the car and almost missed her stop.

Consequently, Annie felt more exhausted than excited when Kathleen greeted her at the kitchen door with the news that she had identified the missing Nellie, and that she, Patrick, and Annie were all going to meet Nate Dawson at a local charity ball to try and talk to her. Kathleen had it all planned out. Patrick would engage a hackney and come by to pick them up so they could get to the ball by nine o'clock. This would give Annie just enough time to bathe and get dressed.

Then Beatrice had stepped in, saying, "Now you just shush girl, you're getting way ahead of yourself! I told you not to pester Mrs. Fuller. There's nothing wrong with you and Patrick going to the dance and searching for that Nellie. But it isn't proper for a lady like Mrs. Fuller. Sides, can't you see she's completely worn out!"

Kathleen had immediately backed off, apologizing for being so thoughtless and not considering how tired Annie would be. Annie wasn't sure whether it was a desire to prove herself in her young servant's eyes, or that Beatrice's words had been so reminiscent of her mother-in-law's constant refrain about what was "proper" for a lady to do, but, in any event, Annie immediately started to defend her right to go to the ball, reminding Beatrice that she had all day Sunday to recuperate. The truth of the matter was that once she had decided to go, she had begun to feel better.

Since Kathleen was adamant that it would be safer if Annie attended the ball as another servant, the question of what she would wear arose. Kathleen had a solution to that as well, saying she had just the thing for her to wear. "My friend Lillian can't fit in it no more, so she let me buy it off her for just five dollars. I was going to start working on cutting it down to my size, but, Ma'am, I just knew it would fit you."

Which is how Annie came to be squeezing through the doorway of the Parker Hotel dressed in an outfit that was a far cry from the virginal white gowns of her days as a proper young woman or the somber clothes of wifedom and widowhood. Her outfit's under skirt, a dark green satin, contrasted with the green and burgundy plaid tarlatan overskirt that swooped back, culminating in a huge matching satin bow over the bustle. While this was a style Annie would never have chosen for herself, she had solemnly agreed with Kathleen when she pointed out how wonderful it was that the satin bow just exactly matched the satin trimming on the dress's short-sleeved cuffs and square neck. The colors were a little dark for summer, but overall she did feel quite festive.

Kathleen's friend Lillian was clearly thinner than she and a good deal shorter because it had taken some very tight lacing of her corsets to get her into the dress, and there was a good deal of ankle left showing. Not just her ankles were exposed, but a substantial portion of her breasts spilled out over the neckline as well. But hers were not the only breasts or ankles showing in this crowd, so Annie stopped worrying about how she looked and just took in the sights and sounds.

She stepped up to Kathleen, who was surveying the dancers with obvious anticipation, and whispered, "It's all quite exciting isn't it, Kathleen? But we mustn't forget we have a job to do, and I'm afraid much of the responsibility for finding Nellie or Jack rests with you and Patrick."

Kathleen wrinkled her brow and nodded once to prove her seriousness. "You're right, Ma'am. I know just what to do. I'll send Patrick to the side doors where the single men gather to smoke. One of them's bound to know Jack O'Sullivan. Meanwhile, I'll go along to the punch tables and ask the servers. The Sisters are very good with names. Then, if we get word that either of them have been sighted here and what they're wearing, we'll be in good shape. Maybe they came in costume--that might make it real easy to spot them."

Kathleen then put her head together with Patrick to give him his orders. Annie regarded them both fondly. Beatrice's nephew, Patrick, seemed different out of his police uniform, a bit older and more sophisticated, with his derby tipped back on his copper-colored hair, and his mustache waxed to dangerous points. Kathleen herself looked quite fetching in light blue poplin, and, while her dress didn't have a satin bow in the back, it did have a very smart blue and white striped satin underskirt. She had made the entire outfit herself, with just a little help from the Misses Moffet, the expert seamstresses at her boardinghouse, and the color she'd chosen made the blue of her eyes even more intense. No wonder Patrick was acting so proud and pleased.

If you didn't count Annie being dressed up as a servant on her night out, none of them had come in costume, but they all had bought masks at the door. Kathleen now turned back to Annie, insisting that she tie hers on. "You don't want to be recognized here. It wouldn't be fitting. Like I said before, Ma'am, a lady like you wouldn't be here, unless as one of the organizers, and then you wouldn't be dressed like this."

Annie looked around and saw the correctness in Kathleen's statement. While there were a number of couples scattered throughout the hall whose evening gowns and top hats and tails proclaimed them as ladies and gentlemen, they were universally standing at the edges, accompanied by black robed nuns or priests. They were clearly supervising, not participating, in the festivities. The other men and women who lined the walls, clustered around the punch tables, and danced down the center of the ballroom were younger, more gaily dressed, and, she thought, having a great deal more fun than their betters.

As she tied the mask on she whispered to Kathleen, "Won't Mr. Dawson be out of place? All the other gentlemen seem to be escorting their wives."

Kathleen shook her head. "No one will pay him no mind. Soon there'll be plenty of young men of his sort around. They come later, after the theater and such, looking for merriment. Our boys don't like it, but what can they do? It's open to the public."

This answer puzzled Annie. But before she could ask Kathleen to explain, she saw Mr. Dawson standing in the entrance to the ballroom, clearly scanning the crowd. Kathleen began to wave madly and darted over to him, Annie following more slowly. When Kathleen had first told Annie that Nate Dawson might show up, since Patrick had seen him earlier that day and told him about finding a lead to Nellie, she had been pleased, thinking that this would give her a chance to discover if he had made any progress tracking down Matthew's assets. Nevertheless, as she walked towards him, she felt apprehensive. She doubted that he would approve of her being here, dressed as she was, and she hadn't thought about the awkwardness of not being able to tell him what she had been doing the last two days.

The first words out of his mouth confirmed her fears.

Nate made an abbreviated bow and murmured, "Good evening Mrs. Fuller. I am surprised to see you here; it was my impression that you were out of town. I don't suppose it would do me any good to point out that your attendance at this affair is totally unnecessary and highly irregular?" Without waiting for a response, he turned his back on Annie and moved further into the ballroom, tying on his mask.

*Why did he have to be such a prig!* Annie said to herself. *It was a shame, because when he wasn't being so stiff and judgmental he could really be quite charming.*

The waltz that had been playing ended at that moment, creating a bustle of activity as people began to leave the floor. Kathleen gave her an encouraging nod and slipped into the crowd of people heading for the refreshment tables across the room. Annie smiled at her retreating back and fleetingly entertained the cowardly thought of following her and losing herself in the throng of dancers. Instead, she straightened her spine, thereby permitting a little more breathing room, and she turned to look at Nate, who was staring out at the dance floor.

The dark silk mask had turned him into a mysterious stranger. His dark eyes glittered in the gas light, and, with his long black hair and dark complexion, the mask gave him the look of a Mexican bandit. She had seen a real bandit once, when she had been a child. He had been a wild, ferocious man with hard brown eyes, tied to the back of a cart in the Los Angeles plaza.

She'd asked her father what he had done wrong and he had replied, "He has had the misfortune of living past his time and trusting in the honor of Americans. He was trying to take back what we stole from him. But he will be tried by our justice and not by his own. And he will lose."

Annie remembered his words because her father had seemed so sad, and because it suggested that life was not always fair, something that life had taught her well in the intervening years. Annie sighed and made her way over to see if she could engage the disapproving Mr. Dawson in polite conversation.

## Chapter Fourteen

After Annie informed Nate that the two of them were to wait near the entrance, while Kathleen and Patrick searched the ballroom, a guarded conversation ensued, where Annie asked Nate questions about how his investigation into Matthew's assets was going, and he gave civil but short answers. She was pleased to discover that after checking with local brokers he had finally accepted that she was right about Matthew's finances, and he even seemed willing to consider as plausible her belief that Matthew had been murdered.

The most surprising revelation came after he asked her politely if she would like to sit down on two chairs that had been vacated near the entrance. Once they were sitting, Annie tucking her feet demurely under her skirt to hide her ankles, Nate had cleared his throat and raised his voice above the noise of the band, saying, "Yesterday afternoon I finally obtained official access to his bank account for the past year. What I found clearly supports your contention that his financial position had been improving steadily."

Annie interrupted, "But didn't you tell me when we first spoke about this that, according to the bank, Voss was insolvent?"

"Yes," Nate replied. "But it turns out this was only because Voss came to the bank last Friday afternoon and withdrew a substantial sum, leaving only enough for day-to-day expenses. He also got access to his safety deposit box and probably removed other paper assets he might have, since it contained nothing of monetary value in it when we opened it on Tuesday."

Here Nate paused for what was clearly dramatic effect. "In fact, we now know that on Friday afternoon Matthew Voss left his bank with over a thousand dollars in bank notes. Possibly a good deal more than that, if he was carrying all his paper assets with him as well! Since there was no sign of this money in his house, the question becomes, of course, what happened to it and his other assets?"

Annie nodded, thinking to herself, that this all began to make sense. Matthew had gathered his assets in preparation for making Samuels an offer. Perhaps trading some of his stock for Samuel's shares in the business. *I wonder why he didn't tell me he was planning all this. Probably worried I would advise against it. The value of his stocks were bound to go up more in the next half year; he might not be getting full value for them if he traded now.*

Nate broke into her thoughts. "Mrs. Fuller, you don't seem surprised at all. Did you suspect something like this? Don't you want to know what he wanted the money for?"

"I already know…." Annie swallowed the rest of her sentence; acutely aware that she had almost revealed information she had learned as a servant. She then continued, "I mean, I know he was up to something. Tell me, what have you learned?"

Annie then listened to Nate repeat what she already knew about Matthew's dinner announcement the night he died and she voiced what she had been thinking since she first heard about these plans, saying, "Jeremy Voss must have been fit to be tied. From what I understand, full control of the business would be the last thing he wanted. Whatever could Mr. Voss have been thinking?"

"He was probably thinking it was about time his son did a little work," replied Nate. "And Jeremy Voss should have been pleased. If his father made him a full partner, Jeremy would get a nice steady income from one of the most prosperous businesses on the west coast. Not a bad start to married life, I'd say. There are plenty of young men who would jump at the chance to be doing so well in their twenties."

"But what about Samuels," she interrupted, "would he have been willing to sell?"

"I think he might have been very pleased to do so. Yesterday, as I made the rounds, several people mentioned that Samuels got himself into heavy waters the year before last. Lived beyond his income for a while when the economy was at its worst. Someone mentioned a few outstanding gambling debts, plus whispers that he was having trouble paying the tailor and such. Not unusual, by any means, but distressing to a man of Samuels' stature in the community. The money Mr. Voss would have given him to buy him out might have come in handy."

"This certainly does seem to rule out the idea that Mr. Voss cashed in all his assets to pay off some huge debt or pay off some blackmailer. He must have planned to use the money to buy out his partner's shares in the business. But why hadn't Mr. Samuels mentioned this to anyone? He didn't, did he?" asked Annie, looking up at Nate.

"No. Samuels was supposed to have dinner with the Vosses the night Matthew Voss died, but he had to cancel because of a business appointment down the peninsula. Instead, he telegraphed from out of town, rescheduling to meet Mr. Voss on Monday morning. Once we knew what to look for, it was all there in Voss's appointment book, the dinner and the rescheduled meeting for Monday morning at ten o'clock. So it is quite possible that Voss had kept his intentions completely secret, and Samuels insists that he had no knowledge of what was planned until Mrs. Voss told him after the funeral."

Annie stood mulling all of this new information, trying to make sense of it, trying to fit it in with what she had learned from her two days living with the Voss family. It appeared that so far she had learned nothing from her sojourn in the Voss household that Nate hadn't learned for himself, with considerably less physical effort!

She turned to Nate and said, "Have you told any of this to the Detective, I believe his name is Jackson, who is in charge of investigating Mr. Voss's death? Doesn't it prove Mr. Voss didn't commit suicide?"

He frowned down at her, but then answered. "Yes, I spoke to Chief Detective Jackson this morning. In fact, that was where I ran into Patrick and found out about his plan to track down the Voss maid at this event. Detective Jackson didn't have much time for me, but he did tell me they were looking into the possibility it wasn't suicide. He expressed interest in what I found out at the bank and in your list of investments as well."

Nate went on, "However, I found their suspicions about Jeremy Voss troublesome. Jackson said Jeremy's been refusing to answer any questions about that night, and he seems to have been pretty much on a steady diet of alcohol since his father's death. Mrs. Voss told me that she is worried his lack of cooperation will get him in trouble."

"What do the police suspect?" Annie leaned closer to hear him more clearly and was momentarily distracted by the interesting scent, a mixture of tobacco smoke and pine needles, which clung to him.

"Well, turns out that Jeremy and his father had an argument right after dinner. Jackson told me they learned about this from the parlor maid. Evidently this Nellie promptly went into hysterics when she came back from her night out and learned that Mr. Voss was dead. Jackson said she went on and on about it being a judgment on Matthew Voss, because of his 'bullying ways.' And that she said there was a terrible quarrel between Matthew and his son in the study after dinner. The lady's maid confirmed this story. I guess she was hanging about on the stairs after dinner to check on the parlor maid. Both women said Jeremy left the house right after the argument, but since he has his own key, nobody knows when he came back."

"Are you saying that because he had an fight with his father the police suspect Jeremy of murder?" Annie pulled back. "From what Mr. Voss told me, disagreements between them happened all the time."

"But Mrs. Fuller, the police don't know that, and that's why Jeremy's lack of cooperation is such a problem. It might help if we could talk to Nellie and see if she can shed some light on the exact nature of the argument."

"I suppose they were fighting over his father's plan to make him a partner. When you think of it, Mr. Voss was, in effect, threatening to put an end to Jeremy's artistic life for good. Maybe he said he'd cut Jeremy off completely if he didn't go along," Annie said. "But I just don't see Jeremy deciding to kill him. Poison seems so premeditated. I could see Jeremy lashing out in anger, hitting his father. But not poison. And why take the money and assets! Much of it would come to him eventually. He's worse off now than if his father lived to carry through his intentions."

Nate remained silent for a second then he said, "I don't know. Maybe he had poison around because he had been flirting with the idea of suicide himself? Just for the romance of it. Who knows what these artistic types will get up to. So, when he has the fight with his father, he leaves the house, walks around and gets himself into a state. Comes home, gets the poison, goes to his father's study, pretends to reconcile, and gets him to drink the poison. Then he forges the suicide note and just goes up to bed."

Annie shuddered at this picture, but she just couldn't reconcile it with the impression she had gotten of Jeremy the previous evening. He certainly felt guilty about something, but she thought a murderer would be more controlled than he was. She said to Nate, "I still don't understand why he would take the money? Why not leave it?"

"Because then there wouldn't be a good reason for his father's suicide. So, he took the money, and the other assets his father had brought home. Maybe he didn't realize that most of the stocks are not negotiable."

"But why would he be insisting, then, that his father didn't commit suicide? I would…."

Nate interrupted, "Where did you hear that he said that his father didn't commit suicide?"

"Oh, well…isn't that what you said, that after the funeral he insisted that his father was well-off? I guess I assumed that he was using this as proof that his father didn't kill himself."

Annie felt a hot blush stain her cheeks, and she hoped that her mask would keep Nate from noticing. This was the second time she had almost revealed information that she shouldn't know. She needed to be more careful.

"I don't know what Jeremy meant, Nate replied. "That's just the point, neither the police nor I have been able to talk to him since Tuesday, and it looks suspicious. As the Voss lawyer, it's my duty to protect him--even from himself. I am hoping that we can find Nellie, learn a little more about what happened, and maybe find someone outside the family that the police can investigate instead."

"But why would Jeremy be so unaccommodating. If he were the murderer, wouldn't he be doing everything he could to appear innocent? I can't imagine he would be that stupid," Annie exclaimed.

"No, I don't think he is that stupid, Mrs. Fuller," Nate replied. "But remorse can cause a man to do strange things. Just consider that if he is the murderer he may be feeling so guilty he wants to be caught. It wouldn't be very pleasant to have your father's death on your hands, now would it?"

## Chapter Fifteen

"I'm sorry Mrs. Fuller," Kathleen said between light gasps, "no one's seen Nellie Flannigan, and with her red hair she should be pretty hard to miss. I've been thinking that if she just got another job she probably hasn't gotten the night off. Patrick found one person who thought he had seen her boyfriend, Jack. Supposed to be wearing a black and white checked suit and a red cravat. Fancies himself a bit, I says, to be wearing a get-up like that. But we haven't spotted him yet. We thought it might help to dance a bit, in case he was on the dance floor. But so far, no luck."

Patrick and Kathleen's arrival broke the rather strained silence that had grown up between Nate and Annie, and she greeted them with relief. "That's all right, Kathleen. I don't have to leave for another hour or so. Keep looking. But go ahead and continue to dance. Might as well have some fun while you're at it."

Patrick wiped his forehead, made a small bow, and led Kathleen back onto the floor. They did look like they were enjoying themselves. Annie watched with some envy, wondering what she would say if Mr. Dawson asked her to dance. When she was much younger she had loved dancing with her father, but her husband hadn't liked to dance. He had usually been found in a back room playing cards or smoking with his cronies at parties.

Nate, who had risen at Kathleen's approach, still stood, and he stiffly asked her if she would like him to get her some punch.

"No, thank you, not yet, but feel free to get yourself some if you

want." *Why am I so disappointed that he didn't ask me to dance?*
Annie thought to herself

Nate hesitated a moment then replied, "Well, maybe I will have
some myself, but I think I'd like to stretch my legs a little first.
Maybe walk around the room; see if I can catch sight of the sartorial
splendor of Nellie's young man. Can't imagine there are too many
men here tonight with red cravats."

Annie looked at him, perplexed by the self-conscious note to his
voice. Then she noticed he had his hand in the breast pocket of his
jacket, where most men kept their cigars, and the light dawned.

"Oh, that is certainly a good idea. And why don't you stop and
have a smoke while you do so? I'll be fine here. Maybe I'll check out
the punch table at that and have a chat with the good Sisters."

Nate looked properly chagrinned and said, "Are you sure you'll
be all right? You could accompany me."

Annie laughed. "Now, Mr. Dawson, I know I am a disreputable
woman, but even I would have some qualms about standing around
with the gentlemen smoking a cigar."

When Nate stammered out that she had misunderstood him, Annie shushed him and sent him on his way, the interchange having
restored her good humor.

For awhile she was content to simply sit and watch the dancers,
but then the lack of sleep the night before started to make itself felt;
so she stood and moved over to the nearby punch table, hoping that
some refreshments would revive her. Handing over the required
nickel for a cup of what looked like pink lemonade, she was startled
when she felt a tap on the shoulder and heard, "Excuse me, Miss.
Would you care to dance?"

She swung around quickly, but her welcoming smile faded when
she realized the masked man standing before her wasn't Nate. Although wearing the evening clothes of a gentleman, this man was of
only medium build, fairly stocky, and his closely-cut, slicked-back

hair and neat mustache and beard were decidedly blond.

"Oh," Annie responded with surprise. "Why, thank you. But no, I've just gotten some punch, you see, and I'm not dancing."

Starting to go back to where Nate had left her, she found her way blocked by the man, who put out a hand to forestall her and said, "Now, honey. You don't mean to tell me you're going to make do with just that sour old nun's punch. I've got a bit of fun in my flask right here, and I'll be glad to sweeten up your drink. Then we can dance. Now come over here and I'll fill you up."

The man showed her that he had a silver flask in his inside pocket; then he took Annie by the left arm and began to her pull her behind him, towards a curtained alcove further along the wall in a darker part of the room.

Annie, confused, followed in his wake, protesting politely, "Please, sir, stop. I am afraid you have mistaken me for someone else. I don't believe I know you. And I do not want anything in my punch."

But instead of stopping and letting her arm go, the man laughed and said, "Sweetheart, of course you know me, I'm the answer to a maiden's prayers. Now stop pretending to be so shy. I know your type. Trying to play hard to get, aren't you? Well, don't bother, I always get what I want."

Annie found it difficult to take in the man's words, as she focused her attention on the problem of keeping the punch from spilling on her borrowed dress. He was obviously inebriated. As she and the man stumbled forward, she muttered with increased irritation, "Be careful. What do you think you are doing?"

When they reached the alcove, Annie placed the punch down on a small nearby table and attempted once more to pull herself away, speaking even more sharply to make her displeasure understood. "Excuse me, sir. Let me go this instant. You forget yourself. I have asked you politely to leave me alone. I must now insist."

Annie felt no fear, just mounting vexation. She didn't want to create a scene, but, from experience with her husband, she knew how difficult it was to reason with someone who had imbibed too much alcohol. On the other hand, he couldn't really do anything in a crowded ballroom, just feet from a number of black robed Sisters of Charity.

Then, abruptly, the situation changed. The man snaked his right arm around her waist and pulled her tightly up against his side, cramming his lips against hers. Paralyzed for a moment by the shock, Annie fought a rising tide of nausea that was quickly re-placed by a white-hot stab of pure anger. She hissed, "I don't have to put up with this," as she shoved hard against the man's chest. Surprised, the man staggered, and as he tried to regain his balance she pulled away. Heading back towards the dance floor, she felt him move up behind her so she jabbed him sharply in the stomach. He growled, "bitch," and then seized her painfully by her upper left arm. Annie began to feel him pull her back, when, miraculously, she was completely free. Someone had swept by her, grabbed the man by the shoulder, and then rammed him against the alcove wall with a thud.

Nate stood there, panting, his upper lip, which showed under the mask, pulled back in a silent snarl. He held the man by the throat with one hand while the other hand was clenched in a fist at his side.

Annie, frightened by the violence she saw in Nate's face, started to intervene when he ripped the mask from the man's face and stepped back, exclaiming, "Good God, Charles Rankin! What in the hell did you think you were doing?"

The man, rubbing his throat, snapped, "Seems that's what I should be asking you, Dawson. Interfering bastard. I saw her first. Get your own bit of skirt and keep your damned hands off me."

Annie didn't hear what Nate replied, because at this moment a woman materialized next to her, distracting her. The woman was large, dressed in garish purple satin, and the reddened hand she placed on Annie's arm advertised that her occupation required a good deal of hard work. But she was young, and her eyes were kind and concerned as she patted Annie's shoulder.

"Honey, are you all right? Did that sorry excuse for a man hurt you? I says they shouldn't let the top hat crowd into these affairs. Decent working girl ain't safe. My Burt will take care of him for you, if you want."

Annie noticed a silent, rosy-faced man standing shyly behind the kind young woman. He was probably a good inch shorter than his female companion, but Annie could see powerful muscles straining his well-worn coat.

She smiled shakily at both of them, as she replied, "No, I'm quite fine now. Everything seems well in hand. But thank you so much for your concern." She then stepped forward and touched Nate on the shoulder. He was still muttering heatedly at her assailant.

Annie said softly, "Please, I don't want to cause a scene. Could you take me to find Nellie? Leave him be."

Nate turned towards her and glanced rapidly up and down her body, as if to check for any overt damage. Then he stared intently into her face, his voice low and fierce. "Did he hurt you? You're safe now. I won't let him touch you."

He grasped her hand lightly, giving it a squeeze, and he delicately touched the corner of her mouth. Annie winced, realizing that her entire mouth felt bruised. Nate's eyes darkened, and she heard the sharp intake of his breath. She stood very close to him, and she fought an impulse to fold herself into his arms. Inhaling deeply, she was just about to repeat her request that they leave when Nate whipped around to confront the man Rankin, who was tugging at his shoulder. Nate continued holding on to Annie's hand, and she instinctively moved up behind him where she felt sheltered.

Rankin stood unsteadily, his cheeks spotted with red, his voice belligerent. "I told you, Dawson, she's mine. Best looker in the place. Get your hands off of her."

Nate replied with icy calmness. "Charles, I'm only going to tell you one more time. Leave the lady alone. She is with me. You're drunk, and that's the only reason I won't haul you in front of the authorities for assault. But don't press your luck."

Hearing the menace in Nate's voice, Rankin stepped back and two men appeared at his side and grasped him by the arms. One of them was the shy friend of Annie's purple-gowned defender; the other was a similarly muscled young man sporting the largest mustache Annie had ever seen.

Rankin laughed uneasily. "For God's sake, no need to call out the vigilantes. My mistake. Didn't know the girl was already claimed. Why Nate Dawson, you sly old dog. Never thought trolling among the low-class potato eaters was to your taste."

Annie felt Nate stiffen. Still afraid the two men might fight, she stepped closer and whispered urgently, "Please, let's go. He will never know who I am. So who cares what he thinks. Just let it be."

Nate turned and looked down at her again, a bit blankly. Then he took a deep breath. Taking her by the arm he led her away, towards the main dance floor. The last glimpse she had of her attacker showed him being hustled out the door of the ballroom by the two young men. Then, with out a word, Nate swept her up into a lively waltz, and for some time Annie was so completely focused on minding her feet that everything else was temporarily forgotten.

## Chapter Sixteen

Annie realized Nate's decision to pull her on to the dance floor was a very sensible move on his part. The vast anonymous throng of dancers provided a sort of instant protective covering for them. The whole incident had taken but a minute or two, but, even so, a small crowd had begun to assemble in response to the altercation. By the time the dance brought them back to that part of the room, the small knot of onlookers had dissolved.

His decision to dance also gave her time to regain her composure. Nate turned out to be a surprisingly graceful dancer, communicating the silent instructions required in dancing clearly but deftly. His technique was confident and Annie's steps rapidly smoothed out under his direction. She discovered her shorter skirt provided distinct advantages. The dress was far easier to manage than the long evening gowns she'd always worn before. By the beginning of the next slow waltz, her feet had started to move with enough independence for her to think about what she would say.

She glanced up and saw that Nate was staring over her shoulder. The mask he still wore made it difficult for her to read his expression. He was probably angry with her. He hadn't thought it proper for her to come, and now events appeared to have proven him right. Yet he had been a gratifyingly effective rescuer. She had to express her appreciation.

Staring resolutely in front of her at the white pleats in his dress shirt, she cleared her throat, which was now quite dry, and said, "It seems insufficient to thank you. But I do. Thank you."

She went on quickly, hoping to forestall a lecture. "Don't say it was all my fault for coming here. I know that's what you are thinking. But I really don't see it. I can't imagine why that man felt he could treat me that way. I certainly didn't encourage him. He just grabbed me. Seemed to think he had the right. You seem to know him. Whatever would make him think that he could get away with assaulting a lady in a public place? He couldn't have been that inebriated."

Nate's grip on her hand tightened and for the first time since they'd started dancing he made a slight misstep. When he began to speak, his words were short and clipped, as if they hurt. "He's Charles Rankin. I went to law school with him. Father's a very prominent manufacturer. He wouldn't have assaulted a lady. Don't you see, he didn't think you were one. Because you were here. Dressed like...." And then Nate stopped, looking down at her.

Annie's steps now faltered as she digested his words, then she replied, "That's ridiculous. Are you seriously saying that because I am showing a little ankle, that this gives a man the license to attack me? If this was a society ball, every woman in the place would be showing a good deal more of her skin than I am."

Annie stopped speaking, for she had let her anger take her well past the point of appropriate speech for a woman. She became aware of Nate's hand firmly placed in the small of her back, holding her close to him. She considered for the first time that if Nate was looking down at her he couldn't fail to see altogether more of her own skin than she was used to revealing. Acutely conscious of the intimacy of his touch, Annie looked up and saw that he was again staring over her shoulder, but his breathing was more uneven than the strenuousness of the waltz required.

Flustered, Annie remained silent, glancing at the couples around them, hoping desperately for a glimpse of Kathleen and Patrick and an excuse to stop dancing. She noted for the first time that there were now a good number of single men in evening dress scattered throughout the ballroom. Some danced, others lounged against the walls staring arrogantly at the couples who waltzed by. Kathleen's earlier comment about young men of Nate's "sort" showing up later was now clear.

Incensed, Annie forgot her embarrassment and she spoke with elaborate sarcasm. "Oh, Mr. Dawson, how silly of me. *Now* I understand. It must be common practice for men like your friend to come here and pester women. What good sport. Let's see, what did he call it, 'trolling' for servant girls or something? What a shame I didn't understand it was just a *game*. I suppose I should apologize to him for not knowing the rules."

Nate jerked her to a standstill and unceremoniously pulled her to the side of the room, dexterously weaving in and out of the other couples on the floor to do so. When they were no longer in danger of being run down he turned, dropped her hand, and began to speak in a gruff voice Annie hadn't heard him use before.

"Listen, Mrs. Fuller, you have every right to be angry. As soon as Miss Kathleen told me why you were here, dressed the way you were, I should have insisted that you return home. And having failed to do that, I should never have left you alone. It was my responsibility to protect you from any sort of harassment. I'm sorry. I failed."

Annie, rather unnerved by his apology, replied, "Nonsense, Mr. Dawson. First of all, it isn't your place to decide what I can and cannot do. It was my decision to come and therefore my responsibility. Not yours. And if anyone is to blame, it was that awful man, not you."

"But don't you see," he continued, "I knew what that sort of man was capable of. You didn't. It was foolish of you to dress beneath your station, but you would have no way of knowing it would put you in danger. You are right; it is common practice. I've frequently heard men brag about their conquests at local events. I never thought about what it would mean to the young women involved. I just figured the girls they spoke of were willing. It was wrong of me to assume an Irish servant girl doesn't deserve the same respect as a woman of my own class. Charles might just as easily have assaulted Miss Kathleen. That wouldn't have made it right."

Uncomfortable with Nate's obvious distress, Annie tried to insert a lighter tone, saying, "Now, Mr. Dawson, if that wretched man had tried anything with Kathleen, she would have given him what for. In fact, now that I think of it, even if you hadn't been so quick to rescue me, I had a number of potential protectors waiting in the wings. I wonder what those two very muscular young men did with your friend Charles? Perhaps he will wish that you had turned him over to the police. They might treat him more gently."

She was gratified to see the bleak look in Nate's eyes soften a bit. But he still sounded quite angry when he responded. "I hope they teach him a lesson he won't forget. He deserves horsewhipping."

It was a sentiment that Annie shared.


A short time later, Annie and Nate got their first glimpse of Jack O'Sullivan, Nellie's reputed beau, leaning nonchalantly against a wall. Quite a dandy, he had dark black curly hair, a handsome mustache, and smiling blue eyes. He also had one arm firmly wrapped around a dark-haired young colleen whose fresh pink cheeks and nervous giggle suggested that she was just off the boat. Definitely not, if Kathleen's information was correct, the Voss's former, red-haired maid, Nellie Flannigan.

"Ma'am, Patrick just found him. He says Nellie's not here. That's some silly girl he's picked up, who thinks she's died and gone to heaven," Kathleen told Annie as they made their way to the couple. Patrick hovered near-by; clearly making sure their quarry didn't up and fly away once they'd found him. When Annie and Nate were in shouting distance, Patrick clapped a hand on Jack's shoulder and proclaimed with assumed heartiness, "Jackie my boy, here are the lady and gentleman who want a word about Nellie."

Jack straightened his red silk cravat, and pushed his shoulders away from the wall. Then he ostentatiously turned away from Nate, who stood in front of him, and gave Annie a quick once over, a wide smile, and broad wink. "Well now, I'm always glad to speak to a beautiful lady, but I'm not so sure I can be of help. I ask myself, Jack my man, what reason does a fine gentleman like this have with the likes of my Nell? And I don't rightly like the answer."

Kathleen intervened. "Now, Mr. O'Sullivan. Mind your manners. Mr. Dawson, here, is a lawyer who works for the Voss family that employed Nellie. He's just trying to find out what happened the night the old gentleman died, and we thought Nellie might help. I'm sure that he will be very appreciative of any assistance you might give him."

As she said this, Kathleen smiled encouragingly at Jack, then she turned away from him towards Nate and Annie and began to gesture frantically with her hands, clearly trying to convey some important message.

Nate stood looking bewildered, while Annie, quicker on the draw, moved forward, offering her hand to O'Sullivan, and gushing, "Oh dear yes, Mr. O'Sullivan, we'd be ever so appreciative to you and Nellie both. Mr. Dawson is very generous, and although I'm sure an upstanding member of the community like yourself would be anxious to help track down the brute that murdered poor Mr. Voss, certainly a monetary reward of some sort would be appropriate."

Nate, catching on, pulled out a thin wallet from his evening jacket and partially extracted a few bank notes, saying, "Yes, Mr. O'Sullivan. I assure you my intentions towards Miss Flannigan are most honorable. I have heard that she might prove a very valuable source of information and I would so like to make an arrangement that would be of benefit to both of us. And of course I would be glad to compensate you as well for your time and bother. That is, if you do know the whereabouts of the young lady in question."

Annie stared at Nate, entranced by the way he had so successfully mimicked his uncle's style in this little speech. Jack O'Sullivan seemed equally entranced, but Annie suspected it was the sight of the wallet that caused a distinct thawing of his attitude.

Sticking out his hand and shaking Nate's enthusiastically he said, "Well now, Mr. Dawson, the Voss lawyer, are you? Let me tell you, I was that glad when Nell wiped the dust of that doorstep from her feet. No disrespect intended, but strange doings in that house, that's for sure. I always say it's not healthy to live in a place where there's been a death. Did'ya say it was murder? Nellie swore she'd a sign that death was coming. Spilled wine at dinner or some such stuff. Queer to think that we were off doing the town when the old man bit the dust. Who knows what might have happened to Nellie if it hadn't been her night out."

Annie longed to pursue what Jack meant by strange doings, but she didn't feel the crowded and increasingly noisy ballroom the best place for elaborate questioning. Besides, anything he'd have to offer would be second-hand. Better to get to the source as quickly as possible. So she got right to the point, saying, "Please, Mr. O'Sullivan, could you tell us where Nellie is working now?"

Jack winked again in Annie's direction, before answering. "Well, Nell's a sly one, she is. Lands on her feet. By the next day she had a new job, a good one. She sent me a note. Got a position as a waitress at Cliff House. Said the job pays five dollars a month more and better hours. Only problem, it's so far away. I work on the docks. Harder to get a message to her when I want to see her. Real bother. But then, I'm never lonely, so it's her bad luck. She wrote that a gentleman got her the job."

"A gentleman? Did she say who?" Annie asked.

"Naw. She likes to keep her secrets. I wondered for a minute if this fellow weren't him." With this he jerked his chin in Nate's direction.

"She'd been hinting for some time she had some gent sniffing around. I just thought she was trying to pay me off for not always being square with her. Talked about the presents he gave her. Never saw any sign of them, so I thought it was all talk. Then when she went off to the Cliff House, well, you know the reputation that place has. Made me wonder. I went to visit her yesterday evening. I said I didn't like it. We had a real go around about it. Truth is, she's a bit put out with me. Got her eyes on better things, she says. Little fool. She'll come back, she always does. Meanwhile, I'm not crying."

At this juncture the young man gave the girl at his side a squeeze, producing a sharp squeal.

"If you want to see her, she said she'd be free sometime tomorrow afternoon. I was going to go, give her a chance to apologize, but I've contracted a spot of work to do. If you see her, tell her if she needs someone to help her spend her newly acquired wealth, I'm the man."

## Chapter Seventeen:
## Sunday, early afternoon, August 12, 1879

Annie sat next to Nate in a carriage drawn by a rather lively pair of matched bays, on the way across the peninsula to the Cliff House Inn to find the Voss family's former servant, Nellie. This establishment, with its views of seals disporting themselves on the rocks just off shore, was a favorite destination for Sunday drives. As a result, the road curving through the Golden Gate Park was crowded, even though the day was partially overcast.

The night before, Annie had been surprised, but very pleased, when Nate had invited her to come with him to find Nellie. By the time they had finished questioning Jack O'Sullivan, it was nearly eleven, and Annie was ready to drop. Every muscle she had used ironing and scrubbing ached, and her head had begun to pound. Not wanting to cut into Kathleen and Patrick's fun, she had announced that she would hire one of the hansom cabs standing outside the hotel and go home by herself. As she expected, Nate insisted on accompanying her. She had been too tired to even attempt polite conversation, much less speculate on what they had learned from Nellie's boyfriend, so the short ride to her house was completely silent.

When they had arrived at her home, Nate had cleared his throat and said, "Mrs. Fuller, I would expect that you might like a chance to interview Nellie Flannigan yourself. So I was wondering if you would do me the honor of accompanying me tomorrow afternoon to the Cliff House. I thought I might hire a carriage. I could pick you up a little after noon. That should give us plenty of time. If this would be acceptable, that is."

Annie had felt a burst of optimism, thinking that tomorrow they might actually find out something that would help solve the puzzle of Matthew's death. She had replied with perhaps more enthusiasm than was proper, saying that she would be delighted and that she was sure that Beatrice would fix them a splendid lunch and that they could have a picnic as well.

So here they were, driving towards the Pacific on a beautiful summer day. Since the team was fresh, Nate concentrated initially on controlling them, letting conversation lapse. Annie bided her time, silently admiring his handling of the reins. She supposed if he grew up on a ranch he was experienced with horses. Like his dancing style, his driving was confident and light-handed.

This thought, of course, put her in mind of last night's events and how they parted. She had no idea what had possessed her, and she hoped Mr. Dawson didn't feel she was too forward in her invitation to a picnic. So far today there was nothing in his behavior towards her to suggest otherwise. She felt, however, it would be important to establish the businesslike nature of the outing right at the start. As a result, as soon as a slight slowing of the carriage and a relaxation in his posture suggested Nate could now be safely engaged in conversation, Annie broke the silence.

"Mr. Dawson, I have been thinking about who else, besides Jeremy, might have been unhappy about the plans Mr. Voss announced at dinner the night he died. I can't really see why Mrs. Voss would be unhappy, except perhaps on behalf of Jeremy. What about his sister? I wonder what Miss Nancy would do if the house were to be closed up while Mr. Voss and his wife were traveling."

Nate shifted the reins from one hand to the other and said, "I'm not sure what you are getting at. You aren't suggesting Miss Nancy murdered her brother because he was going to close up the house?"

Annie thought to herself that Nate obviously hadn't had much conversation with Miss Nancy, but he did have a point. "I know it seems absurd. But what if she held some deep-rooted sense of grievance, and his thoughtlessness on this occasion proved the last straw. After all, according to my friend, Mrs. Stein, it was Miss Nancy's dowry that had subsidized his trip out west and formed the initial capital for the furniture business. Without a dowry, she never married. Instead she took care of her aged parents until they died and then came out west and kept house for her brother. No life of her own, no home of her own. And now, her brother announces he's closing up his house, without a thought to what she might want. Well, I know I'd be furious."

Nate laughed but then replied more seriously. "I don't know that I agree with you. Seems to me he took pretty good care of his sister all these years. Gave her a roof over her head, something important to do. Not as if he made her take care of the house single-handedly. And he thought enough about her to leave her some shares of the company."

Nate stopped, apparently struck by a thought. "Now, I suppose that might be a reason. If she knew about the will, she might have killed him to get her hands on her inheritance. Of course, that brings us back to the same old question of what happened to Voss's assets. Too bad you aren't really clairvoyant."

Annie chuckled and said, "I know. When I'm being Sibyl I think that all the time."

Conversation ceased as Nate maneuvered around a slower carriage containing a large boisterous family who were clearly on a Sunday outing. Since the sun had finally broken through the usual morning mist, Annie wondered if she should put up her parasol, since the small straw hat she wore sacrificed function for fashion, doing little to shade her face. All of her freckles would come out by mid-morning if she didn't, and Beatrice would scold.

*Oh, well*, she thought, *it really was a nice parasol*. It was made of the same pink chambray as her dress, and she particularly liked that the bands of ruching on it matched the flounces on her skirt and that the rose satin ribbons that twisted down its handle were repeated in the overskirt decorations. Both the parasol and the dress had been birthday presents from Mr. and Mrs. Stein, and, together with the stylish hat, they made Annie feel quite the picture of modern womanhood.

She hadn't had an occasion to wear the outfit before now, and Kathleen had surprised her this morning when she had laid it out for her to wear. All had become clear later when Beatrice had made much ado about how nice she looked and what a pleasant day it was for a picnic with a fine gentleman like Nate Dawson. Not even Annie's fervent assurance that the ride was strictly on behalf of her investigations into Matthew's death had done anything to wipe the pleased look off Beatrice's face.

In trying to put up the parasol without distracting Nate from his handling of the horses, Annie was reminded of how intimate an experience riding in a carriage could be. This carriage, a lightweight two-seater with its top folded back, seemed very small. The low bustle at the back of her dress required that she sit slightly sideways on the narrow seat; as a result, the motion of the carriage frequently jostled her knees against her companion's leg. When they swept around curves she even had to put out a hand against him to steady herself. The muscles in his upper arm suggested that his ranching days weren't completely behind him.

Realizing that she had become uncomfortably warm, *it was August after all*, Annie let her shawl slip from her shoulders. She thought that Nate, encased in the double layer of wool suit jacket and vest, must be terribly hot. Noticing a small sheen of moisture on his upper lip, she tipped her parasol so that it would shade the both of them.

Nate glanced over at her then and smiled. "Thanks. Looks like we'll have a nice day after all. We should be at the coast in ten minutes or so. The fog is almost gone, so the view should be spectacular. Have you been to the seal rocks often?"

Annie shrugged and said, "Not really. I have a vague memory of visiting them once when I was a child. You know, I was born in San Francisco, but we moved to Los Angeles when I was only six, so most of my memories are from visits to my aunt and uncle during the summer. I did get out once last winter. Mr. and Mrs. Stein took me for a ride. But the day stayed cold and foggy, so we didn't see much. I'm afraid that working as Sibyl and doing what I can to help Beatrice run the boarding house doesn't leave much leisure time."

Annie stopped speaking. Just mentioning the boardinghouse stirred up the frightening thought that she might lose it. Driscoll would soon be in San Francisco, maybe as early as next week, and she still had no clear idea what to do. If only Matthew's assets could be found, for his family's sake, as well as hers.

Clearing her throat, Annie said, "Mr. Dawson, do you think that the Voss family will be able to survive financially if the money and assets are not recovered?"

Nate looked surprised at her change of subject. "I'm not sure. Not that they will be poor. Certainly, in time, we should be able to recover some of the paper assets, declare them stolen, get new documents issued, and so forth. But that can be a very time-consuming process."

"How long?" Annie asked.

"Could be six months to a year, particularly with the irregularities surrounding Mr. Voss's death. There may be some difficulty proving they were stolen. I am afraid that would go for your mining stock as well. But even worse for the family is the fact that I think we will have to assume the money is gone for good, unless someone is charged with his death and the money is still in the murder's possession and can be recovered. That leaves the profits of the company, or sixty percent of the profits, to be exact, which is simply not sufficient for the three of them to maintain their current standard of living."

Six months, Annie thought with despair. Would Driscoll be willing to hold off for six months until she could claim the stocks? Or would a bank be willing to loan her money on such a risky proposition? She wished that she could ask Nate about her legal options, but she felt too embarrassed to admit that she had such a mercenary motive for trying to find out what happened to Mr. Voss. Even if she knew in her heart that it was of secondary importance to her, he might not see it that way.

Noticing that Nate was looking at her curiously, she tried to restart the conversation. "Do you think selling the company would help? Mr. Voss clearly indicated the furniture business had picked up. That was why he felt comfortable speculating in stocks."

'That's a bit of a mystery," Nate replied. "Uncle Frank swears that his business partner said the company was doing well when he first talked to him on Tuesday. Yet when I talked to him again on Friday, Samuels seemed to be supporting the suicide because of financial difficulties theory. Said again that Matthew hadn't mentioned word one about buying him out and that he doesn't believe that Matthew had the resources to do so."

Annie interrupted. "Did you tell him about the investments Mr. Voss had been making?"

"Yes, but it was a little awkward. I thought it better not to mention you as the main source of our information. I mean Sibyl. So I remained rather vague, and I don't think I was very convincing."

"You mean you felt silly telling him you heard it from a fortune teller!"

"No," Nate replied sharply. "Don't be so touchy. I was just afraid he would want to track you down himself, and I thought that might prove very sticky! Don't you agree? In fact, I think we may have a little trouble with the police in the matter of Sibyl. I didn't get a chance to tell you last evening, but it seems they just got around to reading Mr. Voss's will. Wanted to know who Sibyl was, so I told them she was a business advisor. Somehow I don't think that sat very well with the Chief Detective."

Annie's heart constricted. "Mr. Dawson, do you think they will insist on talking to me? I really don't want to. The papers might get hold of the information and make the connection between Sibyl and myself. It's not that I am ashamed of what I do. And of course my boarders have been fully informed. It's just that I would feel uncomfortable if the knowledge was widespread. And to be in the newspapers...."

Annie stopped, abashed by the note of fear that had crept into her voice. But she knew that any chance of getting a loan or even a mortgage on the house to pay off her debt would fly out the window if she became the object of notoriety.

Nate slowed the horses to a walk and turned to her, sounding distressed. "Please, Mrs. Fuller, don't worry. I am sure we can put off the police. I didn't mean to alarm you. I just wanted you to understand why I hadn't brought up Sibyl to Mr. Samuels."

Annie replied softly, "I'm sorry. Yes, of course you were right. Why do you think he is insisting it was suicide? You would think he'd be glad to hear that his partner didn't kill himself and that there is at least the possibility of the family recovering some of the assets."

"Yes, I thought it was odd too. He tended to go on and on about the problems of doing business on the west coast. Lectured me about the high cost of wages and the trade unions. Kept calling them 'damned radicals.' I know my uncle thinks he's very sound, but I find his manner extremely patronizing. I wouldn't mind if he turned out to be the murderer. Too bad he was out of town."

Annie laughed. "My goodness, Mr. Dawson. How fierce. He really must have upset you!"

Nate sounded a bit sheepish when he replied. "Well, he kept treating me like I was a child, when I'm nearly thirty. I've been practicing law in California for almost seven years, and there is no reason for him to treat me like I'm wet behind the ears. But I guess that isn't a good reason to suspect a man of murder."

"No, but, Mr. Dawson, it should give you a clue to how I feel when people assume I know nothing about business because I am a woman."

"Well," Nate laughed, "I can promise you I'll never make that mistake again." He then rushed on, saying, "Mrs. Fuller, I wonder if you would consent to calling me Nate. I would hope that you are feeling friendly enough towards me to have gotten past the formality of last names. I mean no disrespect by it...but if we are going to continue to work together to solve this puzzle, well...."

As Nate's explanation petered out, Annie, without thinking, placed her hand gently on his arm and said, "Yes, I'd like that, but only if you agree to call me Annie. I don't know why, but I feel like I've known you forever."

Annie surprised herself by that last statement and paused. What she had said was true. She found it difficult to believe she had met Nate Dawson only six days before and that this was only the fourth time she had been in his company. She felt surprisingly comfortable in his presence, even when she was furious with him, and all this formality of last names seemed so stuffy. Yet, she didn't know when she had ever called a man by his first name, except for her husband, that is, and that was only after they married. For older men, even those like Mr. Stein or Matthew Voss to whom she felt very close, the age difference was a barrier. They might call her by her first name, as Mr. Stein did, out of affection, but it would be disrespectful for her to reciprocate and call him Herman.

What about men her own age? Truth be told, she had never had a male friend before. She had been her father's hostess from the age of fourteen, but that meant making small talk with men her father's age, or trying to get his tongue-tied clerks to speak a few words when they came to dinner. There were the young men she met at social functions, but their conversation hadn't gone much beyond vapid comments about the weather. John had been her first real beau, and their courtship had been a whirlwind that ended four months later in marriage. She had fooled herself that the stiffness of his conversations with her was the result of natural reserve, and that after marriage they would develop the kind of warm friendship she believed had existed between her father and mother. This was the first of many disappointments in her marriage. To be fair, she had probably disappointed John in many ways as well.

Snapping back to the present, she told herself that it should be perfectly proper for two adults of the opposite sex to develop a friendship. *It was nearly the eighteen-eighties after all, and being a mature widowed woman should provide some advantages.* She looked over at Nate and saw a hesitant look on his face, and she smiled encouragingly.

He then took up his earlier topic saying, "Now that I think of it, Samuels said something that made me curious. Part of his diatribe on labor costs was directed at the furniture factories owned by the Chinese merchants. He said they hurt the Voss and Samuels Company through unfair competition because they used contract labor. Almost as an aside, he remarked that Mr. Voss's manservant, Wong, could tell a tale or two about what went on among the Chinese who make up the Six Companies. Seemed to imply that if there was wrong-doing, Wong might be involved."

"But hadn't Wong left the house before Mr. Voss died, and weren't the doors still bolted in the morning, so he couldn't have gotten back in during the night?" Annie responded.

"Yes," Nate replied. "Additionally, Wong's movements after he left are fairly well accounted for. Seems that he is a well-known and recognized figure to all the police on their beats between O'Farrell Street and Chinatown."

"And did they report seeing Wong that night?"

"Sure did. One police officer saw him walking down Geary on Sunday evening around eleven o'clock. Like Samuels, he has an al-ibi as well, although Detective Jackson didn't seem convinced he could trust the word of the men who said Wong was with them in a night-long card game. The Detective seemed quite put out that he couldn't immediately haul him in for questioning."

"Well, too bad," Annie replied with some heat. "I can't stand the attitude that all the problems of San Francisco can be laid at the doorstep of the Chinese. Mrs. O'Rourke and I simply can't talk about this issue--it's the only time we have had a serious falling out. It is purely baseless ignorance to say that the Chinese are evil and must be kept out of the United States. I certainly hope that you aren't in the exclusionist camp?"

Nate urged the horses back into a trot and then responded. "No, Mrs. Fuller, I mean, Annie. I don't think that a Chinese Exclusion law would be a good idea. I also disagree with men like Samuels who feel that the Chinese are bad for business. But I can understand the frustration of Dennis Kearney and his Workingmen's Party. It's hard to be unemployed and see the Chinese taking jobs."

"Pooh! I would think Irishmen like Kearney should be ashamed for blaming the Chinese for all the economic difficulties of the past few years. Better to blame the banks-they caused the panic and de-pression. And it was not that long ago the Irish faced the same charges, that they force down wages and cause unemployment."

Nate interjected, "But the Irish are being accepted now. They practically run the city government and make up half the million-aires on Nob Hill. I just don't see that happening to the Chinese."

"Well, the Irish may be more accepted out west," Annie replied, "but there are lots of people who still refuse to see them as equal. I can just hear my mother-in-law back in New York explaining why she refuses to hire Irish maids. She'd stick her nose up in the air and say 'I'd never let a dirty, dishonest, drunken Catholic in my home. They live in filth and breed like pigs, and they should go back to Ireland where they belong.' Which is just as untrue as what is being said about the Chinese."

Chagrined, Annie paused, realizing she had gotten on one of her hobbyhorses. Just as well that she hadn't mentioned her own speculations that Nellie, or someone else in the house for that matter, could have let Wong back into the house later. Nate could have rightly accused her of inconsistency.

"All right," Nate chuckled. "Tell me, have you ever considered giving up the business of clairvoyance for the practice of law? I'd hate to argue against you in court."

Before she could adequately respond to this blatant provocation, the carriage swept around a sharp curve, and the Pacific Ocean spread out before them. Nate pulled the carriage to a halt at the side of the road. They could see to the horizon, where the soft faint mist of August obliterated the edge where the sea met the sky. Only an indefinable difference in the quality of the blue above them testified to the continued separation of air and water. Annie imagined that if she contemplated those far reaches for too long she would completely lose her understanding of up and down, tumbling forever in a world without boundaries.

"Oh, how extraordinarily beautiful," she said quietly. "It goes on forever." Annie found herself breathing deeply, her ribs pushing against the snug stays of her corset. Spontaneously, Annie turned to Nate and exclaimed, "Oh, can we get out and walk along the cliffs? I want to be able to see down to where the waves break against the rocks. I can hear them. I want to see them."

Nate laughed. "In a minute, but first things first. We need to go on to the Cliff House and see if Nellie Flannigan is available. I promise you, before we go back, you can walk along the cliffs. Along the beach, too, if you want."

Nate started the horses again, and they made their way slowly up a steep, curved incline. Around the curve and halfway up the hill they saw the Cliff House Inn perched on the edge of the road, overlooking the ocean. There were a good number of carriages and horses standing out front.

As Nate jumped down to hitch their horses to the rail, he asked if she would mind if he left her alone while he went into the Cliff House to find Nellie. "When I find her, I'll bring her out so we can both speak to her. She won't want to talk in the restaurant where she can be overheard."

Annie agreed. It was nearly one now, and Nellie might be working, since it was clear that Sunday dinner was still being served. She also suspected this was Nate's diplomatic way of keeping her out of the Inn. When first built, the Cliff House was a very reputable hotel. But it had changed ownership several times and become famous as a place where men and women who were married, but not to each other, might conduct liaisons. Respectable people still patronized its dining room, but Annie knew many of those same respectable people would be scandalized if a widow of indeterminate social status, such as herself, ventured into the Cliff House with a single man. Personally, she thought the whole question of a woman's reputation ridiculous, but she was not prepared to fight that battle with Nate today, especially since she knew he was under a strict charge from Beatrice in this matter.

Nate looked rather relieved when Annie didn't protest his decision, and in a few minutes he returned alone and climbed back up into the carriage.

"Well, she's not here. One of the other waitresses said Nellie received a message this morning from someone, and then she begged to trade shifts so she could be off before noon. She's due back at work at four."

"I wonder who she is meeting? Perhaps Jack changed his mind and decided to come today after all."

Nate shrugged. "I wouldn't put it past him to have decided to coach Nellie so she can make up something and soak us properly."

"Oh, dear. I suppose that might have happened. Shall we wait for her here, or try to go look for her?"

Nate turned to Annie and said, "I've got an alternative, if you're agreeable. Since there are three hours until she arrives back, and we haven't the faintest idea what direction to go to look for her, maybe we could drive up a piece and see what Mrs. O'Rourke packed for us as a snack. There are some rocks overlooking the shore, and we can spread the food out, and you can walk a bit. Then at a little before four we'll come back here. The girl I talked to seemed to think that we could talk to Nellie even after her shift started, because at that time there is very little business. Does that sound all right?"

"It sounds wonderful. I confess I didn't have much of a breakfast, and I'm starved. And it's such a beautiful day for a walk. I suspect that Nellie right this moment is wishing that she never had to return from her afternoon off."

Annie suddenly shivered. Disconcerted, she looked up and saw that a tiny scudding cloud had temporarily blocked the sun; she hoped this wasn't an omen of bad weather ahead.

## Chapter Eighteen

Nate felt Annie shiver beside him and hoped she wasn't too cold. The sun had been shining quite brightly for some time, but the breeze off the ocean was sharp. He had wondered at her choice of clothing when she stepped out of the boarding house this morning. Not that her dress wasn't nice enough, but the material seemed awfully flimsy for a carriage ride in August. The weather could be so chancy this time of year.

So far the day had been warm. Looking over at Annie, he could see her smiling, no doubt in anticipation of her housekeeper's lunch. Such a hearty declaration of appetite was wonderful. He'd never quite understood why it was supposed to be indelicate for women to express hunger. Glancing at her again, their eyes met and he smiled, noticing, not for the first time, the dimples on either side of her mouth. He wrenched his gaze away from her face and brought the horses to a standstill along side a hitching post next to the side of the road. They were at a small turnoff a short way up the hill from the Cliff House.

"I brought my youngest sister, Laura, here one afternoon at the beginning of the summer," Nate commented. "She was visiting me for a week, between sessions of the state normal school she is attending in San Jose. She dragged me all over San Francisco. We explored Chinatown, walked and looked at the mansions being built on Nob Hill, ate fish at a little restaurant by the docks; but I think I enjoyed the afternoon we spent here the best. She clambered all over the rocks collecting specimens for her future students. She's going to make a really first rate teacher!"

There was a single, rider-less horse hitched to the post, but no one in sight in the small grove of cypresses at the top of the cliff or on the huge slabs of rock that giant-stepped part of the way down to the sand. He thought that, with luck, they'd have the place to themselves. He got out of the carriage, and, after he tied up the horses, he went around to help Annie down.

"Watch your step," he warned, as Annie lifted her skirts in one hand and held on to the carriage seat with the other. One of the carriage wheels must have been poised on a rock hidden in the dirt, because the carriage unexpectedly lurched forward. Annie let go of her skirts and reached out with her hand to steady herself on his shoulder, while clinging to the carriage back with the other.

Without thinking, Nate grabbed her and swung her down. She landed lightly, springing up slightly on her toes before settling. He was surprised how easy it had been to lift her. The material of her dress was thin and rather slick, and his hands slipped up from her waist so that he could feel the swift contractions and expansions of her rib cage. For the briefest of moments they stood looking at each other, her hand still on his shoulder, his hands still around her, as if they were about to dance. Then he released her, shocked at the nature of his physical response.

Nate swallowed a few times before words came out in a rush. "I'm sorry, I didn't mean to startle you. I was afraid you'd fall."

Annie stepped a little away from him, fussing with the collar at her throat, and she replied rather breathlessly. "That's quite all right. Thank you. These tighter skirts can be a bother." Looking around her, she went on. "This looks like a beautiful spot. Is there something I can carry? Oh, and could you hand me my parasol?"

Nate pulled the basket out of its place under the carriage seat and said, "Certainly, and if you would carry these blankets Mrs.

O'Rourke gave us, I'll bring the basket."

Annie walked beside him as they picked their way carefully down a steep rocky path that ended in a particularly flat outcropping half-way between the road and the beach below. The beach itself was still invisible, but you could hear the waves crashing over the rocks and see the miniature islands to the south, where seals and sea lions were sunning themselves on the rocks. Fault lines crisscrossed the light brown slab of rock on which they stood, and from the crevices delicate wild flowers the color of mustard, amethyst, and rose peeked shyly. The off-shore wind played capriciously with the ribbons on Annie's straw hat and swept Nate's hair into his eyes, and the steady surge of the sea isolated them from the sounds of all other mankind.

Annie dumped the blankets at her feet and, lifting her arms, breathed deeply in unselfconscious delight. Nate grinned at her in response. He then made his way back up to the carriage to tend to the horses while Annie spread the blankets and unpacked the food. When he returned he noted she had sensibly found small rocks to hold down the corners of the blanket, leaving only the edges to rise and fall in abortive attempts at flight. Annie herself was sitting awkwardly, with her left arm propping up her weight, which was all on her left hip, while her legs were folded off to her right, modestly encased in long folds of her skirt. Her position looked rather like those of mermaids he remembered from children's books; and the very incongruity of this thought made Nate laugh out loud.

Annie's eyes flashed, and then she wrinkled her nose and chuckled. "Nate Dawson, don't you laugh at me. I know I look ridiculous sitting here. But I can't figure out how else to do it and remain respectable."

As Nate sat down across from her, arranging his legs tailor fashion, she pointed to him and continued. "See how easy it is for you! It almost puts me in charity with Amelia Bloomer. Women's fashions today are not designed for any real-life activity. Why, my mother's hoops were more practical. I remember as a small child, when we went out with father for trips into the mountains, mother had no trouble sitting down. Her skirts and crinolines just poofed up around her like a tent. I'll admit she did look rather like a gigantic spider, but under those hoops she could do anything with her legs she wanted, and no one would know."

Annie stopped, and Nate could see that she was blushing furiously as she continued, "Oh, dear, I said legs. I'm sorry, my mother would have been furious with me if she knew I had referred to that part of her anatomy in the company of a man. Do forgive me."

Nate tried to compose his features as he replied. "I doubt seriously that people in the spirit world sit around monitoring our manners. And I think you have done quite splendidly in preserving your modesty. Now, if your left arm doesn't collapse and toss you over, you should be fine. Luckily it looks as if most of the food Mrs. O'Rourke sent us can be eaten with one hand. But if you get in trouble, please let me know and I'll feed you."

She just shook her fist at him in mock anger and then began to move food onto the dish in front of her. Nate thought how charming she could be, and how rare and precious was the ability to laugh at oneself. He then turned his attention to the food that her housekeeper had provided. Obviously, Mrs. O'Rourke was a notable cook. The range of delicacies she had prepared on short notice was dazzling. There were buttermilk biscuits, already buttered and still warm, along with a crusty loaf of sourdough bread. She had sent three kinds of jams: cherry, currant, and green gooseberry. And there were pickled beets, pickled corn, and spiced tomatoes. For the main dishes there were thick slices of cold ham and jellied breasts of chicken. Another dish revealed a cold veal pie with a wonderful crumbly crust. And then for dessert there were slices of a towering, three-layered chocolate cake. To wash this abundance down, Mrs.

O'Rourke had provided tightly corked jugs, apple cider for the lady and ale for the gentleman.

Nate, who boarded with his uncle in a house with a parsimonious housekeeper and an indifferent cook, sighed in ecstasy as he surveyed his choices, and for a quarter of an hour the sounds of the ocean faced no competition from him as he concentrated on sampling everything. Annie ate more sparingly and he could tell she was watching how much he ate.

Finally, she laughed and said, "Gracious, you must have been starved. However do you keep so lean, eating that way? Beatrice will be beside herself; she loves a hearty appetite. Here I thought we were going to have to give most of the food away to the gulls so she wouldn't be offended. But I can see that this won't be necessary."

Nate washed down the last of the veal pie with a deep draught of the ale and again sighed with satisfaction. Wiping his mouth with the linen napkin Mrs. O'Rourke had also provided, he said, "That was wonderful. I haven't eaten so well since I was last back home." He then pulled out his pocket watch and flipped open its lid. "It's only two-thirty. Why don't we go for a bit of a walk, and then maybe I'll have room to do justice to the cake before we have to go back to the Cliff House to see Nellie."

Annie nodded in agreement and began to put all but the cake and plates back into the basket. He stood, brushed crumbs off of himself and stretched, filled with a profound sense of well-being. Last night he'd half regretted making the offer to take Annie with him to find Nellie, afraid of the awkwardness that might exist between them after the Rankin incident. But everything had turned out very pleasantly.

He leaned over and offered Annie a hand as she scrambled to her feet. She laughed, saying, "There, wasn't that gracefully done?" as she twitched her skirts straight. "I'd better put up my parasol or I'll get a scold from Beatrice when we get back. She can count the minutes I've been in the sun by the number of freckles that appear on my nose." She then bent over, scooped up the parasol, opened it deftly, and began to wander towards the edge of rocks to look down. Nate moved the basket to the center of the blanket, hoping to insure that it didn't blow away while they were gone, and walked after her.

He called out, "Don't go too near the edge. I'm too full from Mrs. O'Rourke's cooking to run and catch you if you slip. We'll take the path down to the beach if you want a better view."

Annie smiled back at him, clamping her hand on her hat as the stronger breeze near the cliff top snatched at it. "What? Not promising to be my knight in shining armor and save me from certain death! How un-chivalrous. I thought better of you."

Nate winced. *That was just it*, he thought. *I'm not a hero*. Her expressions of gratitude last night had made him feel ashamed. Ashamed because his whole behavior had been reprehensible. First of all, he should never have left her alone at the dance. He'd realized his mistake almost immediately, thrown the cigar away after two puffs, and come right back, but it was too late. He had no memory of how he got to Annie's side and only a hazy memory of slamming Charles against the wall. The depth of his anger still shook him.

It wasn't as if he'd never been angry before, and no boy grew up without a fair number of fights. Hard to avoid them living on a ranch where the cowboys seemed to feel it was their duty to initiate a youngster into manhood by frequent rough and tumbles. But this feeling had been different, primitive. He'd wanted to kill the man who dared touch her. He'd like to think he would have been angry on behalf of any woman; he hadn't been lying to Annie when he'd told her that every woman at the ball deserved to be treated with respect. But that was principle; the reality was that it was the violation of Annie Fuller that was unforgivable.

Nate felt his hands clench as the scene replayed in his mind, then he realized that Annie had spoken to him and was looking back at him with a curious expression.

"Why, Nate, what's making you look so grim. I thought you said it would be all right if we went on down to the beach?"

Nate smiled weakly, unclenched his fists, and hurried up to her, apologizing for his inattention. "I'm sorry, I was thinking of something else. Certainly we can go down, but do be careful not to slip. Perhaps I'd better go on in front."

Annie chuckled. "Oh, that's a good idea. Then if I should tumble down, you'd be there to slow my descent. We could be a regular Jack and Jill."

Nate moved ahead, trying to find the easiest path down, pointing out obstacles that she should be aware of as they went. Annie kept up a steady stream of chatter about what they were seeing, exclaiming about a sand piper that fluttered overhead, and then stopping to pick some of the various wild flowers along the way.

Once they achieved the beach, she turned and said, "Oh, it is beautiful. Now which way should we walk?"

Nate looked down south past the Seal Rocks and saw that the beach in that direction seemed fairly populated. Some children and a dog were running in the surf, and scattered outposts of blankets and large umbrellas testified that a number of family groups were taking advantage of the warm weather. Up north, however, the narrower beach seemed deserted, and that is the direction in which he pointed.

"Let's go this way. If I remember correctly, around the headland that sticks out just there, there is a nice little cove and some interesting rock formations. We seem to be nearing low tide, and there may be some tide pools exposed. You can add to your treasures."

Annie turned her steps in the direction Nate had pointed. The two walked in silence for some minutes, with Annie stopping from time to time to examine or pick up shells. The sand was damp and packed and made easy walking; since the tide was still going out, they didn't have to worry about errant waves catching them as they went along.

Here and there the remnants of foot prints from two other walkers who had passed this way earlier had been spared by the waves and preserved in the sand, each print filled by a diminutive lake of sea water. The sun, now lower in the horizon, battled mightily with the wind to keep them a comfortable temperature, although Nate wished he could take off his suit coat. Sand pipers and terns frantically scurried in front of them, sweeping first in and then out of the ebb and flow of the waves.

Nate looked at his watch again and said, "We probably have just about enough time to get around the base of this outcrop, scout around the rocks for a few minutes, and then we will have to turn back. That is, if we want to leave time for Mrs. O'Rourke's cake before we look for Nellie."

Annie looked over at him and shrugged. "Whatever you say. I confess I've been enjoying myself so much that I've been avoiding the real purpose of the outing. I suppose we ought to talk a little about what we are going to ask Nellie."

Nate expressed surprise. "What is there to discuss? I thought we had agreed that we wanted to hear her version of what happened the night Matthew Voss died, find out about the argument Jeremy had with his father." Picking up a stone at his feet, Nate skipped it out across the waves. "Anyway, what other questions do you think we should ask?"

Annie had stopped and was staring out toward the horizon. When she didn't reply, Nate glanced at her, startled by how wistful she looked. All the animation in her face had vanished, and there was a dispirited droop to her shoulders. Before he could ask what was wrong, the sound of men's voices interrupted. Two men, roughly dressed, strode up the beach towards them from the Cliff House, each carrying pails, nets, and fishing rods. Nodding greetings as they passed, Nate waited to speak until they were out of sight around the jutting wall of the cliffs to the north of them. Looking back at Annie, he could see that her eyes were brimming with tears.

"Annie, what's the matter?" Nate stepped up to her, and, seeing that she was ineffectually trying to open up her purse, he gently removed her parasol and her bunch of flowers and shells so that she could pull out her handkerchief.

Meanwhile she was uttering disjointedly, "Oh, forgive me. You are too kind. I really am quite all right."

Nate successfully fought his desire to take her into his arms. Instead he said, "It's all right. But please tell me what is wrong."

Annie stood still and spoke softly to his chest. "You see, when I thought about what to ask Nellie, I realized how little I really know of Matthew's, I mean Mr. Voss's, life; we were just becoming friends, you see, and now he's gone. I've met so few men since my father's death that I could trust, and Matthew Voss was one of them." Annie glanced up at Nate, giving him a shy smile and squeezing his heart painfully.

She again addressed his shirtfront. "I suspect the friendship of older men has been particularly important because of the close relationship I developed with my father after my mother's death. She died when I was twelve. After that, until I married, my father and I were inseparable. He tutored me himself until I was sixteen. Even when I went on to the Academy, I lived at home. He took me on most of his business trips and was constantly teaching me about the law, and accounting, and the stock market."

Nate let a soft exclamation escape at the picture her words drew, and Annie gave a tremulous smile.

"I know, not your usual subjects for the improvement of a young girl's mind. At night we'd pour over the financial pages of the paper, and we'd decide what to buy and what to sell. Of course, in my case these were pretend transactions. Then we'd see whether my decisions would have brought in a profit or loss. We kept a running total, and over the years my profits finally began to overcome my losses.

Then father let me invest some real money. I loved it, and I did quite well too. He was so proud of me."

Nate marveled at what a strange childhood she'd had. He thought of his family. His parents, younger brother and sister, and always at least two or three visiting friends or relations, not to mention the ranch hands, who were always around. In comparison, Annie's life seemed unbearably lonely. More importantly, he couldn't image growing up without warm support and guidance of his mother. No wonder Annie didn't always behave as other women.

Standing back from him, she took the diminutive handkerchief she had retrieved from her bag and resolutely gave one good final sniff, saying, "Now, I really think we should return to our picnic spot to collect our things and get back to the business at hand. If we are to solve this mystery, we shouldn't put off finding Nellie any longer."

Nate then saw Annie stiffen. Almost immediately he heard a shout. Looking up, he saw one of the fishermen who had passed them a brief time ago running towards them waving wildly and yelling something unintelligible. As he came abreast of them, Nate grabbed him and commanded, "Get your breath, man, and then tell us how we can help."

The man was sweating profusely, and he was soaked with seawater as well. As he stood panting before them, he took out a damp cloth and wiped his face. Finally he began to speak.

"Jesus, sir. We found her lying by the rocks, body all broken. Could hardly tell who she was. My mate's staying with her. I've got to get someone from the Cliff House. Won't help her any, poor girl. She's dead, looks like she drowned! It's that new waitress up there, Nell. I can't believe it, she was such a lively one. Saw her just this morning. But now she's dead."

## Chapter Nineteen

*Nellie dead*! Annie couldn't comprehend the words at first. She had never met Nellie, but she had developed a strong image of the lively redheaded servant, even a sort of sympathy for her, after doing her work and sleeping in her bed at the Voss house. *Dead, how could that be?*

Nate's voice recaptured her attention, as he gruffly said, "Please go back and pack up the picnic things and take them to the carriage and wait for me there. I'll try to get back as soon as I can."

Annie shook her head slightly and noticing that both the fisherman and Nate were staring at her, she gathered her scattered wits. What had Nate said? She was to return to the carriage and wait. No! She would not be banished like some frightened child. If Nellie was indeed dead, she needed to know the details.

Taking a deep breath, Annie lifted her chin and said, "Mr. Dawson, I don't think that will do." Turning to the fisherman, she used her most authoritative voice. "Good man, now that you have caught your breath, please run on to the Cliff House and notify the owner, and make sure he sends a message to the nearest police station. This gentleman and I will walk on and come to your friend's aid. We'll make sure no other people on the beach interfere until the authorities come."

The man looked to Nate, who nodded agreement, and then he tipped his cap to Annie and began a steady trot up the beach. She was glad he'd acquiesced so readily, because the expression on Nate's face indicated they were about to have an argument, and she preferred not to have an audience.

"Annie, listen. You must not go with me. This is not the place for you. I've no time to debate this, so, please, go back up to the carriage."

"No, Mr. Dawson, I will not. First of all, we don't even know for sure if it is Nellie's body that was found. That man was so upset that he might have made a mistake. Perhaps she's not even dead, just hurt, and I could be of help. If it is Nellie, and she's dead; well, I need to know what happened. In any event, since I can't get back up the steep hill to the carriage with all the picnic things on my own, I might as well accompany you."

Seeing the truculent look on Nate's face, Annie decided her best tactic was simply to ignore him. Instead she began to walk briskly in the direction the man had come from, forcing Nate to follow. When he caught up with her, he reached out and grabbed her elbow. She glared at him, trying to pull away, and they stood that way for a short time, their eyes engaged in a wordless duel. Abruptly Nate looked away, muttered a short oath, and then he let go of her and started to walk rapidly towards the edge of the headland that divided them from the next cove.

Annie ran to keep up, thankful he'd abandoned the fight. She tried not to think about how much she had enjoyed the sense of warm sympathy and understanding that had been building between them all afternoon, and what her actions now would do to the budding friendship. She trailed after him in silence, concentrating on picking her way through the partially submerged rocks and the pools of captured tide that littered this place where cliff met ocean. She could tell Nate was still furious, since he made no attempt to help her over the awkward places. Once, when her foot slipped and she involuntarily let out a cry, he simply looked back to make sure she wasn't hurt, and then he turned back to his own slow progress.

Fortunately the tide was still going out, since at high tide there would be virtually no beach at all, just the waves smashing against the cliff wall. Annie felt a trickle of sweat down her back, and she wished for the hundredth time she wasn't so tightly corseted. She used her parasol to divine which pocket of sand was hard enough to bear her weight without turning into liquid. She shuttered to think of what this walk was doing to the flimsy umbrella or the edges of her skirt.

A slight shift in the direction of the breeze on her cheek made Annie look up to see they had successfully made it around the headland. The length of the next cove spread out before them. The beach was narrower here, and there were periodic low arms of rock reaching out from the cliff face into the water, as if some monstrous animals sat in a row, staring out to sea. The second fisherman sat huddled near the end of one of the largest of those arms, about three hundred yards away. He'd seen them and gave a shout, waving his arms frantically. Nate waved in response and began to run toward him, while Annie walked more slowly, looking intently at the sand at her feet.

Because of the narrowness of the beach at this point, all of the sand was the wet, hard-packed kind that readily showed footprints. Annie found the tale fairly easy to read. There were two sets of footprints, going in the direction she was walking, probably made when the tide was higher. Both sets of shoe prints showed slightly pointed toes, but she thought one set might belong to a man because of the size of the shoe print and the longer stride. She thought the other prints were more likely made by a woman, being much smaller, more closely spaced together, and because they included the deeper indentation that a woman's heel might make.

Much nearer the water's edge, there was another set of footprints, both quite large, also going north. Once again clearly two people, probably walking together, but in this case their similar size, shape, and spacing suggested the companions were both men. No doubt the two fishermen. There were two other sets of prints that went on top of the fishermen's prints. One set, she could see, were Nate's. The other set, however, went in the opposite direction, going south, back around the headland towards the Cliff House. Probably the fisherman who'd stopped to give them the news, but there was a slight chance they were from the first man who had been accompanying the woman.

Annie stopped at this point, moved towards the cliff to stare at the first set of what she found herself calling the man's prints, measuring them with her parasol and noting again the slightly pointed toes. She then went to the prints of the man running the other way and saw they had the rounded toe and were the size of one of the fisherman's prints. So, Annie thought, with a slight quickening of her pulse, this left the question of where the man with the pointed-toed shoes had gone, assuming it was his female companion that the fishermen had found among the rocks.

She knew it was cowardly to continue to search the sand rather than to go over to where Nate stood in earnest conversation with the fisherman. She had, after all, insisted on coming. Nevertheless, Annie turned toward the cliffs to pick up the man and woman's prints. She followed them until she came to the arm of rocks upon which Nate and the fisherman stood. There the footprints vanished. She scrambled up onto the mound of rocks and peered over, but saw no sign that the footprints continued on north. The couple must have walked toward the water on the rocks, which thrust up a good way above the beach here and were flat enough to walk on with some safety. Following along these rocks she kept a sharp look out to her right for any prints going north. If the man and woman had come to the rocks soon after the high tide had begun to ebb, and stayed on the rocks for any length of time, they might have left the rocks at a point closer to the water as the tide receded. But she had still seen no prints when she got to the water's edge. Since the tide was still ebbing, unless they had waded in the water, their prints should be still visible.

Annie stared north for a minute, letting the splash and hiss of the waves breaking along the rocks obliterate the sounds coming from Nate and the fisherman. Watching the waves gave her an idea, and Annie ran back along the rocks to where she could find an easy way down on to the sand. It had occurred to her that if someone walked just along the wave line, a few laggard waves might obliterate their prints in places. Sure enough, about ten feet to the north she found the half-erased prints of the man's pointed-toe shoes, and further on she saw where those prints turned at right angles to the water and went towards the cliff face. They showed the characteristics she now associated with haste, and no other prints accompanied them.

She followed them, until the prints disappeared at the edge where sand met the sandstone wall that rose above her. Frustrated, she walked a little to the left and then to the right, looking for the prints to reappear. They didn't. Then she looked up and saw what she had missed at first. A narrow fissure in the cliff, no wider than a doorway, contained one perfectly formed print in the sand on its floor, surrounded by debris.

Annie stepped closer, feeling the cooler temperatures of the rock face enclose her and noticing for the first time the strong odor of rotting seaweed. Looking around she noted that at about knee-height, in the left-hand wall of the fissure, there was a small outcrop of rock, just large enough to hold the toe of a foot. Glancing up, she saw a narrow ledge just above her head that held a scraggly bush. She put down her parasol, pulled up her skirts with one hand, and fitted her foot to the outcrop. Then she stretched, trying to grab the bush to pull herself up to the ledge. She couldn't reach it, but she bet that a man, taller, and unencumbered with skirts, could.

But to what end? She picked up her parasol and backed out of the fissure, searching the rock face to her left. Then she saw it. A faint narrow path snaked down the cliff side, disappearing where she had found the ledge. Plainly it had been a regular path down to the beach until some winter storm had eroded its last length. No doubt the man whose prints she had been following had gone up that path, and he'd gone alone.

Elated by the success of her investigations, Annie ran back to the arm of rocks and clambered up, waving her parasol to get Nate's attention. He and the fisherman were now both crouched down, looking into the waves at their feet. Nate obviously hadn't heard her approach, because when she shook his shoulder to get his attention, he jerked up and whipped around, a grimace distorting his face. Straightening, he grabbed her shoulders to force her away. But he was too late. She had seen.

Annie felt the sight of the woman imprint itself on her eyes, in an instant, like the after-image produced by a photographer's flash. Oddly, the garish vermilion, dark plum, and sickly ochre of the seaweeds that wrapped the still body provided the only color to the picture. Everything else seemed shades of black and grey, like a faded tintype. One black high-buttoned shoe, sporting a pointed toe and a French heel, peeped coyly out from under the seaweeds, and a sodden black dress provided a stark background for the gaudy colors of those same watery weeds. Little of the woman's flesh actually showed--the hand that lay pathetically open, palm up; a high cheekbone with the skin pulled tightly across it; and the lips parted ever so slightly--and all of these were shades of grey.

It was as if all the original skin tones had been sucked up to preserve the only splash of color left on the body that could compete with the ocean's bright harvest, the woman's mass of blood-red hair. Hair that abruptly came alive, writhing and twisting, imparting life to the rest. The hand now lifted in supplication, the cheek turned, and the lips opened in a soundless cry. In another instant all life departed, the pale grey body lay still, inert, until another foamy wave came in to resurrect it once more.

# Chapter Twenty

Annie slapped the side of the carriage furiously. "Of course someone murdered her. Don't even try to argue it was an accident! Though no doubt whoever killed her hoped that would be the conclusion of the police. I can just hear them say, 'Poor girl, slipped on the rocks, broke her neck.' Or better yet, whoever killed her probably hoped the tide would take her out, and she'd never be found. That fisherman said bodies disappear all the time off the coast. The police probably wouldn't have even been interested then. 'Oh, just a flighty servant, probably just ran off without giving notice. Good riddance.'"

Annie winced, her voice sounding too loud and shrill, even to her. She should stop talking, but she couldn't stop. She had been going on and on and on, ever since Nate had returned to the carriage and they'd begun their trip back to town. Nate remained silent beside her, grim-faced, driving the horses at a dangerously fast pace. Already well past seven, the dusk approached rapidly, and he most likely wanted to get to the lighted streets of the city before sundown. He probably wanted to get rid of her as quickly as possible as well.

What a nightmare. Would she ever be able to erase that picture of Nellie's body from her mind? As soon as Annie saw the dead woman's red hair, she'd known it must be Nellie. Had she really ever doubted it? She'd been a fool to insist on coming with Nate and the fisherman. Standing there trembling uncontrollably, seeing the strained look on Nate's face, she knew he'd been right from the beginning to demand she return to the carriage. She could do nothing there to help. She couldn't stay around until the police came just to point out the tracks she'd found, because she didn't dare get involved. The police were already looking for Sibyl. They'd find it very suspicious if she turned up at the death of the Vosses' former maid. And if it came out that she had also been posing as a maid for two days in the Voss household! The papers could certainly construct a juicy scandal out of that connection!

So, she had meekly told Nate she would return to the carriage and wait for him, winning only a weak shrug from him as a reward. Her trip back up the steep path from the beach had been extremely difficult without Nate's help, which had made her feel utterly useless. After taking two trips to retrieve all the picnic things, she had been forced to sit and wait, for what had seemed like forever, until Nate had made his way back to the carriage. Her nerves stretched to the breaking point, she had complained to him about how long he'd been gone. He hadn't bothered to reply but simply unhitched the horses and got them on their way.

Annie tried to calm down, hoping if she sounded more in control that she'd get some response from him. "What did the Cliff House owner say when he got down to the beach? Did you ask him if he knew who had met Nellie this morning?"

"No," Nate said. "I didn't ask him anything. That's a job for the police. My main concern was to hand the mess over to someone else so I could get you home. I also thought the sooner I got to town the better, so I could personally alert Chief Detective Jackson."

"Then you do agree Nellie's death is connected to Mr. Voss's murder? Even the police can see that. She met someone, by arrangement, and walked to the rocks. I found a set of footprints along side hers, so that proves it. Then, whoever walked with her to the rocks killed her, probably tossed her body off the end of that breakwater, and then he went north and climbed up that track I told you I found. Nellie must have been involved in Mr. Voss's death, and she had to be killed by whoever was her accomplice before she could implicate them."

Nate's silence continued, so Annie rattled on. "Who do you think killed her? Probably was a man, because of the size of the footprints. Although I don't suppose that means the same person killed Mr. Voss; that could have been a woman. There could have been more than two people involved. Nellie's boyfriend, Jack, could be the murderer. I suppose if Nellie and Jack had been together on some scheme connected to Mr. Voss's murder, he might have felt the need to eliminate her once he knew we were looking for her. "

Nate slowed the horses and answered, irritation plain in his voice, "This mindless speculation is absolutely useless."

"But who else besides Jack would have known where she was and that we were looking for her?" Annie asked.

"Doubtless everybody," Nate snarled. "I couldn't have done a better job of making sure that the murderer knew she was a danger if I had tried. When I dropped some papers off late yesterday afternoon for Mrs. Voss to sign, I told her I was looking for Nellie. Who knows whom she might have told. Jeremy, Miss Nancy, Wong, the lady's maid...the delivery boy, for all I know."

Annie cringed at the anger in his voice. Nate slapped the reins, putting the horses back into a fast trot, spitting out at her, "But why narrow our suspects to these few, why not include the whole Catholic population of San Francisco, since we made our interest in her so clear at the dance. I can't believe I wasn't more careful. I guess I didn't really believe that she had any information that would have been of use. And now she's dead."

Annie froze beside him, trying desperately to find something to say. How could she tell him not to feel guilty, when guilt consumed her as well? All her silly investigations of tracks in the sand, her fury at Nate's high-handedness, her own non-stop chatter couldn't distract her from the truth. *She*, not Nate, was to blame. She'd been acting out of self-interest from the start. Hunting for the missing assets to solve her own petty financial problems, searching for proof to clear Matthew's name from the scandal of suicide because she would rather think him murdered than that he killed himself. Now Nellie Flannigan lay dead. And it was all her fault.

## Chapter Twenty-one:
## Monday, early morning, August 13, 1879

Annie yawned uncontrollably. She didn't even bother to hide her weariness as she sat slumped on the hard wooden bench that ran along the center of the horse car. It was a little before five in the morning and the fog had thickened overnight. Annie stared sightlessly out at a world of unrelieved grayness that lacked any points of reference beyond the periodic flare of gas light from the street lamps. She felt marooned, suspended with her fellow travelers in some sort of netherworld. Only the muffled sound of the horses and the unremitting action of gravity hinted that the vehicle was moving at a sharp pace up one of San Francisco's hills. A clammy sheath of condensation, which welcomed rather than repelled the cold morning air, enshrouded her, making her thoroughly miserable. It had taken all of her strength of will to rise at four this morning and don her servant attire in preparation for her return to the Voss household.

Beatrice and Kathleen had been up to get her breakfast and see her on her way, but neither woman had much to say. They had said all they could the night before to dissuade her from continuing her investigations as Lizzie, the Voss's maid. When Nate had dropped her off at home last evening, she had hoped to escape to her room and marshal her resources before seeing any one, but she should have realized that Kathleen would have been lying in wait for her to find out how the excursion to the Cliff House had gone. No sooner had she entered the front door than Kathleen had greeted her and drawn her downstairs to the kitchen, bombarding her with questions all the way. One look at the dear faces of Beatrice, Kathleen, and Mrs. Stein, all turned towards her with bright expectation, and she had broken down in sobs. This, of course, made it all the more difficult for her to get out the news of Nellie's death. When the three women finally understood exactly what had happened, their universal response was that Annie should not under any circumstances return to what Beatrice began to call the "Death House."

At least their adamant opposition to her plans had put an end to her tears, as she rallied her strength to combat their arguments. She knew she had appeared stubborn and childish in her angry refusal to budge from her position that she was responsible for Nellie's death and must therefore do everything she could to find her murderer. But finally they had given in, extracting only the promise that she leave the house the moment she felt in danger. This morning, sitting on the hard seat of the horse car, she remembered that it was Monday, the dreaded washday, and her spirits sank even lower.

The faint chimes of nearby St. Mary's Cathedral interrupted these thoughts, and she noticed a newsboy, revealed by an overhead lamp, trudging up the sidewalk, a stack of papers on his shoulder. Would the news of Nellie's death be in the morning paper? Would the Voss household have been already informed of their former maid's death?

She fervently hoped that the chance to observe how everybody reacted to Nellie's death would make going back worthwhile. What about the police? If Nate was correct and the police now believed that Matthew was murdered, they would suspect that Nellie's death was somehow connected. *Heavens, they will probably begin to question members of the household about their whereabouts yesterday afternoon! What should I say if they question me? I can't tell them where I was, that I was the woman with Nate when the body was found! If only I could ask Nate's advice.*

Annie pulled her shawl closer and shivered. There it was, the core of her misery, Nate Dawson. How could she ever expect to continue their new friendship after this? Unbidden came the memory of his strength as he lifted her down from the carriage and the warmth of his smile. *Well, I just have to work harder to find the missing assets and determine who was responsible for Matthew and Nellie's deaths, and then maybe I can convince myself, if not Nate, that all these deceptions will have been justified,* she thought.

At least there had been no news from Driscoll, and Mrs. Stein had promised to consult her husband Herbert as soon as he returned from Portland about how Annie could raise the funds to pay off the loan. Her difficulties with Driscoll now seemed trivial compared to Nellie's death.

Annie noticed that the horse car had just passed Larkin Street and she stood and pulled the cord. The driver slowed the horses down and pulled over towards the curb. Annie thanked him kindly. Gathering up her skirts, she stepped lightly down, being careful to miss the dried dung that lay scattered along the edge of the road. She stepped up on the wooden sidewalk and turned to watch the horse car pull past her, looking up at the Voss house that was gradually emerging in the faint light of dawn.

Matthew's house sat squarely in the middle of the 1100 block of Geary, an elegant, three storied building, narrow and tall, unusual only in the fact that it contained bay windows on both the first and second floors. The windows were tightly curtained against prying eyes, so she couldn't see if any of the rooms had lights on. A peaked roof hid the fourth-floor attic where her room was located. This block of Geary was on a sort of plateau, which put it above most of the morning fog. Looking west, she could just make out the tops of the sandy hills that stood between this edge of the city and the Pacific. With a pang she realized that due west was the beach where Nellie had died.

Shaking off that thought, Annie crossed the now deserted street.

Remembering she was playing the role of a servant, she moved past the gate that led to the front door to enter the gate to the right marked "tradesman's entrance." Opening this gate, she continued on a flagged walk to the side of the house around to the back until she reached a series of three steps that led down to the basement kitchen, where Cartier was supposed to let her in. She needed to get the cook stove going so it would be ready for Wong when he arrived at five-thirty.

Miss Nancy had said sternly, "Mr. Voss always insisted that the maid be back from her night out by five to fire up the stove so that breakfast would be ready by seven sharp."

Annie grimaced at the thought of the long day of work that lay before her. Why couldn't Cartier start the stove if she was going to have to get up anyway to let Annie in? For that matter, why did Wong need to start cooking that early in the morning? It wasn't as if Matthew was still there, needing his breakfast early so he could be at work by eight-thirty. As far as Annie could tell, Jeremy certainly wouldn't be up that early, and no one else in the household had anything of pressing importance to do. *Such stupidity*, she thought peevishly, longing for her warm bed at home and a few more hours of sleep. Her level of irritation rose dramatically when she discovered that Cartier had not yet done her part, and the kitchen door was still locked.

She knocked softly at first, in case Cartier was simply sitting in the kitchen waiting for her arrival. Then she knocked more loudly. Perhaps the woman had fallen asleep? Then she added her voice to her summons, resisting the desire to yell loudly at the top of her lungs. She desisted when neither her voice nor her pounding did anything more than prompt a volley of barks from the neighbor's dog. She didn't really want to wake everybody up, although it would serve Cartier right if Miss Nancy heard. No doubt she would give Cartier an earful.

Annie passed several minutes contemplating this pleasant eventuality, when the thought came to her that perhaps Cartier had meant to open the front door for her. This would have been highly unusual and inconvenient, but, then, maybe this was Matthew's special routine? The household seemed to have gone on following his maxims to the letter, even after his death. She couldn't count how many times either Miss Nancy or Cartier had prefaced one of their instructions to her by, "Mr. Voss said" or "The Master said."

In the growing light Annie walked back along the narrow walkway between the house and the neighboring hedge. As she did, she looked upward for some sign of life in the house, but found none. When she got to the front, she tried the doorknob, tapped lightly with the front knocker, and, when nothing happened, she rang the bell. It was amazing how guilty she felt to be around at the front, so when she got no response, she returned quickly to the back door and tried again, knocking and calling Cartier's name, more loudly this time. Still nothing.

A small worm of anxiety wriggled its way down her spine. *Why wasn't anybody answering*? Shouldn't someone have been roused by the noise she had been making? Between herself and the dog next door, they had produced sufficient racket to 'raise the dead,' to use one of Kathleen's favorite terms. A horrible image crawled, unbidden, into Annie's mind. Everybody in the household, stretched out in hideous rigor, silent, and lifeless, murdered like Matthew and Nellie.

Annie began to pound on the door, yelling frantically. Shifting to the kitchen window, she crouched down to see if there was any movement inside. The kitchen was in the basement, and the window, although placed at shoulder height over the sink, was at ground-level from the outside. Although strong metal bars made entrance or exit through this window impossible, it was always kept open a crack, and she remembered that the back door key hung on a hook fairly near by. In her alarm she had some vague thoughts of perhaps reaching in the window and grabbing it. Falling down on her hands and knees, she thrust her right arm, which just barely fit, between two of the bars, stretching left towards the back door, where the key should be hanging. Pressing her face to the bars and extending her arm to its full length, she swept her arm in a semi-circle along the back kitchen wall, encountering nothing but a splinter.

Then two things happened at once. A soft calm voice from behind asked, "Miss Lizzie, may I be of help?" while from up above, the squeal of wood sliding against wood, followed by a sharp bang, heralded an outraged shout of "Who's there, stop that caterwauling this instant!" Startled, Annie pulled back from the barred window so abruptly she lost her balance and flopped down on the wet grass. Wong, who stood looking down at her, reached out a hand to help her up. As she rose, she glanced up at the window above her and saw a pale blurred oval topped by what she speculated must be a massive white night cap. In the misty morning light, the only discernable feature was a sharp beak of a nose, so Annie took her chances and called up.

"I'm sorry, Miss Nancy. It's me, the maid, Lizzie. I didn't mean to wake you. But Wong and I are here and Miss Cartier hasn't opened the door as she said she would. I was afraid you'd be angry if the stove wasn't ready and breakfast was late. Please, Miss, could you see that Cartier comes down and opens up for us?"

For an answer she got a gruff "Well, I never!" and the window banged down with equal fury. Annie turned to Wong and shrugged.

"Has this happened before? Cartier forgetting? I suppose I should have just waited, but I got the shivers, afraid maybe something had happened to them all."

Wong frowned slightly at her words, but then his expression smoothed out and he responded with equanimity. "Yes, Miss, this has happened before. The good woman who tended to the mistress before, she never forgot. In fact she often started the fire herself. But not Miss Cartier. She refuses. She also sleeps like a dragon dives, very deeply. The other maid, Nellie, had a problem at first. I would find her on the back steps waiting every week. But then the trouble stopped. I don't know what happened. But she would always be inside the kitchen, with the oven going, when I arrived."

## Chapter Twenty-two

Four hours later, Annie glanced at the mirror that hung in the front entrance hallway; her first chance to check to see if her braid was still neatly coiled at the nape of her neck. She had just turned away the third caller that morning with the standard formula that the mistress was not at home. Mrs. Voss was at home, of course, as each visitor had known, but she was still not receiving. They wouldn't have called this early in the day if they had expected to be seen. Afternoon was the time for serious visiting. Each caller had left their card; one had even brought a hideous molded lemon jelly that Wong had taken from her with arched eyebrows and a soul-wrenching sigh. Annie hoped fervently he wouldn't feel obliged to serve it to the staff for lunch. She had never found pale, wiggly water very sustaining, and today she would need all the sustenance she could get.

Thank goodness, none of the callers had been Nate Dawson, or a policeman for that matter. There had been no mention of Nellie's death in the morning paper, and as the day progressed, Nellie's death was becoming less and less real to Annie as she moved about the quiet house doing her chores.

It was only mid-morning, yet already she had lugged steaming jugs of heated water to the two ladies of the household, cleaned out and re-lighted four fireplaces, served breakfast, washed the breakfast dishes, made beds, and scrubbed, rinsed, and hung out two loads of wash to dry. It was no wonder that the long hairpins that were supposed to be holding her bun in place had become derelict in their duty. Annie wrinkled her nose at her image, then poked and prodded at her hair, which served only to release more of the sharp smell of bluing that clung to her.

She now had about an hour before it was time to serve Mrs. Voss her morning tea, and she planned to make the most of it. Knowing that Miss Nancy had just left the house to do some marketing, and that Cartier was helping Mrs. Voss dress, Annie thought this would be a good time to clean and search Miss Nancy's room. She hoped to eliminate this room at least as a place where the missing money or assets were hidden and look for any evidence of the items that someone had taken from Matthew's hidden shelf.

Annie took a pail of water up the back stairs with her and slipped into Miss Nancy's room, putting the pail up against the door that she left just slightly ajar. Now, if anyone tried to enter, they would have to push the door and the heavy pail aside, and Annie would have time to close whatever drawer or cupboard she had been poking into and appear to be conscientiously engaged in performing her proper duties. That was the plan, at least.

Annie stood for a second surveying Miss Nancy's room, which was across from Mrs. Voss's bedroom on the second floor. The smallest bedroom on that floor, it served as both her bedroom and sitting room. Annie wondered at this since there were several larger rooms on the second and third floors that were vacant. Well, most likely she didn't want a bigger room. A true old-fashioned Yankee, Miss Nancy probably viewed comfort as a vice and discomfort as a virtue. In fact, never had Annie seen a room where the old Calvinist doctrines had been more rigorously followed. The room was dark; heavy brown velvet curtains drawn across both windows, and the dark mahogany of the hallway continued into this room, with wainscoting that went halfway up the walls. The wallpaper was a light brown, with a narrow darker brown stripe, and the wooden floor was bare of all save an oval rag rug in which grays and blacks predominated. Annie stared at the rug and muttered, "However did she find so many old mourning clothes. She must haunt funerals and beg for scraps!"

A single bed, with a plain headboard, again in mahogany, was pushed up against the wall to her left. Matching wardrobe and dresser filled the remaining walls, and, on a small table next to the window overlooking the back yard, lay a huge Bible. Open, Annie saw, as she crossed over to it, to *Revelations*. A rocking chair, with no seductive cushions to mar its wooden seat and back, sat next to the table. The air smelled slightly of camphor.

Annie pulled back the curtains and pushed up the window a crack to let in light and to make it easier to hear if Miss Nancy returned from her marketing. She then took her dust rag and attacked the bed, being careful to slip her hand between the mattress and the headboard and then under the mattress to discover any hidden banknotes or stocks and bonds. She then wiped clean the mantel over the room's fireplace, noting both the absence of any of the usual knick-knacks and the presence of a beautiful Seth Thomas clock. There were no suspicious ashes in the fireplace, but she had already learned that Miss Voss did not believe in having a fire during the summer, which explained the chill in this room that rivaled Annie's attic hideaway. The washstand's only secret was the chamber pot, not surprisingly of plain white enamel to match the equally utilitarian basin and pitcher that stood on its surface.

Annie continued dusting. The rocking chair revealed no hidden recesses and the wardrobe contained only a depressing number of black old-fashioned dresses, two black hats, and two pairs of black high-buttoned shoes. *Such extravagance!*

Annie's attention swerved back to the shoes. Picking up one of the shoes from the wardrobe floor, she measured it against her own foot. Miss Nancy had significantly larger feet than Annie, which wasn't surprising, considering her greater height. Her shoes were also slightly pointed. While she had difficulty picturing Miss Nancy struggling with Nellie on the beach, she supposed this was not impossible. And Nellie might have been more willing to meet a woman alone. What she couldn't imagine was Miss Nancy climbing up the rocky path Annie had found, and there certainly didn't seem to be any sand or water marks on these shoes.

At least shoes should eliminate Wong as Nellie's killer. There was no way that his black cloth slippers could have made the marks she had found in the sand. Unless he had changed shoes! *Oh dear,* she thought, *obviously shoes were not going to provide any definitive answers.* Annie put back the shoe she had been holding.

Startled by the soft quarter chime from the mantel clock, Annie swiftly turned to the last piece of furniture in the room, the dresser, fearful that Miss Nancy would return before she had finished searching. Palms beginning to sweat, she went through each of the drawers, sifting through the neatly piled underclothes, aprons, spare linen and the extra blankets found there. Nothing! No bundles of bank notes, no stashes of stocks, no revelatory packet of old love letters or hidden diary that would reveal all.

Straightening up, she was again reminded of her tired muscles and a growing sense of futility. This was her third day in the house, and she really hadn't learned anything of substance. As Sibyl it was so much easier to ferret out information because she could ask questions, glean insight from how a person reacted to her predictions. As a servant, she had to be content with what the mute furniture of the place had to tell her. Sighing, Annie pulled her dust rag from her pocket and began to dust the top of the dresser, looking closely at each of the objects on it, a simple bone comb and brush set, with a small matching mirror. Clearly Miss Nancy saw no need for a fuller look at herself. Beyond a button hook and a small pincushion, nothing else was on the top of the dresser but pictures--pictures that proved very illuminating.

Each was in a heavy silver frame, gleaming with frequent polishing, and worth, perhaps, more than all the other furnishings in the
room together. The largest was a faded family portrait, a daguerreo-
type from the late 1840s, judging by the style of clothing. An older
man and woman who looked remarkably like Matthew and his sister
sat stiffly on two chairs, and a young man and woman stood behind
them. Annie peered closely at these two young people. She knew
they must be Matthew and Miss Nancy, but it was difficult to reconcile these images with the images she had of them now. Matthew as
a young man had been straight, tall, and broad-shouldered. His bi-
ceps appeared to strain the arms of his suit-coat, and the hands that
gripped the back of his father's chair looked massive. For the first
time, Annie could imagine Amelia Voss falling in love with him.

As for the young woman in the picture, Annie could see it was
Miss Nancy, whose hairstyle and clothing had not changed a whit in
thirty years. But her face was so much softer, exhibiting a sweetness
that was completely missing in the present.

Putting this picture down carefully, Annie picked up a second,
which contained a city scene. It featured a two-storied building on a
steep hill. A sign that read *Voss and Samuels-Fine Furniture* extended clear across the front of the building and a wagon stood in
front piled high with what looked like chairs. Next to the wagon,
standing on the sidewalk in front of the building, were three people.
Having just seen the family portrait, Annie had no difficulty distin-
guishing Matthew. A slouch hat on his head and casually dressed in
his shirt sleeves, he stood beaming into the camera, with what
looked like a chisel and plane clutched to his still powerfully built
chest. Next to him was a man more formally dressed, who stood in a
swaggering pose; derby cocked back on his head, extravagant mustache, and the suit jacket pulled aside to reveal the tiny line of a
watch chain across the vest. Malcolm Samuels was immediately
recognizable, even though Annie had only seen him briefly at the

funeral. Samuels didn't look like he had aged a day since this old picture had been taken.

The woman who was the third person in the picture hadn't been so fortunate. Miss Nancy, standing slightly apart from the two men couldn't have been much more than a decade older than in the first family portrait, but time had already begun to carve severe lines on her face, deep enough to be captured by the camera. Miss Nancy, like her brother, seemed to be holding something clutched to her chest. On closer examination, Annie saw that the objects were several large ledgers. This suggested that Miss Nancy kept the books for the company in the early days, an interesting piece of information. But the most startling aspect about the picture was the expression of yearning the camera had captured on Miss Nancy's face as she looked over at the two men to her side. Could it be that Miss Nancy had been in love with Malcolm Samuels? *If so, how sad*, she thought, because Annie couldn't imagine the virile, confident man in this picture looking twice at his partner's spinster sister.

She gave a final wipe to the rest of the dresser top, noting that all the other pictures seemed to be of Jeremy Voss, and that his mother did not appear in a single one of the photographs. This prompted another thought. What if Miss Nancy's expression had been directed at her brother? From her first glimpse of Miss Nancy at the funeral, everything had pointed to a corrosive jealousy on her part, directed at her sister-in-law. Several times in her work as Sibyl she had encountered marriages poisoned by siblings or parents who were never able to accept their new in-laws. Her own mother-in-law had done everything she could to undermine her relationship with John, and then practically accused her of driving him to his death at his funeral. Remembering that awful first year of widowhood when she was forced to live with John's parents, battered daily by her mother-in-law's grief-fueled fury, Annie wondered how Amelia Voss had stood all these years of living under the same roof with a woman who so obviously disliked her.

Recalling the scene in Mrs. Voss's sitting room Friday night and Miss Nancy's chilling biblical quotation, she moved across the room to give the large Bible sitting next to the window a second look. It was one of those Bibles that you would normally find on a pulpit, and Annie wondered if Matthew's father had been a preacher. Since the Bible was opened to *Revelations,* the last book of the *New Testament*, the left side was very high. Too high, Annie realized, as she carefully tried to lift the front cover without letting the pages slide to the right. Underneath were three slim volumes, and when she slid them out they were immediately recognizable as accounting ledgers, very much like the ones Miss Nancy had been holding in the picture on her dresser. However, looking at the front pages of each, Annie saw the dates covered the last year and a half. Voss and Samuels, Fine Furnishings, was embossed on the front cover of each. Annie felt sure that these were the objects that she had seen being removed from Matthew's study, and that it must have been Miss Nancy who removed them. *Miss Nancy, what are you up to?* Annie thought to herself. *And why did you need to remove these ledgers in the dead of night?*

## Chapter Twenty-three

"Girl, what are you doing on this floor?"

Annie, who had her back to the hallway as she closed the door to Miss Nancy's room, was so startled she almost dropped the pail of water. Swinging around she confronted her nemesis, Cartier, who had evidently just come down the stairs from her own room on the third floor.

Cartier stood in front of Annie, hands on hips in clear disapproval. "I said, girl, what are you doing up here on the second floor? Why aren't you in the kitchen doing the washing? I can't believe you've finished."

Cartier was wearing a strikingly handsome dress of plain dark green wool, with a tight-fitting long draped overskirt. *However did she get the money for such expensive outfits? She can't possibly afford such an elaborate wardrobe on a servant's salary!* Annie repressed a sudden desire to slap the other woman's face, just to wipe the condescension off of it for a second. Instead, she dropped a short curtsey and answered her, trying to sound as dim-witted and loquacious as possible, which she had discovered infuriated Cartier.

"Lord and Saints preserve us, Miss! You scared me right out of me shoes. Why I thought the ghost of the dead master had come to catch me. I couldn't sleep a wink my first night in that attic, all by my lonesome. Last place I worked, I shared my cot with the nursemaid. Do you think I could come share your bed if I can't sleep? I cleans my feet every night, promise. I..."

"Don't be impertinent, girl. I don't care if you wash all over, though I doubt the likes of you have ever seen the inside of a tub. I wouldn't share a place at the table with you, much less my bed. Now answer me sharp or I'll take you by your ear straight to the mistress and see what she has to say about you snooping where you don't belong."

Annie sniffed loudly, remembering to wipe her nose on her sleeve, and then began to whine. "Please Miss, don't crab at me so. I didn't mean no harm. I'm just doing my duty. The old Miss, she said I was to do her room this morning. That's the Lord's truth. Go ask her yourself, if you're not afraid she'll snap your nose off. Me, I'd be afraid to rile her again, what with her already being so put out that you forgot to open the door for me and Wong this morning. But if you want to, let's go together. She'll tell you just what I told you, but if you don't believe me...."

"Good heavens, girl, that's enough, get back down to the kitchen. It's time for Mrs. Voss's tea."

Anne watched with some satisfaction as Cartier turned to knock softly on the door to her mistress's sitting room. She sincerely doubted that Cartier would take the trouble to ask for a confirmation of her story from Miss Nancy, since the women's mutual enmity meant they spoke to each other as little as possible. Annie also hoped the threat of getting Miss Nancy upset would convince Cartier to stay out of her way for awhile.

Carrying the pail of water down the back stairs, Annie stopped at the small mirror in the back hallway to check to see that she didn't have any smudges on her face from cleaning. She could hear Miss Nancy's voice float up from the kitchen, and she wanted to make sure she didn't give the irascible old woman any reason to complain about her lack of neatness. She was just in the midst of replacing one of her hairpins when the shrill sound of the front door bell made her jump and stab the hairpin painfully into her scalp. Muttering an unladylike oath, Annie smoothed her apron and regained her composure. She pasted on the demure, subservient expression she had gradually perfected as her "servant-look" and opened the front door. The degree of relief that she felt when the man at the door did not turn out to be Nate Dawson told Annie how much she had been dreading this possibility.

But relief turned to surprise when she realized that the man standing in front of her was Malcolm Samuels, his picture come to life. As instructed, she began to mouth the polite fiction that her mistress was not at home. Ignoring her formulaic phrases, Samuels skillfully side-stepped her, both verbally and physically, and moved from the doorway into the hall and then into the front parlor in several long strides.

As Annie ran indignantly after him, she was again struck by how much younger he seemed than his late partner, Matthew. At close range she could see that Samuels was nearer to Matthew's age than she had thought at the cemetery, but he was still a remarkably vital and handsome man.

Once inside the parlor, Mr. Samuels turned to look down at her with a marked twinkle in his eye, and he assumed an exaggerated air of seriousness, saying, "Well, young lady, you have been fibbing. You and I both know that Mrs. Voss is at home. But since you are obviously the new girl, I will forgive you this time. But you must learn that I am not a person to be fobbed off with polite fabrications."

Breaking out in a friendly smile, seemingly designed to assure Annie that he was teasing, Mr. Samuels went on to say, "You just run up and tell Mrs. Voss that Mr. Samuels is here to see her, and if she doesn't stop moping around in her fancy boudoir and come down to see me, I'll just have to come up there!"

Annie couldn't help smile in return, and, since she knew that Samuels was a close friend of the family, she put up no more resistance. Instead, she asked him to make himself comfortable while she saw if the mistress would receive him. As she went upstairs on this errand, she wondered how she might contrive to overhear what these two people would have to say to each other. What if she pretended to do some cleaning in the large formal parlor? It was across the hall from the smaller morning room that Samuels had entered, so she might be able to hear if both doors were left ajar. Another near collision with Jeremy Voss, outside his mother's sitting room door, drove all thoughts of eavesdropping temporarily from her mind.

Jeremy made no attempt at apology this morning. Annie decided that the weekend had brought no solace to the young man. Instead, his mood seemed to have darkened considerably. He was carelessly dressed, his clothes hanging from him as if he had lost flesh overnight. His pale skin was drawn very tightly across his cheekbones, accentuating the dark smudges that circled his eyes. Annie wondered whether he had slept at all. The smell of stale whiskey clung to him and brought back unwelcome memories of her husband in the last months before his death.

John would stumble in late, drunk, and disheveled, rising the next morning still bleary-eyed and even more belligerent than the night before. Outwardly he would pretend such confidence, loudly asserting that this day his luck would turn, that all he would have gambled away the day before would be gained back again, doubled in worth. In time Annie realized that the bravado was just that; it hid a fear and guilt that consumed him. Jeremy exuded a similar miasma of anxious remorse, and that troubled her.

Jeremy impatiently demanded to know who had been at the door.

"Was it another one of those damned women, come to sniff out the scandal in the house? Why don't you just tell them all to go to hell," Jeremy growled. "Wouldn't I just like to see their faces if you did. Maybe I should answer the door the next time it rings. I'd give them all something to gossip about."

When Annie murmured something about Mr. Samuels to see Mrs. Voss, his face brightened, and he turned and began to go down the steps to the first floor, saying, "Uncle Malcolm? What a relief! He'll know how to get us out of this mess."

Annie knocked gently on Mrs. Voss's door, amused by Jeremy's sudden optimism. She hoped that his faith wasn't misplaced. Perhaps Samuels was just the strong masculine presence Jeremy needed. Despite her sincere affection for Matthew Voss, Annie had always wondered if he might have been as much at fault as his son in their misunderstandings. She also wondered just what Jeremy meant by "mess." Was it just the financial uncertainty he was talking about, or did they need the help of Malcolm Samuels to straighten out a more serious problem, like Matthew's murder?

Annie found Mrs. Voss up, dressed, and ensconced in her sitting room, again working on some embroidery. She also looked like the weekend had not brought much repose. Even though the dress she wore was fashionably cut and trimmed with lace, its dull black sheen tinged her pale skin grey this morning. Cartier was not in the room, so Annie assumed she was tidying the adjoining bedroom. Annie was surprised when Mrs. Voss frowned at her announcement that Mr. Samuels, joined by Master Jeremy, was waiting in the morning room. The reason for the frown became clearer when she asked Annie to bring a strong pot of coffee, as well as tea, to the downstairs parlor, and to get Wong to unwrap some of the fruitcake to serve as well. Jeremy's mother must have some inkling about his state this morning.

When Annie reached the kitchen, Miss Nancy was gone, and she wondered if she would also be present for tea. She hoped so, because, after looking at the pictures in Miss Nancy's room, she was curious to see how the older woman acted around Malcolm Samuels.

Annie found her wish fulfilled when she entered the parlor with the coffee, tea, and cake. Miss Nancy had preceded her and was already engaged in a bitter exchange with Samuels. Again clothed in unrelenting black, she stood stiffly, with her hands twisted in front of her, saying in a voice cracking with emotion, "You would like that, wouldn't you. To take over the company. Run it into the ground, most likely. But why stop at the business? A fine ambitious man like you. 'All day long the wicked covets, but the righteous gives and does not hold back.' Proverbs 21."

Amelia Voss, who was standing at Samuels' side, placed her hand on his arm, as if to restrain him, and Annie could see that she was gripping the cloth tightly. Miss Nancy glared at her and then turned and again addressed Samuels, saying, "I know there are other things of Matthew's besides the business that you have always coveted."

Jeremy threw a startled glance at Samuels, whose good-humored smile seemed frozen in place, and then he walked over to his aunt, taking her hands in his. "Now, Aunt Nan, don't go all religious on us," Jeremy cajoled. "Uncle Malcolm doesn't deserve it. He is just trying to help. You are the one who is most against selling the company, but if we don't sell, we will need his help. I can't run the factory side of the operations all by myself. I'm just not good at business. Here is Uncle Malcolm offering to help me, and you get all upset. If you want to be angry with someone, be angry with me; I'm the fool who has gotten us in this mess."

As Jeremy spoke, she shook her head in denial. She then spoke in a tone so low that only Jeremy, and Annie, who was behind them setting out the cups, could hear. "You could run the factory without his help. I'd help you. If we stick together, you and I, the true Vosses, we can do anything we put our minds to. You shouldn't go talking down about yourself. That was your father's fault--he always undervalued those of us who loved him the most. He was the fool, putting his trust in a ne'er-do-well like Samuels instead of his own flesh and blood. I would have done anything for him. Did he care?

No, I was never a pretty young thing, my looks was all used up caring for others. What was I to do while he and that fine wife of his went gallivanting all over Christendom? What did it matter to him if I had to live the rest of my life with strangers? It wouldn't be the first time I had to leave home for Matthew. Like Moses, 'I have been a sojourner in a foreign land.'"

With this, Miss Nancy turned away from her nephew, and Annie saw that tears ran down her face. When Miss Nancy turned, it brought Annie into her view and the older woman glared furiously at her and rasped out, "Stop your gawking, girl, and skedaddle. You still have the wash to attend to, and help Wong with lunch."

Annie looked over at Mrs. Voss for permission to follow Miss Nancy's orders and caught an expression that looked like fear reflected in those beautiful blue eyes, but when Mrs. Voss saw she was under observation, this look vanished. Instead, Mrs. Voss summoned forth one of her enchanting smiles and nodded to Annie, saying, "Yes, Lizzie, that will be enough here; you must get back to your work. But before you do, please ask Wong to come to my sitting room. I need to consult him about dinner."

After Annie curtsied and was leaving the room, she heard Mrs. Voss go on to say that she was sorry to end Mr. Samuels' visit, but that she had to attend to some household duties. Annie paused outside the door, having remembered this time not to shut it all the way. Jeremy was expostulating with his mother, saying that they had to come to some decisions, and Malcolm Samuels was supporting him.

Mrs. Voss went on pleasantly but firmly, saying, "No, Jeremy, I am afraid we shall just have to postpone any further discussion. It is really all too complicated for my poor understanding. But it seems to me that we shouldn't do anything precipitate until our lawyers, Mr. Hobbes and that nice young nephew of his, get back to us. I feel sure that there must be some stupid mistake and the money will be found. We mustn't rush into anything until we have all the facts."

Mrs. Voss's voice quavered at this point, and Annie heard her give a sad little laugh. "Now, didn't that sound just like Matthew? Maybe some of his good sense rubbed off on me after all."

Alerted by the rustle of skirts approaching the door, Annie left her eavesdropping post and slipped down the hall to the back stairway. As she entered the kitchen to deliver the message to Wong, she thought to herself, *At least I have learned two things. If Miss Nancy ever did have romantic feelings for Malcolm Samuels, they are long gone, and I was right to think that she was hurt and angry that Matthew hadn't considered her in his plans for the family. But is that enough motive to have killed him?*

Nate had been sitting on a hard wooden bench outside Chief Detective Jackson's office for nearly an hour, and he was beginning to lose his temper. Last night, after he had dropped Annie off at her home, he had gone right to the central police headquarters to inform Jackson of Nellie's death. But of course, Jackson had already been apprised of the discovery of a dead Cliff House waitress and was on his way to the scene. Nate had been left to sit for hours waiting for the detective's return, but he never got to see him. Instead, Nate was eventually questioned by a Sergeant Thompson and then spent another hour writing out his statement. He didn't get home until well after one in the morning.

After he caught a few hours sleep, he'd got up and spent a tedious three hours drafting wills. At lunch he had had a very unpleasant conversation with his Uncle, who couldn't understand why he would have taken Mrs. Fuller to question a waitress at the disreputable Cliff House. Nate, himself, wondered why he'd been so foolish. Now, after being summoned by Jackson to come back to police headquarters this afternoon, he'd been left cooling his heels, like a naughty boy called to the principal's office.

The detective's door opened and out came Sergeant Thompson, escorting a man that Nate was startled to recognize as Nellie's boyfriend, Jack. Today Jack wasn't wearing his natty checked coat or red silk cravat, nor was he sporting his jaunty attitude. The only similarity between his Saturday night finery and the sweaty work clothes he was wearing today was the red of the bandana around his neck. His eyes were swollen, his mustache drooping, and when he saw Nate he growled, "I wish I'd never seen you, you bastard. Gent's like you don't give a damn about a girl like Nell. If you didn't kill her you got her killed and I'll see you in hell."

The sergeant, not unkindly, herded Jack down the hall, while saying over his shoulder to Nate, "Chief will see you now. Go right on in." Nate stood for a moment, watching the two men, and then he walked into the small cluttered office. Chief Detective Jackson had been in the detective division for over twenty years, and his office appeared to have files from every case he ever worked on during that time. When Nate's Uncle Frank had first asked him to be the liaison with Jackson on the questions about Matthew Voss's death, he had secretly been elated. He chaffed under the limited scope afforded by working as the junior partner of his uncle's firm, feeling more like a glorified clerk than a true partner, and he had nurtured hopes that a good working relationship with one of the most powerful men in the city would lead to opportunities. Jackson, while a Republican, maintained cordial ties with both the Democratic Party and the upstart Workingmen's Party. His good opinion went far in San Francisco. As Nate stood in front of the Chief Detective, who failed to even acknowledge his presence as he wrote methodically in a small black notebook, his hopes turned to ashes. Standing there as the minutes crawled by, the feeling he'd had in the hall of being treated like a naughty schoolboy reappeared, and out of the ashes burned a fierce determination not to be patronized by this man.

"Sir, I believe *you* wished to see *me*," said Nate. "But I can see you are busy. Perhaps I should come back at a later time, when you aren't so preoccupied?"

"Mr. Dawson, take a seat, I will be with you in a minute," said Jackson.

Nate briefly contemplated walking out, but instead pulled a chair closer to the desk and sat down.

A few moments later Jackson put down his pen and looked up, saying, "Well, I've read your report, Mr. Dawson. You took it into your head to meddle in the investigation into Matthew Voss's death, and now a young woman's dead. What do you have to say for yourself?"

*Well, he certainly wasn't pulling any punches,* Nate thought, *but I'll be damned if he will intimidate me.* "Sir, I sincerely regret if my actions contributed to Nellie Flannigan's death. I would never have made the effort to find and speak to her if I had thought this would put her in danger. I assume that the police had come to a similar conclusion, since you hadn't made any effort to find her in the week following Mr. Voss's death. It appears we both underestimated her importance and possible complicity in Voss's murder. You do accept that Voss was murdered now, don't you?"

"Well, that really isn't the issue at hand, is it?" Jackson said. "We haven't determined anything, except that Miss Nellie Flannigan was found drowned. Whether this was the result of an accident, or if the unfortunate young lady took her own life, or was killed by someone else, it is too soon to tell."

"You can't think this was anything but murder?" Nate leaned forward. "She must have been involved with whoever robbed and killed Mr. Voss; whoever was her accomplice must have felt she was a danger and got rid of her. What did her boyfriend Jack have to say?"

Jackson snorted. "He said a slimy lawyer feller named Dawson tricked him into telling him where Miss Flannigan was, and then killed her! Lucky for you, the evidence is pretty clear that she died yesterday afternoon, sometime between twelve and one, when you were evidently on the way to the Cliff House. The stable where you rented your carriage says that you didn't leave the city until just before noon, and it would have been difficult for you to get to the Cliff House much before one, which is confirmed by the waitress you talked to there. Now of course it would help if we could also have the name of the young woman who was with you for corroboration."

'Sir, I am afraid I must refuse your request," Nate replied, stiffly. "The lady is a friend of mine, a respectable widow, and I simply can't in good conscience drag her name into this affair. I can, however, assure you that she had nothing to do with the death of either Mr. Voss or Miss Flannigan, and there is really nothing that she could add to the details I have already given in my report."

Jackson stared at him for a second then gave a quick laugh, saying, "Well, I suspect you are in enough trouble with the lady for dragging her out on a Sunday picnic as a cover for interviewing a servant girl and then subjecting her to a dead body, so I guess I won't get you in any more hot water." Jackson then poked his index finger in Nate's direction, saying, "But believe you me, if this whole thing should ever come to trial, and her testimony is needed, you will tell me her name. For now, the inquest is going to be sometime Wednesday morning, and I expect you to be there to give your testimony."

Nate, feeling much easier now that he had made it through the dicey question of revealing Annie Fuller's name, nodded, and asked, "Do you think that there is the possibility that Miss Flannigan's boyfriend might be involved in either death?"

"There doesn't seem to be much chance of that. The night of Mr. Voss's death he and Miss Flannigan were at an all-night party at Shannon's dance hall, with at least a hundred witnesses. The afternoon of Miss Flannigan's death he was down in the hold of a ship, welding, along with twenty other men. That's not to say he doesn't know more than he's saying. But beyond his tale that she was getting favors from a young gentleman, like yourself or Mr. Jeremy Voss, he hasn't been all that helpful."

"Chief Detective, why drag Jeremy Voss into this? Seems to me that if someone killed Miss Flannigan that it would be someone outside the household. Someone who would need her help as a servant to get into the house and locate the stolen money and assets, maybe some confidence man that hooked her into his scheme. I know you've dealt with cases like that."

Nate watched with irritation as Jackson leaned back in his chair and smiled and then said, "Well Mr. Dawson, I will say this for you, you do a good job of trying to protect your clients. But consider this, maybe if someone did kill Miss Flannigan, and I'm not saying we have the evidence to conclude that yet, maybe it wasn't for what she did, but for what she knew."

## Chapter Twenty-five:
## Monday, late afternoon, August 13, 1879

"Wong, thank heavens, I think I am finally done." Annie folded the last sheet and stood up straight, put her hands against the small of her back, and bent backwards slightly, groaning. Wong had tried to help her out as much as he could by assisting her in lifting the large kettles of water off the stove to pour into the tubs and then later helping her carry the tubs out to the back to drain. But he was pretty well occupied the rest of the time with preparing, serving and cleaning up after lunch. *That settles it*, she thought. As soon as she got back home, Beatrice was to start looking for a good washerwoman to come in on Mondays and Tuesdays to do the laundry and ironing. Kathleen could still help out with the occasional light load of delicate clothes, but never again would Annie ask her to do a full wash by herself. That is if Driscoll didn't succeed in taking the boarding house away from her! Pushing that defeatist idea away, Annie stretched again and thought about a more immediate problem, with every muscle in her back aching, she had no idea how she would get through serving dinner tonight.

Wouldn't Kathleen laugh at her, a few loads of wash and Annie was feeling like a decrepit old woman. Oh, how she was homesick for that laugh. She also couldn't help but wonder what Nate was up to, if he had met with the police again, if he had been successful in keeping her name out of their investigations. It had been less than ten hours since she left her home, but, if it wasn't for the regular tradesmen who came to the back door making deliveries, she might well believe the rest of the outside world had disappeared. She'd never realized how isolated a servant might feel, unable to simply leave the house to take a walk or visit friends whenever she wanted.

Thinking of tradesmen reminded Annie of one strange occurrence that happened right before lunch. Cartier had come to the kitchen with some excuse about making sure that Annie took care of a stain on one of Mrs. Voss's dressing gown cuffs, but then she had hung around for awhile, simply getting in Wong's way as he prepared the noon meal. She didn't seem interested in talking, but when the young boy who delivered the meat knocked at the back door, she bustled over to unlock the door to take the wrapped beef from him. This was so out of character that Annie had stopped her washing and stared at her, getting a glimpse of a folded piece of paper that Cartier slipped to the delivery boy before sending him on his way.

*Who would have imagined it,* she thought. *The refined Miss Cartier engaged in some sort of secret correspondence with a delivery boy. What a come down.* Then her amusement had been swept away by the thought that maybe this event was more sinister; if Cartier had been involved with Matthew's murder, maybe she was communicating with an accomplice, someone she had let into the house to steal Matthew's money and kill him. If this was true, it wasn't a stretch to imagine Nellie finding out, and maybe that was why she had to die.

As she picked up the basket of clean clothes and moved to put it at the base of the back stairs, she stopped to listen for a minute, struck by the oppressive stillness of the house's upper floors. It was as if the kitchen, filled with the hiss of fat dripping off of the roast in the oven, the gentle bubbling of soup stock, the steady click, click, click of Wong's vegetable knife, contained the only sounds of life in the place. Jeremy had left the house with Malcolm Samuels before lunch and was probably now well on his way towards another night of depressed debauchery with his friends, so his quarters would be dark and silent. All three of the women in the house had retired to their respective rooms before dinner. Annie imagined Cartier, holed up in her room, writing to her unknown correspondent. As for Miss Nancy, Annie pictured her crouched and muttering over that massive Bible. Mrs. Voss would be sitting quietly in her lovely sitting room, her chatter temporarily stilled. Annie imagined her embroidering fantastic scenes of medieval chivalry and hiding her fears behind her unreadable, beautiful eyes.

The door chime interrupted these thoughts, and Annie looked over at Wong, who was sitting at the kitchen table while he chopped. He looked up, then said, "Miss Lizzie, I will answer the door, if you would but please sit and finish dicing these carrots."

"Oh, Wong, would you? I will gladly chop up every vegetable we have in the house if it would mean I could sit down for a while."

Glancing at the kitchen clock, Annie was surprised that it was already near six o'clock, a very odd time for callers, and a very inconvenient time for Wong. He seemed to have planned a more elaborate menu than usual this evening, and Annie assumed this was in honor of Mrs. Voss, who was finally eating her dinner downstairs. He was going to start with an asparagus soup, then a fish course of marinated salmon followed by fricasseed quails, and finally the roast beef. For dessert he had made an orange cake. Annie's job was to assemble a fresh salad of greens and steam the carrots and peas. The smell from the simmering quail sauce permeated the kitchen, effectively eliminating the smell of bluing that had dominated the room for most of the day and making Annie's stomach rumble. *I must remember to get the recipe from Wong*, Annie thought to herself. *Whoever the visitor is, when he smells dinner, he'll wish he'd been invited.*

Hearing the slight whisper of Wong's cotton slippers on the stairs, Annie, without looking up, said. "So, Wong, what lovely offering has one of the neighbors delivered to us this time?"

"Miss Lizzie, Mrs. Voss has requested that we delay the dinner preparations and has asked that Miss Cartier, that she...."

Startled by the odd tone in his voice, Annie looked up from her cutting board to see Wong standing at the bottom of the back stairs, apparently staring into space, one of his long graceful hands touching the base of his throat just where the two sides of his mandarin collar met, and he seemed to have lost the rest of his sentence.

"Wong, what ever is wrong? I am sure that dinner will be fine; we have barely started. Who was at the door, was it someone for Cartier? How odd!"

"Miss, I am sorry, I did not make myself clear. It was a Chief Detective Jackson and his sergeant. They came to inform Mrs. Voss that Miss Nellie has died. I find myself very distressed by the news. I am to prepare tea, and you are to go to Cartier's room and ask her to come down to speak with the Detective. They wish to talk briefly with everyone in the household who knew Miss Nellie. I can only assume that there is something out of the ordinary about her death."

With that statement, Wong moved over to the stove where he began to fill the kettle from the hot water reservoir. Annie rose and started to go over to him, but something about the stiffness of his back stopped her in her tracks. *What could I say? He worked beside Nellie for over two years. Coming on top of the loss of a master that he had served for goodness knows how long, what must he be feeling?*

She realized that most of the day she had been able to push thoughts of Nellie's death away; as if it hadn't happened as long as the people around her didn't know it had happened. But here it was, all the pain and sadness and guilt she had been feeling just twenty-four hours ago. The tragedy of a young woman's death, made real by the evident pain of an old Chinese servant. How she wished she could tell him the truth, confess her guilt over the maid's death, promise him that Nellie's murderer would not go unpunished.

Wiping the tears that had come unbidden to her eyes, Annie cleared her throat and said, "I am so sorry, Wong. I will get Cartier. But please let me serve the tea when it is ready. Then you can do what is needed for dinner." *And I can at least give you some time to grieve in peace*, she thought.

## Chapter Twenty-six

A few moments later Annie stood knocking on the door to Cartier's third floor room.

"Please, Miss Cartier, you are wanted in the parlor." The sound of the key in the lock alerted Annie that the door was about to be pulled open, so she stepped back into the hall.

"Yes, girl, what is it? I thought I explained to you when you first arrived that this is my hour to rest before I must prepare the mistress for dinner. You'd better have a very good excuse for disturbing me. Heaven knows why they hired you? You are hopeless. Even that impertinent girl that ran off was better trained than you!"

Cartier stood, her back straight, looking down at Annie with her usual expression of condescension. She had changed from the outfit she was wearing that morning, and this time her dress was of watered silk. The rich dark purple of the material glowed in the afternoon sunlight, yet was properly somber for a house of mourning. The dress set off the woman's pale skin admirably, as did the rich chestnut curls that served as bangs that framed her face. Her eyes were a dark shade of brown, her nose was straight and aristocratic, and her lips were soft and full, except when they thinned in disdain, as they did now.

Initially with no more idea than of wiping that sneer off of Cartier's face, Annie decided to see if she could create a little fear in the woman, saying in her best Lizzie voice, "Lordy Miss Cartier. I'd be sore 'fraid to speak ill of the dead like that! Not when there's a copper downstairs asking to speak to you about that Nellie, so's that's why I knocked. But I can go down and tell'em you aren't to be disturbed. "

The effects of these words were so dramatic that Annie actually felt a bit ashamed. Cartier staggered against the doorframe and her hands flew up as if to ward off a blow. Annie noted that all color had fled her lips, which she licked nervously, eyes darting to look down the hall to the front stairs. Yet, while Annie watched, Cartier visibly gathered herself together, stood up straighter and said, "Heavens girl, don't be ridiculous. Of course I will go downstairs to attend my mistress if she wishes it. I can assume that she is in the front parlor? Now get yourself down stairs to the kitchen and make yourself useful. I would strongly suggest that you keep that wretched little nose out of my business if you know what is good for you." And with that she pulled the door to her room closed behind her, carefully locked it, and swept down the front stairs.

By the time Annie had made it down from the third floor to the kitchen, Wong had assembled the tea tray. It was really too heavy for her to carry safely up to the first floor by herself, but she nearly grabbed it from Wong in her anxious desire not to miss what was going on. Instead, she picked up the tablecloth and napkins and indicated that Wong precede her up the stairs. When they got to the front formal parlor the door was still slightly open, and they could hear Cartier's raised voice from within. Annie didn't bother to knock but marched right in, sketching a curtsey and announcing, "Tea, Ma'am," as she made her way over to the tea table, hoping that Wong was following her lead. She knew this was completely inappropriate behavior for a servant. However, apart from Miss Nancy, who had given Annie a ferocious frown, everyone else in the room seemed enthralled by Cartier, who held forth in the middle of the room.

"...are unbelievably insulting. I have never been so outraged in my life. Mrs. Voss, I can not believe you would let this person speak to me in this way. This is not the treatment I am used to, and I can assure you such disgraceful behavior would have never had happened in the Burnett-Jones household. My former mistress knew my value. My day off is sacred, and it is no one's business but my own...."

At this point Annie looked up from the table cloth she was straightening and saw that Cartier had extracted a delicate lavender handkerchief from some where about her person and was pressing it against her lips. Her magnificent bosom was heaving and there were two bright spots of red in her cheeks, which did not compliment the deep purple of her ensemble. Stealing glimpses at the rest of the room's inhabitants as she began to unload the tea tray, Annie noted that Mrs. Voss had moved next to Cartier and was ineffectually patting her on her shoulder, while Miss Nancy looked for all the world like she had just discovered a disgusting insect in the middle of the parlor floor.

The two gentlemen in the room were exchanging amused glances. Annie immediately recognized Chief Detective Jackson from the newspapers, whose illustrators had found his generally leonine profile of high forehead, unruly head of hair, exuberant sideburns and large mustache easy to caricature. In person the reddish hair, liberally streaked with grey, and the sharp white teeth that his faint smile revealed, made the comparison with the king of the jungle even stronger. He looked to be somewhere in his fifties, above average in height and solidly built. The browns and grays of his smart four-buttoned, cutaway suit complimented his coloring in a way that showed a remarkable eye for detail. His sergeant, in contrast, was non-descript. An older man in his sixties, with close-cropped grey hair, abbreviated mousey mustache, regular features, he was wearing an undistinguished dark grey suit. Annie doubted if he would ever get his picture in the papers.

Yet it was the sergeant who had the temerity to address Cartier again. Waving his small worn black leather notebook, he said, "Miss, we meant no insult. But duty requires that we investigate when there is some question about a death. Now, if you please, will you give an accounting of your whereabouts and actions during the day light hours of Sunday, August 12th. That would be yesterday. In addition, we would be interested if you have any information that might indicate the recent state of mind of the former parlor maid, Miss Nellie Flannigan."

Annie, placing the last cup and saucer on the table, heard a sharp intake of breath, she thought from Cartier, when Mrs. Voss's said, "Please Mr. Jackson, can't we postpone these questions. We are all distressed to hear the news of Nellie's death. I am sure...."

Miss Nancy broke in impatiently. "Oh, Amelia, don't be such a hypocrite. The girl was pert and sly and I know you were as relieved as I was when she ran off. But she's dead, god rest her soul, so we should answer these men's questions and let them go. I'm sure they have better things to do, like finding out who killed our Matthew, than stand around an listen to a common servant putting on airs. So, my good man, you want to know what I did yesterday. I got up at five-thirty in the morning, read the Bible, and after breakfast I left the house to attend church. My sister-in-law was supposed to go with me, but being such a delicate person, she decided at the last minute not to go. I arrived at St. Catherine's shortly before the eleven o'clock service started, but I found that I was not in the proper frame of mind, so I took the Geary Street car to Laurel Hill and took some flowers to my brother's grave. I got back to the house around 2:30 and had Wong bring me tea in my room, where I stayed until dinner. And, before you ask, no, I didn't meet anyone that I knew while I was out, and I hadn't seen hide nor hair of Nellie since she left our employ, without notice, on Monday last."

Miss Nancy glared at no one in particular and strode over to the tea table and began to pour herself a cup of tea.

"Miss Voss, thank you for your cooperation," the Chief Detective responded. "Now Mrs. Voss, what did you do after your sister-in-law left for church? I'm sure we can all sympathize with how difficult this past week has been for you."

Mrs. Voss made a little dismissive motion with her right hand, moved slightly away from Cartier, and then began haltingly to speak, her voice so soft that Annie found herself leaning forward to try and catch her words.

"Thank you, Chief Jackson. I had intended, as my sister-in-law mentioned, to go to church. Cartier, my maid, had helped me get dressed and had already left for her day's outing when I realized I just wasn't ready to face anyone outside the family circle. So, instead, I sat in my room and tried to read a little. But I was feeling restless and really quite annoyed with myself for my failure of will, so I left my room and went to Matthew's...to my late husband's dressing room where I knew I would find Wong. I had asked him at breakfast to begin to sort through my husband's things. I had planned to pack up most of his clothes to give to charity, but thought that I might box up and keep some of his favorite...."

Mrs. Voss's voice faltered and she began to weep silently into a black embroidered handkerchief that Annie was surprised to see had not yet slipped to the floor, where most of Mrs. Voss's handkerchiefs ended up resting. The Chief Detective made a move towards her, but stopped when she held up a hand and began to speak again.

"See, how silly of me. This is exactly what happened when I joined Wong. Standing there in that small room, surrounded by all his suits and shirts, smelling his pipe, I just broke down. I told Wong it was too soon, and that perhaps we should put off making any decisions. I found that I felt very tired. You see I haven't been sleeping well. Anyway, I told Wong that I was going to retire to my bedroom until two, when he could bring me some tea. As for Nellie's state of mind, I have no idea, Mr. Jackson. I thought she was happy with us, and I am still mystified by her decision to leave so abruptly last week. Perhaps if I had known she was unhappy, I could have done something." Here Mrs. Voss's voice broke again.

"There, there, Mrs. Voss. No need to get upset. I am sure that you are a very kind and sympathetic mistress. But, could you tell us exactly when this conversation with your manservant took place?" the Chief Detective asked gently.

"Why I think around eleven o'clock. Yes, when I lay down I heard the chimes from the clock in my sitting room. I fell deeply asleep and was rather disoriented when I awoke. I remember being surprised when I got up to discover it was already three o'clock, so I rang the kitchen and Wong came up with the tea tray in a few minutes."

Abruptly, the attention of everyone in the room shifted to Wong, who was standing quietly next to the door to the hallway, waiting to be dismissed.

"Three o'clock, an hour late you say?" Chief Detective Jackson barked out. "Well, Mr. Wong, what do you have to say for yourself?"

"Sir, I did come up to Mrs. Voss's room at two and knocked lightly on her door. But when I got no reply, I returned to the kitchen to await her call."

"So you say, and what exactly did you do between eleven and three o'clock?"

"Well, sir, I took a few of the pieces of my late master's clothing down to the kitchen with me after Mrs. Voss retired. Some of the suit coats needed to be cleaned. I straightened up the kitchen, then went out to the vegetable garden out back, to do a little weeding, but came back in around noon because I didn't want to miss the bell if Mrs. Voss should change her mind and wish for lunch. I stayed in the kitchen doing some mending in preparation for washday. Except for when I went up to check on her at two, I didn't leave the kitchen until I took up her tea at three. Oh, and Miss Cartier returned from her afternoon out at four. I was once again in the kitchen working on dinner when she came to the kitchen door to be let in."

"So, you were actually alone between eleven and three, and we have only your word for it that you were even in the house?" Chief Jackson said, sounding skeptical.

"Yes, sir, unless someone in one in the neighboring houses happened to see me when I was in the garden."

"Oh, Chief Detective Jackson, I am sure that Wong is telling you the truth! You might just as well say that you have only my word that I didn't slip out of the house during those times, and I am sure you don't mean to suggest that, do you?" Mrs. Voss then let out a charming little laugh and walked over to the tea table, where she turned and said, "Please Chief Detective, may I offer you some tea? I have been very remiss as a hostess. And if you are finished asking Wong questions, I really must insist that he return to the kitchen, where I fear the dinner preparations have been put sadly awry."

Cartier at that moment chose to delicately clear her throat, and Annie wondered if the lady's maid was actually feeling put out at having temporarily lost her audience. Whatever her intention, this sound diverted everyone's attention from Wong, who, Annie noticed, wasted no time in slipping out the door.

"Excuse me, Mrs. Voss," Cartier said, while she held the back of one hand pressed against her forehead. Her voice revealed just the tiniest hint of a sob in it as she continued, "I really do believe that I must ask to be excused as well. One of my headaches, you know. I am feeling quite faint."

Again it was the sergeant who responded to Cartier, and Annie wondered if this in itself was a kind of insult, that somehow Cartier did not warrant the attentions of the Chief Detective.

"Miss Cartier, we will be glad to let you retire, just as soon as you have answered our questions. Mrs. Voss has said that you had left the house by eleven o'clock and Wong has verified that you came back at four. Did you perhaps attend religious services?"

"Well, yes I did. I attended the eleven o'clock service at Grace Cathedral; I find the Anglican High church liturgy so uplifting," Cartier answered, appearing to find some solace in the upper-class nature of her religious affiliation.

"And did you stay for the whole service, and perhaps sit with an acquaintance who can vouch for you," the sergeant responded encouragingly.

Cartier hesitated a fraction before responding. "Well, actually I sat alone at the back of the church because I knew I would have to leave before the service was over. I was meeting a friend for lunch at noon, and that's really all I have to tell you about my afternoon. It was such a beautiful day that I chose to walk home, which did take some time, and I believe I did arrive at the house sometime around four."

"Splendid. Then if you would be so kind as to give us that friend's name and address and the name of the restaurant, you can be on your way." The Sergeant stood beaming at Cartier, his notebook at the ready. Cartier, in contrast, frowned and began to dither.

"Well, that is simply impossible, I couldn't…who I met with is really none of your business, it's my private…well, actually who it was is quite beside the point. They were unable to keep the appointment. I waited…I don't know why they didn't show, there must have been a…in any event I ended up simply walking the grounds. I was at Woodward's Gardens; there was a band. I enjoyed the music and walked among the flowers. Then, as I said, I walked home. Now, Mrs. Voss, if you please, I must insist that I be given permission to retire to my room. Being hounded like this is beyond anything."

The Chief Detective intervened at this point, forestalling Mrs. Voss, who had begun to speak. In a bluff hearty tone he said, "Well,

well, Miss, don't fret. I am sure there is a perfectly reasonable explanation for why your *friend* failed to show. And I am sure we can find *someone* who can remember you strolling the grounds, a fine figure of a woman such as yourself, unescorted in a public garden. Now if you would just tell us a little about the girl, Nellie Flannigan. Was there anything bothering her that might explain the frame of mind she was in when she left here? You being the other female servant in the house, stands to reason you would be the one closest to her, a friend she might confide in. For instance, did she communicate with you at all once she left? Maybe write a little note to tell you how she was getting on at her new position, eh?"

Cartier was literally rendered speechless in response to the Chief Detective's words, pressing the handkerchief once again against her mouth and closing her eyes as if the headache had temporarily blinded her. Then, she drew herself to her full height and with exaggerated politeness deigned to answer him. "Sir, I am afraid that you are sorely ill-informed about the running of a superior establishment and the exceptionally important status of a lady's maid such as myself in that establishment. Not surprising from one of your class, living in a provincial city like San Francisco. But, let me assure you, that a woman in my position would never share confidences with a common domestic like Nellie. I don't suppose I exchanged more than two words with her outside of passing on orders from my mistress. I certainly would not be the person she would write to, if she were literate, which I sincerely doubt. Now, again, I must insist that I be permitted to retire." And not waiting for a response from Mrs. Voss, Cartier swept out of the room.

"Tsch! Good riddance!" Miss Nancy spoke with disgust. "Amelia, I don't know why you put up with her, surely you can find someone else who can do up your hair to your satisfaction." Then, noticing that Annie was still in the room, Miss Nancy turned her gruff attention towards her, saying, "Girl, what in the dickens are

you still doing here? We can pour our own tea, so get yourself down
to the kitchen."

Annie, feeling the attention of the two police officers turn in her
direction, began to fuss with the sugar and cream pot, not daring to
look up.

"See here, young lady. Before you go, let's hear what you know
about this business. You've been pretty quiet there in the corner.
First, what's your name?" the Chief Detective asked with a kind
heartiness.

"My name's Lizzie, sir, and I don't know nothing about anything,
sir." Annie squeaked out.

"Well, that's for me to determine, isn't it my girl. Was yesterday
your day off as well?"

"Yes, sir, I had the weekend off, didn't come back until this
morning."

"And where did you go on your time off? You didn't happen to
see Nellie Flannigan anytime recently, did you?"

Annie froze. *What should I say? He couldn't possibly know who I
really am, could he? No, this was a natural question of a servant,
really the same one he had asked Cartier.* Annie didn't want to lie to
the Detective, but suddenly her whole masquerade seemed threatened and the frightened note to her voice when she began to speak
was no longer an act.

"Sir, I don't know what you mean. Why would I see someone
called Nellie? What are you saying?"

"Chief Detective, do leave the child alone," Mrs. Voss's soft
tones intervened. "She never met Nellie, she just started working
here last week as Nellie's replacement. She came highly recom-
mended by the wife of Herbert Stein, who I am sure would vouch
for her if necessary. Now Lizzie, be a good girl, and go down and
help Wong in the kitchen. Tell him that dinner will be served at
seven."

Annie was never more in charity with Amelia Voss than at that moment, and she made her escape without waiting to see if the Chief Detective objected. She was not, however, so flustered that she didn't leave the parlor door cracked and linger outside in the hall long enough to hear the Chief Detective say, "Well, that's all we can do for now. Are you sure that your son Jeremy won't be home soon? I would like to see him before the inquest, which will be Wednesday morning. I must impress on you that it is of the utmost importance that he drop by the station. Just for a little chat. I must say he has been a difficult man to get hold of, and I won't take it kindly if we have to come back hunting for him."

## Chapter Twenty-seven:
## Monday Evening, August 13, 1879

An hour later, Annie came into the kitchen with more bad news for Wong. "I am so sorry. Mrs. Voss sends her most sincere apology, but she must ask that you delay dinner an additional half hour, until eight-thirty. Master Jeremy has come in and needs some time to get ready. I am to take water up to him, so that you do not have to leave the kitchen at this time." Annie smiled ruefully at Wong. She had just returned with the last of the tea things.

Wong took the news with fortitude, for which Annie was thankful. Her mother-in-law had once employed a cook who in the same circumstances would have purposely burned all the courses to register her disapproval. Wong simply nodded and went to work trying to salvage what he could of his original menu. The asparagus soup would be fine, since it was to be served at room temperature; and he hadn't put the salmon on to broil yet, not planning on doing so until Annie took up the soup course. But the roast would soon pass from succulence to desiccation, and Annie couldn't imagine how Wong intended on saving the fricasseed quails.

Having had the dubious pleasure of relieving an unsteady Jeremy of his hat and coat when he came in the house, however, Annie appreciated Mrs. Voss's desire to give her son time to regroup, no matter what the cost to the quality of the meal and the temper of the cook. Annie doubted whether a half-hour would be sufficient time to sober him up, but it was better than nothing. Wong had the presence of mind to insist that Annie take up cold water instead of hot for Jeremy.

"It will wake him up to his responsibilities as a dutiful son and nephew," Wong said, with a hint of a smile.

As Annie watched Jeremy towel off his water-soaked head, she had to admit that it certainly seemed to do the trick. She suspected that this was not the first time that Jeremy had resorted to this remedy, because the young man didn't protest at all when she gave him the pitcher filled with ice-cold water, which she had drained from the icebox. Instead, he had actually managed to produce a ghastly grin for her benefit when he raised his head from dousing it thoroughly.

Normally Wong would have acted as valet to Jeremy, and, as she handed him a towel, she felt uncomfortable standing so close to him in his bare-chested state. Jeremy was only moderately muscled, and a bit thin for his height. Annie couldn't help but compare him to the only other man she had ever seen in this state of undress, her late husband. John had been of medium height and weight with rather narrow shoulders, but he had held himself very tall and erect, thrusting out his chest as if waiting for a medal to be pinned upon it. Annie remembered being charmed at first with the way this had given him a rather bantam-rooster sort of stance, but in time she had begun to associate it with a particularly bullying sort of male arrogance. All things considered, Annie thought to herself, she preferred Jeremy's tall, thinner frame.

She wondered what Nate would look like stripped to the waist. She suspected that, although he was as tall as Jeremy, his wide shoulders were probably more muscular. He had certainly felt very strong when he helped her out of the carriage on Sunday, and she remembered how hard and solid his chest felt as he had pulled her into his arms when they danced.

All of a sudden, the complete impropriety of her thoughts struck her. Looking up, she saw that Jeremy had finished toweling his hair and was staring at her. Annie immediately blushed, which Jeremy seemed to find quite amusing. Furious with herself, she snatched up the basin and pitcher, thereby spilling some of the water, and fled the room. The sound of Jeremy's laughter wafted after her. Once out of Jeremy's sight she slowed down, in part because it was awkward to carry a basin filled with water and a pitcher at the same time, but also because she was wrestling with thoughts she found contradictory and confusing. It had occurred to her that no one would find it terribly immoral for a servant to be alone with a half-dressed man. Female servants routinely were expected to serve their masters in the privacy of the bedroom, lighting the fire, bringing up the water or perhaps a cup of coffee in the morning, even if the master was still in bed. There had probably been ample opportunity for Jeremy to become intimate with Nellie if he had wished, and, from her boyfriend's description, Nellie might have welcomed these attentions. Jeremy definitely could be the gentleman who was giving her gifts.

Such thoughts, intriguing as they might be, had to be put aside when Annie reached the kitchen. She had the misfortune of arriving just as Cartier did, complaining loudly over the fact that she hadn't yet received dinner. She had been waiting in her room, where she was accustomed to take her meal on a tray. Evidently Cartier hadn't heard about Jeremy's arrival and the further postponement of the meal, and she was incensed that Annie hadn't come to tell her.

Since Annie had always been fairly friendly with her own servants, not hesitating to work side by side with them at some domestic chore, or sharing a cup of tea with them at the kitchen table, she felt Cartier's assertion of special prerogatives as an upstairs maid absurd. So, it was with little sympathy that she listened to her complaints this evening. Fortunately, before Annie lost her temper completely, Wong stepped in front of her and disarmed the situation by thrusting a fully laden tray into Annie's hands. With his back to

Cartier, he rolled his eyes and wrinkled his nose in a comic piece of mime, then softly asked Annie if she could carry the tray upstairs to Cartier's room by herself.

Annie grudgingly acquiesced, and when she returned from taking the tray upstairs, she thanked Wong for intervening. "I don't know how you deal with that woman with such equanimity, Wong. She is so condescending."

"Well Miss, I find that by being patient with her face-to-face, my mind is easier when I am forced to give her the less desirable portions of food. Otherwise, I might feel very bad that it was she who got for dinner the breast of quail that burned a bit on the edge of the pan and will get for dessert the molded lemon jelly that was so thoughtfully given to us this morning by a neighbor."

Annie nearly laughed out loud at Wong's subtle form of revenge, but before she could comment she was distracted by the ringing bell that signaled that the Voss family was finally ready to be served dinner. For the next hour Annie had no time to think about Jeremy's relationship to Nellie, or Wong's attitude towards Cartier, as she shuttled trays and platters up and down stairs between kitchen and dining room. Feeling her arms and legs grow wearier and wearier, she greatly feared that she would trip and fall on one of the journeys or that she would let one of the plates crash to the floor as she made her way around the table.

To make matters worse, the dinner conversation remained firmly in the realm of innocuous discussions of the weather, so she didn't learn anything that could help her investigations. This could have had as much to do with Jeremy's attempt to appear sober in front of his mother and aunt as it did with any desire on the family's part to hide things from the servant. Still, Annie was dismayed by the lack of any comment or concern over the news of Nellie's death. Finally, Mrs. Voss signaled that dinner was ended and that Annie might begin to clear the table.

"Jeremy, would you please join me in my sitting room, the police have been here with some distressing news, and we need to talk. And Lizzie," Mrs. Voss spoke over her shoulder before leaving the dining room. "I know that with the wash and this late dinner it has been a very long day for you, and for that I apologize. Just get the table cleared and the room straightened before you retire."

"How very kind," Annie said under her breath, as Mrs. Voss left. She then stuck out her tongue at the closed door and turned and viewed scene before her with a depressed sigh. It would take a good twenty minutes to clear the room and probably as many trips up and down the stairs. She had barely gotten four hours sleep last night, and she was actually looking forward to the cold hard bed that waited for her in the attic.

Just then the door opened slowly and Wong stuck his head in cautiously and entered. He was carrying a large tray, which he waved in front of her and said, "Miss, would you mind if we traded duties for tonight? I can clear the table. You can dry and put away those dishes that are already washed. I get very tired of the kitchen."

Annie's heart warmed once again to this kind man, wishing she could be completely truthful with him. "Bless you, Wong, I wasn't sure if I could make the trip between here and the kitchen one more time without accident. I would be glad to wash and dry all the dishes if you would just be the one to bring them to me."

And so, as the large kitchen clock chimed out ten o'clock, Annie was putting the last dessert dish on the shelf, while Wong entered with the dining room tablecloth draped over his arm. Her smile of greeting died when she saw the troubled expression on his face.

"What's wrong, Wong? Have I forgotten to do something?" she asked looking around the kitchen with confusion.

"No Miss, it is nothing that you or I have done. It is this house. I am afraid that the omens are not good for a return to harmony."

He then silently held out the tablecloth, which Annie could see held a dark red splotch in one place, hideously like blood. Although she knew that the stain must be from the burgundy that had been served at dinner, the hair on the back of her neck still rose.

She sternly told herself not to be so fanciful, and she chided Wong. "Why Wong, that is a rather dire conclusion to draw from a simple household accident. Don't tell me no one has ever spilled wine at dinner in this house before?"

Wong stared without blinking at her for a second, and then he replied, his voice barely above a whisper. "Yes, Miss. Someone has. The night the master died. The mistress spilled her wine, as she did tonight. That was the first time that she ever did in all my years of service, Miss. The servant Nellie, it was her night out. She asked me to get rid of the stain. I did. I had to scrub long and hard, but I did. That night the master died. Now Nellie herself is dead. And here the stain is back. The omen is not good, Miss. I am afraid death will come again."

As day followed night, the day after washday found Annie iron-ing. Some of the routine morning chores, like raking the coals out of the kitchen range and delivering breakfast trays, had become easier with practice, on this her fourth day as a servant. But ironing was a different matter, and she was finding the second time around that ironing was even more difficult than it had been last Friday. Lifting the heavy irons badly exacerbated the pain in her shoulder and arms. Try as she might, she seemed unable to determine which of the four irons heating up on the top of the stove was the right temperature. The only reason she hadn't yet ruined any of the sheets she was ironing was that she carefully tested each iron on a scrap of cloth before using it, but this was enormously time consuming. To make matters worse, the day was unusually hot for San Francisco in August, and the whole kitchen felt like the inside of an oven. The only advantage that the ironing of sheets and handkerchiefs had over some of her other chores was that it gave her a little time to think about what she had learned the day before.

While she hadn't had success in finding the missing assets, she did feel she had found some important information about the mem-bers of Matthew's household. Everything she had seen or heard reaf-firmed Annie's impression that Miss Nancy didn't like Matthew's business partner, Malcolm Samuels, and that at the very least she was extremely jealous of her sister-in-law, Amelia. If either of them had turned up dead, Annie would put the angry old woman at the top of her list of suspects. But kill Matthew? Because he decided to close up the house and take his wife to Europe? It seemed unlikely, unless the older woman was deranged. And the ledgers Miss Nancy had taken suggested otherwise; it was more like she was looking for proof that either Samuels or her sister-in-law were responsible for Matthew's death. On the other hand, the ledgers may have been simply the household accounts, and Miss Nancy may have just remembered where they were and acted on impulse. Annie needed to get a better look at them. Maybe she would get a chance the next morning when Miss Nancy left to do the marketing.

Then here was Jeremy, who was acting like a young man with a guilty conscience, but she still felt his motivation seemed weak. Despite Nate's suggestion that Jeremy might have killed his father in a fit of anger over his thwarted artistic dreams, this seemed rather far-fetched, since he was clearly worse off now than when his father was alive. While Annie could imagine either Jeremy's mother or his aunt killing Nellie on his behalf, if they thought she was threatening Jeremy in some fashion, she was having difficulty imaging either one of them killing Matthew to protect his son.

Then, maybe she was looking for too complex a motivation. According to Nate, Matthew had brought home nearly $1,000 in cash on Friday night, an enormous temptation to someone like Nellie or Cartier, and they would have had twenty-four hours to arrange with someone from outside to help stage a suicide to cover a plain and simple robbery. This seemed a rather more sophisticated murder than she would associate with Nellie or her boyfriend Jack. She again speculated that the mysterious gentleman in Nellie's life who prompted Jack's jealousy was some sort of skilled confidence man or professional burglar. The same scenario could fit Cartier as well. Annie found Cartier's emotional response when the police questioned her about Nellie's death, combined with her secret correspondent, very suspicious.

Thinking of mysterious gentlemen reminded Annie of the gentleman who had been hanging around the alley Friday night. He said he was looking for Jeremy, but that could have been a form of misdirection. Perhaps he was the *friend* Cartier was supposed meet but who stood her up on Sunday. If he was her accomplice in Matthew's murder, she might have even made up the story about him not showing. The Chief Detective certainly hadn't appeared convinced by her description of how she spent her Sunday afternoon off. For that matter, no one had seemed to have a very convincing alibi for Sunday afternoon, and Annie didn't envy the police in their job of trying to confirm the truth of everyone's stories.

*Oh well, that is their job. My job is to make sure I have searched every nook and cranny of this house for the missing assets,* Annie thought, as she folded another less than adequately ironed sheet and put it in the basket at her feet.

So far, she had been able to pretty much rule out the basement areas and the first floor as hiding places. Even with the threat of Miss Nancy or Cartier dropping in to oversee her work, the excuse of giving everything a thorough cleaning had permitted her ample opportunities to systematically look in cupboards, dressers, side boards, and book shelves, behind mirrors, pictures, and under tables, couches and chairs. Miss Nancy had actually been so impressed with Annie's diligence in dusting that she had been moved to give her a compliment. There had been sufficient occasions as well when Wong wasn't in the kitchen for her to look through all the cupboards, bins, and boxes in the kitchen and scullery. He had walked in a few times to discover her with her head stuck in the depths of a back cupboard, but he hadn't challenged her airy excuse that she was just trying to figure out where all the pots and pans went.

She had been able to check out all the guest bedrooms while stripping their sheets and dusting; she also felt pretty sure she had done a thorough search of Miss Nancy's room yesterday. Mrs. Voss's rooms had been more difficult to search, since she went downstairs so seldom. Annie had given her sitting room only a piecemeal investigation, snatching the chance to look in the ornate cabinets and small writing desk when she came in to clean out the fireplace and do a light dusting each morning. Tonight, however, Annie would be attending Mrs. Voss after dinner because it was Cartier's night out, so she might find some chances to complete her search, particularly in the bedroom. That left Cartier and Jeremy's rooms on the third floor. Somehow, in the next two days, she needed to get to those rooms because when she left the house tomorrow evening for her night out, she would really like to shed her servant masquerade for good.

Annie got her chance to examine Jeremy's rooms in the early afternoon, when Wong offered to spell her at the ironing. She had just dried the last of the lunch dishes and hadn't been able to suppress a deep sigh as she turned and looked at the mound of shirts, table linens, and petticoats she still had left to iron.

Wong had smiled gently at her and said, "Miss Lizzie, I think that it might be a more efficient use of our time and talents if I took charge of ironing the more delicate items, while you made up the beds on the third floor and cleaned master Jeremy's room, now that he has finally left the house. You may have to take over for me when we get closer to dinner time, but by then there should only be table linens."

Annie refrained from going over and hugging him but simply said, "Thank you Wong, I think that is a wonderful suggestion, and I will be glad to help in any way I can with dinner."

She then went to the corner where the cleaning implements were kept. She put four dust rags, the bar of soap, a scrub brush, and the tin of furniture wax into an empty pail, then picked up a bucket of

hot water and a broom, which was leaning against the wall, nodding
to Wong as she started up the back stairs. When she reached the
third floor, she stood for a minute, undecided about which of the
three rooms dedicated to Jeremy's use she should start cleaning first.

She wished she were sure Cartier was downstairs with her mistress, so she could try to open her door. She had been able to try
twice in the past two days, when she was sure Cartier was occupied,
but each time she found the door locked, which was suspicious in
itself. With Cartier leaving for her night, Annie hoped for a lot more
time to find a way to search the room. Maybe she could get Miss
Nancy to agree that she needed to get in the room to tidy it before
Cartier came home in the morning. Given the enmity between the
two women, she just might be successful. Thinking about this plan,
Annie picked up her pails and entered Jeremy's rooms.

He had the whole south side of the third floor for himself, with
just Cartier's room and two guest rooms across the hall. Annie had
been in his dressing room at the front of the house last evening, but
not his bedroom or the large back room that acted as his studio. The
dressing room was easily searched; Wong evidently kept this room
in order. Apart from wiping some water drops from the washstand
and giving it a good polish, and sweeping the bare wooden floor,
there wasn't much to do. She did go through his wardrobe, even taking the time to run her hands through his pants and jacket pockets,
and tipping over his hats to see if she could find anything. But either
Jeremy had not developed the habit that both John and her father
had possessed of depositing any stray bit of flotsam and jetsam into
their coat pockets, or Wong was very thorough in cleaning out those
pockets when he put Jeremy's clothes away. She also noted that Jeremy's shoes came in all styles; and, although most had rounded toes,
there was at least one pair of evening pumps that had pointed ones.
Annie had a difficult time imaging him wearing these shoes on a
rendezvous with Nellie on the beach.

The next room proved to be equally unrewarding. She dusted, but apart from the usual toiletries on the dresser, there was nothing of interest in Jeremy's bedroom. After stripping off the sheets, she checked under the mattress, finding nothing. Again, Annie had the strong impression that Wong had been there before her. The room was neat, there was very little dust, the clothes in the dresser draw-ers were carefully arranged, and there was absolutely no clutter in the room.

In fact, Annie felt little of Jeremy's presence in the room at all; it reminded her strikingly of the guestrooms she had cleaned earlier in the week. Open, airy, fashionably furnished, but sterile, and not a scrap of paper that might represent a piece of evidence.

Annie was quite curious about Jeremy's artistry. She thought it strange that none of the artwork that hung elsewhere in the house was by him, not even in his mother's sitting room. Even if he were a wretched painter, you would think that a parent would be willing to hang a small example of his work, at least in the private rooms in the house. Presumably Jeremy's art had been such a sore subject with Matthew that Amelia didn't dare exhibit it anywhere, or maybe he just talked about painting, but never actually painted. In any event, Annie opened the door that connected the bedroom to the studio next to it with a great anticipation.

Her first thought was that Wong had clearly not had free rein in this room. Her second thought was that, although incredibly untidy, the room bore impressive signs that Jeremy was really a working artist, not just the dilettante that Annie expected. Unlike the rest of the house, where dark paneling or fancy wallpaper predominated, these walls were painted plain white and hung with a variety of striking pieces of art. A good number of canvasses, their backs to the walls, were leaning all over the place, and paint tubes, turpen-tine-drenched rags, and brushes obscured the surfaces of every table in the room. A *chaise longue* sat against one wall, and an easel containing a blank canvas stood squarely in a shaft of sun. Yet, despite the sunshine, the room seemed rather gloomy and cold, giving off a feeling of abandonment. Apparently no fire had been lit in the fireplace for several days.

Aware of time passing too swiftly, Annie first looked hurriedly at the paintings and etchings hanging on the walls. She determined that they all had been done by people other than Jeremy, many of them with French names. While most of the paintings were rather small, they were all quite lovely, if unusual. Among the oils, pale pastels predominated, and most intriguing of all, she found that when she came up close to some of the paintings the scenery dissolved into mist or broke up into motes of light. Annie recalled that one of John's uncles had brought a painting like this back from a trip to Paris in '74, by someone named Monet. Sure enough, several of the dissolving paintings bore this signature. All the work hanging on Jeremy's walls was so different from the dark formal paintings to which she was accustomed that she had difficulty tearing herself away from them. But she knew she had to get back to her task, before Cartier or Miss Nancy came in to find out what was taking her so long.

Despite her initial impression that the room would be difficult to search because it was such a jumble of miscellaneous objects, Annie found there were actually few hiding places. A container with pipe-smoking equipment on the mantel, a handy wooden carrying-box for Jeremy's painting gear, and a large trunk that seemed to hold an assortment of props were all easily ransacked and found innocent.

Finally Annie discovered that one of the pieces of furniture that she thought was a table was, in reality, a small desk, almost entirely hidden by stacked blank canvasses. This was crammed full of papers, along with two palette knives, charcoal, pencils, chalk, a ruler, a drawing compass, an empty tumbler with a dusty scum on the bottom, sealing wax, and a small photograph of Mrs. Voss, apparently posed along the seaside. Her fingers trembling in haste, Annie shuffled through the papers. Most seemed to be bills for art supplies, or bills from a tailor and a boot maker, including a diplomatically worded request from the former for Jeremy to please pay off some of the debits on his accounts. There were also a few letters, with Paris postmarks, that seemed innocent enough, although Annie's grammar school French was very rusty. But nowhere was there evidence of the thick rectangular sheets of paper that stock certificates were normally printed on, nor of the bank notes issued by the Bank of California, nor any packets of a mysterious powder marked cyanide.

Annie sighed with relief. She knew that the absence of evidence in the rooms she searched might simply mean that anything incriminating had long since been gotten rid of; it had been, after all, over a week since Matthew Voss had been murdered. Annie had to note ruefully how contradictory it was for her to be relieved that she found nothing, since her reputed goal was to find something that would not only prove who killed Matthew but would restore some of the missing assets. Nevertheless, Annie was pleased that she hadn't found anything suspicious among Jeremy's things. In her heart she knew she wanted the murderer to be a stranger, not one of Matthew's loved ones.

This left the paintings themselves as possible hiding places, since she supposed that the back of frames might be a good place to stuff a sheet of paper or bank notes. Trying to be systematic, she first walked around the walls, taking each piece of artwork off of its hook and looking at its back. Thankfully, all of the work was cheaply framed and easy to examine. She dusted as she went, figuring she might as well make herself useful while she was hunting.

She turned next to the unframed canvasses that were leaning here and there. Annie had left them for last, hoping to discover some sample of Jeremy's own work among them. She started to walk over to a dark corner where she saw a few small canvasses were leaning against a cluttered table that was rammed up against the back wall and then she stopped, gasping. Reality as she knew it had just vanished.

There was no table, its top littered with objects, there were no blank canvasses leaning up against its legs. Instead, between the two windows, there stood a large oil painting that so accurately reproduced a table and leaning canvases that she had mistaken them for the real thing. She leaned forward, trembling fingers out-stretched, and touched the canvass. Up this close she felt foolish at her mistake. Of course it was a painting; it was flat, the oil surface shiny, the paint strokes obvious. But when Annie stepped back, the illusion reasserted itself. The painter had so cleverly captured each nuance and shadow of reality and so perfectly recreated the lines of perspective that from a distance she once again found herself staring at what looked like three-dimensional objects.

Annie whirled around to look at one of the tables on the other side of the room that she had searched earlier, and confirmed that it was the original subject of the painting. There it was, the same three canvasses leaning up against the same scarred legs and the same old paint smattered smock hung up on a peg, providing a rich brown backdrop for the dirty rags, tubes of paint, stacked dusty books, scattered candle stubs, rusty knives, a button hook, and the tin of shoe polish that crammed the small table's surface. The only difference was that the real table did not have Jeremy's initials carved into one of its legs; the table in the painting did.

Unwanted, a thought niggled its way into her mind. Here before her stood the work of a great artist, the work of a man of incredible drive and discipline, a man whose father had called him a fool. Here before her stood an excellent motive for murder.

## Chapter Twenty-nine:
## Tuesday evening, August 14, 1879

The rest of the day Annie continued to pursue her thoughts about Jeremy and whether he might feel that his father's plans were such a threat to his art that he was justified in killing him. While she couldn't reconcile the premeditated nature of Matthew's murder with her impressions of Jeremy Voss, the precision of his painting revealed a depth in him that she would never have imagined if she hadn't seen the work itself. It was a puzzle. However, right before dinner something happened that drew her attention away from this line of thought.

Shortly before seven, Cartier came down to the kitchen to ask Wong to open the door so she could leave for her night out. Annie, who had been chopping vegetables, waited until Cartier was out the door, and then she ran over to Wong. She asked him to keep the door unlocked while she stepped out to look for a missing bag of clothespins she thought she had dropped while taking in the washing. Once outside, she moved to the back of the yard. Having noticed earlier that this put her out of sight of the kitchen window, she then nipped through the back gate and into the alley. She thought that Cartier would certainly have made it to the street by that time, and she simply planned on running down the alley to see if she was waiting for a horse car or was walking up or down Geary. Annie was very surprised when she saw that Cartier was just standing at the end of the alley. She immediately stepped back into the bushes next to the gate, peeping carefully out to make sure Cartier hadn't seen her. In less than a minute a carriage pulled up, filling the end of the alleyway. The carriage door opened, a man's arm reached out to assist Cartier inside, the door closed and the carriage was on its way before Annie had a chance to blink.

Knowing it would be impossible to follow the carriage, she returned to the kitchen, mulling the implications of what she had just seen. Cartier had been meeting a man, a man of some means if the carriage was any indication. This must be the *friend* she had been planning on meeting on Sunday. Had her message to the delivery boy yesterday arranged for this meeting, or was this something that happened every Tuesday on her night out? Who was he, and could he possibly be involved in Matthew and Nellie's murders? She so wished she could talk about this with Nate. Annie had half been expecting either Nate or his uncle to arrive all day, given the intrusion of the police yesterday afternoon. As far as she could determine, Mrs. Voss hadn't sent off a message to her lawyers, so perhaps they were unaware of what had happened.

The need to begin serving dinner precluded any more thought on the subject, and this was a dreary repetition of the night before. Wong was even more silent than usual during dinner, handing each serving to her wordlessly. The two ladies she served upstairs in the dining room were equally silent. Mrs. Voss ate very little of what Wong had prepared, and, while Miss Nancy ate everything served, it was with no sign of enjoyment. Maybe each was wondering if the other had killed Matthew or Nellie, or perhaps both were worrying that Jeremy was the guilty party.

Jeremy certainly did his best to act the part of the guilty son when he came home right after dinner. Annie, removing the dessert dishes from the dining room, heard sounds from the front of the house. Mrs. Voss had skipped dessert and already gone upstairs to her sitting room, and Miss Nancy was just crossing into the hall. At the sound of the key in the door, Annie put down the dishes in her hand and slipped over to look out into the hall, doing so in time to catch the sight of the front door banging open and Jeremy staggering in, almost knocking his aunt off her feet.

Jeremy stepped back from Miss Nancy with a gruffly muttered apology, and then, after fumbling to lock the door behind him, he turned to make his unsteady way upstairs. Miss Nancy took one stride forward, grabbed him by the shoulder, and turned him back to face her. Annie noted how very tall the older woman was, and that her grip looked like it had considerable strength to it. Jeremy stood, swaying slightly, looking sullenly down at his feet, while Miss Nancy began to berate him in her harsh twang.

"Drunk again, young man. Have you no honor? To shame this house, this family, and your father, who is barely cold in his grave? I have held my tongue, Jeremy, forgiven you and forgiven you, as God has commanded. Blamed everyone else, including your father for being so hardheaded about your painting and your mother for her sinful ways, her heartless neglect. But I can keep still no longer."

Jeremy looked up at this point and sneeringly said, "When have you ever kept still? Oh, yes, Aunt Silence, that's you. You never interfere. All forbearance, the silent martyr."

Miss Nancy jerked her head as if Jeremy had slapped her. She then pulled him closer to her, and she hissed out, "God said, 'Wine is a mocker, strong drink a brawler; and who ever is led astray by it is not wise.' *Proverbs* 20. And the Lord said to the sons of Moses, 'Drink no wine or strong drink, lest you die.' *Leviticus* 10. Don't you see? You must repent. Confess your sins. Only then will God help you."

Jeremy pulled sharply away from her grasp and stumbled backwards, his right hand flung upwards as if to ward off further verbal blows. Annie was appalled at the look of agony that contorted his face. Miss Nancy must have been moved as well, because her stance softened, and she muttered, "My poor child," as she moved towards him with her arms outstretched to embrace him.

But Jeremy shouted, "No, don't touch me!"

Then he turned and began to stumble up the stairs. Annie had to move closer to the dining room door at this point to keep him in view, so she was only a few feet behind Miss Nancy when his next words came. Halfway up, he had leaned over the railing and in tones of loathing lashed out.

"Confess? Oh yes I'll confess. *Mea Culpa. Mea Culpa.* I'm to blame. I'm a drunken loafer. A good-for-nothing. No talent. No ambition. No ability. Except to make everyone miserable and kill my father. I was very good at that. He kept saying it. 'You'll be the death of me. You'll be the death of me.' You heard him."

Jeremy sobbed once at this point but then went on in a rush. "But I am not the only one to blame. I can quote the Bible too. You made damn sure of that."

He continued in a singsong voice, "And Christ said, 'let him who is without sin cast the first stone.'" Laughing harshly, Jeremy pointed a finger at his aunt. "I had help in making his life miserable, didn't I? Why do you think he was in such a rush to turn the business over to me? So he could get away from you. Take my mother away from your never-ending complaints, your black moods, your petty jealousies. God, we were a wonderful family to him. A failure for a son and a harpy for a sister. No wonder he couldn't stick it any more. The only joy in his life was Mother, and you tried to poison that too, didn't you? Well, don't try it with me. I'm not your child and I never will be." With that, Jeremy turned and lurched up the stairs.

## Chapter Thirty:
## Wednesday morning, August 15, 1879

Annie shifted back on her haunches and viewed the gleaming flagstones of the kitchen floor with pride. Miss Nancy had announced this morning at breakfast that she wanted all the kitchen and scullery counters, cabinets, and floors washed, and all the wood work on the first floor cleaned and waxed. So, while Annie had been downstairs in the kitchen, scrubbing away, up to her elbows in sudsy water, Wong had been upstairs polishing away, on his hands and knees.

Despite the physical demands of the work, Annie was in an improved state of mind from the day before, helped considerably by the fact that she had had a decent night's sleep. Last night, after helping Mrs. Voss get ready for bed and letting Wong out of the house, Annie was able to retire to her room by 9:30, and she had fallen asleep quickly. Which was surprising, considering all the interesting information she had gathered that day. Not only could she have been kept awake going over Jeremy and his aunt's fight, but two subsequent incidents should have been enough to disturb her sleep.

First of all there was the mysterious letter to Jeremy. Annie had noticed that in his argument with his aunt that he had overlooked two letters that were waiting for him on the hall table. Oddly they had both been slipped through the mail slot well after the afternoon mail delivery, and, although she had no desire to interact with him in his inebriated and overwrought state, Mrs. Voss had instructed her to make sure he got these letters when he came home. So, as soon as Miss Nancy made her way down to the kitchen, presumably to give Wong his orders for the next day, Annie had crept out of her hiding place in the dining room and snatched up the letters, hoping she could catch Jeremy before he made it all the way to his third floor room. As she mounted the back stairs, she looked at the letters, seeing that one of them was from Malcolm Samuels, which wasn't that odd. The other letter, however, had no return address. The neat delicate handwriting practically shouted female correspondent, and Annie wasn't surprised at all when she lifted the envelope to her nose to smell a light scent. When she handed the letters to Jeremy, who had been unsuccessfully trying to turn his door handle, she noted that it was the scented letter that he fixated on. He first stared at the envelope, as if it was a dangerous serpent, and then he snatched it to his lips, and the pain she saw reflected on his tear stained face still haunted Annie the next day.

The second unexpected occurrence that should have kept her awake was the return of Cartier, who for some reason cancelled the rest of her night out. When Annie returned to the kitchen after helping Mrs. Voss get ready for bed, Wong informed her that she had just missed Cartier, who moments earlier had arrived at the kitchen door, asking admittance. Curious, Annie made a detour to the third floor on her way up to bed and knocked on Cartier's door. She planned on asking the lady's maid if she needed anything, but it was really an excuse to see if Cartier would explain why she came home early. Cartier never answered her knock, and, as Annie stood listening outside the door, she thought she heard a muffled sob. Finally, Annie trudged up to her own narrow bed in the attic, where her body's fatigue triumphed over the evening's stimulating surprises, and she instantly fell fast asleep.

She had slept through the night dreamlessly, and when she rose at five she had felt much refreshed. In addition, the day's work was less frustrating than the ironing had been, and this improved her mood considerably. Scrubbing was hard physical labor, but it was easy to do it well. Overall, she just felt more optimistic. She was now confident that Cartier would turn out to hold the key to the puzzle of the two murders. As for the other people in household, Matthew's loved ones, today it was easier to believe that Miss Nancy's insinuations that Mrs. Voss and Malcolm Samuels were responsible for Matthew's death were the imaginings of a bitter and jealous woman, and that Jeremy was simply overcome by guilt about disappointing his father, not consumed by guilt over killing him.

And tonight she would be home! Perhaps for good. She had felt so lonely these last three days, hearing nothing from her friends. Not even a glimpse of Patrick on his beat. She had hoped that he might be able to stop by the kitchen on his rounds, maybe be able to tell her how everyone at home was doing. She would be so relieved to get back into her work as Sybil, and she worried a bit about a few of her clients who might unravel if she missed more than one appointment with them. Those she advised on financial matters didn't worry her, although she might lose their business if she missed too many sessions. It was women like Margery Dunhill, struggling to placate an exacting mother-in-law and worried about her husband's fidelity, that she regretted most having canceled. But with luck she would be able to meet with her Friday clients and only have missed a week.

She also wondered what Nate was doing, if he had tried to see her. Probably not. After the disastrous carriage ride back from the beach, he most certainly would feel well rid of her. Anyway, she would have to decide tonight how to best convey what she had learned about Cartier to the police, whether to try to go through Nate or perhaps his uncle. But this would require her to explain how she had obtained her knowledge of the household. Maybe it would be safer to tell Patrick and see if he could relay the information without revealing its source. She also needed to decide if she should find another maid to replace her here at the Vosses. Sunday night she had asked Beatrice and Kathleen to be on the look out for a replacement. Annie knew she couldn't afford to delay Sibyl's return to work much longer. But would it be right to send some poor girl into the house that might very well contain a murderer? *Well*, Annie thought to herself, *all these questions will be much easier to answer tonight when I'm home, bathed, and completely rested. Meanwhile, just look at how clean the floor is!!*

Everyone else in the household, even Cartier who was red-eyed and unusually subdued this morning, seemed to be finding solace in the details of everyday life as well. Perhaps that is why Miss Nancy had herself started a thorough rearrangement of the linen cupboards that had produced a pile of mending for Cartier to do, and Annie had been shocked when the lady's maid hadn't objected. *Unprecedented!* Mrs. Voss spent most of the morning in the front parlor, apparently answering the stack of condolences that piled up in the past week. Stranger still, Jeremy had risen exceptionally early, announcing that he was going to his father's office at the furniture factory. *Maybe his aunt's words about his drinking had finally gotten through to him. Or maybe there was something in the anonymous letter that had improved his disposition!* Annie had overheard Mrs. Voss tell Miss Nancy at breakfast how pleased she had been when Jeremy had agreed to meet Samuels at the factory in the morning to go over some of the decisions that had to be made about new orders and the factory production schedule.

In fact everyone had risen early. Wong had arrived a little before five-thirty and had barely gotten the bread in to rise and Cartier's breakfast tray to her, when Jeremy had rung for him to bring him water for shaving and a tray of coffee and biscuits. Jeremy must have slipped out soon after that to go across town to the factory, because at 7:30, when Wong had gone up to Jeremy's room to tell him that Malcolm Samuels had stopped by to accompany him to the office, he had already left. Wong told Annie later that Samuels had just laughed and made some remark about how forgetful Jeremy could be. He didn't seem terribly put out; in fact he had asked Wong to bring him some coffee, since he had skipped breakfast, figuring he'd have it with Jeremy.

In any event, Samuels had already had his coffee and left the house by the time both Miss Nancy and Mrs. Voss rang for service at eight o'clock. This wasn't early for Matthew's sister, but it was much earlier than Mrs. Voss had gotten up during the time Annie had been working there. Mrs. Voss had begun her correspondence right after breakfast and was still at it when Annie came to her sitting room to announce that lunch was ready.

Lunch was not one of Wong's better efforts. First of all, neither Annie nor Wong had time to prepare much for the meal. Wong had barely gotten the carpets laid back down in the dining room when it was time to fix lunch, and Annie had been caught in the middle of scrubbing the scullery floor when it was time to serve. She very hastily changed to a clean apron, but she couldn't hide the damp stains at the edge of her skirt and cuffs, and she was sure she smelled strongly of carbolic acid. The food itself was uninspired; the cold cuts were left over from the dinner the night before, the rolls were a bit burnt around the edges, and there was no fresh dessert, so he had brought out one of the neighbor's condolence gifts, a rather sad-looking pudding. Neither Miss Nancy nor Mrs. Voss seemed to care. They were too busy arguing with each other to notice what they were eating.

*Well, arguing wasn't perhaps the correct term,* Annie thought to herself as she took the dessert dishes down to the kitchen. Miss Nancy had been reproaching her sister-in-law, and Amelia Voss, for once, didn't seem willing to listen patiently. Annie had been able to hear only bits and pieces of the conversation, but what she had heard had been intriguing. As she had entered the room with the first course, she heard Miss Nancy say that she thought that at twenty-three Jeremy was altogether too young to marry.

She'd gone on, ignoring Annie's presence, "I don't believe in a man marrying so young. You and Matthew were pushing him into it." Miss Nancy was dressed in her habitual black, and Annie thought she looked even more cadaver-like, if possible. The older woman shook her finger in the direction of Mrs. Voss, who was sitting quietly across the table from her. Clearly not expecting any answer from Mrs. Voss, the old woman went on in the same accusing voice. "Rushing him to grow up. He's just a boy. Why, Matthew himself was near twice his age before he tied the knot."

Annie almost dropped the plate she was placing on to the center of the table when Mrs. Voss suddenly replied, a distinct note of sarcasm in her soft drawl.

"Well, dear sister, we both know how you feel about Matthew's judgment at that mature age. I've heard for over twenty years about how a man plays the fool when he marries in middle age. I would have thought you would be glad that Jeremy was going to avoid that mistake."

Miss Nancy was so taken aback she had sputtered. Amelia Voss had quite kindly asked her sister-in-law if she'd caught something in her throat, and if she could be of any help dislodging it. It was said with such sweet sincerity that Annie couldn't tell if Matthew's wife was making fun of the older woman or not. Apparently Miss Nancy was unsure as well, because she just sat silently staring at Mrs. Voss, as if she were a garden snake metamorphosed into a viper.

She evidently didn't remain speechless for long, because she was again haranguing Mrs. Voss about Jeremy when Annie came to clear off the main course and bring in the dessert. This time the subject seemed to have shifted from when Jeremy married to whom he should marry.

Miss Nancy was again shaking her finger as she catalogued Judith Langdon's faults. "She's nothing but a scatterbrained girl, and vain. Did you see the jet beads on her earrings at the funeral? I would have been ashamed to be seen flouncing myself around like that when I was her age. Of course, what would you expect from the daughter of that woman? Mrs. Langdon is a professional widow. I know the type. Trade on their misfortune so they don't ever have to do an honest day's work. I say she should be glad she had the comfort of a good man, and she should stop sniveling because she had the bad luck to lose him. Her husband probably died of neglect. Can't imagine she was a very good housekeeper. Too used to the good old days back on the plantation when she was waited on hand and foot by her slaves."

Here Miss Nancy jabbed her spoon into her pudding with a flourish, and Annie envisioned her as a young Yankee soldier, bayoneting a Confederate with equal relish. The older woman then looked up at Mrs. Voss with a sniff and went on. "Young Judith won't be any better, brought up in boarding houses, dens of iniquity every one. No, Judith Langdon is no fit wife for my nephew, and I aim to tell him so. He won't have any trouble getting out of the betrothal. I am quite certain Mrs. Langdon would love to be shut of us--hasn't had the decency to call since Matthew's death. We're clearly not prominent enough a family for her blue blood."

Annie had her back turned to the table as she stacked plates onto the tray that was resting on the sideboard, so she didn't get to see the expression on Mrs. Voss's face when she replied. But the sense of iron beneath the polite phrases was chilling.

"Dear Sister, I am afraid I must disagree with you. I have found Judith to be a sweet, honest, and refreshingly practical young woman. And as a daughter of the South myself, you can't expect me to see this as a fault in her mother. Judith sent me a note yesterday afternoon, and she made it perfectly clear that she dearly loves Jeremy, as he loves her. I do hope that you will reconsider your decision to try and turn Jeremy against her. I would hate to see you do anything to estrange yourself further from him. I do know how important he is to you, and I promise you that I will fight you on this, and I will win."

Then, without missing a beat, Mrs. Voss's voice changed and she continued sweetly, "Now, Lizzie, would you please finish clearing the table and then bring me some tea in the front parlor. I find that I cannot bring myself to try this pudding. Mrs. Walters is a good soul, but I fear she has an inept cook."

Annie had then fled the room so she didn't hear if Miss Nancy had managed a response to the thinly veiled challenge her sister-in-law had thrown down. Later, remembering the unexpected coldness in Amelia Voss's voice, Annie believed, for the first time, that this woman was capable of murder if she thought her son was threatened.

## Chapter Thirty-one:
## Wednesday afternoon, August 15, 1879

Annie knocked on the parlor door, resting one edge of the heavy tray against her hip. It was nearly two o'clock in the afternoon, and Mrs. Voss was entertaining a visitor. Although this news had piqued Annie's interest, most of her attention was focused on not dropping the heavy tray as she opened the door and entered. She had already discovered how daunting a task it was to carry a fully laden tea tray without having the china set up a cacophony of clinks as they shimmied to and fro. Consequently, she carefully kept her eyes on the tray as she crossed over to the tea table, where she began to gently lower the tray to its resting place. All her care was cancelled out by the clamor the cups and saucers emitted when, upon recognizing the visitor's voice, she released the ponderous sliver tray to drop unchecked the last two inches onto the table.

The unexpected noise of clashing crockery caused the visitor to slew around in his seat and stare at her. Time literally slowed, giving Annie ample opportunity to watch the gentleman's first reaction of astonished recognition turn into anger, an expression that was becoming distressingly familiar in connection with this man. How incredibly stupid she had been to think that Nate wouldn't recognize her when she was playing the part of a servant.

Annie never thought so quickly before in her life. While the time it took Nate to recognize and react to her presence in the room seemed interminable, her own mind seemed to be clicking along at a terrific rate. He must not tell Mrs. Voss who she was. She must find a way to speak to him. Convince him not to betray her. How to do it? She must get Mrs. Voss out of the room. No, it might be easier to get Nate out of the room. If only he would cooperate.

Before the sounds emanating from Nate had time to form into speech, Annie looked past him to Mrs. Voss and said, "I'm sorry ma'am, the tray slipped. I'm afraid I'm terrible clumsy. Please forgive me."

Pausing only for a second to acknowledge Mrs. Voss's soft protest that it didn't matter, Annie went on, improvising as she went. "Please ma'am, I'm afraid that there's something that requires the gentleman's attention. A boy, he came to the back door, ma'am. Said that he was sent to find a Mr. Dawson. Wong said the gentleman was with you. Said I should fetch him when I brought the tea. I put the boy in the small back parlor. I hope I haven't done wrong, ma'am, seeing that I'm new and don't always know how things are done here."

Annie spilled out this entire speech in a frightened sounding squeak, and she decided that it should be appropriately ended with a tearful sniff.

"Why Lizzie, you have done just fine," responded Mrs. Voss with such kindness that Annie felt a momentary twinge of contrition at her outrageous charade. "Please escort the gentleman to the back parlor and see that he has everything he needs."

Annie curtsied and went to the door to the hallway and opened it, turning back to see if Nate would follow. He rose and mumbled disjointed phrases about how sorry he was, how he hadn't known, how Mrs. Voss must believe that he had no idea. Mrs. Voss stared at him with a mild expression of surprise, and Annie felt sure that he was about to give everything away. If she could just get Nate out of the room, maybe Mrs. Voss wouldn't notice. Just possibly she would assume he had been flustered by her beauty and distraught at having to leave her side. She supposed Mrs. Voss was used to tongue-tied men and would not find Nate's behavior so very remarkable. Annie threw out a sharp sounding "Sir," from her position at the door. This drew Nate's attention back to her, and she captured his gaze. With every ounce of will she could summon, she commanded him with her eyes to follow her, while she retreated slowly out of the room. Dazedly he obeyed, and in what seemed to be an eternity he was safely with her in the hallway with the door to the parlor closed.

Annie grabbed his hand and drew him down the hallway towards a small sitting room tucked back at the end of the hall. Nate regained his wits half way down the hall and stood stock-still. He snatched his hand from Annie's grasp and said, "Mrs. Fuller, Annie, what in the hell are you doing here? Mrs. Voss clearly thinks you are some sort of servant. Damnation, what possible explanation could you have for this ...."

Nate stopped and stammered, "Oh I'm sorry, I didn't mean ...." Then he uttered another oath under his breath and continued, "No, I take that back, I won't apologize for swearing. Why should I care about your ladylike sensibilities? You never behave like one. This time you have gone too far. I will not condone ...."

Annie ignored him and grabbed his arm, this time at the elbow, and tugged, all the while whispering urgently, trying to strike on the right phrases to convince him of the need for secrecy. "Please, Mr. Dawson, just come with me. We can't talk here, not in the hallway. I will explain everything, but do come where we can be private. You don't want to disturb Mrs. Voss. She wouldn't understand why you were struggling with her servant! It would cause a scene that would distress her; you don't want to do that, do you?"

This last argument achieved the desired effect, and Nate permitted himself to be hustled into the small dark room. Annie shut the door firmly behind her, resting her back against it momentarily as if to gain some strength from its solid presence. She saw only the barest outline of Nate, but she could hear him breathing softly. She felt her way to the curtains, opening them to let in the afternoon sun. The room was chill, so she then went to the fireplace and lit the small bundle of firewood she had laid down just this morning after dusting. While performing these simple actions she could feel Nate's glare boring into her back. Alerted by his swift intake of breath that he was about to launch into speech again, Annie swung around and forestalled him by beginning to speak herself. She tried to keep her voice light, as if they were merely in the middle of a mild disagreement.

"Now, Mr. Dawson, you mustn't get in such an uproar. I'm just trying to help out. It was you, yourself, who gave me the idea of helping Mrs. Voss with her servant problem. They really were struggling when I got here. You wouldn't believe how worthless Cartier, her personal maid, has been. Now Wong, Mr. Voss's man-servant, has been wonderful. But in a house this size, you can't expect one servant to do all the work. So you see, it is quite fortunate that I could help out."

Throughout this speech, Nate stared at her as if she was demented, but when she paused for breath he snorted in what Annie felt was a very unbecoming manner. She really expected that he would say something at this point, but when he persisted in just staring at her, Annie continued nervously.

"Now, I know that what I have done might appear slightly unorthodox. But it seemed to me that, while helping out, I could also find out what I needed to know to track down Matthew's money and his murderer. And I couldn't very well do that if I showed up as Annie Fuller, a complete stranger. At the start it didn't seem to be working out very well. You have no idea how hard being a servant can be, and at first I didn't seem to be learning very much. After Nellie was killed, I just couldn't give up, and I have begun to discover a good deal. For example, Mrs. Voss seems frightened, although I don't think she is as fragile as she appears. I think she may be worried that Jeremy was involved with his father's death. And, you wouldn't believe what an amazing artist Jeremy turns out to be; it really is a shame that his father failed to appreciate his talent. Then there is Miss Nancy! She took some company ledgers out of a hidden shelf in Matthew's study in the dead of night, and she has practically accused Mrs. Voss and Samuels of having something to do with Matthew's death, but I think she is just jealous. Wait until I tell you about the lady's maid, Cartier. She has some sort of secret relationship with a man, and she keeps her door locked, and last night I heard her crying. Did you know the police were here yesterday, and I think...."

By this last sentence, Annie had begun to falter. She found Nate's icy stare unnerving, and she couldn't help feel that she wasn't doing a very good job of justifying herself. If he was going to shout at her, she wished he would get on with it.

Annie stared back at him, lifting her chin a bit. *It really wasn't any of his business what I do*, she said to herself. *Of course, to be fair, the Voss family welfare is his business. But it is hurtful of him to think that I would purposely injure any of them in any way.* For a moment the vision of Nellie's lifeless body flashed in front of her, but Annie pushed it away, telling herself she was doing this for Nellie as well.

It was Nate who finally ended the impasse. Shaking his head slowly, he said, in a tone of amused disbelief, "Annie, Mrs. Fuller, you are impossible! I just don't understand you. When I think how I bent over backwards to keep your name from Chief Detective Jackson, trying to protect your reputation. And Uncle Frank rang such a peal over me for taking you to see Nellie. If he could only have seen that performance; he certainly wouldn't have recognized Edward Stewart's respectable daughter. Oh, lord! Wherever did you get that atrocious accent? For a minute, I really thought you were some dim-witted scullery maid!"

Annie focused on the only point that seemed of importance in Nate's speech, saying quickly, "So you have spoken with the police? And you didn't tell them about me? Oh, I appreciate that so much. Did the Detective tell you about coming here and asking everyone where they had been on Sunday? Thank goodness they didn't have any interest in me, since I hadn't been in the house when Nellie worked here."

"No, they didn't tell me," Nate replied. "In fact, that Jackson is a sly one. Interviewed me on Monday afternoon. Dashed unpleasant. Treated me like a suspect, then practically told me to go out to play and stop meddling in police affairs. Made me promise that I wouldn't inform anyone, including the Voss family, about Nellie's death until after the inquest, which was this morning. Implied that he wouldn't be interviewing anyone until after there was a determination made on how Miss Flannigan died. Appears that as soon as I left the station he hot footed it over here and questioned them. I should have been here as their counsel. I didn't even find out they had been questioned until I got a note from Mrs. Voss this morning. Makes me look incompetent."

"That's awful," Annie said. "Although, I must tell you they didn't learn very much. Nobody seems to have had a very good alibi, and Jeremy wasn't even here to be interviewed. They didn't really think you were involved did they? What happened at the inquest?"

"As usual with these things, there wasn't much detail. A waitress from the Cliff House told about Nellie saying she was meeting someone at noon on the beach. The fishermen described finding the body. I was simply asked to confirm their testimony. The coroner reported that she had drowned, but there was a contusion on the back of her head. There was some inconclusive discussion about whether or not this could have been done before she drowned or afterwards. The finding was death by misadventure, which can mean she died of an accident, suicide, or murder. Pretty standard when there is a suspicious death."

"Oh Nate! I can't believe they won't accept that she was murdered."

"What they think and what they can prove are two different matters." Nate replied. "To tell you the truth, I think they do believe her death is connected with Voss's death. However, my primary responsibility is to ensure that the Voss family isn't adversely affected by any of this."

Relieved that his anger seemed mainly directed at Jackson, Annie moved towards Nate, saying, "Oh, of course that is your concern; I am so glad you aren't too angry with me. You do understand what I have been doing here?" she asked hopefully.

Nate put up a hand as if to stop her physically from coming any closer and replied, "I am sorry if I mislead you, because, quite frankly, I'm furious with you. I think what you have done was at the very least misguided, and probably unlawful, and very possibly dangerous. What most disturbs me is your willingness to deceive a respectable and good woman like Mrs. Voss; that seems unconscionable to me."

Annie, taken aback by his change in tone, stood mute for a moment. As she opened her mouth to respond, he cut her off brusquely,

"No, Annie, don't say a word. You asked for my opinion, and for once you are going to keep still and listen to it. I am angry with you, but I do understand in part why you have done what you have. And, for now, I will not divulge your identity."

"But..."

Nate continued to disregard her attempts to speak. "Please, Annie, it is important that you understand why I have made this decision. First of all, I think that the knowledge of how she and her family have been taken in by you would be very distressing to Mrs. Voss, as you yourself so perceptively and, I might add, reprehensibly pointed out to me a few minutes ago in your attempt to black-mail me into silence. Secondly, I have no desire to damage your good name or embarrass you, although I'm not sure that the experience wouldn't be salutary. I realize your behavior was not motivated by any malice, but by a misdirected attempt to get at the truth. But I will keep your secret only on the condition that you remove yourself from this untenable situation as quickly as possible. Mrs. Voss ...."

The mention of Mrs. Voss suddenly recalled Annie to her circumstances and surroundings. Her heart beating, Annie interrupted Nate to ask the time, since there was no clock in the room. She had left her small pocket watch at home, judging that this would be a luxury few domestics could afford.

Perplexed by the question, Nate drew out his watch. "It's quarter to three. Oh, my God," he gasped. "How long have we been in here? What must Mrs. Voss be thinking?"

"Look," Annie said hurriedly. "It will be all right. As soon as I have gone down the back stairs, you go back to Mrs. Voss. Let's hope that she hasn't been ringing for me. Tell her that you had to send a written message, and I had to get you some writing materials. That will explain the delay. Tonight is my night off. I should be home by seven. Meet me there and I will tell you more about Cartier and everything else I have learned. And don't worry, I have already decided not to return tomorrow, so you don't have to worry about distressing Mrs. Voss further, although I don't think she will thank you for the loss of her housemaid. But now I must go."

## Chapter Thirty-two:
### Wednesday evening, August 15, 1879

The rest of the afternoon passed by uneventfully. Annie assumed that Nate had been able to explain his absence satisfactorily to Mrs. Voss, and she found herself going over the brief conversation, trying to remember just how he had looked and what he had said. She couldn't help but chuckle when she thought of how dumbstruck he had seemed when he first saw her as Lizzie. He may have been angry, but he had seemed to find some amusement in the situation as well. This thought then led to memories of how he had teased her during the picnic lunch near Cliff House, and, before she knew it, the rest of her cleaning chores were done. By five o'clock Wong had dinner preparations well in hand, and Annie was washing lettuce while he went upstairs to lay out clothes for Jeremy, on the off-chance he actually made it home for dinner on time. Annie had just finished drying the leaves when she heard the front doorbell peal impatiently. She thought she ought to go up to answer it in case Wong hadn't heard it on the third floor. As a result, she was just coming through the green baize doorway at the rear of the house when the policemen began to stream in through the front door.

At first impression, Annie thought there must be at least fifty of them, but later she figured out that there were only six, in addition to the Chief Detective and his Sergeant. Wong stood pressed back against the wall where one of the policemen had shoved him in passing, while the Chief Detective instructed him to get his mistress. Without looking to see if he was being obeyed, he marched into the front parlor and closed the door behind him. Meanwhile, the rest of the police spread throughout the house, accompanied by muffled bangs and shouts. Wong threw Annie an agonized look and then proceeded upstairs, so rattled that he neglected to take the servant's stairs. Mrs. Voss, who was hurrying down, followed closely by Miss Nancy, met him halfway.

Her fear palpable, Mrs. Voss stopped next to Wong and took him by the hands, crying out, "Whatever's happened? What are the police doing here? Do they know who killed Matthew?"

Wong answered, his voice shaking ever so slightly, "Please, Mrs. Voss. It's that Detective, Mr. Jackson. He came to the door with a paper that said he had the right to search the house. I tried to stop him, but they all came in at once. I'm sorry, but he is in the front parlor. He wishes to speak to you. Please, Mrs. Voss, let me send for Master Jeremy. I will go telegraph both the factory and his club and be back before they even know I'm gone. It is only right that your son be here with you."

Mrs. Voss looked relieved and gave Wong a warm smile, telling him that was an excellent idea. When she asked him if he would need money, he smiled slightly and said not to worry. Then she fished her husband's door key from a pocket and slipped it into his hand, and he was gone before Annie could blink. Surprisingly, Mrs. Voss then turned to her sister-in-law, who had stood rooted to the steps above her throughout this exchange, and reached out her hand, saying "Sister, will you please help me entertain the Chief Detective. I would appreciate your support."

Miss Nancy scowled and descended the two stairs that divided them. Ostentatiously ignoring Mrs. Voss's outstretched arm, she pushed her way past and made her way down the stairs alone. Mrs. Voss gave a slight sigh and followed her sister-in-law the rest of the way down the steps. When she got to the foot of the stairway where Annie had been standing as a mute witness, Mrs. Voss turned to her and asked her to bring tea into the parlor and then to ask Cartier to go down to the kitchen and stay there until called.

An outraged screech from upstairs testified that Cartier had already discovered that the house had been invaded, and Annie thought to herself she would probably not have to go to Cartier, but that Cartier would soon be down to the kitchen to find out what was going on.

After bobbing a curtsy in reply, Annie turned and flew back to the kitchen where she stopped abruptly when she glimpsed the blue of a police uniform. Her alarm turned to relief when she saw the man standing in the kitchen was Beatrice's nephew, Patrick. She ran to him, swiftly surveying the rest of the kitchen to make sure they were alone before speaking.

"Patrick, what is going on? Why is the Chief Detective having the house searched?"

"Mrs. Fuller," Patrick whispered urgently, "I hoped I'd get a chance to see you alone. The Chief's hot to make an arrest. He got new evidence this morning. Of course, the top brass don't tell us nothing specific, but the rumor is that someone from this house was seen at the Cliff House near the time Nellie was drowned. And some letter came in the mail this morning that fingered the same person for the Voss killing.

Annie gasped, "Who Patrick? Who do they suspect? Is it the servant Cartier?"

"Dunno. Didn't tell us. We're just supposed to look through the house and look for anything suspicious."

Patrick, who continued methodically to look through the cupboards and pantry shelves while talking, sounded apologetic when he next spoke. "You know, we didn't really do a thorough search of the place first time around because everyone thought it was suicide. Everyone but you! But the Chief got a court order for a search just this afternoon, based on this new evidence, so here we are. I'll try not to make too much of a mess down here. I know how my ma or Aunt Bea would feel about some man traipsing around in their pantries."

Annie laughed feebly. "That's all right, Patrick. You're just doing your job. But I don't really know what the Chief Detective expects to find, unless it's in Cartier's room. I've been looking myself for these past three days, and I haven't found anything in the rest of the house."

Just then the sound of footsteps interrupted them and Cartier swept indignantly into the kitchen. Annie was fully occupied for the next quarter of an hour getting the tea ready to take upstairs and trying to calm Cartier's hysterical outburst. She thought it was significant that the woman seemed to think the whole search was a direct attack on her. Annie found herself hoping that it was, and that it would turn out that Cartier's ever-locked room held the evidence Annie had been searching for.

In any event, Annie was so busy that she had no further opportunity to speak with Patrick. At some point Wong came in the back door, nodded to Patrick and then silently began to help Annie with the tea things. The two of them took the tray up together, which gave them a chance to whisper quietly on the stairs. Wong said briefly that he had sent the telegrams, but that he had not waited to see if there was a reply. Annie told him what Patrick had said, and then they were at the parlor door.

When they returned to the kitchen, Patrick seemed to have finished his investigations, and had been joined by another policeman. The two whispered together and then left. Cartier had lapsed into silence, stirring her tea and staring rigidly in front of her. Annie helped Wong clean up after the mess Patrick made. When the kitchen clock struck six o'clock, Wong finally spoke, saying to the room in general that he supposed that dinner was once more going to be delayed. They could hear the sounds of thumps and voices that testified that the police were still at work.

Shattering the silence, the bell for the parlor rang, and Annie went upstairs to see what was required. When she entered the parlor, Miss Nancy and Mrs. Voss were sitting stiffly, side by side on the sofa. Apparently Mrs. Voss's abundant social skills had failed her. The Chief Detective and his Sergeant were huddled with two uniformed policemen looking at something that rested on the tea table. Their bodies screened whatever they were looking at from Annie's sight. However, their voices sounded excited, and, when the Chief Detective glanced over at their entrance, she saw tangible signs of suppressed elation in his expression. His sergeant and the two other policemen were just leaving the parlor, taking whatever they had been looking at with them, when the sounds of a commotion reached them from the hallway and Jeremy and Malcolm Samuels burst into the room.

Jeremy ran straight to his mother and aunt, kneeled down and, taking is mother's hands in his own, exclaimed, "Mother, Aunt Nan, are you all right? What has happened?" Mrs. Voss's soft words were quickly drowned out by Miss Nancy's harsh exclamations, and Annie could see that Jeremy was thoroughly bewildered. Meanwhile, Samuels buttonholed Chief Detective Jackson and upbraided him for invasion of privacy and a general lack of good manners. Jackson ignored him and walked over to Jeremy and began to speak in a clearly ironic tone.

The other voices died down and Jeremy rose to stand before the Chief Detective who said, "Excuse me, Mr. Voss. How kind of you to come. You have saved me the trouble of tracking you down. I have here a court order permitting me to search these premises in connection with the deaths of Matthew Voss and Nellie Flannigan." The Chief Detective drew a sheaf of papers out of his coat pocket and handed them to Jeremy, who looked at them vaguely and then passed them over to Samuels, who had come to stand by his side.

Jackson continued, "My men have just completed the search, and, as a result of what they've found, I would like to invite you to come with me to my office downtown to answer a few questions. I would suggest that you have Mr. Samuels here get in touch with your lawyer, so he can meet you there."

This last statement was met with at first silence and then outraged protest from both Miss Nancy and Malcolm Samuels. Mrs. Voss simply rose and stood mutely next to Jeremy, her arm sliding around his waist protectively. Jeremy said nothing but stood frozen for a minute; and, then, running his long fingers through his hair and taking a deep breath, he began to talk softly as he put his arm around his mother's shoulder.

"Chief Detective... Jackson, it is, I believe. I'll be glad to answer any questions you might ask. I know I haven't been as cooperative as I could have been in the past. I apologize. However, I wonder if we couldn't go over what you want to know here. We could use my father's...." At this point Jeremy's voice broke, and then he continued, "...his study, we would be private. But then my mother wouldn't worry so much. I don't really think that my lawyers need to be present. I'm not guilty of anything. But if you insist, I'll have Wong go for them."

The Detective smiled grimly and shook his head. "I'm sorry, young man. The time for informal chats has passed. I'm afraid that it must be done at headquarters. Now, I can't force you to come at this time. But I think that you would prefer to come voluntarily. Better for everyone."

Samuels again began to protest, stepping up close to Jackson and poking him in the chest with his finger, his mustache bristling in his anger. "This is an outrage. You've completely overstepped your authority. You are just trying to hide the fact you've bungled this investigation from the start. Well, I can assure you, you won't get away with it. Mayor Bryant will hear from me tonight."

Jeremy reached out and put a restraining hand on Samuels' shoulder. "No, Uncle Malcolm. That's enough. The Detective is just doing his job. But please. You stay here with mother. She'll need you. Send for Mr. Hobbes and Mr. Dawson. They'll know what to do."

Then he turned to his mother and gave her a swift hug. Annie could now see his face and felt a sharp pang when she saw how drawn and frightened he looked. His mother only reluctantly let him go, and she whispered something in his ear that made him chuckle weakly. Next he stepped over to his Aunt, who had also risen, and gave her a hard hug, saying, "Now, take care of Mother. I depend on you."

A moment later he was gone, taking the Chief Detective with him. Mrs. Voss, cutting off Miss Nancy and Samuels, both of whom had begun to speak, turned to Annie and said, "Please, Lizzie. Could you take the tea things and then ask Wong to come up here. I will want him to run an errand for me. Would you feel capable of carrying on with dinner alone for a while?"

Annie nodded and Mrs. Voss said, "Good girl. And could you also ask Cartier to come upstairs to my bedroom. I will be retiring for a while before dinner, which we will have at 7:30 tonight. Oh, I am sorry, but I am afraid that we won't be able to spare you this evening, but I promise that you will have your night out tomorrow night. I am sure all this misunderstanding will be straightened out by then. That will be all for now, thank you." As Annie left the room she heard Mrs. Voss say that she hoped that Samuels would stay to dinner.

Annie did as she had been told, first telling Cartier that she was wanted in Mrs. Voss's rooms. Then, when Cartier was gone, she told Wong what had been happening upstairs. "I think that they must have found something, something that they feel implicates Jeremy. The Chief Detective was practically bursting with glee, and he essentially threatened Jeremy with arrest if he didn't come willingly.

Oh, Wong. His father would have been so proud of him! Jeremy handled himself magnificently."

Annie stopped then, silenced by Wong's penetrating stare, and she realized that she had forgotten to refer to Jeremy as the master or Mr. Jeremy. Even worse, he must be wondering why she would profess any knowledge of what Matthew would think about his son. They stared at each other for a second, and then Wong shrugged, turned, and went upstairs to see his mistress.

When Wong returned to the kitchen he gave her instructions on how to finish the meal preparations and told her that he was to go out and telegraph the family lawyers.

"Oh Wong, is there any way you could also send a message to my friends as well. They were expecting me home this evening, and I wouldn't want them to worry. If you can wait a minute I will run up stairs for some money."

"Miss Lizzie, don't worry about the money, just write out the address and your message, and I will be off."

As Annie wrote out Beatrice's name and the boarding house address she thought hurriedly how to write the message in such a way that if Nate was already there he would be alerted to the fact that he and his uncle were needed at the police station. She finally determined that the blunt truth would work best, so she wrote under the address, "Will not be home this pm. Master taken by police for questioning. Mistress requests my presence." She hoped that Wong would not take exception to her revealing Jeremy's business to her friends, but she didn't know any other way to insure that Nate would get the message, without actually telling Wong she knew Mr. Dawson and where he would be at this hour. Wong simply nodded when she gave him the message, and slipped quickly out the back door. She wished she had a clue to what he was thinking, about the accusations against his new master or about her presence in the household.

During the next few hours, time limped along like an arthritic ancient. It took forever for Wong to return from the telegraph office, and Annie became increasingly ineffective in her attempts to carry out all of his instructions for the meal. Serving the dinner itself seemed to last for days, with Annie's shoulders and arms stiffening up more and more with each course. By ten o'clock, they finished washing the dishes, and Annie found herself sitting at the kitchen table with her head held between her hands, trying desperately to stay awake. When the doorbell rang again, Wong went up to answer it. Jeremy hadn't come home yet, but there was no reason for him to ring the bell. Annie got up and began to pace, waiting for Wong to come back and wondering what was going on.

Wong returned and started to brew another pot of coffee, reporting, "It was Mr. Dawson. He and his uncle have just come from the police station. I'm to take some of Master Jeremy's clothes down to him tonight on the way home. They're keeping him overnight."

Annie took a deep breath. "Then they've arrested him? Oh, Wong. This is awful. I can't believe he would kill his father." As she spoke, she realized she had never really believed Jeremy could have been the murderer. She wanted desperately to talk to Nate and find out what was going on.

As if in answer to her unspoken wish, Wong continued. "I don't know if he is arrested. Maybe Mr. Dawson will inform you. He asked me to request that you meet him at the back gate at 10:45. He wants to speak to you."

Wong did not look up from his task; neither did his voice express any surprise or curiosity when he conveyed this message. Annie didn't know what to say. The explanation for why the family's lawyer would want to hold a private conversation with her was too complicated, and she didn't want to insult Wong with lies. So after a pause she just said, "I see. Well, if you see him before that, tell him I'll be there. If any one can find a way to protect Mr. Jeremy, I am sure that Mr. Dawson can do it."

Wong finished with the coffee and took it upstairs, saying he would go on up and gather together Jeremy's things. Annie later wondered if she had possibly fallen asleep, because before her tired brain had gone beyond repeating to itself that Jeremy was innocent, Wong was back down beside her with a packed bag in one hand and the tray of coffee cups in the other.

After putting the coffee cups into the dishpan to soak and getting on his jacket, Wong spoke again in his inflectionless voice. "Mr. Hobbes and Mr. Samuels have left the house and Mrs. Voss and the old Miss have retired to their rooms. Cartier has also gone to bed. The front is locked, and you are to let me out the back and lock up after I have gone. I believe that it is now time for your meeting with Mr. Dawson; I will tell him you are on your way as I go by."

And with this Wong took down the key from its hook next to the back door, unlocked it, and gave the key to Annie before slipping out into the night.

## Chapter Thirty-three

Wong's exit from the kitchen galvanized Annie into action. She dashed to the washbasin in the corner, where a small mirror hung. She flung some of the water in the basin onto her face, and, while toweling it dry, peered to see how she looked. The light in the kitchen at night was too poor for her to see very well, and she chided herself for even caring. She then hastily poked and prodded at her hair to try and produce some semblance of neatness. All she succeeded in doing was dislodging a few more pins, and a few more strands escaped from the braid coiled at the nape of her neck. Muttering a very unladylike phrase, Annie hurried to the door, snatched a shawl that hung over a kitchen chair on the way, and, stopping to make sure she had the back door key in her pocket, she too slipped out into the night.

As she stood for a second on the top doorstep to let her eyes adjust to the darkness, Annie looked around. It was a typical August night for San Francisco: cold, foggy, damp. No stars were visible, and the moon was a faint, misty sliver. There was a slight breeze and shadows loomed and clumped and slithered in various parts of the yard, causing Annie to rethink her decision not to bring a lamp. But, no, the chances of someone seeing its light from the house and coming to investigate were too great. Making her way down the path in the faint moonlight, she tried to think of what she would say to Nate. She smelled the acrid scent of smoke and located the tiny glowing ember of a cigar about a foot away from her. She whispered Nate's name. The ember arced over the back gate into the alleyway, and then a tall shadow detached itself from the universal blackness and came toward her, slowly revealing the figure that was becoming so familiar.

Without thinking, she ran up to him and placed her hands against his chest, as if to steady herself and said, "Oh, Nate, I'm so glad you've come. What are we going to do? The police can't really think Jeremy's the murderer? Tell me, is there anything I can do to help!"

Annie's rush of words faltered as she felt Nate stiffen and then pull away from her. Chagrinned, she scolded herself for her behavior. *What was she thinking of, throwing herself at him*! Yet, for a brief moment she'd felt his warm breath against her cheek. Annie thought sadly that it must have been her imagination.

Trying to cover her hurt, Annie resumed her questioning. "Have they arrested Jeremy? What did they find when they searched the house? Please tell me, I need to know."

Nate responded in a tense, quiet voice. "It looks bad. They haven't formally arrested him, but they will probably press charges sometime tomorrow. Really don't have much choice; the evidence is pretty strong against him. Someone has testified that they saw Jeremy last Sunday afternoon on a path above the beach where Nellie was killed. And when they searched the house they found a small bloody wooden club stuffed down among the paint rags in his room. They figure this was used to knock out Nellie."

Annie gasped. "No, Nate that's not possible. Jeremy couldn't have killed her. That would mean he killed his father as well, and I just can't believe that."

Nate interrupted her, "That's not all. They also found a bundle of bank notes and some of the stock certificates that were missing. Even more incriminating, they found a small vial of potassium cyanide in his room, the poison used to kill his father."

Annie, speechless for a moment, began to crumple her shawl in her hands. Then she fired off a series of questions, giving Nate no chance to answer them. "Where did they find the bank notes and stock certificates? Patrick said the police got some sort of letter in the mail. What did it say? And where do they think Jeremy would have gotten the cyanide? How could they think that anybody would be so stupid as to leave that kind of evidence around? It just doesn't make any sense."

Nate put a hand out and briefly touched her shoulder, saying, "Slow down. One question at a time."

Annie paused, catching her breath. Nate's hand had felt so warm through the thin damp wool of her dress that she realized how chilled she was, and she pulled the shawl around her shoulders, shivering.

Nate continued. "First of all, they found the money and assets stuck among his bills in his desk. The vial of cyanide was among his painting gear. And yes there was a letter, anonymous, that purported to be from someone who Jeremy had approached about selling some non-negotiable bonds."

Annie burst out, "Someone is trying to frame him. All of this is a lie. Yesterday I went through his rooms from top to bottom, and there weren't any stock certificates in his desk and there certainly wasn't any blood-stained wooden club. As for the vial of cyanide, I can't believe that if he were guilty of poisoning his father that he would keep the cyanide in his rooms. He had nearly two weeks to get rid of it. Where would he have gotten cyanide in the first place?"

"Well, the police say the vial came from the furniture factory. Evidently they use potassium cyanide in the furniture-making process."

Annie snorted. "Well, that just proves the cyanide wasn't used by Jeremy. As far as I can tell, before today he has rarely set foot in the place, and I don't see him being able to recognize any chemical from the factory, much less knowing it was a poison."

"I'm sorry, but the police don't see it that way. Turns out that the factory uses the cyanide in the mixture of certain pigments and stains for some of the finished furniture. So Jackson figures that, as an artist, Jeremy would be familiar with cyanide and its effects on the human body. And as for his hiding the money and missing assets in his room, well, I suppose he might have hidden them somewhere else but thought that enough time had lapsed that it would be safer to have them closer to home." The neighbor's dog barked again, and Nate turned aside, looking at the back gate.

Annie grabbed Nate's coat lapels, pulling him back around while she furiously spat out. "Look at me! You believe he did it, don't you! You've always believed it was him. I can't believe you would be so stupid."

Nate grabbed her hands and held them to his chest. "Listen to me, Annie; don't jump to conclusions. I'm just as upset about all this as you are. You didn't have to sit and explain all this to his mother. God, I felt helpless, and she was so brave. But even if you are right about none of this making sense, we have to be realistic. I am telling you how it looks to the police. And on the surface the evidence seems fairly overwhelming."

He then let her go, and Annie turned slightly from him and wiped her eyes with the edge of her shawl. Taking a deep breath, she turned back to him and said as calmly as possible, "All right, I'm trying to get this straight. What did Jeremy say to their questions? He didn't confess to the police, did he?"

Nate sighed. "No, but he just said he was innocent, over and over. And you would think that if he was the murderer, he would have come up with a better story by now, although I am pretty sure he was lying about one thing. But then that didn't make sense either."

"What do you think he was lying about?"

"About his whereabouts Sunday afternoon when Nellie was killed. He told the police that he went down town and wandered around, but I don't know; something was wrong. He stiffened, and, when Jackson pressed him, he got angry. It was the only time he showed any real emotion throughout all the questions. He even seemed quite calm when they took him over the night of his father's death. He stuck to the tale he had told the police earlier, about walking all the way down to the docks and back that night. He didn't seem uncomfortable with that story, even though it was as weak and unsubstantiated an alibi as the one he had for Nellie's death. I think he is hiding something about Sunday, but if he isn't Nellie's murderer, I don't know what it is."

Annie thought for a minute. "Maybe he was doing something else he was ashamed of Sunday. I don't know, maybe he was drunk in some dive or in a prostitute's crib on the Barbary Coast. Doesn't want it to come out. Of course it would be idiotic of him to withhold information that would prove him innocent, but I could see him doing just that in a misguided attempt to keep from embarrassing his mother or his finance, can't you?"

Nate sounded skeptical. "Remember, they have a witness that says Jeremy was near the Cliff House on Sunday afternoon."

"But *we* where there, and we didn't see anybody. Who said they saw Jeremy?" Annie cut in.

"A man who works as a hostler for the Cliff House. Said he was taking a walk along the cliffs that overlooked that part of the beach. Said he saw a young man, dark curly hair, mustache, scrambling up to the road to the north. They brought him to the station house tonight, and he said it was definitely Jeremy that he saw."

Annie exclaimed, "That's ridiculous! How could he be sure from such a distance? Jeremy's looks are not all that distinctive. Most of the young men in this city have mustaches, and I dare say half of them have dark curly hair. Besides, how do we know we can trust that someone who works for the Cliff House is telling the truth? Maybe he was bribed to say he saw Jeremy."

"But by whom?" Nate shot back. "I don't have any strong faith in the integrity of the hostlers of the Cliff House, but who would do such a thing?"

Annie sniffed impatiently, "The real murderer. Who else? And for the same reason the real murderer must have sent the anonymous letter and planted the bank notes, the bloody club and the poison. To shift the blame on Jeremy."

Nate repeated, "But who? Who could do all those things?"

"Cartier, Mrs. Voss's maid, could. She was in the house the night Matthew was killed, she could have poisoned Matthew in order to get the money, or let in an accomplice to do the job. Her room is the only one I haven't been able to search, so maybe she had all the missing assets the whole time. Did I tell you she passes messages to someone through the meat delivery boy, and that she was supposed to meet someone on Sunday on her afternoon off, but he didn't show? Maybe her mysterious *friend* couldn't meet her at Wood-ward's Gardens because he was busy killing Nellie."

Annie felt her excitement rising. "Listen, I just had a thought. It was Cartier's night out last night, and some man picked her up in a carriage. If that man was her accomplice, either he or she could have mailed the anonymous letter to the police. Then, Cartier came back to the house last night around 8:30, cancelling her night out. Maybe her accomplice gave her the evidence, forced her to plant it in Jeremy's room. It would have been easy; her room is right across from his. Oh this makes perfect sense."

"Slow down Annie. Do you have any proof of this? What am I supposed to do? Tell the police that the parlor maid, who just happens to be the same person who was with me when I discovered Nellie's body, and just happens to be the mysterious Sibyl they have been looking for, suspects the lady's maid because she keeps her door locked and came home early from her night off. Face it Annie, Jeremy is still the most obvious suspect as her accomplice."

As Annie started to protest, Nate silenced her. "Please, just let me review the facts, which is what the police are going to consider, not speculation on what might have been. Matthew Voss came home Friday night, evidently with a great deal of money and his paper assets, having planned on meeting Samuels the next night to buy him out. At dinner on Saturday, he announced his plans, including his decision that Jeremy was to end his artistic career and take over the business. According to Nellie's statement to the police, Jeremy and his father quarreled, his father threatened to cut him off if he didn't submit, and then Jeremy left the house around seven. Nellie left the house around eight for her night out; Wong followed her around eleven, by which time the three remaining women in the house had already retired to bed. Voss was alive at this time, since he locked the door behind Wong, as was his habit. Jeremy says he returned around twelve o'clock, letting himself in with his own key, and that his father's study lights were on, but that he didn't go in to see him, he just went up to bed.

"Sometime between eleven and the next morning, someone poured Voss a shot of whiskey laced with cyanide. He was found dead the next morning by his wife, and since the doors and windows were all still locked, the assumption must be that either one of the three women in the house or Jeremy killed him. And do you honestly think that any jury would believe that his wife, or sister, or the lady's maid got up, came down stairs, and convinced Matthew Voss to have a drink? I don't think so. But a jury could certainly be led to believe that Jeremy might have spent the time between seven and twelve o'clock working himself up into a rage and getting the cyanide. Then, when he got home, he could have pretended to make up with his father, offered to have a night cap with him, poisoned him, and then carefully set up the scene for a suicide by taking the money and other assets and hiding them."

Annie remained absolutely still during Nate's recital, but now she whispered urgently, "Do you believe this is what really happened?"

Nate shrugged, ramming his fists once more into his pockets. "Annie, I just don't know. Contrary to your belief, I don't want it to be him. He's my client! And, if he is guilty it will destroy Mrs. Voss. But I can't ignore the reality that Jeremy had a reason to kill Voss and certainly the best opportunity."

Annie's stomach lurched, and she suddenly feared she might become ill. She walked shakily over to a garden bench, sat down, and hunched over, pressing her hands to her cheeks, taking in deep breaths, trying to quiet her nausea.

"Annie, are you all right?" Nate sat down beside her on the bench.

"It's all my fault. I should have left well enough alone. I just *know* Jeremy didn't kill his father, but you've just shown me that he could be found guilty anyway. If I had just let it alone, you, the police, everyone might have been willing to let it rest as suicide. I thought I was helping. Trying to clear Matthew's good name. I wanted to do something to preserve my memory of him as a kind and wonderful friend. But I haven't even done that. The longer I live in this house, the more I can see that Matthew himself was to blame for much of the unhappiness I see here. I mean, there is Miss Nancy, a bitter old woman who lived her entire life for her brother, and I can't see that Matthew cared two figs for her. And he let her turn her bitterness on his wife. Maybe Amelia Voss acts like such a foolish and naïve woman because he insisted she be that way. Who am I to despise a woman for giving into an autocratic man? I was no better at standing up for myself to my husband. And Jeremy—well, it would have been a crime to put an end to the career of someone with the artistic talent that Jeremy has, just to satisfy some vain idea of a son carrying on the business."

Annie had begun to rock back and forth in her despair, her last words coming out as a kind of lament, "I should have left Matthew to rest in peace. But now Nellie's dead, Matthew's son might be hung, the Voss family will be destroyed, and there will be no peace. It's all my fault."

Slowly through her misery, Annie came to realize that she was being rocked in Nate's arms, her face pressed up against his chest, where she could feel the warmth of his skin and hear the beat of his heart through the fine linen of his shirt. One of his arms was tightly wrapped around her waist, and with his other hand he was gently stroking her hair. All the while he was murmuring to her.

"Annie, hush now, hush. You're not to blame. It's not your fault. Please don't cry. I'm sorry, please don't cry. It will be all right, hush now."

Annie pulled away and sat up straight, groping for her handkerchief. She blew her nose, unable to look him in the face. Nate, while he did loosen his hold on her, kept an arm around her, and now pulled her chin up at him so she had to look him in the eyes.

"Annie, you must believe me when I say you are not responsible for any of this. You know as well as I do that the police were already suspicious of Voss's death before I went to see them, and I've learned that they had already sent out word to find Nellie for further questioning. From the beginning they suspected Jeremy, so you had nothing to do with that. What you've been doing at this house might have been misguided, but it certainly hasn't made anything worse. And perhaps I'll be able to use some of what you've learned about Cartier to at least mount an effective defense for Jeremy.

"And you mustn't be so upset about what you've learned about Mr. Voss. So he wasn't perfect. He made mistakes. But they were not heinous crimes. He behaved the way men are supposed to. He wanted to take care of his wife, he wanted to make sure his son grew up to be able to support his own wife. You shouldn't be so hard on him. Ninety percent of the men in this city act the way he did, and none of them have been murdered. He didn't deserve that. And he would be grateful that he had a loyal friend like you who cares enough to take personal risks to find his murderer."

Annie gave him a quick hug, whispering, "Thank you."

She felt his arms tighten around her, and she felt the warmth of his breath travel slowly down her forehead, her eyes, her mouth....

The neighbor's dog again barked, and Nate broke away from her and stood up, peering around. Silence reasserted itself, providing a counterpoint to the thump of Annie's heart. She waited, hoping that he would sit back down beside her. Instead, he turned and reached his hand down to her in an offer to help her to her feet, saying as he did, "Come, let me escort you home now. You have the back door key, don't you? Well, lock up and take it with you. First thing in the morning Kathleen can bring the key back and get your things. You can write a note, make some excuses. You won't have to see anyone in the house. It will be all right."

Annie snatched her hand away as she stood up. "What do you mean? I can't leave now. I promised Mrs. Voss I would stay. And it's more important than ever to see what I can learn to help save Jeremy."

Nate grabbed Annie suddenly by the arms, startling a gasp from her.

"No!" Nate was almost shouting, which prompted another series of barks from the neighbor's dog. Then he lowered his voice, although it was no less intense. "Your days as maid are over. Leave this to me. I want you out of this house now; it's too dangerous. If Jeremy isn't the murderer, then the murderer, whoever he is, could be in that house right now. It's just not safe for you to stay. One servant in this house has already died. I will not permit the same thing to happen to you. I should never have let you stay in the first place. It's not right. You shouldn't be exposed to this sort of danger."

Nate's vehemence was so unexpected that Annie was at first speechless. Then as she pulled away from him she said, "Nate Dawson, get your hands off of me! You have used that tone of voice on me once too often. I'm not your sister, *thank goodness*, so you can't boss me around. You have no authority over me whatsoever. And I don't take kindly to threats."

Nate instantly stepped back, and she rubbed her arms where he had held her. He reached towards her and then backed away again, saying, "Oh, Annie, I'm sorry. I didn't mean to hurt you. Please forgive me. I meant no offense. But don't you see, I'm worried about you. What if I promise that I'll look into your suspicions about Cartier first thing tomorrow? Maybe you are right and she and some man were in it together. You must realize you have done what you can here. It's time for you to leave the investigation to others."

"You mean leave it to some man, don't you." Annie snapped back. "But you're wrong; there are things I can do to help here, even though they may not seem important to you. I have to be there in the morning to let Wong in and to get the kitchen oven going. You don't expect Mrs. Voss to do those things? And she isn't going to be able to get a new servant in a day, not one they can trust, not with the publicity that Jeremy's arrest will generate. Wong can't do everything himself and you wouldn't want me to leave Mrs. Voss with only Cartier, who might be a murderer, to serve her. Anyway, if it is dangerous, I can't just expect some young innocent girl to take my place. I have got to stay, at least for tonight. You see that don't you?"

"No, I don't see it," Nate said flatly. "But it's useless to argue with you. You are the most stubborn woman I have ever met, or ever hope to meet" He took a deep breath, and said, "All right, you are probably safe as long as Jeremy is with the police, safe from Jeremy if he is the killer, and if he isn't, the real murderer isn't going to do anything while the police have him in custody. But, I want you to promise that you will leave by tomorrow evening, and I want you to promise, no snooping around in the meanwhile."

Annie bristled, muttering, "No promises." There was a charged moment of silence; then she said, "Look, I have a responsibility here, and being female doesn't release me from it. Please try to understand. Since I am at least partly responsible for the danger Jeremy is facing, no matter what you say, it is only right that I should take some risks to try and help him. I only wish I could do more. I know you probably disagree, but I happen to believe that what's right for a man to do is right for a woman. If you feel that makes me less of a woman, I'm sorry."

She whispered, more to herself than to Nate, "I can't change, not for you, or for anybody," and, before Nate could reply, she turned and fled back down the path to the kitchen door, half-afraid he would attempt to stop her and half-afraid he wouldn't. She'd left the kitchen door open slightly, so it took but a moment to slip inside and bolt it with the key. Then she stood leaning against the door, the silence of the night pooling around her.

# Chapter Thirty-four:
## Thursday morning, August 16, 1879

*Wong was late.* It was nearly six in the morning and Annie had already removed and sifted the cinders from the grate and rekindled the fire in the kitchen stove. *Wong was never late.* She should be opening up curtains upstairs by now, then setting and starting the fire in the dining room, cleaning out the fireplace in the front parlor and making sure that room was dusted and ready to be used. But she didn't dare leave the kitchen since it was her duty to let him in. Instead she sat at the kitchen table, barely able to stay awake, trying to think of what to do. By now Wong would have been making bread. Annie supposed she could try to get it started, but her bread-making attempts at home, even under Beatrice's tutelage, generally ended in disaster. Kathleen had suggested last time that they should use the dense brick-like loaf of rye she made as a doorstop. *Heavens, how I want to be home!*

And she was so tired. After Nate had left and she retired to her attic room, she had lain for hours, going over what he had told her, looking for proof that Cartier or some mysterious stranger was responsible for the murders. At least she could remove Miss Nancy or Mrs. Voss from the list of potential suspects. While they might have had a hand in killing Nellie, or even Matthew, in order to protect Jeremy, they would never have participated in an attempt to wrongly accuse him of these murders.

A muffled shout from the back yard snapped Annie from her reverie; her heart pounding, she grabbed the lamp beside her, took the key from its hook and unlocked the back door. With the door open she could clearly hear the neighbor's dog barking and what sounded like several voices raised in anger. She ran up the back steps and could barely make out two men at the back gate who were struggling to hold a third man. Without thinking she raised the lamp higher and ran through the back yard, shouting, "You there. What's going on?"

When she realized that the man who was being held was Wong, she stopped short and yelled, "Let him go. He belongs here. If you don't let him go, I'll have the police on you."

One of the men turned towards her and said something that was drowned out by the ever more frantic barks of the neighbor's dog, but he didn't release his hold on Wong. Instead he pushed Wong to his knees, while yanking on the old man's long braided queue. Fearless with rage, Annie snatched up a rake that was leaning up against the garden fence and one-handedly began to wail at the back of the man holding Wong. With each swing of the rake she grunted out, "Let him go, let him go."

Simultaneously there was the sharp crack of a window shade being drawn up and a man's voice bawled out "King! Shut up you worthless hound!" and the dog's barking ceased. The man who's back Annie had been assaulting dropped his hold on Wong and ran through the back gate. Once he put the fence between himself and Annie, he shouted at the other man, saying, "Ned, let him go. She'll have the whole neighborhood awake. It's not worth it, the old Chinaman's not going to talk anyway."

The other man gave a half-hearted kick at Wong, who was struggling to his feet, and then removed himself from the back yard, joining his friend behind the fence. His courage apparently bucked up by the sight of Annie dropping the rake in order to help Wong to his feet, the first man leaned over the fence and said, "Hey missy. No need to get all in a bother. We just wanted to talk to the old man, but he didn't seem to understand us, guess his English isn't all that good. We're just looking for a story, got a deadline for the afternoon editions. Damned *Chronicle* got a jump on us. Seems like the police think that old man Voss was killed by his son. So tell us how's his mother taking the news? Did she faint or something? Hysterics? Why'd ya think he did it? For the money? Did he have help? Just tell us something and you'll get your name in the papers. We could make it worth your while. Now come on, don't go, we're not going away, and if you don't talk to us, someone else will!"

This last was shouted at Annie and Wong's retreating backs as they stumbled together down the three steps and into the kitchen; Annie slammed the door shut and locked it behind them.

Putting the lamp down, Annie began to brush the dirt that clung to Wong's jacket, saying, "Wong, are you all right? What happened? What was that man shouting about? Has Jeremy been arrested?"

Wong, who had been completely silent up until this moment, said quietly, albeit a little breathlessly, "Please Miss, give me a moment."

He walked over to the stove and drew out water from the reservoir into a pitcher that was sitting on the stovetop. Then he went to the washstand in the corner and added fresh hot water to the basin sitting there. He bent and brushed dirt from the knees of his trousers, took off his coat and shook it, hanging it on the peg beside the washstand, and he began methodically to wash his hands and face. After he was done, he carefully folded the towel and hung it over the rod on the side of the stand and flipped his queue neatly over his shoulder. Only then did he turn and come quietly over to Annie where she still stood before the door. He placed his two hands together, raised them to his forehead, and bowed slowly to her, saying, "Thank you."

Embarrassed, Annie motioned dismissively and began to ask him again to tell her exactly what happened. Wong said, "Miss Lizzie, I am afraid that the newspapers have become interested in this family's misfortunes. Those two men were reporters and they were lying in wait for me at the end of the alley. They took exception to my unwillingness to answer their questions. I regret that you became involved."

Annie started to exclaim, but Wong held up his hand and cocked his head, saying, "Please Miss, let us not discuss this further. We have our morning chores to attend to, and if my ears are not deceived I believe that we are about to receive a visit from Miss Nancy. It would be good if she would find breakfast preparations underway."

## Chapter Thirty-five:
## Thursday afternoon, August 16, 1879

Later, Annie would think of this early morning event as the beginning of the siege. Miss Nancy did indeed burst into the kitchen, still dressed in her night things, demanding to know the cause of the commotion that had wakened her. Annie didn't wait around to hear Wong's explanation and instead scurried up the stairs to attend to her morning duties before Miss Nancy had a chance to admonish her. While she opened the dining room window curtains and knelt to start the fire in this room she tried to recall what the reporter had said, something about the *Chronicle*. Perhaps Miss Nancy would ask Wong to go out and purchase a copy of the paper, but that would put him in danger of being accosted by the same two men. Thinking about this as she moved into the front parlor to clean out its fireplace, it occurred to Annie to peek out the window that looked out on the street. With a sense of inevitability, she noted two different men were standing on the railings of the front fence, peering up at the house as if trying to determine if anyone was up. She wondered if they were also newspaper reporters and if they would be brazen enough to actually come to the front door. Before breakfast was over, she had her answer.

They, and the three or four other men who soon joined them, *were* newspaper reporters. They not only repeatedly rang the front bell but they knocked on the kitchen door, climbed the fence and stood in the flower beds at the side of the house to peer in the windows, and intercepted the men delivering milk and ice to the house. It was the iceman who thoughtfully smuggled in a copy of the morning paper, confirming what they had already guessed, that Jeremy's questioning by the police was front-page news. Thank goodness the house had indoor facilities, because Annie shuddered to think about what it would have meant if they had had to use an outhouse. Miss Nancy, Mrs. Voss, and Cartier chose to remain upstairs all morning, each having their breakfasts in their own rooms, so they were spared the inconvenience of dealing with these interlopers, but neither Wong nor Annie had that option. First of all, they were forced to keep all the first floor windows closed and locked and the curtains drawn, on what, perversely, proved to be one of San Francisco's loveliest sunny August days. Consequently, Annie and Wong sweltered in musty darkness. Secondly, much as they would have liked to, they couldn't simply ignore the front door bell, since it might have been someone with legitimate business. So, each time the doorbell rang, both Annie and Wong dropped whatever they were doing and went into action. Annie would run up to the second floor and nip into the front guest bedroom, where she could see the front stoop from a window. After determining that the person ringing the bell was no one they knew, she would stamp her feet twice, which Wong could hear from his position in the hallway, and they would both return to their chores.

Needless to say, everything took twice as long to accomplish, and Annie was already physically and emotionally exhausted from the events of the previous day. That was probably why she screamed and dropped one of the good china plates she was drying after lunch when the face of a reporter suddenly appeared at the kitchen window. Wong was just covering the window with a thick towel, when the bell for the front door pealed again.

"Oh, Wong. I can't stand this much longer. Please, please, can't I drop the contents of the slop jar on the top of their heads? I promise

I'd scrub the front steps on my hands and knees when this is all over."

Annie was heartened to see that she had finally won a smile from Wong. He had clearly been shaken by his early morning adventure. As she took her place at the front look-out, she was so busy wondering how they were going to get the day's marketing done that Annie almost didn't register that the person standing at the front door wasn't a reporter, but that it was Nate. He was ringing the doorbell repeatedly while being shouted at by the gaggle of reporters along the front sidewalk.

Annie disobeyed all the rules and flew down the front steps to skid to a stop in front of a startled Wong, saying, "Open the door quick, it's Mr. Dawson. Maybe he has news of Jeremy. I'll tell Mrs. Voss he's here."

As she went down the back hall to the servant's stairs she could hear the sudden rise in the noise level as Wong opened the front door, and she turned to watch as he and Nate put their shoulders to the door to shove back the men who were trying to push their way in. Assured of their success, she made her way to the back stairs to ascend to the second floor. At first Annie had found the requirement that servants only use the back stairs amusing, then extremely irritating, and now, with less than a week as a servant, it seemed normal to her. What also seemed normal was the way her heart began to misbehave at the sight of Nate. She wasn't sure which idea was more upsetting, that she had adapted so well to the rules of domestic service or that a man once again could have that sort of effect on her.

"Miss Lizzie," Wong looked up from a tray on the kitchen table, where he was laying out the tea biscuits he had by some miracle found time to make this morning, "Mr. Dawson informed me that he should be with Mrs. Voss and Miss Nancy for no more than a half hour, and that if you would await him in the kitchen, that he would try to have a word with you before he leaves."

Annie had just come back down to the kitchen from notifying Miss Nancy that her sister-in-law had requested her company in the front parlor where she was entertaining Mr. Dawson. This had prompted the usual scowl and grudging acquiescence on the old lady's part. All the way down the stairs Annie had been so absorbed with concocting a scheme that would win her a few minutes conversation with Nate that Wong's message took a second to sink in. When it did, Annie found herself blushing furiously.

"Oh, Wong. Thank you. Yes, I will be here. Is there something that I can be doing to help you prepare dinner? Annie hesitated and then rushed ahead, fearing that if she slowed her courage would fail her. "Please Wong, I would like to explain. I know that Mr. Dawson's request to see me, last night and today, must seem highly irregular. I assure you that there is…I mean he is the complete gentleman and there is nothing wrong. It is just that we have, well you might say, a prior acquaintance, and he…."

"Please, Miss Lizzie, there is no need. Even a blind man could see that you are more than a simple maid and that the purpose of your sojourn here goes beyond simple service. I trust in your pure heart, and if you and your young lawyer friend can but lift the cloud of misfortune from this family, I am content. I need know nothing more. Now I will take up the tea. When the bell is rung to escort Mr. Dawson out, I will direct him here, while I pack up more of Master Jeremy's things. It seems he must suffer being away from his home for at least one more night."

Annie watched with eyes blurred by tears as Wong picked up the loaded tea tray as if it weighed no more than a feather and disappeared up the stairs.

Barely twenty minutes passed before Nate was sitting at the kitchen table across from her. He looked tired, and she wondered at the toll all of this was taking on everyone.

"I just came from visiting Jeremy," said Nate. "Jackson's been questioning him all morning. I told his mother he looked well, but that was a lie. I tell you, Annie, he looked awful. Pale, eyes sort of bruised. Doubt if he slept any. Who could under the circumstances? I asked him, did he need to see a doctor? He said he was fine, but I don't know." Nate sat at the kitchen table across from Annie, shaking his head.

"Have the police charged him yet?" asked Annie.

"No, and they have forty-eight hours to hold him. You know, I think Jackson is a bit spooked by how Jeremy is behaving. He has continued to be very polite, none of his previous blustering. From what I could tell, he's remained very consistent in his story about what happened the night his father died and where he was last Sunday. He didn't even seem upset when Jackson sprung on him the evidence they found in his room--the bloody club, the money and investments, and the poison. He just acted bewildered!"

Annie broke in, "Of course he did. I told you, I searched those rooms on Tuesday, and I would swear nothing incriminating was there until someone put it there, probably after Jeremy left for the factory the next morning. I bet Wong could verify that as well."

"I know, but as I said before, I don't relish the thought of telling Chief Jackson that a respectable widow, posing as a servant, swears the evidence was planted. But if this thing does come to trial I may have to consider getting you and Wong to testify to that fact. I've got to tell you, though, Jeremy's response to the questions about the cyanide really flummoxed Jackson. First, Jackson thought he finally had won a confession from him this morning when Jeremy admitted that he knew that cyanide could be found in paint, and that he probably had some in his rooms. I wanted to stuff a handkerchief in his mouth when he came out with that statement, incriminating himself like that.

"But then, when Jackson pressed him further, asking if he had taken the vial of cyanide from the factory and if he had given it to his father, Jeremy just frowned and said, 'Vial, what vial?' He then proceeded to tell Jackson how Prussian blue comes in a tube, not in a jar. Something about not keeping oils in a jar, cause they'll get all gummy. Then Jeremy said, 'I don't think it would kill you unless you ate it. But father would never have fallen for that. It would turn the whisky blue! He wasn't blind, you know.'

"Hang it all, Annie, I thought Jackson would have apoplexy. Jeremy said he'd never heard of potassium cyanide, the white powder that is used in the furniture factory and was used to kill his father. What he did know all about was this special oil-based paint that he said contained...I think it was ferrous cyanide-I'm not sure about that, since that sounds like it would be rust colored. Anyway, I guess this kind of cyanide makes a special kind of blue paint. Jeremy went on for a good half hour about the usefulness of this color blue for painters...well, let's just say Jackson wasn't too pleased. In fact he said to me later that if Jeremy had gone on for one more minute, extolling the virtues of Prussian blue for seascapes, he was 'going to make him eat a tube of it, just to see if works the same as the potassium stuff!'

"He made light of it, but I think this particular interchange really shook him. You know, this case could be a real feather in Jackson's cap. Charges of patricide, missing money, poison, a double murder. As you know, it's already generating lots of press, which Jackson seems to like. But he could be ruined if he turns out to have made a mistake. I think he expected Jeremy to crumble after one night in a jail cell, and he hasn't. That's probably why I was able to get Jackson to postpone charging him until tomorrow. He wants to make dashed sure of his facts.

"It means at least another night in jail for Jeremy, but Jeremy said that was all right if it would help me look for evidence that would exonerate him. Actually he was much more concerned for his mother and aunt than he seemed to be for himself. I've got to admit, my estimation for him has gone up considerably."

"But what about Cartier?" Annie broke in impatiently. "Did you tell Jackson about her! Her note to the meat delivery boy, the fact that she could have been the author of the anonymous letter?"

"Yes, yes I did. And Jackson said they would look into it. See what the delivery boy has to say for himself. He also said they had already established that Cartier was where she said she was last Sunday, and that she was alone. I gather she and a gentleman are regular customers at the restaurant at Woodward's Gardens on Sunday afternoons, and that she is not a favorite with the staff. The general opinion seemed to be that she was rude. Evidently there was some bad feeling about an accusation she made about over charging. She does sound like a piece of work! Anyway, there had evidently been some rather spiteful comments passed between waiters this past Sunday when her gentleman friend didn't show up. Some speculation that she had been jilted, so they had clear memories that she was there, and alone."

"But, don't you see, this could prove that she could have had an accomplice, that...."

"Wait, Annie. I said Jackson would look into it, but you have got to realize that from his perspective, if Cartier is involved and she had an accomplice, it was probably Jeremy."

"But Cartier and Jeremy, that's ridiculous! Anyone who knew either one would...."

"Annie, calm down. If Jackson finds that Cartier has been corresponding with someone else, and I think this is likely since there would be no reason for her to pass notes to Jeremy through the meat delivery boy, this might help a lot. It would mean that it was less likely that Jeremy and Cartier are involved in this together, and it might provide an alternative suspect. But we just have to leave this to the police. Jackson assured me he would look into this today. He's no fool and the last thing he wants to do is wrongfully charge a wealthy young man like Jeremy of murder."

"But there must be something we can do, we can't just leave it to the police, not if they don't really believe in his innocence. Jeremy could die!" Annie paused, knowing that she was sounding frantic.

"Annie, I swear to you, I will do everything in my power to see that it doesn't come to that. It would make everything simpler if Cartier and an accomplice were guilty, with a straightforward motive of money; but, just in case her actions turn out to have a more innocent explanation, I think my time would be better spent looking further into other possible suspects. Samuels, for example. Maybe he is Cartier's mystery gentleman."

Annie cocked her head and said pensively, "Samuels? What makes you think that? I know that Miss Nancy seems convinced that somehow Mrs. Voss and Samuels are to blame for Matthew's death. I even overheard her accuse Mr. Samuels of wanting both Matthew's business and his wife, but I just don't know. It seems that he would have been better off financially with Matthew alive and buying him out of the business, unless he really did want Mrs. Voss to be a widow. He does appear very solicitous of her, and she is a beautiful woman. But then why implicate Jeremy? That would be the worst way to win Jeremy's mother."

Nate replied, "Well, what I started wondering is if Samuels really did have a financial motive. Remember that I said I thought Samuels wasn't being straight with me about the health of the furniture company when I talked to him last week? Well, it occurred to me that, if there had been anything improper about his business dealings, he might have been afraid this information would come out if Matthew Voss took over complete control of the company. That might give him a reason to kill Matthew. Anyway, before I joined my uncle at the jail with Jeremy this morning, I called on a couple of Voss's competitors. What I learned was damn…dashed interesting.

"Coleman Rawlings, you may have heard of him, he owns the Marin Furniture Company, he was quite surprised at some of the prices I quoted for the cost of lumber that Samuels had been paying over the last six months. He said Samuels had been paying nearly five cents more a board foot than Coleman had for the pine he got from Redwood City Lumber. Coleman actually said, 'Either Malcolm Samuels is losing his touch, or he's got a swindle going on.' Now he did go on to admit that Samuels could be trying to lock out his competitors by outbidding everyone else, but that was really a risky proposition in this kind of business climate."

"Or he could have been falsifying the books, buying the wood for the usual amount, telling Matthew the price had gone up and pocketing the rest," Annie stated with some surprise.

"Yes, that's what I thought. If we could prove that, it would certainly provide a clear motive that would interest Jackson; but there is still the problem of his alibi, and of course how he got in and out of the house that night. Anyway, I thought I might take the train down to Redwood City, which is where Samuels said he was the night Mr. Voss was killed, and look into that alibi."

Nate consulted his pocket watch and then rose from his seat, saying, "And now I really should go. I still have to stop by the police station to deliver Jeremy his clean things, and I would like to make the late afternoon train."

Annie scrambled to her feet and said, "Oh, of course. Thank you for taking the time to tell me how things stand. We are feeling so isolated here, and that makes everything seem more hopeless. You saw what it's like with the newspaper reporters. Is there anything that can be done about that? It is terribly stressful for Mrs. Voss and I am not sure how we are going to even get meat for tonight's dinner."

Annie knew her babbling reflected a reluctance to let Nate leave.

"I'll try. I'll ask Jackson to put some men on the house. Can't really keep them from the public road, but that should keep them off the property itself, give you all a little privacy." Nate paused, then he said, "Annie. Can I assume that you are still planning on going home tonight?" He raised his hand as if to forestall a response, although Annie had remained quiet. "I'm not telling you what to do. I just thought that it would be good to be able to consult with you about what I learned in Redwood City, and I wondered where I might best be able to get hold of you tonight when I returned."

Annie chose her words carefully, trying to match the calm tone Nate had used. "Yes, it is my intention to take my night off as promised tonight. I haven't decided about tomorrow. That will depend to a certain degree on whether or not either you or Jackson have discovered anything that might result in Jeremy's release."

Annie suddenly noticed that Wong stood at the bottom of the back stairs, holding a packed carpetbag, and she wondered how long he had been standing there. She walked around the table holding out her hand to Nate, saying "Thank you again for your time. Here's Wong with Master Jeremy's things. I hope your trip meets with success."

Nate started to say something, clearly thought better of it, and instead he took her hand in both of his and shook it firmly, looking straight into her eyes, and said, "I trust that you will keep yourself well. Until tonight then."

Annie watched Nate consult briefly with Wong about something, and then the two of them ascended the stairs where Wong was evidently going to let him out the front door. Annie found that she was holding her right hand to her cheek, as if to preserve the coil of warmth Nate had deposited there.

## Chapter Thirty-six:
## Thursday, late afternoon, August 16, 1879

Usually Nate found the swaying rhythm of a railroad car soporific, and he had hoped to nap during the little more than an hour it took to get to Redwood City from San Francisco. This afternoon the train seemed to be having the opposite effect. Each click, click of the wheels on the rails ratcheted his nerves tighter. He'd not gotten much sleep last night. He had stayed up late, going over the company books of Voss and Samuels once more, looking for something that might support his gut feeling that Samuels had something to do with the murders. After talking with Annie this afternoon, he was feeling more optimistic about at least finding some evidence that might convince the police they had the wrong man. While he was having trouble picturing the lady's maid, Cartier, as the mastermind of a double murder, Samuels he wasn't so sure about.

However, it was entirely possible that Samuels was indeed executing a new business strategy, and that he'd been doing it with Matthew's blessing. It would be very difficult to prove otherwise. Nate needed definitive proof one way or the other about Cartier or Samuels or needed to find some hint that there was another person outside the household involved so that he could weaken the case against Jeremy and get Annie to leave the Voss household for good.

Nate stared idly out at the passing countryside, thinking about Annie. Christ, she was infuriating. But smart. She argued like a man, never let up. It seemed to Nate that they'd been arguing constantly since the trip to the Cliff House. She could make him so mad. But then she'd say something funny, or smile that sweet sad smile, and the anger would just sort of slide away. She had this habit of tugging at his coat front when she was excited. Her hands were so small. He didn't know where he stood with her. Did she see him as just a friend, or something more? If that idiot dog hadn't barked last night, he knew he would have kissed her. She probably would have slapped him, and he'd have deserved it.

But the dog had barked, and then she'd gotten angry again and stood there, voice shaking, telling him that she believed that women were the same as men. Did she really expect him to accept that? But he did have to admire her integrity. He couldn't fault her there. Not many women, or men for that matter, could look honestly at the facts and accept responsibility. But it made her a damned awkward companion.

Shifting in his seat, Nate tapped impatiently against the window of the railroad car. Well, when he got back from Redwood City to-night, no matter what he'd found, he'd force her to leave the Voss house. If necessary he'd get the Steins and Mrs. O'Rourke to back him up. If Annie got angry with him, so be it. He had responsibili-ties as well. And whether she liked it or not, her safety was one of them. When the whole mess was over, she could go her own way if she wanted. That would probably be better for both of them, any-way. It was absurd even to think of developing a friendship with a woman, and he was in no financial position to think of anything else.

Nate's thoughts were interrupted by the hissing of the brakes as the train slid into the Redwood City station. Detective Jackson had given him a copy from the police report on Samuels' supposed whereabouts for the time of Matthew Voss's death. It was pretty straightforward, and now all Nate had to do was confirm that every-thing Samuels had said was true. Samuels said he had come to Redwood City on the morning train, Saturday, the day Voss was killed. According to the police report, he stayed at Baker's Hotel, did business, missed the five-thirty train back to San Francisco. He said he then telegraphed Matthew at their place of business, cancelling on dinner, and let him know he'd meet with him in the morning when he got back. Samuels had returned Sunday morning by train, even having the stub confirming this to give to the police when they asked him for it.

As soon as Nate got off the train, he went straight to Baker's Hotel. The owner, Fred Popper, was standing behind the desk in the hotel lobby, and he was delighted to be of service to Nate. Popper, a skinny bean-pole of a man, twirled his mustache and twinkled his eyes merrily when Nate asked him if he could confirm that Malcolm Samuels had been at the Hotel on Saturday, August fourth, and that he didn't leave until the next morning.

"Well, now, young feller, what's all this now? Some of those crooked San Francisco police wondering if they can pin old Matt Voss's death on his partner? Sorry to be disobliging. But Samuels was sure enough here and not in San Francisco when Voss died. Now I'm right sorry about Matt's death, particularly sad for his wife. Sweetest lady I ever met. But Matthew Voss could be a tight-fisted, stubborn old man, and, down the peninsula, we always felt that Samuels was the smart businessman of the two."

Nate mumbled something about how it might be hard to remember exactly when Samuels visited, if he visited that often, and Popper had laughed. "Maybe so, but you can bet when we heard the news of Voss's death, we all said to ourselves how lucky old Samuels was to be here with us, or for certain someone would be wondering if he'd have a hand in it. If Samuels was to be believed, those two seldom saw eye-to-eye. Anyway, I got proof for you if that's what you want."

At this point Popper pulled over the register and showed Nate the line where Samuels had signed in on August fourth and then signed out again on August fifth. "I remember he came in off the morning train, dropped by for breakfast, said he'd not be staying the night this time, since old Matt wanted him back for some important meeting. Samuels told me he thought his partner was getting senile, making a big mystery of everything. About eleven he left, I assume to make some calls. Then around three he came back, had some lunch and got tied up in a poker game. There's always one going on, most of the men who played with Samuels that afternoon are probably sitting in my dining room right this minute."

Nate interrupted. "Why did Samuels change his mind about going back to town? Was that unusual?"

Popper ran his hands through his thinning hair, slicking it back. "Well, it wasn't the first time he got involved in a game and forgot the time. Anyhow, I was bringing the boys some refreshment when Samuels pulled out his watch and swore a blue streak when he realized he'd missed the 5:30. That's the last train to San Francisco on Saturdays, you know. Anyway, he asked me to send a telegraph to Voss. Here, I'll show you."

At this point Popper went over to a cabinet and pulled out a large grey ledger, similar to the one for the hotel register. He rifled through the pages and turned the book around so Nate could see, pointing out an entry.

"See, I've got it all written down, date, time, address where it was sent, message itself. Just in case one goes astray or gets transmitted wrong, want to protect myself, you know. We're the only hotel around that has a telegraph operator on call 24 hours a day. I can tell you it's a great service to our guests."

Nate looked at the entry, which confirmed everything. This didn't really surprise Nate, since he had seen the notation in Matthew's own business diary of the cancelled and rescheduled meeting. But before he went in to interrogate the card players, he thought he'd better pin down the information about when Samuels had departed the hotel.

Nate gave the hotelkeeper a warm smile and said, "Thank you, Mr. Popper, you have been more than helpful. Could you just please tell me what you know of Samuels' movements after he finished his poker game and before he left for San Francisco the next morning?"

"Well, now, I'm not right sure. I know the card game broke up pretty soon after. Many of the men live outside of town and have to get home for supper. But I do know that he was in my dining room by seven the next morning. If I rightfully remember, he ate a sight more than usual. He's a man who watches his weight, he does. Hard not to overdo it when you're on the road a good deal, I can tell you. He had steak and a large stack of flapjacks. I can recommend the food we serve at Baker's, if you'd like some supper. We got a damn fine cook."

Nate responded that he was hoping to get back on the early 8:30 train that made the trip to San Francisco on weeknights, but that he'd be sure to try the steak before he left. And he had to admit later that the steak at Bakers was good; it was just too bad he hadn't been able to eat in peace. He had asked Popper to send any of the men who'd played poker with Samuels over his way, and by the time he had eaten his dessert he'd had his back slapped by no fewer than six men, all of whom had very sharp memories of Samuels' last visit. It appears that Popper's hotel was the favorite gathering place for both the local businessmen and those from out of town. There had been only one suspicious circumstance in all their information.

None of the men Nate talked to had seen Samuels between seven, Saturday evening, when the poker game broke up, and seven the next morning, when Samuels had come down to breakfast. Some of them remembered that Samuels had something planned for the evening, some vague memory of him hinting at a late night ahead of him, drinking with some old pal from the gold rush days. But nobody was very clear on it; they didn't know if it was somebody at the hotel, or even if the person was in town.

Nate didn't know what to do. On the surface, Samuels appeared to have been exactly where he was supposed to be, in Redwood City, twenty miles away from where Matthew was killed. Yet Nate hadn't found anybody who had actually seen him at the crucial times, since the police were putting the time of Matthew's death between at 11 p.m. and 3 a.m. There was a slight possibility he could have ridden back to San Francisco and been back in time for breakfast the next morning, but that would mean that somehow he had to get a horse. So the first thing to do was to see if he could rule out Samuels using any of the stables in town. The town wasn't all that big, it shouldn't take very long, and he still might be able to make the eight-thirty back to the city that night.

Nate began a round of visits to the local stables. After the second stable, which had been filled, as had the one before, with hostlers who were either drinking or poker playing buddies of Samuels, Nate was ready to give it up. Although nobody remembered seeing Samuels two weeks ago, everyone had a story to tell about him. If Nate had to hear one more off-color story or salacious joke that Samuels had told, he thought he'd get ill. Nate really had begun to dislike Samuels, but, to be fair, that wasn't proof that the man was a murderer.

Finally, with only twenty minutes to train departure, Nate hit pay dirt at the third stable. This one was near the edge of town, and what he learned there caused Nate for the first time to take the idea of Samuels as Voss's murderer seriously. It was a small stable, only seven stalls, and the owner, Jasper Steckle, was not a good friend of Samuels. Actually, it turned out that Jasper was the Grand Knight of the local Sons of Temperance and, while he remembered Samuels as clearly as everybody else, his memory was due to both a general dislike of all hard-drinking businessmen and a more specific grievance against Samuels. Jasper Steckle said that Samuels had mistreated the horse he had rented Saturday before last, the night that Matthew Voss died, and that he, Jasper Steckle, planned on filing a suit for damages.

"Durned fool man said Jenny was lame when he took her out, but she weren't. She was lame when he brought her in, and winded like I never seen before. He'd whipped her too. She's a gentle one, no need to whip her. Man treats an animal like that ought to be horsewhipped himself. It's not the money I'm after. She'll be all right if I give her enough rest. But it's the principle."

*Wait until Annie hears this*, thought Nate. Here was a possible hole in Samuels' alibi. He had been out on horseback on Saturday night, and he had ridden hard. It would take six to eight hours to get to San Francisco and back by horse, but Samuels could have done it. According to Jasper, he'd rented the horse at seven-thirty that night and had not brought her back until six-thirty the next morning. Nearly twelve hours! Theoretically he could have been in San Francisco between ten at night and two the next morning, in time to commit a murder and still get back to Redwood City in time for breakfast.

Jasper continued, "He had some tall tale about riding over inland to a friend's ranch to visit. The Johnsons, they have a spread about an hour west of here. Then said when he got there he discovered they were down country for roundup and the ranch was empty. So he rode back after getting a few hours sleep in the barn. He looked like hell, but I don't think it was from sleeping in a barn; more'n likely he'd spent it with his head in a bottle, and that's why he'd mistreated Jenny."

*Unless he'd spent it riding to San Francisco to murder his partner*, thought Nate.

## Chapter Thirty-seven:
## Friday morning, August 17, 1879

The old scarred kitchen table was covered with fourteen oil lamps, standing in neat rows as if soldiers on parade. Each base had been cleaned and refilled, with the silver burners polished to gleaming brightness, each wick had been trimmed or replaced and was standing at attention, and the glass chimneys had been thoroughly scrubbed with soda and water so that not a speck of soot marred their surfaces. Annie sat slumped in a chair looking at these neat rows. It had taken two hours of hard work to achieve this martial scene of perfection, and these were only the lamps from the first floor. She still had two more floors of lamps to clean, and, even if she put off cleaning the rest of the lamps in the house, she still had to return the lamps to their proper places before lunch. Which meant going up and down the back stairs fourteen times, since she could only carry one lamp at a time, filled as they were to the brim with oil.

But first she had to clean up herself. She held up her hands for inspection, and noted with little surprise that they were covered in greasy black splotches and that her fingernails were etched in black. Without thinking, she began to tuck in a stray curl of hair that had escaped and dangled over her right eye, when she snatched back the offending hand.

With a short laugh that threatened to disintegrate into a sob, Annie smoothed back her hair with both hands. *What difference does it* make? I'm sure that my face and hair are already polluted by now. I* *must look like a chimney sweep. What I wouldn't give for a bath!* Annie shifted forward to prop her head in those grimy hands, lean- ing her elbows on the table and causing her army of lamps to clink and rattle, as if preparing to march. *If only they could march them-* *selves right up the stairs to take up their duties throughout the* *house.*

In this new position, Annie was forced to notice a sour smell that emanated from her skin and mingled with the sweeter smell of the oil. She had put on her last clean chemise and drawers yesterday, thinking that she would be going home last night. But she hadn't gone home, despite her promise to Nate. Mrs. Voss had asked Annie as she cleared the dinner dishes if she would postpone her night out again, with the promise that she could have tonight off, and half of Saturday as well.

Annie had nodded yes, mentally defending herself to Nate. *What* *else could I have said to Mrs. Voss? No, I can't stay and help out,* *despite the fact that you have learned today that your son may be* *arrested for murdering your husband, despite the fact that you face* *a night alone in this house with no one but your sister-in-law, who* *hates you, and a lady's maid who may be the actual killer?*

She had sent another note with Wong, again informing Beatrice that she would be staying another night, again hoping that Nate would get the message as well. As a result, here she was, her fifth day as a servant, and she wasn't sure that her black jersey waist and skirt would ever come clean of the accumulations of carbolic acid, bluing, coal dust, and kitchen grease. Before she had to serve lunch she would have to see if the under things she had washed in the morning were dry yet, and switch back to her black wool dress that she had hung out to air. But she didn't think that anything but a bath would really remedy the way she smelled or felt. And a bath was a good eleven hours away, since she didn't think she would be able to get away before nine tonight. *Saints above, I hope I didn't smell this way yesterday afternoon when Nate was sitting across from me. Or the night before on the garden bench!* Annie shuddered.

She didn't know how Wong kept looking so clean, given all the work he did. And, Cartier, it was hard to imagine her with dirty hands or soiled clothes, although she must have done some harder domestic work at some time. For the hundredth time Annie wondered about Cartier's background. Did she come from a wealthy family fallen on hard times, which might explain her attitude of superiority. *Where was Cartier anyway?* The lady's maid had unexpectedly volunteered to do the marketing, but she should have been back by now. Annie hoped some newspaper reporter hadn't stopped her. This morning the presence of the patrolman that Nate had requested had the newsmen away from the front of the house. Or maybe they had simply lost interest. The *Chronicle* had been full of some awful carriage accident that had happened in Golden Gate Park.

Annie looked at the clock on the wall and realized with a start that Cartier had been gone for nearly three hours. With sudden elation, Annie realized the best explanation for Cartier's extended absence would be that she had fled the house, perhaps the city. *This was as good as an admission of guilt!*

Energized by the thought that Cartier's disappearance would shift the attention of the police away from Jeremy, Annie began the long process of returning the lamps to their allotted places throughout the first floor. As she did so, she tried to figure out the best way to alert the police. She decided that if Cartier still hadn't returned by lunchtime that she would tell Mrs. Voss; she could express concern about Cartier's safety and suggest the police should be notified. It would be even better if Nate stopped by, because she knew he would take Cartier's disappearance seriously. She had been rather expecting that he would show up this morning, if only to find out why she hadn't gone home as planned last night. She couldn't help wonder what he had found out about Samuels. Whatever it was, it seemed irrelevant now, unless it turned out Samuels was Cartier's mysterious gentleman friend.

Much to Annie's disappointment, Nate didn't come, and she didn't have a chance to talk to Mrs. Voss at lunch, since Miss Nancy had taken one look at Annie's smut-covered person and decided that Wong should do the serving at this meal. While Wong had informed his mistress that Cartier had not returned from her errands, it did not appear that Mrs. Voss had done anything about this information. So it was with some anticipation that Annie entered Mrs. Voss's sitting room mid-afternoon with the afternoon tea. Here was her chance to convince Mrs. Voss that she needed to inform the police about her missing lady's maid. She had just gotten up the nerve to say something, when there was a discreet knock at the door and Wong came in and handed Mrs. Voss an envelop, saying that there was a gentleman downstairs who had asked to speak with her.

"Oh, Wong, you don't think it is one of those prying newspaper men do you?" Mrs. Voss asked anxiously, taking the envelop from him while simultaneously dropping her embroidery scissors.

As Annie watched Mrs. Voss open the envelop, she thought to herself that the woman had aged years in the two days since her son had been lead off by the police. And Miss Nancy was no better off, becoming, if possible, even grayer than before, slipping around corners, clutching a Bible that appeared to give her no solace. When Jeremy had been taken away, it was as if the flame that burned within her had been snuffed out. Only the occasional gleam of fury in her sunken eyes revealed that those embers still glowed. Annie had thought that the threat to Jeremy would unite these two women, if only in a temporary truce; but Miss Nancy's insistence that she have breakfast and lunch in her room separately from her sister-in-law suggested that even the polite fiction of a family had dissolved with Jeremy's absence.

A sharp exclamation from Mrs. Voss caused Annie to look up from the tea she was pouring, spilling some of the tea into the saucer.

"Oh, my! Yes, Wong, do bring Mr. Wellsnap up." Mrs. Voss continued to read the letter, shaking her head and emitting periodic little out bursts of "My heavens."

As she mopped up the spilled tea, Annie's curiosity was thoroughly aroused. *Who could this mysterious visitor be*? But the man Wong ushered into the sitting room turned out to be one of the least mysterious looking men Annie had ever encountered. Mr. Wellsnap appeared to be in his mid-thirties, although his round, clean-shaven face, rosy moist lips, baby-fine blonde curls, and soft soprano voice may have caused Annie to underestimate his age. Standing uneasily just inside the sitting room door, his hands fidgeting behind his back, Mr. Wellsnap looked for all the world like a young boy trying to avoid being punished for some prank. A young *well-to-do* boy, since his dark navy suit, Annie could see, was of a soft light wool, probably an expensive cashmere, and was finely tailored to fit his short, very round frame. The gold that gleamed on his pudgy fingers, and at his cuffs and collar, completed the impression of wealth.

This young man bowed deeply and then said, "Mrs. Voss, I would like to introduce myself. I am Ambrose Wellsnap, and I apologize for intruding upon you in your time of grief. But I knew you would be worrying about Bertha, that is my fiancé, Miss Cartier, and so I had to come. I laid out all the bare particulars in the note, which I see you have in your hand, just in case you were not able to see me; I am most gratified that you have permitted me to apologize to you in person. I am afraid that I have imposed on you egregiously, by engaging in a clandestine courtship of Bertha. I know that there is a bond between a lady and her maid, which should not permit the withholding of secrets. And I know that my own dear mama would have found it unbearable to think that her Theresa had embarked upon an engagement without her blessing. I want to ensure you that I shoulder all blame because my lovely Bertha would never have done so if I had not imposed upon her the strictest silence. Please say you will forgive me?"

At this point Mr. Wellsnap had whipped out a tasteful pale blue silk handkerchief and mopped his slightly moist brow, giving Mrs. Voss a chance to speak.

"Dear Mr. Wellsnap, please calm yourself, I am sure there is nothing to forgive. Please sit down, and let Lizzie pour you a cup of tea. Am I to understand from your note that you are a neighbor, and that you and Miss Cartier met through a mutual interest in gardening?"

Annie had thought that Mrs. Voss sounded just a wee bit incredulous at that point, but she herself had been willing to believe anything was possible now that she knew the first name of the imperious lady's maid was *Bertha.*

As Annie poured and served him tea, Mr. Wellsnap went on to tell a tale of heart-felt sentimentality. How Cartier, passing by his house, which was just two blocks down Geary and where he lived with his *darling mama,* had complimented him on the roses he was tending, at first mistaking him for the gardener since he was dressed for this task in his very oldest clothes. How this first conversation had led to others, then an invitation to walk in Woodward's Gardens, and eventually to love. How Mr. Wellsnap had wrestled with the difficulty of how to acquaint his delicate mother with the news that her devoted son had found another woman with whom he wished to share his life, while convincing her that this had not lessened his affection for her.

Then there had been the terrible misunderstandings, when his mother, upon learning of his *beloved Bertha,* had suffered a shocking collapse. This was really all his own fault, he assured Mrs. Voss, because he had been so desirous of being able to offer his *beloved* a haven from the terrible tragedies that had visited the Voss household that he might have been a tad too forceful with his mother. The result had been that he had been prevented from making his usual rendezvous at the Gardens this past Sunday and his poor *beloved Bertha* had thought he abandoned her. This in turn had lead to an unfortunate lovers quarrel on Tuesday evening. But all had been explained and forgiven this morning when he accosted his *beloved* as she passed his house on the way to do the marketing. And now the engagement was public and he was here at the home of his *beloved's* esteemed employer to gather her things and install her in his own home, pending their marriage, which would occur as soon as his *dearest mama's* health permitted.

Mr. Wellsnap concluded his tale by saying, "My dear Mrs. Voss, I assure you that Miss Cartier had wanted to return and tell you about these events herself, but I insisted that my *beloved* be spared the heartache of saying good bye in person to the mistress she loves so. I can only hope that you can forgive me for stealing your precious maid away."

Mrs. Voss, who had remained silent and unnaturally still during this recitation, stood up and moved with her usual grace towards Mr. Wellsnap, her hand out stretched, and said, "Oh dear Mr. Wellsnap, what wonderful news for Miss Cartier. Of course I forgive both of you, but please let Miss Cartier know that I would love to be able to call on her once everything is settled."

*I only hope that I can be so forgiving*, Annie thought, as she moved to pick up the handkerchief that Mrs. Voss had dropped, *since you have blown apart my theory that your beloved was behind the murders of Matthew and Nellie.*

## Chapter Thirty-eight:
## Friday morning, August 17, 1879

Nate would have enjoyed this chance to be on horseback again, but as he made the ride east to find the Johnson ranch, which was located in the San Bruno foothills, he couldn't shake the feeling that he was wasting precious time. Yesterday evening, after speaking with the irate stable owner Jasper Steckle, he felt obliged to look further into Malcolm's alibi. While the story that Samuels had given Steckle about the deserted ranch had a ring of truth to it, he would still have to check it out. This had meant he had to stay in Redwood City over night, which bothered him. He had really hoped that he would be able to see Annie at her home and convince her not to return to the Voss household this morning. But he knew that if he went back with the story about Samuels sleeping in the Johnsons' barn, but no hard proof, she'd insist on doing something rash, like asking Samuels himself. As soon as he got back to the Baker Hotel, he'd telegraphed his Uncle Frank to find some diplomatic way to ask Samuels what he had actually been doing Saturday night.

After sending off his telegram, Nate had made a brief stop at the Hotel bar and retired early, eager for a good night's sleep. Unfortunately, about eleven, soon after he'd dropped off to sleep, there had been a knock on his room door. The Baker Hotel's twenty-four hour telegraph service was in top form. Popper stood at the door with a telegram from Nate's uncle, who had evidently gotten right on Nate's request. It read as follows.

SAMUELS RODE TO JOHNSON RANCH STOP JOHNSONS AWAY STOP SPENT NIGHT IN BARN DRINKING WITH OLD SOUSE NAMED POCO STOP POCO MAY NOT REMEMBER VERY WELL STOP FRANK

Nate had groaned and spent the next hour or so wrestling with the problem of what to do if an old drunk named Poco was able to provide an alibi for Samuels. If Samuels was the murderer, he was a God-damned clever one. He could have ridden out to the ranch first, knowing no one would be there that time of year but Poco. Anyone with a slightest knowledge of ranching would know this was round-up time. He could have then given the old man a bottle of whiskey and snuck off as soon as Poco had begun to nod. If questioned, the old man would probably swear that Samuels had been with him all night. Meanwhile, Samuels could have ridden on to San Francisco and the whole detour would only add an hour or so to the trip. Not impossible.

It wasn't a perfect alibi; might even be a weak one if you ever got Poco on the stand, but it was a hell of lot better than Jeremy's nonexistent one. Of course, there was also the problem of explaining how Samuels could have gotten into and out of the locked house. He might have gotten Matthew to open up for him, but how did he get out of the house, leaving the doors locked behind him, without a key? And everyone swore the doors were locked and the keys all accounted for in the morning. This is another reason the police were so convinced Jeremy must be the murderer. He had a key. Nate had finally fallen asleep some time past one o'clock in the morning and consequently had woken up much later than he'd intended.

His late start meant that he would be lucky to make it back to Redwood City by noon and then he still had to catch the train to San Francisco. While he knew his uncle was there to handle things if Jackson decided to go ahead and charge Jeremy, he felt bad about being gone this long, and he really minded not having made his promised meeting with Annie last night. As his horse came over the crest of the last hill, Nate sighed with relief to see that the Johnson ranch was far from deserted. The corrals were half-filled with cattle, smoke rose from the main house, and the clang, clang of metal came from the barn, all suggesting that the Johnsons were definitely at home and maybe he would be able to get some definitive answers.

Nate had grown up on a ranch, and it wasn't difficult to see that this was a place in the midst of fall round-up. A tall young man with the characteristic bowed legs of someone who was more used to riding than walking strolled over to where Nate was tying up his horse. Nate tipped his hat, stated his name, made a few intelligent comments on the herd in the corral in front of him, and then he asked if he could speak to Mr. Johnson or whoever was in charge. The young man smiled and tossed his head in the direction of the main house.

"Mr. Johnson's my Pa. He's in the house; reckon you can hear him from here, swearing up a storm. Ma will be right glad for some company. Pa's horse slipped out from under him up country and bust up his leg. He's so ornery we practically had to rope and tie him to get him back home. Now he's so fidgety being tied to the house that he's ready to bite nails."

Within a few moments of making the acquaintance of Mr. and Mrs. Johnson, Nate felt completely at ease. Here were people he could understand. Knowing how people like the Johnsons worked, he didn't try and rush them, but let the conversation meander around the weather, price of hides, the recent hay crop, and the unfair railroad rates before he got to the point. Then, after he felt that he had sufficiently established his credentials, not as a lawyer, but as a rancher's son, Nate brought up the question of Malcolm Samuels.

"Now Ma'am, Sir, I'd sure like to tarry longer, but I need to head on back to Redwood City soon to catch the afternoon train. So if you don't mind, I'd like to ask a few questions about the last time your friend, Malcolm Samuels, visited here. As I told you, I represent the

estate of his late business partner, Matthew Voss. And, not to put a
too fine point on it, there are some problems. The police have decided that there are some suspicious circumstances surrounding Mr.
Voss's death, and they have taken into their heads that his son might
be involved. Now you can imagine the distress this has caused Mrs.
Voss. Poor woman, widowed like that unexpectedly, and now to
have her only son pulled in by the police for questioning."

Here Mrs. Johnson expressed her heartfelt sympathy and Mr.
Johnson frowned. Nate thought to himself that this couple would be
particularly sensitive to the plight of Matthew's widow. Mr. Johnson's accident had been very humorously recounted, but Nate knew
that it had been only been luck that was Johnson's leg and not his
neck that had been broken. Not wanting to distress them further, he
continued; hoping to wrap things up quickly now that he'd gotten to
the issue at hand.

"Mrs. Voss has asked me to look into things, just make sure the
police have all the facts. That is why I'm attempting to track down
the whereabouts of everyone on the night Mr. Voss died, Saturday,
August fourth. Now, Mr. Samuels said that he stayed here that Saturday night, drinking with one of your ranch hands, Poco, and I'd
wondered if you could ask Poco, if he is around, to step in and confirm this for me."

Nate caught a startled look between the Johnsons that sent a chill
up his spine. Mr. Johnson moved restlessly in his chair, rubbing his
thigh above the splinted leg, as if it ached. But when he began to
speak his tone was light, although Nate thought the jocularity a bit
forced.

"Well now, Mr. Dawson, it seems to me that old Malcolm must
have gotten his dates mixed. I've told him time and again, he'd better
watch it. If he keeps up with that hard living, he'll turn out to be as
forgetful as old Poco. Samuels makes it down to Redwood City on
business at least once a month. He knows that we're usually gone all

of August, and he's nice enough to stop by and check on Poco for us; although I wish he wouldn't feel the need to bring Poco his little gifts. I have a lot of affection for that old man, and he'll live a lot longer if he gets only his bottle of beer every night. The binges aren't good for him. When we got back to the ranch this time, Poco said Samuels had been by to visit the week before and they'd had a good old time. Frankly, I'm surprised Poco remembered that Malcolm was here at all, and I wouldn't be surprised if Malcolm might be a bit hazy about it all if he kept Poco company. That was probably what happened."

Nate interrupted. "You're saying Malcolm did come to visit Poco, but not on the Saturday night that Matthew Voss died?"

"Not if Voss died on August fourth. That was a night I won't forget because that was the night my wife and sons brought back half the herd, with me laid up in the wagon as useless as a broken-down horse. My sons spent all night getting the herd settled, with a very sober Poco's help, and we didn't see hide nor hair of Malcolm Samuels all that night. And you can be damn sure there's nothing wrong with my memory."

# Chapter Thirty-nine:
## Friday evening, August 17, 1879

"Well, girl, don't leave me standing on the doorstep for all the yahoos out here to stare at, let me in."

Annie moved to the side, letting Malcolm Samuels into the front hallway. She had just finished cleaning herself up for dinner and had been on her way down to the kitchen to help Wong when the front door bell rang.

Handing his hat, walking stick, and light overcoat to Annie and turning to go into the front parlor, Samuels said heartily, "Good girl. I'll show myself in. Run upstairs and announce me to Mrs. Voss, and then get me a whiskey. You better tell Wong to prepare for an extra place at the table."

Annie found herself bristling at Samuels' highhanded tone. *But to be fair, he's probably always acted this way, as the oldest family friend,* Annie cautioned herself. *I'm going to have to be very careful not to see nefarious meanings in ordinary events. I can't afford to make another mistake like I did with Cartier and find evidence of wrong doing on Samuels' part just because I want somebody else to blame besides Jeremy.*

Ten minutes later, Annie entered the front parlor with a tray bearing a glass, whiskey bottle, and chips of ice. Wong, who was simultaneously stirring a thin consommé, deboning some trout, and washing vegetables, had merely nodded when Annie told him Samuels appeared to be staying for dinner. He hadn't raised any objections when she offered to take Samuels a drink, just pointed to the right bottle and mentioned that Mr. Samuels preferred his drinks with ice.

Mrs. Voss had preceded her and was sitting in a chair next to the fireplace, which as yet remained unlit, testament to the lingering heat of the day and the fact that the windows in the room had remained closed. She had brought her embroidery with her, but this lay unattended while she looked intently at Samuels, who was standing by one of the front bay windows, looking out through a slit in the curtains and talking over his shoulder.

"No, I do not think it wise for you to visit Jeremy tomorrow. It is my understanding that, now that they have charged him, he will be arraigned tomorrow. And, no, I don't think you should be at the arraignment. Is that what that young lawyer fella, Nate Dawson, suggested? Because I have to tell you, I wouldn't take advice from a boy like him. His uncle's all right for business matters, but that nephew, I don't care for him. He hasn't much experience and he strikes me as a bit underhanded. Frankly, I think we should consider getting a lawyer with more trial experience, the Dawson firm just isn't...Girl, put the tray down over there, but first, give me the glass." Samuels took the glass from Annie's hand, giving her one of his quick smiles.

"Malcolm, her name's Lizzie." Mrs. Voss said. "Thank you Lizzie, if you would now kindly let Miss Nancy know that we would appreciate her company in the parlor. And then inform Wong that Mr. Samuels will be staying for dinner. Oh, and could you please bring Miss Nancy and me a cup of tea? Would you like anything to eat, Malcolm? I am afraid that dinner will be delayed." Mrs. Voss smiled at Annie as she delivered her orders.

"No, had a late lunch, I'm fine. As I was saying, I've a good man in mind; he's done lots of criminal defense work. I don't think you should bury your head in the sand, Amelia, Jeremy's in a tough spot. I'll...."

Annie could no longer hear Samuels as she made her way down the hall, but she carefully examined the implications of what he had been saying as she went downstairs to the kitchen. Jackson must have finally arrested Jeremy! She wondered why Nate or his uncle didn't come by to inform Mrs. Voss, and why Samuels was trying to steer Mrs. Voss to a different lawyer. She supposed that Nate might seem inexperienced to an older businessman like Samuels, and Annie had no way to really know how good he would be if it came to mounting a defense for Jeremy. On the other hand, if Samuels was the murderer then maybe he was simply trying to get Mrs. Voss to rely on someone else, someone who he could better influence.

It was nearly twenty minutes later that Annie finally made it back to the parlor with the tea, and it appeared that Miss Nancy had just come down, since she was still standing when Annie arrived. She had scowled and muttered when Annie had conveyed Mrs. Voss's invitation, but Annie was certain that the older women wouldn't pass up on the chance to provide disapproving chaperonage for her sister-in-law and Samuels.

Mrs. Voss had risen, dropping her embroidery frame, a few of the bright blue and green threads clinging to the dull black silk of her underskirt. "Please, dear sister, won't you sit down. Dinner will be delayed and I've asked Lizzie...." Mrs. Voss suddenly noticed Annie as Miss Nancy moved. "Oh there you are, Lizzie, please come in and put that heavy tray down." Turning back to Miss Nancy, she continued. "Samuels has been to see Jeremy this morning. He said that they only permitted him a few minutes with our dear boy, and then not alone. But...."

Samuels interrupted her, "That damned interfering detective, Jackson, said that only Jeremy's lawyers and family members could see him in private. That's another example of Frank Hobbes and his wet-behind-the-ears nephew not doing right by Jeremy. They should've seen to it that I was granted permission to see him.

Crommer, the man I spoke to you about, Amelia, he would've gotten me in."

Mrs. Voss fluttered over to the tea tray, where Annie had begun to pour the tea into two cups. Taking one cup she turned and handed it to Miss Nancy saying, "Please, do sit down. I thought that you would want to hear from Malcolm what Jeremy said when he saw him this morning, and then I thought that we might discuss what we should be doing to help him. Malcolm, how did Jeremy look? Do you think he is eating enough? Did the Chief Detective say whether or not Jeremy will be able to come home tomorrow?"

Mrs. Voss took a cup and returned to the chair she had vacated, absent-mindedly picking at the threads on her skirt, while Miss Nancy chose to remain standing by the door.

Samuels tossed off the last whiskey in his glass and said with some irritation, "Amelia, I told you, Jeremy looked terrible, I don't care what Dawson said yesterday."

At this point Samuels moved over to where Mrs. Voss was sitting, softening his tone. "Listen, Amelia, I love the boy like he was my own, but the evidence is so strong, it's shaken me. To make things worse, its quite possible the judge might make the bail so steep that I'm not sure we could raise the necessary amount. It might be better to conserve what little resources you have to help pay for his defense." Pulling a chair next to Mrs. Voss Samuels leaned forward and took her hands in his, saying, "Dearest Amelia, you need to prepare yourself. I'm not saying give up. We will fight this thing together, the two of us. But ignoring the truth isn't going to help Jeremy, and you must protect yourself. You're not strong, and you need to...."

Miss Nancy let out a noise halfway between a growl and a snort, and then said. "You two make me sick. I...."

"Oh dear, I think I've lost my embroidery!" Mrs. Voss exclaimed, standing up suddenly, which forced Samuels back in his

chair. She turned and patted the chair cushions, muttering disjointedly, "Was I sitting on it? No, not here. Then wherever could it be? I
live in fear that someone will impale themselves on one of my needles. Oh, Lizzie, you've found it, clever girl."

Annie had to admire the way Mrs. Voss had defused what looked
to be a nasty fight between her sister-in-law and Samuels, but she
noticed that Mrs. Voss's hand was shaking as she took the piece of
embroidery from Annie.

Mrs. Voss continued to fidget around her chair, supposedly looking for the needle that Annie had clearly seen stuck in the material,
until Malcolm Samuels finally made a sound of disgust and got up
and went and poured himself another drink.

"Oh, there, I've found it," Mrs. Voss exclaimed and then said,
"Lizzie, we are fine here, but I suspect that Wong could use some
help in the kitchen," which gave Annie no choice but to leave the
three occupants to their own devices.

Half an hour later, when Annie served the first soup course, it appeared that little conversational progress had been made. Miss
Nancy sat rigidly at attention, evidently trying to test the accuracy of
the old saying "If looks could kill." Samuels was still trying to convince Mrs. Voss of the necessity of finding another lawyer and hinting that the house might have to be sold in order to raise the necessary defense funds.

By the main course a new topic had been found, the surprising
news about Cartier and her beau. Samuels evidently found the story
of Mr. Wellsnap extremely amusing.

"Wellsnap's the name you say? And you say he appears to be
well to-do? Wellsnap? Nancy, wasn't there a Wellsnap back in the
fifties? Made his pile selling shovels to the miners if my memory
serves me. Old man probably dead and gone by now, wasn't any
spring chicken back then. Well, if I'm right, your fancy maid's done
a good sight better for herself than she deserves. Sour face and nasty

tongue she had on her. I hope for Wellsnap's sake that marriage will sweeten her up a bit."

"Malcolm, there is no need to denigrate Miss Cartier in that fashion. She's had a very hard life, and I am delighted she has contracted an advantageous marriage. Mr. Wellsnap seemed a very kind and sensitive man."

"Oh Amelia, stop talking such tripe," Miss Nancy snapped. "She's fooled some idiot into thinking that he's some kind of hero rescuing a damsel in distress, and Malcolm's just angry because the one time he tried to pinch her bottom she slapped him silly."

Annie nearly dropped the platter of trout she was serving, which would have been a shame after all the work Wong had put into it. But this interchange did lighten her mood considerably.

## Chapter Forty

After dinner was over, Annie scrubbed at a pale pink spot that stained the scarred and pitted top of the kitchen table. It had been blood red; at least she had made that much progress. But it didn't look as if the stain would ever completely vanish. There had been beets with dinner, and she had clumsily permitted some of the juice to spill when she had been transferring them from the pan to the serving dish. Wong and she had already washed up the pots and most of the dinnerware, but they were waiting for dessert to be over so she could finish clearing off the table and ask to be dismissed for the night. Finally, she was going to get her promised maid's night out, and she could barely wait to escape from the house.

Off and on during the day, Annie had found herself thinking about what the various members of her own household might be doing. In the morning she imagined the Misses Moffet having their morning tea, sitting in their matching chairs next to the parlor window, stitching intricate and precise seams. At mid-day, she thought of Lucy Pringle, eating one of Beatrice's substantial lunches because she claimed that the high-priced food at the restaurant where she worked was too rich for her stomach. In the afternoon she saw Barbara Hewitt sitting on the front porch, trying to grade high school essays while keeping an eye on her son Jamie, who would be playing with his new dog. Now, she yearned to be walking in her kitchen door, to see Beatrice making up dough to rise all night for morning sweet rolls, Kathleen, sweeping the back steps, and Mrs. Stein, sitting in the kitchen rocker, knitting and laughing over the antics of the kitchen cat.

Annie longed so to be with them, longed for her regular days dispensing advice as Sibyl. Heaven knew how Sibyl's Friday clients would react to having been turned away once again, but that was something she just couldn't deal with now. Just as she couldn't face the thought that she still had not figured out how to raise the funds to pay Driscoll without losing her home. What she had to concentrate on was finding some solution to the mystery surrounding Matthew's death that didn't result in his son being hung for murder and his wife and sister left penniless. Maybe her earlier speculation that Nellie had been in league with some confidence man, who then killed her, was the right angle to pursue. There was that strange man who was hanging around the back gate last Friday. She had forgotten all about him! She wasn't sure she had even told Nate. He had asked for Jeremy, but maybe the man came out with Jeremy's name as a blind; he had really been loitering around to see if Nellie was still working at the house. If she had been, that was her night out, and he might have been trying to talk to her, or even murder her in the back alley! Now that she thought about how the man had loomed over her and then just vanished, Annie was struck by how sinister he had seemed. She couldn't wait to tell Nate.

Annie's thoughts then shifted to Samuels. What if Nate was right, and he was the murderer? From the moment Samuels had entered the house this afternoon he had rubbed Annie the wrong way. He was still charming, but she was no longer feeling quite as charmed. Maybe it was just that he had said such cutting things about Nate. For once she found herself in sympathy with Miss Nancy, who, no matter what her youthful feelings for him had been, now clearly despised Samuels. *But did that make him a murderer?* If Nate was able to find proof that Samuels had been embezzling money that would cinch it in Annie's mind. But would it be enough to convince the police? Probably not as long as Samuels had an alibi and there was no proof that he had any way of getting into or out of the house the night of Matthew's death. But that's what made Nellie's murder so significant. If she had found a way in and out of the house, then that would explain why Matthew's murderer had to kill her.

What if Nellie's gentleman admirer *was* Samuels? Actually, if the *murderer* were Samuels, this would explain something that had bothered Annie when she cast Cartier and some unknown lover of hers as the villains. Even if Cartier had been able to let her accomplice into the house the night Matthew died, how would a stranger get Matthew to sit down and have a drink with him? But if the murderer were Samuels, he could have sent a second telegram, this one saying that he would be by the house late to discuss Matthew's plans. Matthew could have let him in, they would have had a drink; Samuels could have destroyed the telegram. *No, too complicated.* When she thought more about it, Annie could see that all Samuels would have had to do was knock on the front door or study window, make some joke about getting back to town late and not wanting to wake the whole house, and Matthew would have let him in and one of the first things he would probably do is pour each of them a drink. But that still left the problem of how Samuels, without an accomplice like Cartier, could have let himself out of the house leaving all the keys in place and doors locked.

Annie sighed. Maybe Samuels had helped Nellie get a duplicate key made so that she could get into the house on her mornings out, and he had gotten one made for himself at the same time! After Matthew's murder, Nellie could have attempted to black mail him and got killed for her efforts. Nate might know how to go about finding out if the keys had been duplicated.

Continuing with her scrubbing, Annie's thoughts strayed again to Nate. She had to admit she was attracted to him. She felt safe with him. But not the kind of safe she felt with Mr. Stein, or her father, or

Matthew Voss for that matter; because Nate also frightened her in a way that none of those men ever did. Remembering how protected and comforted she had felt each time he held her in his arms, Annie could also feel the under current of fear that had bubbled just below the surface. And she could hear that panicked fear reverberate through every argument she had had with him. Fear that Nate would try to dominate her, the way John had, demanding obedience in every aspect of her life.

But yesterday afternoon, sitting across from her at this kitchen table, when he had essentially apologized for that behavior by saying that he wouldn't tell her what to do, Annie had felt even more frightened. If she was honest, she feared herself more than Nate. She was afraid of her own weakness and need to depend on someone else. It had been Annie, herself, who had rejected her father's suggestion of a marriage contract that would keep control of her dowry in her own hands; it was she who had given her husband the power of attorney to oversee the money she inherited from her father; it had been her fear of being left alone that had kept her from demanding a divorce; and it had only been the terrible years of complete dependence on John's family that had taught her the true value of standing on her own. Now she was so frightened that all it would take is the soft comfort of a strong man's arms to....

Wong, who had just returned from serving Samuels his after-diner port, interrupted these thoughts.

"Miss Lizzie, the Mistress has asked me to stay tonight, and she has given you permission to leave for your night out immediately. I will let Mr. Samuels out when he has finished his drink."

Annie wanted nothing more than to go home and be with the people who loved her, but she felt it was cowardly to go and leave this unhappy household. So she said, "Oh Wong, do you think I should? Doesn't Mrs. Voss need me with Cartier gone?"

Wong came over and took the scrub brush from Annie's hand,

saying softly, "Go, I will see to the mistress. I can do this at least for my master, take care of his home and his family as he always took care of me."

Annie left the kitchen and hurried up the four flights of stairs to the attic. She had already packed her bag, putting everything she had brought with her into it, just in case she didn't come back. Even if she had to return, it would be good to exchange all her clothes for clean things. She tossed her apron into the bag, gathered up her shawl, and grabbed her purse from the top of the wardrobe. She stuck the purse under her arm as she left the room hurriedly, not sure of what time it was.

When she came into the kitchen she was relieved to see it was just a quarter to nine and that she had a good fifteen minutes before the horse car was due. She smiled warmly at Wong who went over to the back door, got the key off the hook, and opened the door for her. She could hear him locking it behind her as she stood on the back steps a moment. Annie took a deep breath and sighed with relief. She was free, if only for tonight. Glancing back, she saw Wong silhouetted against the kitchen window. She waved before turning; then she went down the path and out the garden gate. She thought, *What if I don't return and I never see him again? That would be so sad.*

With the evening fog moving in and the light failing, Annie had to make her way carefully. She could see better once she exited the alley, for on Geary at least the street lamps made some stab at penetrating the gloom. She noted the activity on the street. A carriage passed by, and she saw several pedestrians on the opposite sidewalk, no doubt hurrying home. It was all so completely normal. She walked slowly to the corner. She had about ten minutes to wait, assuming the horse car was on time, but she didn't mind. The damp air felt cool on her cheeks and refreshing after the close confines of the house.

Annie put down her bag and opened her purse to get out the five-cent fare, so she would be ready to give it to the conductor. She realized instantly that there was something wrong; the purse was too light. In fact it seemed empty. Scrabbling around in the bottom of the purse she encountered only one thing in it, a long thin object that seemed metallic. *How odd,* she thought, when she held the object up to the light. *It's a long buttonhook.* Whatever was a buttonhook doing in her purse? She never carried one with her. Usually hers resided on her dresser, along with her combs and brushes. Of course, now it should be safely packed in her bag. Puzzled, she held the purse up to the light as well and saw with a shock that it wasn't hers. Although identical in size and shape, this purse had a different pattern of beading on it than hers.

Staring at the empty purse and the buttonhook, Annie felt at a loss. The only thing she could figure was that there must have been somebody else's purse along side hers in the top of the wardrobe, probably Nellie's. Annie wondered why the previous maid had left it. The top shelf of the wardrobe was way above eye level; perhaps it was a spare and Nellie hadn't noticed it when she left.

Well, there was nothing else to do. She'd have to go back and fetch her own purse to get the fare. Picking up her bag, she strode back down the street and back down the alley, hurrying this time. The light was almost gone now, but her eyes had become adjusted to the dimness, so she didn't have too much difficulty making her way through the garden path up to the kitchen door. As she went along she thought more about the purse. It must have been Nellie's, since she had been living in that room for nearly two years. As she came up to the back door, Annie mused over the oddity of the buttonhook, wondering why Nellie had carried one in her purse.

Leaving this conundrum be, she knocked on the back door to the kitchen, but heard no movement from within. She moved to the window on the right of the door and, crouching down, she peered in through the bars. She saw no sign of Wong. He must have been called upstairs. *What a bother!* She didn't want to make her way all the way round to the front of the house and ring the bell. She went back to the kitchen door and knocked again, more loudly, and then went back to the window to observe the result. Still nothing.

Later Annie wondered why she did what she did next, since her actions weren't really rational. Remembering the key that hung on a hook next to the back door, she stuck her right arm through the barred window and reached for it. She knew her arm wouldn't reach; she'd tried it several times Monday morning, when she'd been locked out. But she was beginning to panic, afraid that if she didn't get into the house soon and get her purse, she'd miss the horse car. She couldn't stand to wait even an additional half an hour to get home. So she tried for the key once more, just the way one tries to open the stopper in a jar, or pulls at a stuck drawer, or reaches down behind a table to pick up a pin, just one more time, in case this is the magical time that will do it.

And like magic, this time her efforts paid off, because this time Annie still had the buttonhook in her hand. As she reached through the window, she realized that not only did the extra six inches of reach this gave her make all the difference, but that the tiny hook on the end of the implement was perfect for snagging the key and bringing it back through the window. It took only a few tries, and then the key was safely in her hand, and she was opening the kitchen door in triumph. She left her carpetbag at the back door and ran through the kitchen and up the back stairs, taking them two at a time, very conscious of the precious seconds that were ticking by. When she opened the door to her attic room she froze. A bright oil lamp placed on the dresser clearly revealed Malcolm Samuels leaning over the bed with the contents of Annie's own purse strewn out on the quilt. Interrupted in his searching he looked up, and, when he saw it was her, he stood up and laughed.

"Oh, it's little Lizzie. I thought you'd gone. I was just checking to make sure you hadn't pinched anything from the house. You know how untrustworthy housemaids can be. For example, I wonder where you got such a valuable piece? Did you steal it, or was it for services rendered from some former master?"

When she saw her mother's locket in hands, Annie exploded. For a week she had put up with being bossed around by Miss Nancy, treated like an idiot child by Mrs. Voss, condescended to by Cartier, and this was the last straw--to have her keepsake from her mother pawed over by Samuels. So, brandishing the buttonhook she still had in her hand, she shouted, "Take your hands off my things and get out of my room. How dare you come creeping in here like a thief?"

The effect this had on Samuels was startling. He threw down the locket, his eyes bulged, and his lips curled back in a snarl as he pointed at her and said, "Where did you get that?"

Bewildered, Annie looked at the buttonhook in her hand. Then, with incredible clarity, she realized that it was Samuels who had gotten into and back out of the locked house the night Matthew died, with a buttonhook. Without a moment's hesitation, she hurled her knowledge at him as if it were a weapon, saying, "So it was you!"

## Chapter Forty-one

Before she had time to say another word, Samuels launched himself at her, snatching the buttonhook from her, hurling her on the bed. As she tried to force her way up to a sitting position, Samuels pressed her back, pinning her arms under her, covering her mouth with his hand. She continued to struggle against him until he flourished a jack knife in front of her eyes and then she felt the sharp prick of metal at her throat. Annie went still. Through the pounding in her head she began to make sense of what he was saying. His voice was low and menacing, but there was a still note of amusement that chilled her heart.

"You've been a bad girl, Lizzie. Spying. Just like Nellie. Selling your little bits of information. You really should have come to me, not to that meddling lawyer. I know you've been spying for him. I talked to Nellie's chum after Saturday's dance. Poor, poor Jack. He's all broken up by her death. He told me that a lawyer fellow, Dawson, had come sniffing around, with some mystery girl on his arm, described you to a tee. That must have been fun, little Lizzie, dancing with a gentleman."

Annie struggled to breath, and Samuels took his hand from her mouth. Having no difficulty sounding frightened she squeaked out, "No, please, Mr. Samuels, you're wrong. I'm a good girl. I dunno what you are talking about. I don't know no lawyers. I was just protecting my stuff."

Samuels slapped her hard across her mouth and then growled,

"Stop your lying. I saw you in the garden with him late Wednesday night, practically sitting in his lap. I wonder what Mrs. Voss would say if she knew what you were doing late at night when a good girl should have been fast asleep. Did he buy you this locket? Was that your payment? I would have done better by you, if you had come to me. I can give a girl a real nice time. I'm no inexperienced boy like our Jeremy or Nate Dawson. Nellie had a good time before she got too greedy."

Samuels laughed again, nastily. "Wouldn't our resident virgin, old prune-faced Nancy, have had a fit if she knew that up above her head I was having carnal relations with her maid. Lively little Nellie." Reaching over on the bed beside Annie, Samuels picked up the buttonhook and slipped it into his jacket pocket and said, "Yes, you were very clever to figure that out. Too clever. Nellie showed me that trick sometime ago, so I could sneak up here nights. She'd tell me what she'd picked up about my secretive partner with her prying and peeking, and I'd pleasure her in return."

Annie despaired. He shouldn't be telling her all this, admitting that he knew how to get into the house, admitting a relationship with Nellie. He meant to murder her like he did Nellie. Somehow she had to get away from him.

Without warning, Samuels heaved her up and back more fully on the bed. Before she could react to the knife's absence, it was back at her throat. But this time Samuels was lying on her with almost all of his full length, his voice husky, and his left hand pulling at the neck of her dress as he whispered, "You bitch, I'll get my satisfaction out of you now, for my troubles."

Then without warning he was off of her, staring wildly over his shoulder. The sound that had startled him came again, and this time Annie recognized it. It was the buzzer that signaled that she was wanted for service in the kitchen. It buzzed one more time and stopped. Wong must have come to the kitchen and seen the back door open and her bag still there and wondered what was going on. Seeing the knife lax in Samuels' hand she twisted off the bed to her feet and lunged towards the door, starting to scream. She was swept up and back against Samuels as if she was a child. One of his arms was crushing her ribs, while the other was around her face. Annie thought she would suffocate. The rough wool of the coat sleeves not only filled her mouth but also pressed against her nose, so that the scent of cigar and cleaning fluid seared her lungs as she tried to suck in air. He was so strong. His fleshy respectability had fooled her. Even with her feet pushing off the floor and her hands clawing at his, she was held tight.

Then the arm was gone from her face and she felt the knife back against her throat. He pulled her arms painfully behind her and held her tightly as she breathed in great gasping sobs. Samuels was saying something about having to postpone his enjoyment until he could get her out of the house and to a place of privacy. Annie's spirits lifted. He wasn't going to try and kill her here. If he tried to take her from the house, someone would see, stop him. He began to push her forward, out through the door from her attic room to the back stairs. With a lurch she stumbled down one or two steps until Samuels brought her up short. She felt a thin trickle of blood begin to run down her neck from where the knife had pricked her, but she felt no pain. Wong was standing unblinking on the landing below her.

Samuels voice ground out slowly. "Just turn around, Wong. Leave this house and leave this city. Never come back and never mention what you've seen; or I swear I will tell everyone you killed your master and raped his servant and the world will be rid of one more dirty Chinaman."

Wong looked for one eternal second at Annie and then he turned and silently slipped away. Annie could not even feel betrayed. She knew as well as he did what Samuels' threat meant. No one in the city would take Wong's word against a respected citizen like Samuels. Even if he were a witness to her murder, Wong wouldn't be able to testify in court. And if Samuels charged him with rape, Wong's case wouldn't even make it to trial; he'd be lynched. Annie finally realized just how incredibly brave Wong had been to continue to serve in this household once Matthew had been murdered, how vulnerable he'd been, and how loyal he had been to the Matthew's family by staying.

The confrontation with Wong had evidently made Samuels change his strategy, because he began to drag her back up the stairs to her room. Her ankles kept banging against the stairs and the knife kept pricking her as her feet got tangled up with her long skirts. Once back on the landing, Samuels pushed her back into the room and onto the bed, this time face first. She landed with her own purse uncomfortably pressed into her chest. She felt him let her hands go, but his knee pressed into her back, making movement difficult, and her skirts kept her from effectively kicking backwards. She heard a tearing sound and then he wrenched her arms back again and she felt him wrap a cloth around her wrists and begin to pull them tightly together.

Abruptly the voice of Mrs. Voss broke through the muttered curses Samuels had been whispering as he tied Annie's wrists. Annie heard her say, "Malcolm, whatever are you doing? Have you gone mad? Let her go this instant. How could you? In my house. This is *my* house, in case you have forgotten, and you will do as I say."

"Like hell I will." Samuels snarled, as he pulled Annie to her feet and placed the knife at her throat again.

Samuels' breathing was ragged, but Annie could feel him trying to get control. He continued more quietly, but if anything more terrifyingly. "Really, Amelia my dear, I think that it is rather late in the day for you to try and act like the mistress of this house. Now what I want you to do is to go downstairs and get that skinny hag of a sister-in-law, and I am going to tell you all *exactly* what you are going

to do. I promise, if you try anything, this girl will be dead and Jeremy will never see the light of day. Now go!"

Half-dragging Annie and half-pushing Mrs. Voss, Samuels
herded them down the stairs to the second floor. As they came out
onto the landing they saw Miss Nancy standing in her doorway, her
Bible clutched to her chest. As she saw Mrs. Voss and Samuels
come out from the shadows she began to point her finger at them.

"Adulterers. I knew it. Slinking around, in the cover of night. Oh,
Matthew, I weep for...." Her harsh accusatory words stopped as she
saw Annie being dragged along behind Samuels. Samuels ignored
the older woman and continued unchecked down the corridor. When
he got to the open door of Mrs. Voss's sitting room he halted and
motioned to her to go in before him. He then shifted so that Miss
Nancy could see the knife he had again placed at Annie's throat, and
he barked at her, "In with you too, or I'll kill you both, with pleasure."

Irresolutely, Miss Nancy stood where she was until Annie whim-
pered when Samuels gave her arms another particularly painful
twist. Then the older woman shuffled hastily into the sitting room,
joining Mrs. Voss. Samuels yanked Annie into the room after him,
and, after awkwardly kicking the door shut behind him, he continued with his orders.

"Amelia, lock the door. I know you have a key, damn you. Then
we can have our little talk uninterrupted."

Mrs. Voss did as he asked, but as she locked the door she began
to speak; Annie could hear the attempt to appear calm in her voice.

"Malcolm, please be reasonable. I'm sure that whatever has happened we can...."

Before she could complete the sentence Samuels shouted, "Shut
up and sit down over there with the hag! No, better yet, before you
do, pour me a drink. And not another word from you. I'll do the talking."

Amelia Voss went quickly to a cabinet in a corner and Annie saw her open the door and pull out a decanter and a glass and then fill the glass with what looked like whiskey. Oddly, Annie thought of Matthew pouring out a drink as he settled down for a quiet evening with his wife. The idea of this evil man partaking of anything that was Matthew's and thereby polluting it was almost more than she could bear. She could see that Mrs. Voss's cheeks were wet with tears as she held the glass out to Samuels, and Annie wondered if she were thinking the same thing. As Samuels gulped the drink down, Mrs. Voss went over and pulled her sister-in-law down beside her on to the sofa across the room.

After draining the glass, Samuels put the glass on the table beside him and jerked Annie over to a chair across from the two other women. He pushed her down on to it, and, leaning over the back of the chair, he again placed the knife at her throat. Annie stared beseechingly at Mrs. Voss and Miss Nancy. From behind her, Samuels began to speak in an odd, matter-of-fact tone.

"You see this is how it is going to be. Miss Nancy will go downstairs in just a minute and get a hansom. When it comes, I will take little Lizzie down to it and take her away. What happens to her then is really none of your concern."

When Miss Nancy began to protest, Amelia Voss put her arm around her and pulled her back, telling her to hush. Samuels laughed. "That's right, my dear. I knew you'd understand. Don't worry. You too will have a role to play. You see, Jeremy is in very real danger of hanging for the death of his father and Nellie. But I just might be able to get him off, if you cooperate with me. I am offering you a deal. Lizzie in exchange for Jeremy."

Mrs. Voss began to speak again, but Samuels waved her silent. "Tut, tut. Remember what I said. No interrupting. You want to know how little Lizzie here can set Jeremy free? Well, I'll tell you. I just thought of it. I was just going to let him hang, but Lizzie here has given me an even better plan. You see, before Lizzie leaves with me, she is going to write a letter."

Samuels suddenly grabbed Annie by her hair and pulled her head back so she was forced to look up at him, "You aren't illiterate, are you? No, of course not, not a fine girl like you. Well, as I was saying, Lizzie will write a letter, two letters in fact. The first will simply say that she and Nellie and a boy friend of theirs conspired to kill Matthew Voss and steal his money, but that when Nellie got greedy, the boy friend killed her. It will also say that she planted the evidence the police found in Jeremy's room. And then little Lizzie will simply disappear. When the police find the letter, they'll let Jeremy go free. Now, that young lawyer Dawson might object. He'll say that poor Lizzie is innocent. Turns out our little Lizzie has been spying for him. But I think you'll be able to convince the police he is mistaken, and I don't think anyone will take him very seriously. They will think he's been made a fool of by another pretty face. And she does have such a pretty face, doesn't she?"

Samuels at this point ran the knife down Annie's cheek, and she closed her eyes, trying desperately to think. Samuels was offering the two women Jeremy's freedom in exchange for her own life. What else could they do but go along? But should she? Would writing the letters for him buy her more time, or sign her own death warrant?

Samuels went on, sounding more and more satisfied with himself. "Now, you ask me, what is the other letter for? Well, in that letter Lizzie here will say that the boy friend was your darling son Jeremy. She can write how first he seduced poor Nellie, and then he killed her. But we won't show that letter to the police, shall we? I'll just keep it as a sort of insurance policy, to make certain that once Jeremy is free that you, Amelia, will marry me, and that Miss Nancy and Jeremy will do the sensible thing and turn over their shares of the family firm to me. As a wedding present! Won't that just be grand? Then Jeremy can go off and starve as an artist in Paris, Miss Nancy here can go off to that Old Ladies home she's so fond of talking about, and you and I, Amelia, will live happily ever after."

Amelia Voss just looked at him and said softly, "Why, Malcolm? Why did you kill Matthew?"

Samuels let out a sharp bark of laughter. "Why? Because I needed money and I took a little extra from the business. Matthew would have found out if he lived, and you know Matthew, he wouldn't have let it go. Did you think it was for your sake, my sweet? Well I'm sorry to disappoint you. I'll admit that I hoped I could convince you to marry me willingly once he was gone, but that was only to get at the rest of the money and because unwilling women are such a bore. But I misjudged you. I thought you'd be glad for a warm bed after all those years with that cold son of a bitch you married. But clearly I'm too much of a man for you. That's all right. Mother's love will do nicely to keep you in line, keep both of you in line."

Annie watched the deepening horror in the two woman's eyes as they saw the cunning in Samuels' words. Miss Nancy appeared to wilt as he spoke, her fingers plucking at the Bible in her lap, her eyes widening in shock. The truth was turning out to be far worse than her bitter imaginings. Amelia Voss looked less shocked, and Annie wondered how much of the truth she had already guessed. As for herself, Annie felt unnaturally calm. Her heart had slowed, her breathing had returned to normal, and while she was still afraid, she was not terrified in the way she had been earlier. She could think and plan. She would write the letters, but she would do it slowly. Time was on her side. The longer it took, the greater chance that someone would come to the house; something would save her.

Samuels' voice shifted unexpectedly, revealing a note of haste it had not held before. It seemed his thoughts had followed a parallel path. Grabbing Annie by the shoulder, he pulled her up and began to push her towards the small writing desk by the window. As he did, he spoke roughly to the two other women. "That's enough talk. Let's get a move on. Amelia, get me paper and a pen, and then, while Lizzie here writes, you sit still and behave. Don't you even think about crossing me! I can kill her in an instant, and I'd say the old lady did it to keep her from implicating Jeremy. Then she'll hang alongside Jeremy. Or, we can do it my way, and you'll get your lives and your precious Jeremy's freedom. Either way I win, so don't push me."

Amelia Voss slipped over to the desk and, opening a top drawer, pulled out several sheets of paper and a pen. After laying them on the desk, she moved without a word back to the sofa, but remained standing beside it. Samuels had Annie sit at the desk, cutting the cloth that bound her arms behind her; then he leaned over her shoulder and whispered in her ear. "Now, Lizzie, my love. You will write what I tell you to. Don't fret about your spelling; this isn't grammar school. But don't think of resisting. You'll do it for me in the end. But you can do it after a lot of pain, or not. It's your choice."

Annie took up the pen and was surprised to see her hand wasn't shaking. Samuels pointed to the top of the paper with the knife and said, "Start here, write 'I Lizzie.' Why, Lizzie girl, I don't know your last name. That will never do. Write it down for me."

Annie's mind went blank. What name had she given when she took the job? No one ever called her anything but Lizzie. Did she give her own name?

Samuels' voice thundered in her ears, "Write, damn you or I'll break your fingers one by one." He took her left arm and pulled it behind her, grabbing her hand and squeezing her fingers between his own until she heard herself cry out in pain. But internally Annie was still calm. She saw that she had blotted the paper with ink, and that a tear had fallen on top of one of the spots of ink, reminding her for all the world like an inky blue sun being eclipsed by a watery transparent moon.

A terrible gut-wrenching shriek from behind her followed by a muffled thud shattered her peace and brought her senses sharply back into focus. The pressure on her hand ceased and, as she turned in her chair, she saw that Samuels, cursing horribly, was warding off a series of blows that Miss Nancy was raining down upon his head with her holy book. Annie shouted out a warning as she saw him lift up his right hand, which was still holding the knife, and aim it in a swiftly descending arc at the older woman's chest. Miraculously, the knife buried itself in the Bible Miss Nancy had thrust forward in protection. With an infuriated bellow Samuels pulled his arm back to strike another blow. But the knife stayed lodged, bringing the book with it, and the additional weight of the Bible on the knife carried Samuels' arm up and back over his shoulder, propelling both the book and the knife out of his hand. They sailed past Annie and crashed against the curtained windows.

Before Samuels could go after his weapon, Annie stood and picked up the chair she had been sitting on, swinging it at him with all her strength. The chair was one of the Voss and Samuels Company's finest decorative chairs, and Annie found no difficulty in slamming it hard against his legs. She heard a distinct crack as it connected with one of his kneecaps. Samuels screamed in pain and as he bent over to clutch at the knee Annie swung again, this time aiming at his head, which was now within her reach. The chair bounced back with a thunk from the solid contact it made with Samuels' skull, and Annie saw a dazed expression temporarily replace the fury in his eyes. As he staggered backward in confusion, Amelia Voss tossed a crocheted afghan that had been on the sofa over his head, successfully entangling his arms and hands in its folds. As Mrs. Voss held on to the ends of the blanket, pulling it tighter around him, Annie again swung the chair, this time onto his back. Samuels toppled to the ground, still struggling with the blanket.

Annie swung the chair down onto his prostrate body two more

times, while Miss Nancy shrieked encouragement. Suddenly, Mrs. Voss shouted, "the carpet," and Annie saw that she was pushing tables towards the edge of the room. She thought for a moment that Mrs. Voss had gone mad, then the ingenuity of the plan struck her. She shoved the chair at Miss Nancy and said, "Keep at it," and then she ran to help Mrs. Voss.

It seemed to take forever to shift the heavy sofa and to tip back the legs of the desk and corner cabinet so the carpet could be freed from under the furniture, ignoring as they did the objects that slid off and crashed to the floor. All the while Annie kept looking over her shoulder, afraid that Samuels would get free. But each time he would begin to rise he would be knocked off balance again by Miss Nancy's thrust and parry with the chair. Finally the thick Persian carpet was clear, except for Samuels who was still thrashing and screaming near one edge.

When Annie turned to look at him she saw that he had managed to pull the afghan from his head and grab onto one of the chair legs. She ran over to help Miss Nancy pull the chair away from him. He rose, with a bellow, but then his face twisted in agonized pain as his knee gave out from under him. Annie once more swung the chair at him, causing him to roll into a defensive ball. She then ran to Mrs. Voss, who was struggling to lift the end of the carpet, and, with muscles that screamed from the week of hard domestic work, Annie flung the edge of the carpet over Samuels and the three women began to roll it and him over and over. Before they knew it, they had him completely bundled up; and they were sitting on the rolled up carpet that humped and lurched and howled beneath them, holding onto each other, laughing and crying triumphantly.

And that is how the four men, Nate, Jeremy, Patrick, and Wong, found the three women when they finally broke through the door that they had been battering at for some time. The men stood a minute, looking at the women in shocked silence, while the women turned and stared blankly at this unexpected arrival of the cavalry. Then Wong pointed at the carpet, saying with satisfaction, "Samuels?" Annie responded with a giggle, and the tableau unfroze, releasing the men into action. Jeremy ran over and helped his mother to her feet, while Miss Nancy leaped up and gave Wong a gigantic hug, and Patrick bent over the carpet and poked it warily with his nightstick.

Meanwhile, Nate strode over to where Annie was rising unsteadily from her seat on the carpet. He lifted her unceremoniously into his arms and carried her out of the room, dumping her back on her feet in the hallway before he began to berate her.

"My God, Annie, I thought Samuels had killed you. I finally broke his alibi, but it took me until this afternoon. Then I had to make it back from Redwood City; it took forever before I could convince the police to set Jeremy free. I had prayed you were safe at home, but then we met up with Patrick and Wong on the way here. Wong said Samuels had a knife on you. And the door, we couldn't get the door open. We could hear screams. I thought he was killing you."

The whole time Nate spoke, he was swiftly examining Annie for injuries. Finally he began to wipe at the mingled tears and smears of blood on her cheeks and to pat the cuts on her neck with his handkerchief, as he muttered fiercely, "You're bleeding, you little fool."

Annie just laughed and said rather shakily, "I'm fine, really I am. You needn't worry about me." Then Nate, evidently further enraged at this response, growled savagely, pulled her close and began to kiss her, confirming quite nicely Annie's earlier speculations on how lovely his lips would feel against her own.

## Epilogue:
## Friday morning, August 24, 1879

*WOMAN'S BODY FOUND IN TRUNK* screamed the headline on the first page of the *Chronicle*. Annie idly calculated how big the trunk would have to be to fit an entire adult female body. *Oh, the body was cut up into several pieces, that would make it easier*, she thought. *Well, this poor woman, who ever she was, had certainly relegated the Voss's tragedy to a back page.* Annie found the short story she was looking for on page seventeen. Under a headline that simply said *Prominent Businessman Confesses*, there was a short piece about Malcolm Samuels pleading guilty to the manslaughter of Nellie Flannigan, a Cliff House waitress. No mention of Samuels' murder of Matthew Voss, the discovery of the missing assets and most of the money, or the role that a housemaid named Lizzie had played in solving the crime. It had taken a good deal of effort on the part of Nate and his uncle, as well as old friends of Matthew's, like Herbert Stein, to ensure that the Voss family name had disappeared quietly and quickly from the story of Samuels' arrest.

The police had cooperated, since it was going to be easier to get Samuels to admit to Nellie's death, which he could claim was accidental, than to Matthew's clearly premeditated murder. Annie suspected that Jackson also preferred to settle the case quickly since he had initially charged the wrong man and hadn't been involved in the capture itself. Embarrassing to let the press get hold of the story that a desperate criminal had been subdued by three women and household furnishings.

Annie smiled at the memory. She hoped that the cooperation that Miss Nancy and Mrs. Voss had demonstrated that night would continue. Miss Nancy's decision to step forward and take over the running of the factory would at least keep her away from the house a good deal, which should ease tensions somewhat. Jeremy would still have to be involved in the business, at least until a replacement for Samuels could be found, but his marriage was to go forward. Evidently Judith's mother had been pressuring her to break the engagement, and the mysterious man Annie had run into Saturday night had been sent by Jeremy's fiancé, Judith, to set up a secret meeting between them. That was why Jeremy acted so oddly when questioned about the afternoon Nellie died. He had been with Judith and was protecting her good name. What a young romantic fool. But she suspected his father would have been very proud of him.

The sound of the door opening caused her to look up. Seeing Kathleen standing there, she folded the newspaper and put it on the table in front of her.

"Mr. Driscoll to see you, Ma'am." Kathleen's prim and proper curtsy contrasted with the saucy wink she gave Annie, who had to take a deep breath to forestall a nervous giggle. She then flashed a glare at Kathleen that said silently, *behave yourself,* while out loud she said calmly, "Thank you Kathleen, and please show Mr. Driscoll in."

Annie had chosen the small parlor where she worked as Sibyl for this confrontation, although she was not dressed as the clairvoyant. At the thought of how Driscoll would have reacted to Sibyl, she was forced to repress another giggle, a sorry indication of how nervous she felt. Annie rose to meet the man who had followed Kathleen into the parlor, and permitted him to take her hand in greeting.

"My dear Mrs. Fuller. How honored I am that you would see me. I realize that I am a bit earlier than I indicated I would be in my letter. But my travel plans changed slightly. When I got to San Francisco, I just had to rush round and see the wife of one my dearest friends, may he rest in peace."

Hiram Driscoll bowed deeply over her hand, and Annie barely repressed a shudder. On the surface he presented a perfectly ordinary appearance. In his early thirties, he was of moderate height, slightly stocky, and his rather unassuming sideburns and mustache nicely complimented his thinning brown hair. His most distinctive features remained his incredibly intense blue eyes. Eyes that always had left Annie feeling naked and vulnerable. Maybe some women liked being mentally undressed; Annie didn't.

What she found truly inexplicable was that husbands had seemed to encourage Driscoll's attentions to their wives. In fact, men in general, her late husband included, appeared totally besotted by him. They competed for a place at his table at cards, counting their losses as gains; they took his tips on races, blaming the horse not the tip when it came in last; and they praised his business acumen, ignoring the fact that the advice he handed out seldom proved beneficial to anyone but himself.

Pulling her hand from his, where he had held it just that faction too long to be polite, Annie murmured, "Oh, Mr. Driscoll, why wouldn't I be delighted to see such a good friend of my husband? It's been ever so many years, I declare, I'd despaired of ever making your acquaintance again. But please do be seated and tell me to what I owe this pleasure."

Annie marked a slightly startled look in Driscoll's eyes, followed by a perceptible frown, as he made his way over to the chair she'd indicated for him on the other side of the table. She had confused him. He didn't know whether to take her words at face value. Driscoll undoubtedly expected to meet the same shy, inexperienced woman he had known back in New York over five years ago. Then, although she'd disliked and distrusted him, she had been still trying to save her marriage; so she had tried, evidently successfully, to hide her disdain. John had made it crystal clear from the beginning he wouldn't tolerate any public display of her own intelligence, exploding in anger the one time she had timidly ventured an opinion at a social gathering. No doubt Driscoll, a man of supreme self-confidence, had assumed her reticence in his company meant either stupidity or awe.

Sitting down across the table from him, Annie decided to pretend a profound naiveté, so she just stared, wide-eyed, at Driscoll, waiting for him to take the lead.

He crossed his legs and straightened his cravat, plainly unnerved by her unwavering gaze.

He then said, "My dear Mrs. Fuller, I must say how pleased I am to see you looking so well. I'm delighted to have this chance to see you again. I am just sorry we have to introduce such an unpleasant subject as business into the conversation. But then, there it is."

Driscoll's speech faltered. Annie wondered speculatively just how he was going to explain trying to collect on a six-year-old debt from a dead man's wife. She smiled encouragingly at him.

He cleared his throat. "I know this must be distressing for you. But it has to be done. You see, John got in such terrible difficulties before he died, but then those were difficult times for us all. And when he asked for my help, I couldn't turn him down. So, despite my better judgment, I made him a small loan. Never, ever could I have foreseen what would... well, such a tragedy. I was devastated, truly devastated."

Annie slowly slid her hands together where she could hide their tendency to curl into fists. Driscoll's portrayal of himself as the faithful friend was proving very difficult to stomach. But, keeping to her role, she only nodded and murmured, "Please, don't distress yourself. You were only too good, and I know John would wish me to thank you for your generosity."

Driscoll appeared stymied by her thanks, again straitening his cravat. Then he seemed to gather himself for the last difficult hurtle.

"Mrs. Fuller, please, I don't deserve your thanks. It was the least I could do. I just wish I could have done more. But now, well, as dear John's widow, you can do something for me. You see, I would never have asked it of you, if I weren't pushed to the limit myself. But I'm afraid I must ask you to pay me back. I've gotten in a bit of financial difficulty myself, and I know John would wish you to help out one of his best friends. As a sort of testimony to that friendship."

Annie stared, not needing to feign astonishment. The outrageous audacity of the man! Driscoll seemed to feel that her expression denoted bewilderment, so he spelled out his meaning in simple terms, so the poor widow would understand him.

"Mrs. Fuller, I am asking that you pay off the loan. My letter explained this. The total sum is significant, but I am afraid I must insist on immediate repayment. I simply cannot continue to carry this debt. I'd be ruined."

Be ruined! What a hypocrite! Annie became impatient with this game; the man made her positively ill. So, she decided to force the issue of the house out into the open. Cocking her head to the side and frowning, she said, "But Mr. Driscoll, John's father must have explained to you that there was nothing left after John died and his debts were paid. Nothing!"

Driscoll leaned over, reaching out to pat Annie's hands consolingly, and it took all her resolution not to pull back in revulsion. His voice was warm and comforting as he responded, "Oh, Mrs. Fuller, don't worry. I've found a solution that will benefit us both. You see, you have this nice little house here, and this will make everything right. If you turn the deed over to me, I will be glad to accept it in exchange for the amount you owe me; even though I'm afraid the value of the house is considerably less than the debt. But no matter. What is money between old friends?"

Annie stared at Driscoll, speechless at the gall of the man, and

Driscoll continued, "Now don't worry. It's all very simple. I have the documents right here. All you need to do is sign, and I'll take care of everything else. And, I know you're worried about where you will live, but that's the beauty of my little scheme. You don't have to move! Since I don't live in San Francisco, and long distance investments are such a worry, I've decided to ask you to remain here, as my manager of sorts. I'd be glad to pay you a small fee for your help, and of course your board would be free, as well. So as you can see, really nothing will change."

*Like hell nothing would change*, Annie said to herself. *Just that you would now own the house, to sell whenever you please. In the meanwhile you'd get the income from the boarders and pay me a pittance to be the boarding house keeper, no doubt firing Beatrice as an unnecessary expense.*

Annie took the papers that Driscoll had taken out of his suit jacket and pretended to look vaguely at what was clearly a document for conveying title to her property to Driscoll. Then she responded in a soft hesitant voice, "But Mr. Driscoll, I still don't understand. Papa Fuller explained it all to me, right after the funeral. How I had to sell my house, all my furniture, even my dresses to pay off all the debts John owed. I remember he put a notice in the paper, so that we could be sure all of the creditors would know to make their claims. Didn't you see the notice?"

Driscoll replied patiently, "Yes, Mrs. Fuller, I was aware of Mr. Fuller's bankruptcy action, but I didn't want to add another burden to your poor shoulders during that difficult period of mourning."

"Oh, Mr. Driscoll that was kind of you, but I'm afraid that might have been a mistake. It did seem unfair to me at the time, but John's father explained that there was only so much money to go around, and that only those creditors who put in a claim would get any of it. You really should have put in your claim then, I believe it was for $300? Then you at least would have been able to get some of your money back." Annie smiled sadly at him.

"Yes, at ten cents on the dollar, no thank you!" Driscoll snapped. Leaning forward, he took out another piece of paper and waved it in front of Annie. "Listen, Mrs. Fuller, I don't think you have quite grasped the situation. I have a piece of paper here that says your husband owes me $300 plus interest, which means you, as your husband's heir, owe me $1,380. Do you have any other assets besides the house that you could use to pay me that amount?"

Annie shook her head in the negative, although it wasn't the complete truth, since the mining stock certificates she had inherited from Matthew now rested in escrow waiting for the will to be probated, but no need to confuse the man.

"No, I *thought* not!" Driscoll said. "But you *do* have the house, so just sign this document, and everything will be fine." Driscoll folded his arms complacently, and then looked startled when Annie rose and handed the documents back to him.

"I'm sorry, Mr. Driscoll, that you have gone to all this trouble. But I will never sign over this house. As I have explained, I fulfilled any responsibility I might have had to John's creditors when I liquidated all the property I owned or had inherited at the time of his death. Your claim comes too late. In fact, I have recently learned that under California law, this house, or any property or income I obtained after my husband's death, is not subject to any of my late husband's creditors. Now, I believe it is time for you to leave. I will have my maid escort you out." Annie went to the bell pull next to the mantel and then returned to stand in the middle of the room.

Gone was the affable smile on Driscoll's face as he stood up and walked past Annie to the parlor door. At the door he turned and spat out, "Don't think that this is the end of this discussion, Mrs. Fuller! I think that you have seriously misunderstood the law. You owe me this money, and I will get it, one way or the other. I'll take you to court if I have to, and I'll win and you will be left with nothing! The lawyer's fees alone will bankrupt you. So, just think about that, and when you change your mind and decide to be reasonable, you can reach me at the Palace Hotel."

Annie smiled, and said, "I don't believe that I will change my mind, Mr. Driscoll. For you see, I do understand the law. I had it explained to me by an excellent lawyer, who is a Harvard graduate and is licensed to practice law in *both* New York and California. Oh, and as for those lawyer's fees, I suspect that any legal action on your part will cost you a good deal more than it will cost me, since that lawyer has agreed to represent my interests in this case, for free."

With satisfaction, Annie saw first surprise and then defeat in Driscoll's face. Then, as Kathleen opened the door and escorted him out, she heard the door to the back room open and in a moment felt a warm hand on her shoulder. Annie Fuller leaned back into the comforting embrace of her lawyer, feeling very safe and only a little afraid.

# About the Author

For over twenty years, the author has been known by students taking U.S. History classes at San Diego Mesa College as Dr. Locke, an enthusiastic and amusing teller of stories about the past. Now semi-retired, she has taken her story telling in a new direction with the publication of the historical mystery, *Maids of Misfortune*. She is currently living in San Diego with her husband and assorted animals, and she is working on *Uneasy Spirits*, the next installment of her series of Victorian San Francisco mysteries featuring Annie Fuller and Nate Dawson. Check out http://mlouisalocke.com/ for more about M. Louisa Locke and her historical fiction.